endless
SUMMER

Also by
Jennifer Echols

♥ ♥ ♥

Major Crush

The Ex Games

endless SUMMER

The Boys Next Door
and
Endless Summer

Jennifer Echols

Simon Pulse

New York London Toronto Sydney

SIMON PULSE

An imprint of Simon & Schuster Children's Publishing Division

1230 Avenue of the Americas, New York, NY 10020

This Simon Pulse paperback edition May 2010

The Boys Next Door copyright © 2007 by Jennifer Stimson

Endless Summer copyright © 2010 by Jennifer Echols

All rights reserved, including the right of reproduction in whole or in part in any form.

SIMON PULSE and colophon are registered trademarks of Simon & Schuster, Inc.

For information about special discounts for bulk purchases, please contact Simon & Schuster Special Sales at 1-866-506-1949 or business@simonandschuster.com.

The Simon & Schuster Speakers Bureau can bring authors to your live event. For more information or to book an event contact the Simon & Schuster Speakers Bureau at 1-866-248-3049 or visit our website at www.simonspeakers.com.

Designed by Mike Rosamilia

The text of this book was set in Garamond 3.

Manufactured in the United States of America

6 8 10 9 7

Library of Congress Control Number 2010922978

ISBN 978-1-4424-0659-9

The Boys Next Door was previously published individually by Simon Pulse.

The Boys Next Door

For my brother

Acknowledgments

Heartfelt thanks to my wonderful editor, Michelle Nagler, and my friends who helped make this book possible: Nephele Tempest, Victoria Dahl, Catherine Chant, Marley Gibson, and Caren Johnson.

Thanks also to everyone who sent me an e-mail or MySpace message saying you enjoyed *Major Crush*. You went out of your way to do this, and I appreciate it so much! You keep me afloat.

Sean smiled down at me, his light brown hair glinting golden in the sunlight. He shouted over the noise of the boat motor and the wind, "Lori, when we're old enough, I want you to be my girlfriend." He didn't even care the other boys could hear him.

"I'm there!" I exclaimed, because I was nothing if not coy. All the boys ate out of my hand, I tell you. "When will we be old enough?"

His blue eyes, lighter than the bright blue sky behind him, seemed to glow in his tanned face. He answered me, smiling. At least, I *thought* he answered me. His lips moved.

"I didn't hear you. What'd you say?" I know how to draw out a romantic moment.

He spoke to me again. I still couldn't hear him, though the boat motor and the wind hadn't gotten any louder. Maybe he was just mouthing words, pretending to say something sweet I couldn't catch. Boys were like that. He'd just been teasing me all along—

"You ass!" I sat straight up in my sweat-soaked bed, wiping away the strands of my hair stuck to my wet face. Then I realized what I'd said out loud. "Sorry, Mom," I told her photo on my bedside table. But maybe she hadn't heard me over my alarm clock blaring Christina Aguilera, "Ain't No Other Man."

Or maybe she'd understand. I'd just had a closer encounter with Sean! Even if it *was* only in my dreams.

Usually I didn't remember my dreams. Whenever my brother, McGillicuddy, was home from college, he told Dad and me at breakfast what he'd dreamed about the night before. Lindsay Lohan kicking his butt on the sidewalk after he tried to take her picture (pure fantasy). Amanda Bynes dressed as the highway patrol, pulling him over to give him a traffic ticket. I was jealous. I didn't want to dream about Lindsay Lohan or getting my butt kicked. However, if I was spending the night with Patrick

Dempsey and didn't even *know* it, I was missing out on a very worthy third of my life. I had once Googled "dreaming" and found out some people don't remember their dreams if their bodies are used to getting up at the same hour every morning and have plenty of time to complete the dream cycle.

So why'd I remember my dream this morning? It was the first day of summer vacation, that's why. To start work at the marina, I'd set my clock thirty minutes earlier than during the school year. Lo and behold, here was my dream. About Sean: check. Blowing me off, as usual: noooooooo! That might happen in my dreams, but it wasn't going to happen in real life. Not again. Sean would be mine, starting today. I gave Mom on my beside table an okay sign—the wakeboarding signal for *ready to go*—before rolling out of bed.

My dad and my brother suspected nothing, ho ho. They didn't even notice what I was wearing. Our conversation at breakfast was the same one we'd had every summer morning since my brother was eight years old and I was five.

Dad to brother: "You take care of your sister today."

Brother, between bites of egg: "Roger that."

Dad to me: "And you watch out around those boys next door."

Me: (Eye roll.)

Brother: "I had this rockin' dream about Anne Hathaway."

Post-oatmeal, my brother and I trotted across our yard and the Vaders' yard to the complex of showrooms, warehouses, and docks at Vader's Marina. The morning air was already thick with the heat and humidity and the smell of cut grass that would last the entire Alabama summer. I didn't mind. I liked the heat. And I quivered in my flip-flops at the prospect of another whole summer with Sean. I'd been going through withdrawal.

In past years, any one of the three Vader boys, including Sean, might have shown up at my house at any time to throw the football or play video games with my brother. They might let me play too if they felt sorry for me, or if their mom had guilted them into it. And my brother might go to their house at any time. But *I* couldn't go to their house. If I'd walked in, they would have stopped what they were doing, looked up, and wondered what I was doing there. They were my brother's friends, not mine.

Well, Adam was my friend. He was probably more my friend than my brother's. Even though we were the same age, I didn't have any classes with him at school, so you'd think he'd walk a hundred yards over to my house for a visit every once in a while. But he didn't. And if I'd gone to visit him, it would have been obvious I was looking for Sean out the corner of my eye the whole time.

For the past nine months, with my brother off at college, my last tie to Sean had been severed. He was two years older than me, so I didn't have any classes with *him*, either. I wasn't even in the same wing of the high school. I saw him once at a football game, and once in front of the movie theater when I'd ridden around with Tammy for a few minutes after a tennis match. But I never approached him. He was always flirting with Holly Chambliss or Beige Dupree or whatever glamorous girl he was with at the moment. I was too young for him, and he never even thought of hooking up with me. On the very rare occasion when he took the garbage to the road at the same time I walked to the mailbox, he gave me the usual beaming smile and a big hug and acted like I was his best friend ever . . . for thirty heavenly seconds.

It had been a long winter. *Finally* we were back to the summer. The Vaders always needed extra help at the marina during the busy season from Memorial Day to Labor Day. Just like last year, I had a job there—and an excuse to make Sean my captive audience. I sped up my trek across the pine needles between the trees and found myself in a footrace against my brother. It was totally unfair because I was carrying my backpack and he was wearing sneakers, but I beat him to the warehouse by half a length anyway.

The Vader boys had gotten there before us and claimed

the good jobs, so I wouldn't have a chance to work side by side with Sean. Cameron was helping the full-time workers take boats out of storage. He wanted my brother to work with him so they could catch up on their lives at two different colleges. Sean and Adam were already gone, delivering the boats to customers up and down the lake for Memorial Day weekend. Sean wasn't around to see my outfit. I was so desperate to get going on this "new me" thing, I would have settled for a double take from Adam or Cameron.

All I got was Mrs. Vader. Come to think of it, she was a good person to run the outfit by. She wore stylish clothes, as far as I could tell. Her blonde pinstriped hair was cut to flip up in the back. She looked exactly like you'd want your mom to look so as not to embarrass you in public. I found her in the office and hopped onto a stool behind her. Looking over her shoulder as she typed on the computer, I asked, "Notice anything different?"

She tucked her pinstriped hair behind her ear and squinted at the screen. "I'm using the wrong font?"

"Notice anything different about my boobs?"

That got her attention. She whirled around in her chair and peered at my chest. "You changed your boobs?"

"I'm *showing* my boobs," I said proudly, moving my palm in front of them like presenting them on a TV commercial. All this can be yours! Or, rather, your son's.

My usual summer uniform was the outgrown clothes Adam had given me over the years: jeans, which I cut off into shorts and wore with a wide belt to hold up the waist, and T-shirts from his football team. Under that, for wakeboarding in the afternoon, I used to wear a one-piece sports bathing suit with full coverage that reached all the way up to my neck. Early in the boob-emerging years, I had no boobs, and I was touchy about it. Remember in middle school algebra class, you'd type 55378008 on your calculator, turn it upside down, and hand it to the flat-chested girl across the aisle? I was that girl, you bi-yotch. I would have died twice if any of the boys had mentioned my booblets.

Last year, I thought my boobs had progressed quite nicely. And I progressed from the one-piece into a tankini. But I wasn't quite ready for any more exposure. I didn't want the boys to treat me like a girl.

Now I did. So today I'd worn a cute little bikini. Over that, I still wore Adam's cutoff jeans. Amazingly, they looked sexy, riding low on my hips, when I traded the football T-shirt for a pink tank that ended above my belly button and hugged my figure. I even had a little cleavage. I was so proud. Sean was going to love it.

Mrs. Vader stared at my chest, perplexed. Finally she said, "Oh, I get it. You're trying to look hot."

"*Thank* you!" Mission accomplished.

"Here's a hint. Close your legs."

I snapped my thighs together on the stool. People always scolded me for sitting like a boy. Then I slid off the stool and stomped to the door in a huff. "Where do you want me?"

She'd turned back to the computer. "You've got gas."

Oh, goody. I headed out the office door, toward the front dock to man the gas pumps. This meant at some point during the day, one of the boys would look around the marina office and ask, "Who has gas?" and another boy would answer, "Lori has gas." If I were really lucky, Sean would be in on the joke.

The office door squeaked open behind me. "Lori," Mrs. Vader called. "Did you want to talk?"

Nooooooo. Nothing like that. I'd only gone into her office and tried to start a conversation. Mrs. Vader had three sons. She didn't know how to talk to a girl. My mother had died in a boating accident alone on the lake when I was four. I didn't know how to talk to a woman. Any convo between Mrs. Vader and me was doomed from the start.

"No, why?" I asked without turning around. I'd been galloping down the wooden steps, but now I stepped very carefully, looking down, as if I needed to examine every footfall so I wouldn't trip.

"Watch out around the boys," she warned me.

I raised my hand and wiggled my fingers, toodle-dee-doo, dismissing her. Those boys were harmless. Those boys had better watch out for *me*.

Really, aside from the specter of the boys discussing my intestinal problems, I enjoyed having gas. I got to sit on the dock with my feet in the water and watch the kingfishers and the herons glide low over the surface. Later I'd swim on the side of the dock upriver from the gasoline. Not *now*, before Sean saw me for the first time that summer. I would be in and out of the lake and windy boats all day, and my hair would look like hell. That was understood. But I wanted to have clean, dry, styled hair at least the *first* time he saw me, and I would hope he kept the memory alive. I might go swimming *after* he saw me, while I waited around for people to drive up to the gas pumps in their boats.

The richer they were, the more seldom they made it down from Birmingham to their million-dollar vacation homes on the lake, and the more likely they were complete dumbasses when it came to docking their boats and finding their gas caps. If I covered for their dumbassedness in front of their families in the boats by giggling and saying things like, "Oh sir, I'm so sorry, *I'm* supposed to be helping *you*!" while I helped them, they tipped me beyond belief.

I was just folding a twenty into my back pocket when Sean and Adam came zipping across the water in the boat emblazoned with VADER'S MARINA down the side, blasting Nickelback from the speakers. They turned hard at the edge of the idle zone. Three-foot swells shook the floating dock violently and would have shaken me off into the water if I hadn't held on to the rail. Then the bow of the boat eased against the padding on the dock. Adam must be the one driving. Sean would have driven all the way to the warehouse, closer to where they'd pick up the next boat for delivery.

In fact, as Sean threw me the rope to tie the stern and Adam cut the engine, I could hear them arguing about this. Sean and Adam argued pretty much 24/7. I was used to it. But I would rather not have heard Sean complaining that they were going to have to walk a whole extra fifty yards and up the stairs just so Adam could say hi to me.

Sean jumped off the boat. His weight rocked the floating dock again as he tied up the bow. He was big, maybe six feet tall, with a deep tan from working all spring at the marina, and a hard, muscled chest and arms from competing with Adam the last five years over who could lift more poundage on the dumbbell in their garage (Sean and Adam were like this). Then he straightened and smiled his beautiful smile at me, and I forgave him everything.

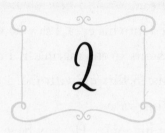

2

"Hey, Buddy," he said to me. I got a close-up view of his strange, light blue eyes and golden skin as he threw his arms around me and kept walking right over me. I had to throw my arms around him, too, to keep from thudding flat on my back on the dock.

"Oh, pardon me!" he said, pulling me out from under him and setting me on my feet again. "I didn't even see you there."

"That's quite all right," I managed in the same fake-formal tone. His warm hands still held my waist. This was the first time a boy had every touched my bare tummy. My happy skin sent shocked messages to my brain that went something like, *He's touching me! Are you getting this? He's touching me! Eeeeeeee!* My brain got it, all right, and put the rest of my body on high alert. My heart thumped painfully, just like in my dream.

But as I looked into his eyes, I saw he was already gone, glancing up the stairs to the marina. If I didn't know better, I'd say he'd been flirting with me. I knew better. He treated all girls this way.

He slid out of my grasp. He may have had to shake one hand violently to extricate it from my friendly vise-like grip. "See you later, Junior," he threw over his shoulder at me as he climbed the steps to the marina.

When we were kids, he'd started calling my brother *McGillicuddy* because he thought our last name was such a riot. It caught on with the other Vader boys, and Cameron had told everyone at school. I'm not sure anyone in town knew my brother as Bill. Thankfully, everyone in town knew me as Lori. The names Sean had made up for me were too long to be practical nicknames: McGillicuddy Junior, McGillicuddy the Younger, McGillicuddy Part Deux, McGillicuddy Returns, McGillicuddy Strikes Back, McGillicuddy's Buddy.

You see what I was up against? Obviously he still saw me as my brother's little sister. I sighed, watching him climb the steps, muscles moving underneath the tan skin of his legs. He was immune to the delicious temptation of my pink tank top. But I had another trick up my sleeve, or lack thereof. Later that afternoon, when we went wakeboarding, I would initiate Stage Two: Bikini.

The dock dipped again as Adam jumped from the boat. I turned to greet him. We did our secret handshake, which we'd been adding to for years: the basic shake (first grade), upside down (second grade), with a twist (fourth grade), high five (fifth grade), low five (seventh grade), pinky swear (eighth grade), elbows touching (ninth grade). We'd been known to do the secret handshake when we passed in the halls at school, and on the sidelines during Adam's football games.

Everybody on the girls' tennis team fetched water and bandages for the football team during their games. It wasn't fair. The football team didn't bring *us* drinks and bandages at tennis tournaments. I never complained, though, because I got to stand on the football field where the action was, which was all I really wanted. The secret handshake had proven surprisingly hard to do when Adam was in football pads. We'd made it work.

But Adam had gotten together with Rachel a month before. Ever since I'd heard a rumor that she didn't want her boyfriend doing the secret handshake with "that 'ho next door," I'd tried to cool it in public. I mean, if *I'd* had a boyfriend, I wouldn't have wanted him doing a secret handshake with anybody but me, especially if he looked like Adam.

Because Adam looked basically like Sean. Up close and in daylight, you'd never mistake them for each other, especially now that they were older. Their facial features were different. At a distance or in the dark, all bets were off.

Adam's hair was longer than Sean's and always in his eyes, but you couldn't tell this when they were both wind-blown in the extreme, like now. If you happened to be watching them from your bedroom window as they got in a fight and beat the crap out of each other at the edge of their yard where their mom couldn't see them from their house—not that I would ever do such a thing—you could tell them apart only because Sean was more filled out and a little taller, since he was two years older. Also, they walked differently: Sean cruised suavely, while Adam bounced like the ball that got away from you and led you into the street after it.

But what I always looked for to tell them apart instantly, when I could see it, was Adam's skull-and-crossbones pendant on a leather cord. I'd bought the pendant from a bubble gum machine when we were twelve. In one of my many failed attempts over the years to become more girl-like, I'd been trying for a Miley Cyrus pendant for myself. The last thing I wanted was a skull and crossbones. I'd given it to Adam because it was made for him.

Suddenly I realized I was standing on the hot wood of the dock, still touching elbows with Adam, staring at the skull-and-crossbones pendant. And when I looked up into his light blue eyes, I saw that *he* was staring at *my* neck. No. Down lower.

"What'cha staring at?" I asked.

He cleared his throat. "Tank top or what?" This was his seal of approval, as in, *Last day of school or what?* or, *Dallas Cowboys Cheerleaders or what?* Hooray! He wasn't Sean, but he was built of the same material. This was a good sign.

I pumped him for more info, to make sure. "What *about* my tank top?"

"You're wearing it." He looked out across the lake, showing me his profile. His cheek had turned bright red under his tan. I had embarrassed *the wrong boy*. Damn, it was back to the football T-shirt for me.

No it wasn't, either. I couldn't abandon my plan. I had a fish to catch.

"Look," I told Adam, as if he hadn't already looked. "Sean's leaving at the end of the summer. Yeah, yeah, he'll be back next summer, but I'm afraid I won't be able to compete once he's had a taste of college life and sorority girls. It's now or never, and desperate times call for desperate tank tops."

Adam opened his mouth to say something. I shut him up by raising my hand. Imitating his deep boy-voice, I said, "I don't know why you want to hook up with that jerk." We'd had this conversation whenever we saw each other lately. I said in my normal voice, "I just do, okay? Let me do it, and don't get in my way. Stay out of my net, little dolphin." I bumped his hip with my hip. Or tried to, but he was a lot taller than me. I actually hit somewhere around his mid-thigh.

He folded his arms, stared me down, and pressed his lips together. He tried to look grim. I could tell he was struggling not to laugh. "Don't call me that."

"Why not?"

"Dolphins don't live in the lake," he said matter-of-factly, as if this were the real reason. The real reason was that the man-child within him did not want to be called "little" anything. Boys were like that.

I shrugged. "Fine, little brim. Little bass."

He walked toward the stairs.

"Little striper."

He turned. "What if Sean actually asked you out?"

I didn't want to be *teased* about this. It could happen! "You act like it's the most remote poss—"

"He has to ride around with the sunroof open just so he can fit his big head in the truck. Where would you sit?"

"In his lap?"

A look of disgust flashed across Adam's face before he jogged up the stairs, his weight making the weathered planks creak with every step. I wasn't really worried he would ruin things for me and Sean, though. Adam and I had always gotten along great. When the older boys picked on us, we stood up for each other as best we could. The idea of me hooking up with Sean bothered him simply because he hated Sean with the white heat of a thousand suns, and the feeling was mutual.

A few minutes later, just as I was helping the clueless captain of a ski boat shove off, I heard footsteps on the stairs behind me. Sean alert! Sensory overload! But no, I saw from the skull-and-crossbones pendant that it was Adam.

On cue, Sean puttered past us in a powerful boat, blasting Crossfade instead of Nickelback for a little variety, looking so powerful himself in cool sunglasses, his tanned chest polished by the sun. He waited until he reached the very edge of the idle zone (Mr. Vader was probably watching from somewhere inside the marina to make sure the boys idled in the idle zone) and floored it across the lake to make another delivery.

I'd forgotten all about Adam behind me until he tickled

my ribs. In fact, I was so startled, I would have fallen in the lake if he hadn't caught me. This was the second time ever a boy had touched my bare tummy, and something of an anticlimax.

Don't get me wrong—the attention and his fingers on my skin were very pleasant. But he was just being friendly, brotherly. He was totally devoted to Rachel, and he knew I was totally devoted to Sean. It was like craving a doughnut and getting french fries. You were left with an odd taste in your mouth, and you still wanted that doughnut afterward.

Mmmmm, doughnut.

For the rest of the morning, I pumped gas. I worked on my baby tan through the SPF 45. At lunchtime I went up to the marina and ate the chicken salad sandwich Mrs. Vader made me and watched *What Not to Wear*, which I'd been studying recently almost as hard as I'd studied for my algebra final this week. I ate veeeeeeeeery slowly, one nibble of bread and scrap of celery at a time, in case the beginning of Sean's lunch coincided with the end of mine.

After Mrs. Vader looked in on me the fourteenth time, I got the hint and galloped back down to the gas pumps. Of course *that's* when Sean and Adam roared back into the marina in the boat.

I gave up. Now that Sean had seen me dry, it was safe to go swimming. *Safe* being a relative term. I knew from experience that before you went swimming off a dock for the first time each summer, you needed to check the sides and the ladder carefully for bryozoa, colonies of slimy green critters that grew on hard surfaces underwater (think coral, but gelatinous—*shudder*). They wouldn't hurt you, they were part of a healthy freshwater ecosystem, their presence meant the water was pristine and unpolluted, blah blah blah—but none of this was any consolation if you accidentally *touched them*. Poking around with a water ski and finding nothing, I spent the rest of the afternoon watching for Sean from the water.

And getting out occasionally when he sped by in the boat, in order to woo him like Halle Berry coming out of the ocean in a James Bond movie (which I had seen with the boys about a hundred times. Bikini scene, seven hundred times). Only I seemed to have misplaced my dagger.

Sometimes Sean was behind the wheel. Sometimes Adam was. I could tell which was which even when I was too far away to see the skull and crossbones. Adam was the one waving to me, and Sean was the one looking hot behind his sunglasses. Maybe Sean was watching me and I simply couldn't tell from his mysterious exterior. He only *appeared* unmoved by my newfound buxom beauty.

Yeah, probably not. There were several problems with this theory, not the least of which was that when they passed by, I never timed my exit from the water quite right for Stage Two: Bikini. Then, in case they did turn around, I had to appear as if I'd meant to get out all along—for some reason other than driving Sean to distraction with lust.

Oh—hair toss—I was getting out to look at teen fashion mags, like a normal almost-sixteen-year-old girl. I examined the pictures and checked this info against what I'd gathered from *What Not to Wear*, plus some common sense (I hoped). High fashion was all well and good, but if it prompted the object of your affection to comment that you looked pregnant or you had elf feet, really it wasn't serving its purpose.

Around four o'clock I climbed the stairs and walked around to the warehouses. I knew the boys wouldn't save me the hike by driving around to the gas pumps to pick me up. Adam might, if it were up to him, but it wasn't up to him.

Just as well. Adam, Sean, Cameron and my brother, all wearing board shorts, stood in a line, pitching wakeboards and water skis and life vests and tow ropes from the warehouse into the boat. Adam, Cameron and McGillicuddy half-turned toward Sean as he related some amusing anecdote that was probably only thirty percent true. In fact, the other boys didn't notice, but Sean had stopped working.

They handed wakeboards around Sean in the line. His only job was to entertain.

I wanted him to entertain me, too. I could listen to Sean's stories forever. The way he told it, a trip to the grocery store sounded like *American Pie*. But I had a job to do. I had a grand entrance to make. While walking toward them, I dropped my backpack, then pulled my tank top off over my head to reveal my bikini.

And just balled up my tank top in one hand as if it were nothing, and threw it into the boat. "Heeeeeey!" I said in a high girl-voice as I hugged Cameron, whom I hadn't seen since he'd come home from college for the summer a few days ago. He hugged me back and kept glancing at my boobs and trying not to. My brother had that look on his face like he was going to ask Dad to take me to the shrink again.

I bent over with my butt toward them, dropped my shorts, and threw those in the boat, too. When I straightened and turned toward the boys, I was in for a shock.

I had thought I wanted Sean to stare at me. I *did* want him to stare. But now that Sean and Cameron and Adam were all staring at me, speechless, I wondered whether there was chicken salad on my bikini, or—somewhat worse—an exposed nipple.

I didn't feel a breeze down there, though. And even I,

with my limited understanding of grand entrances and seducing boys, understood that if I glanced in the direction they were staring and there *were* no nipple, the effect of the grand entrance would be lost. So I snapped my fingers and asked, "Zone much?" Translation: *I'm hot? Really? Hmph.*

Adam blinked and turned to Sean. "Bikini or what?"

Sean still stared at my boobs. Slowly he brought his strange pale eyes up to meet my eyes. "This does a lot for you," he said, gesturing to the bikini with the hand flourish of Clinton from *What Not to Wear*. Surely this was my imagination. He didn't *really* know I'd been studying how to be a girl for the past year!

"Sean," I said without missing a beat, "*I* do a lot for the *bikini*."

Cameron snorted and shoved Sean. Adam shoved him in the other direction. Sean smiled and seemed perplexed, like he was trying to think of a comeback but couldn't, for once.

Off to the side, my brother still looked very uncomfortable. I hadn't thought through how he'd react to the unveiling of the swan. I hadn't thought through *any* of their reactions very well, in case you weren't getting this. I wanted Sean to ask me out, but I didn't want to lose my relationship, such as it was, with everybody else. Like

The Price Is Right: I wanted to come as close as I could to winning Sean without going over.

"Team calisthenics," McGillicuddy called. I understood he wanted to change the subject, but I'd hoped we could skip team calisthenics now that we were all grown up. Mr. Vader used to make us do push-ups together before we went out. The stronger we were, the less likely we were to get hurt. When my brother and Cameron got their boater's licenses and we started going out without Mr. Vader, we kept doing push-ups before every wakeboard outing. It was a good way for the rest of the boys to keep Adam and me in our places.

No hesitation, no complaint—this was part of the game. I dropped on my hands on the concrete wharf just as fast as the rest of them, and started doing push-ups. All five of us did push-ups, heads close together, with limited grunting at first. And absolutely no grunting from me or from Adam. We stayed in shape, because we cared about the calisthenics.

And because we both were in training for sports. Adam might start for the football team this year. I was just trying not to get kicked off the tennis team by an incoming freshman. My game was okay, but I was nowhere near as good as Holly and Beige, who had just graduated. Or Tammy, who would be a senior this year, and team captain. Plus, there was an unfortunate incident last year. I didn't train all winter, got to our first meet, overexerted myself, and barfed on the court. I went on to win the match 6–2, 6–1, but nobody seemed to remember that part. Since then, I'd made sure to stay in shape.

Today I held my own in push-ups. After about fifty, I was nowhere near my limit. Cameron's grunting increased. I tried to concentrate on my own self, but Cameron was hard to ignore. His face turned very red. His arms trembled, and finally he collapsed on his bare stomach. My brother hadn't trembled or grunted as much, but he took the opportunity to lie down on his stomach, too, hoping no one would notice as Cameron drew the fire.

Cameron cursed and said, "I don't know why I can't get my ass in gear today."

Between push-ups, I breathed, "About twelve ounces too much frat party for both of you."

Cameron scrambled toward me. I knew I was in trouble, but it was too late to get up and run. One solid arm circled my waist. With his other arm, he held my legs so tightly I couldn't wiggle or, better yet, kick him in the gut. He took two steps toward the edge of the wharf.

I managed not to plead or scream. After almost sixteen years with boys, I had a lot of control over my natural girl-reactions. It wasn't until he pitched me off that I remembered I *did* want to react like a girl today. Then, as I hit the water, I realized I hadn't screened this swimming area for bryozoa. "Eeee—"

I plunged in. Almost before my toes hit the bottom, I was pushing up through the water, toward the sunbeams and the platform on the back of the boat, which was less likely to harbor bryozoa than any part of the concrete wharf. Ugh, ugh, ugh, I could almost feel a heinous mass squishing past my skin—but I made it safely to the surface.

And slapped myself mentally as I climbed up on the platform. If I'd pulled off my new siren act, Cameron wouldn't have tossed me into the lake. I would have been too delicate and too haughty. He wouldn't have dared to touch me. On the other hand, he did recognize that I was a girl, on some level. If I'd been Adam, he would have just shoved me in instead of picking me up.

By the time I stood on the platform, I remembered I was now wearing a *wet* bikini. I collected myself enough to make jumping down into the boat look halfway svelte. But nobody was looking at me anymore. Cameron and my brother stood over Adam and Sean still doing push-ups.

Adam, eyes on the concrete, kept pushing himself up in an even rhythm. Sean watched Adam with a little smile and gritted teeth, turning redder and redder. The bulging muscles of Sean's tanned arms trembled.

Oh God, Sean was going to lose.

3

He fell on the concrete with a groan, followed by eleven choice curse words. Adam kept doing push-ups, probably because these games we played tended to change without warning. Sean might claim Adam was required to do five more push-ups per year younger. Adam was no fool. He made sure. Sean stood, and Adam was *still* doing push-ups.

"We've created a monster," my brother said.

Adam did one last push-up for good measure and stood up slowly. He clapped his hands together to brush off the dust. And then—*don't do it, Adam, don't make Sean any angrier than he already is*—he gave Sean a grin.

"I don't believe it!" shouted Cameron. "You know what else? Adam is taller! Stand back-to-back and let me make sure."

Sean refused to stand back-to-back with Adam. They goaded him and called him names that I can't repeat, but that had to do with Sean being a girl, the worst insult imaginable. So Sean and Adam stood back-to-back. Sure enough, Sean was more muscular and filled out, as always, but Adam was half an inch taller.

Adam turned and gave Sean that grim look with dropped jaw, trying not to laugh. "I'm the biggest."

"Ohhhhhh!" Cameron and my brother moaned like Adam had gotten in a good punch on Sean in one of their boxing matches. I'll spare you the full five minutes of size jokes that ensued. Tammy and some other girls on the tennis team had told me they were so jealous of me growing up around boys, because I had a window into how boys thought. This, my friends, was the deep, dark secret. The size jokes went on and on as if I weren't there, or as if I weren't a girl. I wasn't sure which was worse.

Sean smiled, wincing only a little when they shoved him. He would keep smiling no matter what they said to him. This was one of the many things I loved about Sean. Surely the boys knew they couldn't break him. They would try anyway.

I was a little concerned about what Sean would do to Adam later. Sean didn't let Adam get away with stuff like that. But I supposed that was Adam's business, the dumbass.

Disgusted, I sat in the boat with my back to them. When they ran out of size jokes for the moment—they would think of more as the afternoon went on, trust me—they piled into the boat and proceeded to argue about who got to drive first. The consensus was that Sean could drive first as a consolation prize because he was a loser.

There was no question about me driving. I got my boater's license when I turned fifteen, just like they did. The problem was that I didn't know my left from my right. This was their fault, really. They taught me to waterski when I was five years old. Nobody thought I'd get up and stay up on the first try, so I wasn't properly instructed on the dismount. I couldn't steer. Too terrified to drop the rope, I ran into the dock and broke my arm.

My *right* arm. At the time, my brain must have been designing the circuitry that told me left from right. Because since then, I'd never been able to hear Sean yell, "Go left!" or my brother holler, "Turn to the right!" without thinking, *Okay. I broke my right arm. This is my right arm. They want me to turn this way,* by which time I had missed the turn, or run the boy I was pulling on the wakeboard into a tree. We found this out the hard way last summer, the first time I tried to pull Adam.

Sean started the engine and putted through the marina waters, and Adam had the nerve to plop onto the seat across the aisle from me. Sean reached the edge of the idle zone and cranked the boat into top speed. Adam called to me so softly I could barely catch his words over the motor, "Close your legs."

"What for? I waxed!" I looked down to make sure. This was okay now, because Sean was facing the other way and couldn't hear me in the din. Indeed, I was clean. I spread my legs even wider, put my arms on the back of the seat, and generally took up as much room as possible, like a boy. I glanced back over at Adam. "Does it make you uncomfortable for me to sit this way?"

He watched me warily. "Yes."

"May I suggest that this is your problem and not mine?"

He licked his lips and bent toward me. "If it keeps Sean from asking you out, it's going to be *your* problem, and you're going to *make* it my problem."

"Speaking of which," I said, crossing my legs like a girl. "Thanks for staying out of my way. How the hell am I supposed to get Sean to ask me out when he's all pissy?"

"You wanted me to lose to him at team calisthenics? That was too sweet to miss."

"You didn't have to win by quite so much, Adam. You knew I needed him in a good mood. You didn't have to rub it in."

Adam grinned. "And you wanted me to stop growing?"

"Do *not* make a joke about your size. If you can't think of anything to talk about except your large size, please say nothing at all."

So we sat in silence until Sean slowed the boat in the middle of the lake. McGillicuddy put on his life vest, sat on the platform, slipped his feet into the bindings of his wakeboard, and hopped into the water. He and Cameron had been the ones to discover wakeboarding, and they did it first while the rest of us were still waterskiing. To look at them today, you'd think they'd never gotten the hang of it. My brother face-planted twice in his twenty-minute turn. Cameron had a hard time getting up. Frankly, I was beginning to worry.

Since we were kids, we'd spent every summer afternoon skiing and wakeboarding behind the VADER'S MARINA boat as advertisement for the business. Sean had even convinced Mr. Vader to go all out with a boat made especially for wakeboarding, which made bigger waves. Bars arched over the boat for attaching the tow rope, and speakers on the bars blasted Nickelback like the music came on automatically with the boat motor. (Once I'd brought the first Kelly

Clarkson album and asked to play it rather than Nickelback while we wakeboarded. They'd laughed in my face and called me Miss Independent for months.)

We held a special wakeboarding exhibition when the lake was crowded on the Fourth of July and Labor Day. But our show during the Crappy Festival in two weeks was the most important, because sales of boats and equipment at the marina were highest near the beginning of the summer. Okay, it was actually the *Crappie* Festival. Crappie is a kind of fish, pronounced more like *croppie*. The Crappie Festival had a Crappie Queen and a Crappie Bake-Off and a Crappie Toss, in which folks competed to throw a dead fish farthest down the lake shore. Sean started calling it the Crappy Festival, which sounded a lot more fun.

But the festival would be no fun at all if we kept wakeboarding like *this*! None of us had been out on the water since Labor Day last year, but come on. I never expected Cameron and my brother to be quite so awful on their first time out. And since Sean would be watching me now, I hoped I broke the cycle.

I strapped a life vest over my bikini. Such a pity to cover my shapely body (snort). Then I tied my feet tightly into the bindings attached to my board. I hopped into the water, wakeboard and all, and assumed the position. I wished my brother would putter the boat away from me a little faster.

The wakeboard floated on its side in front of me as I crouched behind it with my knees spread. Talk about needing to close my legs! The embarrassing stance had caused me to get up too quickly and face-plant more times than I cared to count, just to save myself a few seconds of the boys cracking jokes about me that I couldn't hear.

Not today. I relaxed in the water. Anyone care for an eyeful? I parted my knees and gave Adam the okay sign. He was spotting. Sean and Cameron watched me, too, as concerned as I was that we *all* sucked and Mr. Vader would pull the plug on our daily outing. No pressure. When my brother finally got around to opening up the engine, I let the boat pull me up and relaxed into the adrenaline rush.

Wakeboarding was pretty simple. I stood on the wakeboard like a skateboard, and held onto the rope as if I were waterskiing. The boat motor left a triangular wake behind it as the boat moved through the water. I moved outside it by going over one of the small waves. Then I turned back inward and used one wave as a skateboarding ramp to take off. I sailed over the wake, and used the opposite wave as a ramp to land.

After a few minutes I mostly forgot about the boys, even Sean. The drone of the motor would do that like nothing else: put me in this different zone. Even though I was connected by a rope to the boat and the outside world, I was all alone with myself. I just enjoyed the sun and the water and the wakeboard.

My intention all along had been to get my wakeboarding legs back this first day. Maybe I'd do tricks when we went out the next day. I didn't want to get too cocky and bust ass in front of Sean. But as I got more comfortable and forgot to care, I tried a few standbys—a front flip, a scarecrow. There was no busting of ass. So I tried a backroll. And landed it solidly.

Now I got cocky. I did a heelside backroll with a nosegrab. This meant that in the middle of the flip, I let go of the rope handle with one hand, reached down, and grabbed the front of the board. It served no purpose in the trick except to look impressive, like, *This only appears to be a difficult trick. I have all the time in the world. I will grab the board. Yawn.* And I landed it. This was getting too good to be true.

My brother swung the boat around just before we reached the graffiti-covered highway bridge that spanned the lake. Cameron had spray-painted his name and his girlfriend's name on the bridge, alongside all the other couples' names and over the faded ones. My genius brother had tried to paint his own name but ran out of room on that section of bridge.

MCGILLICUDD

Y

Jennifer Echols

Sean wisely never painted his girlfriends' names. He would have had to change them too often. For my part, I was very thankful that when most of this spray-painting action was going on last summer, I was still too short to reach over from the pile and haul myself up on the main part of the bridge. I probably had the height and the upper body strength now, and I prayed none of the boys pointed this out. Then I'd have to spray-paint LORI LOVES SEAN on the bridge. And move to Canada.

It was kind of strange Adam hadn't spray-painted his name with Rachel's in the past few weeks. Maybe he didn't consider it daring enough, if Cameron had managed to do it. Adam *had* painted in red letters in the very center of the bridge, WASH ME. The bridge was a big part of our lake experience. Wakeboarding underneath it would have been cool. But driving the boat under the bridge while towing a wakeboarder was dangerous. Adam had been the one to discover this (seventh grade).

My brother pointed the boat for the rail. A few summers ago, the boys had pulled the guts out of an old pontoon boat that also said VADER'S MARINA down the side. They anchored it near the shore and built a rail sticking out from it, topped with PVC pipe. You could really hurt yourself on this contraption (Adam: eighth grade) but my ride was going great, and I was in the groove. I zoomed far out from the wakeboarding boat, popped up onto the rail, slid across it on the board, and landed nice and soft in the water on the other end.

Adam raised both fists at me. (Nice, but no love from Sean?) If Adam yelled, I couldn't hear him over the boat motor. What I *could* hear as my brother paralleled the shoreline was the Thompsons and the Foshees, our neighbors hanging out on their docks. They came out to watch us practice a lot of afternoons. Cha-ching! Two sales we'd as good as made for Vader's Marina when their kids got a little older.

Then came my family's dock, the Vader's dock at their house, and finally the marina. Dad had gotten home from work, I saw. He and Mr. Vader sat in lawn chairs on the marina dock, holding beers. I really shouldn't have done this if I was trying to be ladylike. But the opportunity was too perfect to resist, and old habits died hard. I arced way out from the wake, aiming for the dock.

My dad saw me coming and knew exactly what was going to happen. He jumped from his chair and jogged up the stairs, toward the shore, so I wouldn't ruin his business suit. His tie flapped over his shoulder. He didn't warn Mr. Vader, who took a sip of beer as I slid past, spraying water probably fifteen feet in the air behind me.

The wall of water smacked right on top of him. I didn't want to turn my head to look, lose my balance, fall, and ruin the effect (chicken salad on bikini, hello). But I saw him out the corner of my eye, T-shirt and shorts soaked, beer halted in midair.

Sean probably heard me cackling all the way up in the boat. Sex-y. I tried to calm myself and concentrate. I wanted to try an air raley, which I'd been working up to last summer but never landed. If there was one good reason for Sean never to ask me out, it was that he couldn't shake the memory of me wiping out after an air raley. Done correctly, I would hang in the air behind the boat for a few seconds with the board above my head. I would then sail down the opposite wake and land sweetly. Done incorrectly, it was a high-speed belly flop.

When I busted ass (or tummy), Sean and the other boys would make fun of me for the rest of the boat ride, and would spread it around their party that night. But they were so far away in the toy boat, and the drone of the motor was like a bubble around me. Nothing could hurt me in here.

I gestured upward, which told Adam to tell my brother to speed up. Adam knew what I planned to do and shook his head at me. What a pain, to stop the boat and *argue* with him about it. *He* didn't consult anyone before *he* tried a trick and busted ass. If we stopped, Sean would insist my turn was over, and I'd be done for the day. I wasn't done. So

I nodded my head vigorously. Adam shook his finger at me, scolding. Then he turned around and spoke to my brother.

The drone pitched higher as the boat sped up. I relaxed, relaxed, relaxed and let the boat and the wave do the work for me. My muscles remembered what they'd tried to do last summer, and this time they were able to do it. I caught miles of air, a huge thrill, and one glance at the boat: four boys with their mouths open. Then I almost panicked as I lost my balance when my board hit its high point behind me. *Almost*—but I kept myself together. I rode gravity down the opposite wave.

Immediately I arced out and back to pick up speed, and did a 360 with a grab. Landed it. Then a 540. Landed it.

I thought I might be pushing my luck. I'd probably break my leg climbing back into the boat. Also, I didn't want my arms to be so sore the next day that I couldn't ride at all. I signaled to Adam that I was stopping and dropped the rope. The handle skipped away from me across the surface of the lake.

As the echo of the motor faded away and I sank into the warm water, I could hear them clapping for me. All four of them, standing up in the boat, facing me, applauding me and cheering for me. "Yaaaaaaay, Junior!"

I had never been so happy in my life.

And it got better.

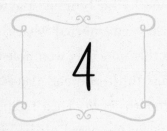

4

I bent over in the water to loosen the bindings, slipped my feet out, and kicked my way back to the boat with my board floating in front of me. As I pulled myself up on the platform, Sean put out one hand to help me—totally unnecessary, since I'd climbed up on the platform a thousand times before with no help.

"I taught her everything she knows," he said loudly enough for the other boys to hear, but looking only at me. He gave me his beautiful smile, a secret smile for the two of us to share, and sat down again.

"That's bullshit," Cameron said.

"I was the one who helped her most with the air raley last summer," my brother said.

"Tough act to follow," Adam told me, shrugging on his life vest. I would have treasured this comment forever if I hadn't been high on Sean.

But I was. So I peeled off my life vest and dropped it on the floor of the boat, sat daintily in the seat where Adam had been, and crossed my legs. Like my fingers had a mind of their own, they bent inward and rubbed my palm where Sean had touched me. I tingled all over again at the thought. Or maybe I tingled because my body was still jacked from how hard I'd worked my muscles out on the water. Either way, I felt so lovely and sated just then, with the sun in my eyes. I wished Adam weren't jumping in for his turn.

Because watching Adam wakeboard was not relaxing. He wasn't careful when wakeboarding. Or in general. He was the opposite of careful. His life was one big episode of *Jackass*. He would do anything on a dare, so the older boys dared him a lot. My role in this game was to run and tell their mom. If I'd been able to run faster when we were kids, I might have saved Adam from a broken arm, several cracked ribs, and a couple of snake bites.

Knowing this, it might not make a lot of sense that Mr. Vader let us wakeboard for the marina. But we'd come to wakeboarding only gradually. When we first started out, it was more like, *Look at the very young children on water skis! How adorable.* One time the local newspaper ran a photo of me and Adam waterskiing double, each of us holding up an American flag. It's okay for you to gag now. I can take it.

But Mr. Vader was no fool. He understood things changed. After the second time Adam broke his collarbone, Mr. Vader put us under strict orders not to get hurt, because it was bad for business. Customers might not be so eager to buy a wakeboard and all the equipment if they witnessed our watery death. To enforce this rule, the punishment for bleeding in the boat was that we had to clean the boat. Adam cleaned the boat a lot last summer.

At the end of the rope, Adam signaled that he was ready to go. I told Cameron, who was driving now. He started too slow, and Adam tried to get up too fast. "Down," I called.

"Come on, LD," Sean muttered as if Adam were right in front of him. Even though I'd heard this joke one billion times and didn't think it was funny, I made sure to look over at Sean and laugh until he saw me laughing. He laughed too.

Adam had attention deficit hyperactivity disorder. This was why I didn't see a lot of him during the school year. I was in all the advanced classes, and he definitely was not. Sean had lots of fun with this. The boys actually called

Adam ADD to his face. They called him LD (for Learning Disability). They called him SAS (for Short Attention Span) and Sassy and Sassafras. They told him the short bus was coming for him. He had a prescription to help him concentrate in school, but he refused to take it because it made him feel dead. In other words, he was perfectly happy with ADHD. Or he *would* have been, if the boys had left him alone about it.

Sometimes I thought he took stupid risks to make up for being slow in school. Or maybe he was just like that. The skull-and-crossbones pendant was perfect for him. The boys told him if he improved his grades, when he graduated he could apply to pirate school.

Cameron brought the boat around and straightened the rope. I told him Adam was ready to go. This time they got it right. Adam got up. Immediately he told me to speed up, and I told Cameron. Adam did a tantrum to blind, which meant he backflipped where he couldn't see and ended with his back to the boat. He preferred tricks with a blind landing. He told me to speed up again, and I told Cameron. Adam did a turn to blind, touched down on the edge of his board, and miraculously managed not to fall.

"Good save!" McGillicuddy shouted from the front of the bow.

"Dumb luck," Sean said.

I smiled at Sean. I would feel guilty later about laughing, as I always did when I laughed at Sean's mean jokes. But while I was there with him, he was so charming, and I couldn't help but laugh.

When I looked back at Adam again, he was in the middle of a 540 to blind, which was fine, but for the love of God, he hardly had time to land before he hit the rails on the pontoon boat. I waved to get his attention, then swiped my finger across my throat: *cut it out*. He signaled for me to speed up.

I told Cameron, "Adam would like to spend this summer in traction. Speed up."

I turned back around in my seat to watch Adam again. Sean was leaning toward me in his seat, watching *me*. "Cold?" he asked me.

Pardon? Yeah, the ninety-degree afternoon and ninety-percent humidity always gave me a chill I couldn't shake. But one delicate, haughty brain cell in the back of my mind told me he was *flirting* with me and I should *feign helplessness*.

"I'm freezing!" I squealed. And just like that, Sean Vader moved across to my side of the aisle and scooted against me in my seat until I made room for him. He put his hot bare arm around my bare shoulders. And I fainted.

No, I didn't really. But I did feel dazed, perhaps from

the hyperventilation. Suddenly I realized Adam had been gesturing wildly at me for several seconds without it even registering with me. He signaled me to slow down. I told Cameron.

Adam did a front flip. Sean said in my ear, "Gosh, I've never seen anyone do *that* before. Makes me want to buy a wakeboard from Vader's Marina!" I giggled. Adam signaled me to slow down more, and I told Cameron.

Adam did a back roll with a grab. Sean put his free hot hand on my bare knee and whispered, "You don't believe Adam's bigger than me, do you?"

This time I missed a beat. I was used to locker room humor. But Sean directing locker room humor at *me*, flirting with *me*? It seemed unlikely that Stage Two: Bikini had worked so quickly. Was I reading him wrong? Adam gave me the thumbs-down, and I told Cameron to slow the boat one more time.

Just as I turned back around, Adam launched into what could only be an S-bend, which was absolutely impossible to land with the boat going this slowly.

Sean, McGillicuddy and I all swore at once, and watched Adam's long, slow death-splash with interest and resignation.

"Down," I called to Cameron.

Sean gave me the funniest look that said *no shit*. I

laughed out loud. He smiled again as he found his board and slipped over the back of the boat to the platform.

Adam emerged from the depths, vaulted over the side of the boat, and stood close to my seat so he dripped on my formerly comfy, sun-dried self. He commented, "S-bend or what?"

"Or what?" Cameron said. "What the hell were you doing, trying it that slow?"

"Sometimes I want to try new things," Adam said. "Sometimes I want to do things I know are bad for me, just for fun and profit. Don't you, Lori?"

I gazed way up at him and gave him a look that said, *Stay out of my net, little dolphin.* He grinned right back at me, defiant.

"Yeah, Adam," I said. "Sometimes I like to stick my finger in a light socket to see what will happen."

He pointed at me. "Exactly." Without another word to me, he took off his life vest and handed it to Sean.

Sean got up on his first try without any trouble. He never attempted any tricks he couldn't do perfectly. We always ended the exhibitions with him. We could count on him to do impressive moves, but nothing he couldn't land.

That's why I watched in disbelief when, after a few textbook flips, he launched an air raley. Surely he wasn't doing it just because *I'd* landed one. Or maybe he was, and this was his way of teasing me. Anything I could do, he could do better.

Except he couldn't. He panicked at the peak of the trick. Overcorrecting, he *did* lose his balance. He face-planted in the lake, rocking the pontoon boat with the splash.

"Down," called Cameron, who was spotting.

"I'll say," agreed my brother.

Adam, who was driving now, brought the boat around. When he cut the motor and the Nickelback, he, Cameron and McGillicuddy hooted and clapped for Sean almost as hard as they'd clapped for me. I wished they would quit. I didn't want Sean mad. Flirting with him was turning out to be a lot harder than I'd thought.

Sean grinned at them from the water. Even though his turn hadn't been very long, clearly he'd had enough. He took off his life vest and tossed it up into the boat. Then he disappeared under the surface.

"What's he doing?" I asked, leaning over the side of the boat, searching for him beneath the water. If the tow rope had gotten tangled, he might need help. And *someone* would need to go in the water with him, perhaps accidentally sliding against him down where no one else could see.

"Boo!" A handful of bryozoa rushed up at me from the lake.

I screamed (for once I didn't have to think about this girl-reaction) and fell backward into the boat. Sean hefted himself over the side with one arm, holding the bryozoa high in the other hand. It dripped green slime through his fingers. "Bwa-ha-ha!" He came after me.

I squealed again. It was so unbelievably fantastic that he was flirting with me, but bryozoa was involved. Was it worth it? No. I paused on the side of the boat, ready to jump back into the water myself. He might chase me around the lake with the bryozoa, but at least it would be diluted. On second thought, I didn't particularly want to jump into the very waters the bryozoa had come from.

Sean solved the problem for me. He slipped behind me and showed me he was holding the ties of my bikini in his free hand. If I jumped, Sean would take possession of my bikini top.

I had *thought* about double knotting my bikini. I'd hoped against hope that Stage Two: Bikini would work, and that Sean might try something like this. Of course, I didn't *really* want my top to come off in front of everyone. Nay, in front of *anyone*. But I'd checked the double knots in the mirror. They'd looked . . . well, double knotted, for protection, sort of like wearing a turtleneck to the prom. I'd re-tied the strings normally.

Now I wished I'd double knotted after all. Sean brought

the dripping slime close to my shoulder. "Go ahead and jump," he said, twisting my bikini ties in his fingers.

"Sean," came McGillicuddy's voice in warning. This surprised me. My brother had never taken up for me before. Of course, none of the boys had ever crossed this particular line.

But that was nothing compared with my surprise when the bryozoa suddenly lobbed out of Sean's hand, sailed through the air, and plopped into the lake. Adam, standing behind him, must have shoved his arm.

Which meant I owed Adam my gratitude for saving me. Except I didn't *want* him to save me from Sean, and I thought I'd made that clear. Saving me from Sean with *bryozoa* . . . that was a more iffy proposition. I wasn't sure whether I should give Adam the *little dolphin* look again when our eyes met. But it didn't matter. When I turned around, he was already stepping over Cameron's legs to return to the driver's seat.

Sean was watching me, though. And Sean wiped the bryozoa residue from his hand across my stomach. This was the third time a boy had ever touched my bare tummy, and I'd had enough.

Through gritted teeth, like any extra movement might spread the bryozoa further across my skin, I told him, "I like you less than I did." I bailed over the side of the boat—

the side opposite where the bryozoa had returned to its native habitat. Deep in the warm water, I scrubbed at my tummy with both hands. A combination of bryozoa waste and Sean germs: it was the best of times, it was the worst of times. Leaning toward worst, because now I had slime on my hands. Or maybe this was psychosomatic. Holding my hands open in front of me in the water, I didn't *see* any slime. I rubbed my hands together anyway.

Something dove into the water beside me in a rush of bubbles. I came up for air. Sean surfaced, too, tossing sparkling drops of water from his hair. "You still like me a lot, though, right?"

"No prob. Green is the new black." Giving up on getting clean, I swam a few strokes back toward the platform to get out again. What I needed was a shower with chlorinated water and disinfectant soap. I might need to bubble out my belly button with hydrogen peroxide.

"What if I made it up to you?" He splashed close behind me. "What if I helped you get clean? We don't want you dirty." He moved both hands around me under the water, and up and down across my tummy.

It was the *fourth* time a boy had touched my tummy! And it was very awkward. He bobbed so close behind me that I had a hard time treading water without kicking him. I needed to choose between flirting and breathing.

Cameron and my brother leaned over the side of the boat and gaped at us, which didn't help matters. I'd been afraid of this. Flirting with Sean was no fun if the other boys acted like we were lepers. Well, okay, it *was* fun, but not as fun as it was supposed to be.

Obviously I would need to give McGillicuddy the *little dolphin* talk. I wasn't sure I could do this with Cameron— Cameron and I didn't have heart-to-heart convos—but I might need to make an exception, if he continued to watch us like we were a dirty movie on Pay-Per-View (which I'd *also* seen a lot of. Life with boys).

BEEEEEEEEEEEEEEEE—

Sean and I started and turned toward the boat. Still behind the steering wheel, Adam had his chin in his hand and his elbow on the horn.

—EEEEEEEEEEEEEEEEEEEEEEEEEEEEEEEEEEEEE

Damn it! I turned around to face Sean and gave him a wry smile, but he'd already taken his hands away from my tummy. The horn really ruined the mood.

—EEEEEEEEEEEEEEEEEEEEEEEEEEEEEEEEEEEE

Sean hauled himself up onto the platform. I followed close behind him, and (glee!) he put out a hand to help me. Cameron and my brother yelled at Adam.

—EEEEEEEEEEEEEEEEEEEEEEEEEP. "Oh!" Adam said as if he'd had no idea he'd been laying on the horn.

He looked at his elbow like it belonged to someone else.

I was in the boat with Sean now, and he was still holding my hand. Or, maybe I was still *clinging* to his hand, but this is a question of semantics. In any case, I pulled him by the hand past the other boys to the bow. We didn't have privacy. There was no privacy on a wakeboarding boat. At least we had the boat's windshield between us and the others.

As I turned to sit down on the bench, I stuck out my tongue at Adam behind the windshield. He crossed his eyes at me.

Sean sat very close to me again. He pretended to yawn and stretch, then settled his arm around my shoulders. I smiled at him and tried to think of something to say. After years of him being vaguely pleasant to me but basically ignoring me, it had never occurred to me that we had nothing in common but wakeboarding—and I suspected wakeboarding might be a touchy subject right now. We didn't need to talk. He kept his arm around me for the short ride back to the marina.

Instead of driving straight to the wharf where we usually parked the boat, Adam slowed at the marina dock so the boys could mock Mr. Vader, who hadn't moved from the position he'd been in when I splashed him, except he'd started on another beer. The boys told him he was all washed up and he should enter a wet T-shirt contest with that figure, and so forth. My brother called to Dad, "Nice save, Pops."

"Hey." Dad tipped his beer to us. "You've got to be fast with Lori around."

"I have to say, young lady," grumbled Mr. Vader. "I was very impressed with all your shenanigans. Right up to the point I got doused. I want you to plan to close the Crappie Festival show until further notice."

Which meant, *Until you screw up.* That was okay. He'd told me I was better than the boys at something for once in my life! I turned to Sean and beamed so big that my cheeks hurt.

Sean squinted into the sun, wearing that strange, fixed smile. Even my brother and Cameron gave each other puzzled looks rather than congratulating me again. Only Adam met my eyes. He shook his head at me.

Oh, crap. Crappy. Holy Crappie Festival! I had upset the natural order. After Adam had already upset the natural order in team calisthenics. I should have thought *all* of this through better.

Sean began, "But I didn't even get a chance to—"

"I saw what happened," Mr. Vader told him. "You had your chance. The Big Kahuna has spoken."

"Race you to the wharf," Adam called. Mr. Vader said

something to my dad, put down his beer, and tried to hurl himself up the steps to the marina faster than Adam idled the boat. The boys were doofuses, and it was genetic. Adam let Mr. Vader win by half a length, touching the bow of the boat to the padded edge of the wharf just after Mr. Vader dashed past. The boys howled, and someone threw a couple of dollar bills at Mr. Vader. He picked up each bill like it mattered and limped back down the stairs toward my dad.

Then Sean jumped out of the bow to tie up the boat. He, Cameron, and my brother tried to trip each other as they took armfuls of equipment into the warehouse with them. No one gave me a single backward glance.

Adam cut the engine. "Now you've screwed up."

"How?" I asked casually, stepping out of the boat. "You think Sean won't want to go out with me now that I've taken his spot in the show?"

Adam just looked at me. That's *exactly* what he thought. I was getting tired of his warnings about Sean. I gathered my clothes and my backpack, turned on my heel, and flounced away. Which was fairly ineffective with bare feet, on a rough concrete wharf.

"You'll see at the party tonight," Adam called after me.

"No, *you'll* see," I threw over my shoulder. Sean and his pride would prove no match for Stage Three: Slinky Cleavage-Revealing Top.

5

As I walked home, balancing on the seawall that kept the Vaders' yard and my yard from falling into the lake, my cell phone rang. I pulled it out of my backpack without hurrying. The only people who ever called me were my dad, my brother, assorted Vaders to tell me to come early or late to work (including Sean, but he always sounded grumpy that he had to call me, so it wasn't as big a thrill as you'd think), Tammy to tell me to come early or late to tennis practice, and Frances. I glanced at the caller ID screen and clicked the phone on. "What's up, Fanny?"

From the time Mom died until I was eleven, Frances the au pair had hung out in the background of my life. Once

Sean overheard someone calling her Fanny, which apparently is a nickname for Frances. We found this shocking. I mean, who has a nickname that's a synonym for derrière? Who's named Frances in the first place? So the boys started calling her Fanny the Nanny. Then, Booty the Babysitter. Then, Butt I Don't Need a Governess. This had everything to do with the nickname Fanny and the fact that she tried not to get upset at being addressed in this undignified manner when she was trying to raise compassionate, responsible children. It had nothing to do with her having an outsized rumpus. Frances had a cute figure, if you could see it under all that hippie-wear.

"I'm on the dock," she said.

I peered the half-mile across the lake and waved to her. I could hardly make her out at that distance, against the trees that sheltered the Harbargers' house, where she nannied now. I could only see her homemade purple patchwork dress, which was probably visible from Mars.

"The children and I watched the last part of your wakeboarding run," she said. "You've improved so much since last year!"

"Thanks! But that's not why you called. You're dying to know what happened with Sean."

Frances was in on my Life Makeover. Not the fashion part—sheesh, look at her. She hadn't even given me advice on what to do. I wandered into the Harbargers' house every week or so and told her how my plan was shaping up, and she told me I was being ridiculous and it would never work. I guess I went to her because I wanted to hear some motherly input. We had the perfect relationship. She wasn't really my mother, so I could listen to her input and then do the opposite. The difference between me and girls with mothers was that I didn't get in trouble for this.

"Let me guess," she said. "When Sean saw you in a bikini, he acted incrementally more cozy to you. Therefore you expected him to profess his love. You honestly did. And he didn't do a thing."

"Rrrrrnt!" I made the game-show noise for a wrong answer. I told her what had really happened.

"What?" she said when I told her Adam beat Sean at calisthenics. "What?" she said when I told her I landed the air raley. "What?" she said when I told her Sean wiped out. As I got to the part about Sean touching my tummy *repeatedly*, she interrupted me so often that I had to pitch a frustrated fit. I threw the phone down to the grass, cupped my hands around my mouth, and hollered across the lake, "LET. ME. FINISH!" *Inish, inish, inish,* said my echo. I picked up the phone and told her the rest of the story, ending with my plan to implement Stage Three that night.

"But you don't really think wearing a low-cut top to the boys' party will solve all your problems, do you?" she asked.

"Of course not. I think wearing a low-cut top to the boys' party will show Sean I'm ready for him."

"Lori, no girl is ever ready for a boy like Sean. How were finals?" Clearly she wanted to change the subject to impress upon me that boys were not all there was to a teen-age girl's life. As if.

"Finals?" I asked.

"Yes, finals. To graduate from the tenth grade? You took them yesterday."

Wow, it was hard to believe I'd played hopscotch with the quadratic equation only twenty-seven hours ago. Thinking back, it seemed like I'd sleepwalked through the past nine months of school, compared with everything that had happened today.

Time flew when you were having Sean.

Mr. Vader let the boys throw a party at their house every Friday night during the summers. He reasoned that if they were home, they weren't out drag racing the pink truck against Mrs. Vader's Volvo. So I'd been to a million of these parties. It should have been old hat. Yet it was new hat. I had put on my seductress bonnet. Ha! Not really.

This would have dented my hair, which I'd blown out long, straight, and bryozoa-free.

We'd had a lot of rain in May, which made the lake full, the grass lush, the trees happy, and the ground soft. Walking through my yard into the boys' yard in high heels was like wading in the lake where the sand was deep, feet sinking with every step. I felt like Elizabeth Bennet in *Pride and Prejudice* (tenth grade English) hiking through pastures to a house party, her petticoat six inches deep in mud. Wait a minute—oh crap, I'd forgotten my petticoat.

And what ho, cheerio, here was Mr. Darcy getting his groove on with Miss Bingley under a massive oak tree. Actually, it was only Adam and Rachel.

I did a double take. Adam pressed Rachel against the tree, kissing her. Deeply.

This shouldn't have surprised me. They'd been together for a month. He was my age, and she was a year younger, so neither of them had a driver's license. But they met at the arcade or the bowling alley. I'd even seen them kiss before, a quick peck. I'd just never seen them kiss like *this*.

Knowing Adam, I would have thought his love life would be like every other part of his life: dangerous. It started that way. Since middle school, he'd followed in Sean's footsteps, coming on to a different girl every week. I had imagined this would continue as Adam got older. The only difference between Adam and Sean would be that Adam would get in a lot of fistfights with the girls' ex-boyfriends in the movie theater parking lot, and occasionally I would hear a rumor about a drive-by that he would swear wasn't true.

Instead, he'd been with Rachel for a month. A whole month. It seemed stable. Even boring. Well! Maybe her own budding womanhood had brought out the pirate in him. Yaaarg.

He broke the kiss, turned, and stared at me as if I had no right to watch what was going on in a public place. That's when I realized *I* was staring at *them*. Standing still in the middle of the yard, just staring, my heels settling in the dirt. Watching him kiss Rachel bothered me, but I couldn't put my finger on why. There was nothing to do but wade to the front porch of his house.

I rang the doorbell.

Nothing happened.

After a few minutes, I pressed my ear to the door and rang the doorbell again. I definitely heard the chime of the doorbell inside, the bass beat from the stereo, and laughter. Why didn't someone come to the door? Maybe they had a closed-circuit camera on me right now and everybody at the party was watching me on TV, taking bets on how long I'd stand there before wading home. I peered into the top corners of the porch for a camera.

Why hadn't I dispensed with the last three coats of eye shadow and gone with my brother to the party when he told me he was leaving the house, like usual? He was a dork, but at least he was totally comfortable in social situations, like Dad. Comfortable, or oblivious, which amounted to the same thing.

The door swung open, revealing Ashton Kutcher. Just kidding! It was actually my tennis team captain, Tammy.

"Tammeeeeee!" I squealed, hugging her. This was what girls did.

"Loreeeee," she said in her husky, low-key voice, playing along. "I figured someone had better open the door, because you obviously weren't going to. Why'd you ring the doorbell? No one's ringing the doorbell. They just walk in. Besides, don't you practically live here?"

Did I? I supposed I knew the territory, and always hoped someone in the house noticed me. This sounded less like I was a member of the family and more like I was a stray dog. I changed the subject. "What are *you* doing here? Are you friends with Sean or Adam or Cameron?"

She knitted her eyebrows at me. "I'm friends with *you*."

"Right!" I said. Was she? I fought the urge to look behind me, like she'd actually been talking to someone over my shoulder the whole time.

"You look great!" she said, pulling me through the

doorway and into the brighter light of the foyer. "Cute top, and your eye shadow looks great!"

"Thanks!" I watched her reaction to make sure she'd said what I'd thought she said. The stereo was loud, and *you look great* was not something I heard every day, or every year.

"You weren't planning to wear mascara?" she asked. "Usually when people wear shadow and liner that heavy, they wear mascara with it."

"I do have some! I forgot! Thank you!" I grabbed her hand. She flinched. I didn't let go. "Will you come with me to my house to make sure I put it on right? I'm serious."

Her eyes moved past me out the door, toward my house. "You live next door, right?" Clearly she didn't want to venture too far from the party with a weird-eyed lunatic such as myself.

"Noooooo," I said sarcastically. "I live on a planet far, far away. Women are from Venus. Come on." I pulled her toward my house until she seemed to be keeping pace with me. Then I dropped her hand. I knew girls pulled each other by the hand and squealed a lot, but it was too weird for me to do it for long.

Adam and Rachel were still making out. They'd moved behind the tree where I wouldn't have seen them unless I'd been looking for them (which I was). I almost pointed them out to Tammy, then decided against it. I didn't want to sound like a fifth grader: *Wow, kissing!*

"You really do look cute," Tammy said, "other than the—you know. Why the makeover?"

I took a deep breath and readied myself for my next step into girldom: spilling a giggly secret. When we'd gotten far enough away from Adam and Rachel that they couldn't hear me, I said, "I have a crush on somebody. I'm trying to get him to notice me."

"Sean Vader?"

I stopped short in my garage, and Tammy ran full force into me. I shoved her and shrieked, *"Why would you think that?"*

"Gee, I don't know," she yelled back. "Maybe because *you have told me this over and over!*"

I blinked. "I have?"

"Maybe not in so many words."

Oh *no!* "So, I've been really obvious at school?" I tried to keep most of the horror from my voice.

"Isn't everyone?" She flipped her hair back over her shoulder with a tennis ace flick of the wrist that I would try later to reproduce (and fail). "Girls fall all over themselves when Sean comes around. He's hot, and soooooo sweet."

"He sounds like fondue." Mmmmm, fondue. I opened the door and led the way into my house.

I didn't think we were being quiet, particularly. High heels may have looked dainty, but they didn't sound that way on a tile floor. Maybe it was just that my dad was so absorbed in the convo on his cell phone. For whatever reason, when we emerged from the kitchen into the den, he started, and he stuffed the phone down by his side in the cushions. I was sorry I'd startled him, but it really was comical to see this big blond manly man jump three feet off the sofa when he saw two teenage girls. I mean, it would have been funny if it weren't so sad.

Dad was a ferocious lawyer in court. Out of court, he was one of those Big Man on Campus types who shook hands with everybody from the mayor to the alleged ax murderer. A lot like Sean, actually. There were only two things Dad was afraid of. First, he wigged out when anything in the house was misplaced. I won't even go into all the arguments we'd had about my room being a mess. They'd ended when I told him it was *my* room, and if he didn't stop bugging me about it, I would put kitchen utensils in the wrong drawers, maybe even *hide* some (cue horror movie music). No spoons for you! Second, he was easily startled, and very pissed off afterward. "Damn it, Lori!" he hollered.

"It's great to see you too, loving father. Lo, I have brought my friend Tammy to witness our domestic bliss.

She's on the tennis team with me." Actually, *I* was on the tennis team with *her*.

"Hello, Tammy. It's nice to meet you," Dad said without getting up or shaking her hand or anything else he would normally do. While the two of them recited a few more snippets of polite nonsense, I watched my dad. From the angle of his body, I could tell he was protecting that cell phone behind the cushions.

I nodded toward the hiding place. "Hot date?"

I was totally kidding. I didn't expect him to say, "When?"

So I said, "Ever." And then realized I'd brought up a subject that I didn't want to bring up, especially not while I was busy being self-absorbed. I clapped my hands. "Okay, then! Tammy and I are going upstairs very loudly, and after a few minutes we will come back down, ringing a cowbell. Please continue with your top secret phone convo."

I turned and headed for the stairs. Tammy followed me. I thought Dad might order me back, send Tammy out, and give me one of those lectures about my attitude (who, me?). But obviously he was chatting with Pamela Anderson and couldn't *wait* for me to leave the room. Behind us, I heard him say, "I'm so sorry. I'm still here. Lori came in. Oh, yeah? I'd like to see you try."

"He seems jumpy," Tammy whispered on the stairs.

"Always," I said.

"Do you have a lot of explosions around your house?"

I glanced at my watch. "Not this early." I passed through my bedroom, into my bathroom, and found the mascara in the drawer. Poised with wand to eye, I realized Tammy hadn't followed me. I leaned through the bathroom doorway.

She stood in the middle of my bedroom, gazing around with wide eyes. I hadn't made my bed. In three years. And the walls were plastered with wakeboarding posters and snowboarding posters and surfing posters (I was going to learn to snowboard and surf someday, too). It all might have been overwhelming at first—not exactly *House Beautiful*.

"Is this McGillicuddy's room?" she asked.

"What! No. McGillicuddy's a neat freak. Also he collects Madame Alexander dolls."

She turned her wide eyes on me.

"Kidding! I'm kidding," I backtracked. Why did I have to make up stuff like that? My family was weird enough for real.

She stepped over to my bookshelf to peer at the stacks of wakeboarding mags and sci-fi novels. Well, let her stare, the bi-yotch. I didn't need her damn help. I swiped the mascara across my lashes and popped back out of the bathroom. "Ready?"

She looked up at me guiltily like she'd gotten caught thumbing through my issues of *Playboy* (stolen from McGillicuddy, and more useful for learning what not to wear than teen fashion mags). But she hadn't found those yet. Standing at my bedside table, she held the photo of my mother.

She set the photo down and narrowed her eyes at me. "*You're* not ready." She came into the bathroom and explained the aesthetic we were going for was not clumps of lashes honed to points and sticking out from my eyeballs like the tentacles of a starfish. Somehow in the purchase of my fine cosmetics, I'd missed out on the idea of an eyelash comb. She used a regular hair comb to tease my lashes apart.

We stomped back down the stairs (no cowbell, but I made air-raid siren noises to warn my dad) and waded across the yard. Adam and Rachel were *still* making out behind the tree, like they hadn't seen each other for a year. Jeez, we'd just gotten out of school *yesterday*.

I tried to look without really looking and letting on to Tammy I was looking. Both Adam's hands were on Rachel's shoulders, holding her in place while he kissed her. Both *her* hands were under his T-shirt, on his stomach—his stomach hard with muscle, his smooth tanned skin . . . I couldn't see this, of course, but I knew it was there.

It had never occurred to me to be jealous of Rachel

before. Suddenly I was burning with jealousy, sweating in the humid night. It must be that I saw Rachel as an understudy for Holly and Beige and all the girls at my school who knew what to wear and how to act or, if they didn't, hid it well. I could totally see a third-grade girl feeling inferior to Rachel and wanting to be Rachel when she grew up. That third-grade girl was thinking someday maybe *she* could have a boyfriend like Adam, who loved her like Adam—

"Argh!" I bellowed as I pitched face-first onto the pine needles. I must have gotten my heel caught in a snake hole.

"Are you okay?" Tammy asked, holding out a hand to help me up. "Nice trick. You should put that in your wakeboarding routine."

"What? And steal Adam's thunder?" I brushed myself off. Did I need to go home and change? I was new to this idea of a "wardrobe," and my supply of Slinky Cleavage-Revealing Tops was limited. Fortunately, my denim miniskirt was made to look dirty. It was very me. And the wild pattern in my top probably concealed any decayed-leaf stains. Satisfied, I walked on with Tammy. I didn't look back to see whether Adam had watched me fall. I hadn't forgotten that stare of his.

"Want to play tennis tomorrow night, after it's cooled off a little?" she asked.

"Sure," I said before I thought. Tammy and I played tennis all the time in school. Why not out of school, too? After I'd answered, I realized that of course Sean would ask me out for tomorrow night and I wouldn't get to go with him! Right. I wasn't lucky enough to have problems like that. Silly me. "You shouldn't have to drive all the way down here to pick me up and then drive me all the way back."

"I don't mind."

Stepping onto the Vaders' porch, I said, "McGillicuddy can come get me when we're through." My brother never had anything to do on Saturday night. It ran in the family.

"McGillicuddy?" she asked.

We walked back into the party. Fluttering my finely separated lashes, I could hardly believe my luck. Usually at parties I wandered in alone and hoped someone took pity and talked to me. Then, by degrees, I faded into the shadows. Tonight I was entering the party *with* someone.

Of course, the instant we hit the wall of crowd and sound, she pointed across the dark room and shouted above the music, "I'd completely forgotten McGillicuddy was coming back from college! I'm going to say hi." The two people I felt most comfortable hanging with, hanging with each other instead!

Except for the kids from Birmingham and Montgomery

who were vacationing on the lake with their parents and had wandered into the party, I knew all these people from school. I'd been in school with most of them since kindergarten. For some reason, this didn't help, and possibly made things worse. I watched Tammy weave between knots of people to hug McGillicuddy. I thought about going after her. But then I might look like I didn't want her to leave me by myself because I wasn't good at talking to people at parties. Imagine!

Suddenly things looked way, way up. I saw Sean in the darkness, next to the stairs, with his back to me. He stood a few inches taller than his friends who'd just graduated too, who surrounded him. Sean was always surrounded.

As I crossed the room to him, folks kept stepping in my way, wanting to say hey and have conversations with me, of all things. The one time I *wasn't* interested in being well-liked. Drat! I made nicey-nicey, go away, and resumed my uphill trek across the room, only to have someone else stop me.

By the time I finally reached him, my heart pounded. But it was now or never. I made myself grin at his friends as I slid my hand across his T-shirt, feeling his hard stomach underneath the cotton. I almost flinched at how good and how intimate it felt, but through the marvel of my own willpower, I did not flinch. I laid my head playfully against his chest, as I'd seen girls do when they claimed to be just friends with a guy but everyone whispered something more was going on.

I half-expected him to shout, "Get off me!" and shove me away. Not because Sean would ever do this to a girl—he had more charming ways of extricating himself from cretins—but because my life generally had been a long series of mortifications, and Sean shouting in alarm at my embrace would fit right in. The other half of me expected him to chuckle gently, but not make a move of his own quite yet. It might take him a while to get used to the new me.

He didn't chuckle. He didn't shove me away. He did *exactly* what he was supposed to. He slipped his arm around my waist and drew me closer against his warm body. I felt him nodding at something one of the other guys said about baseball, but he didn't say a word to me or anyone. As if a greeting like this from me were the most natural thing in the world. He smelled even better than usual, too, just a hint of cologne. A woodsy scent with undertones of musk and gunpowder.

I snuggled against him, nose close to his warm, scented chest, and enjoyed a few more seconds of this tingling paradise. What heaven if my whole summer could be like this—

His low voice vibrating through my body, he asked his friends, "Have you been watching the Braves? Awesome pitcher or what?"

Oh God, I was hugging *Adam*!

6

I jerked away from him. Almost instantly I realized I shouldn't jerk away from him, because the situation would be slightly less mortifying if I pretended I'd known it was Adam all along.

The damage was done. Worse, I didn't have a chance to burst out the front door and run—not walk, *run*—all the way home, dash upstairs to the computer in my room, and book a one-way ticket to Antarctica, to join the commune there for teenagers too socially challenged for the chess club. Before I could take another step away, he caught my elbow.

"Later," he called over his shoulder to the guys. He

pulled me into a corner and bent down to whisper in my ear, "You're blushing."

I opened my lips. I didn't seem to be taking in enough oxygen through my nose. "I'm sunburned," I breathed.

"You thought I was Sean." The little dolphin was smiling, enjoying my discomfort too much for my taste.

"No, I didn't." I made an effort to slow down my breathing through nose *or* mouth. My bosom was heaving, I tell you. I had a heaving bosom!

And Adam noticed. He focused on the V of the Slinky Cleavage-Revealing Top Meant for Another, and slowly, slowly dragged his light blue eyes up to meet my eyes. "I should have said something. I didn't realize what was happening at first. And then, when I did, I was *really* enjoying myself."

"Shut up. I didn't think you were Sean."

"You thought I was Sean, because I'm as big as him." He winked at me.

There was no mistaking him for Sean now that I was staring up at him. I tried to figure out what had fooled me into assuming it was him without checking his face and the length of his hair. It could have been his height compared with the boys two years older than him. But something else was different about Adam. He was more confident. More relaxed. More tingle-worthy, like Sean had always been. Those friendly prickles spread across my chest again as Adam's fingers moved a little, reminding me he still held my elbow.

I pulled reluctantly out of his grip. "It's not funny, Adam. What if somebody tells Rachel?"

"She won't mind. She knows we're friends."

From my end, the hug hadn't felt like we were friends. It had felt like we were teetering on the very edge of friendship, about to tumble down a waterfall into depths unknown. With rocks hidden underneath the water. Hard ones.

Or *I* was about to take a tumble, by myself. *He* still stood in his living room like always, at the edge of his crowded party, laughing down at me, thinking, *The Slinky Cleavage-Revealing Top has cut off the blood supply to Lori McGillicuddy's brain.*

I reached up to his neck. Surprise finally flashed in his eyes—ha!—but he let me pull the skull-and-crossbones pendant on the leather string out from under his shirt.

"You make sure this shows at all times," I said. "It's your cowbell. It tells me when you're coming." I patted his chest, which I should not have done if we really were just friends. As we've established, my brain was walking a few steps behind my body and couldn't quite catch up. Face still burning, I took a few steps into the crowd. Where would

Sean most likely be? Flirting with Holly and Beige simultaneously, pitting the best friends against each other to see what would happen. But no, they were dancing together at the edge of the crowd in the living room, without Sean.

I stopped suddenly.

Walked back to Adam, who was still watching me.

"What's wrong?" he asked.

"You're right," I breathed, my words sinking into the pit of my stomach. "Rachel won't mind us hugging."

"What do you mean?"

"She's in the side yard, making out with Sean."

By the time I'd kicked off my (dirty) heels and dashed after Adam outside, he'd already gotten himself pinned flat on his back under Sean on the pine needles. I winced as Sean shifted to get better leverage and pressed his forearm harder across Adam's neck.

"Sean!" I hollered, running all the way around them, trying to find a way in. Sometimes I couldn't pull Sean off Adam, or I even got hit myself. There was a time when I would have tried anyway, disregarding my personal safety. This was back when we were all very small and made of rubber. Nowadays, hollering was more effective, unless they were really into it, in which case nothing would work.

They were really into it. Adam managed to kick Sean

off him and get in a blow to Sean's chin. Usually they didn't hit each other in the face because Mrs. Vader would see the bruises and they'd get in trouble. Adam must be angry enough tonight not to care.

Sean came right back with a punch to Adam's gut. While Adam was absorbing that one, Sean pinned Adam's arm high behind him, tripped him, forced him to the ground, and put one knee on his back. Tonight Sean was more aggressive than usual, intent on causing more pain.

Or—Something wasn't right. Had they switched shirts? Surely not. Sean didn't let Adam borrow his clothes. Slowly it dawned on me that Sean was Adam and Adam was Sean. For the first time ever, Adam was kicking Sean's ass.

"Holy shit," I said helpfully. "Adam, let him go."

Adam looked up at me, blue eyes shadowed in the dark between the trees, skull and crossbones swinging at his neck.

This gave Sean the opportunity to buck Adam off. He snatched Adam down to the ground and punched him.

"Sean," I said, stepping close over them again. They weren't listening to me. I looked over at Rachel, who had her hands over her mouth and her toes turned in. She looked exactly like a James Bond girl from the pre-Halle Berry era, one of those ditzes who stood safely in the corner and *never* had a dagger when she needed one, like Honey Ryder, or Plenty O'Toole. "Rachel, a little help?" I called.

She stared at me with big doe eyes like she had *no idea* what I was talking about. She'd been with Adam for a month and she'd never seen one of his fights with Sean?

"Call Adam off!" I yelled at her. "Or Sean. Whichever one you can get!" Both.

"Sean, stop," she said in a whiny little voice that couldn't have reprimanded a Chihuahua.

"Forget it." I knelt down on the pine needles and shouted directly at Sean and Adam, on their level. "I'll go get your dad. Your dad will come down into your party and cuss at you and spit on the ground in front of your friends."

They didn't even slow down. Whoever was on top had the other in a choke hold so real, the victim was turning red.

"I'll go get your mom!"

Adam gave Sean a final shake and stood up quickly, before Sean could catch his leg and pull him down. "What is the *matter* with you?" Adam screamed.

Yeah. What was the *matter* with Sean? He was making out with Rachel, that's what. This was terrible! It blew my theory out of the water that Sean had never asked me out because I was too young for him. Rachel was a year younger than *me*!

Normally I would have given up, slunk home, and broken out the Cheetos. I would have immersed myself in *I, Robot* for comfort (again) and put it down after every paragraph to wallow in my own outrage and loss. He'd flirted with *me* just that afternoon! He'd wiped bryozoa on *me*!

Luckily, this was no normal night. Tonight I was on a mission. So I reasoned that all wasn't lost. Maybe Sean had flirted with me because he was overcome by my charms and wit (ho ho), but he didn't see me as the girlfriend type. After all, I'd never been anyone's girlfriend. Rachel didn't have this problem. Sean had watched Rachel go out with Adam for a month.

Sean stood up more slowly than Adam had, taking deep, ragged breaths, clearly hurting. I waited for Adam to decide Sean had had enough of his wrath for now, and turn to Rachel. I looked forward to hearing what Adam would call her, to save me the trouble. But he never even glanced in her direction. He said again, still to Sean, "What the hell is the matter with you?" His voice broke.

Now Cameron and McGillicuddy came jogging through the trees, with Tammy behind them, and more interested spectators from the party bringing up the rear. Even though the fight was over, McGillicuddy stepped between Sean and Adam. A smart move, because these things had been known to flare up again. Which was exactly what the ring of spectators hoped for. Tammy tried to catch my eye. I shook my head.

Cameron took Adam's face in both hands and peered at the big smudge under his eye. He let Adam go and hissed at me, "Get rid of him in case Mom comes down."

I felt honored to be included in the intrigue. But why couldn't Cameron ask me to get rid of Sean instead?

That was okay, for now. Adam needed me. I put my hand on his back and said, "Walk away." We moved through the yard, toward the side of the house. A pine needle hung from one of his brown curls in the back.

After fifteen paces, his breathing had slowed almost to normal. I felt him start to turn. "Don't look back," I said.

He took a deep, calming breath through his nose. He was fighting the part of ADHD that made him short-tempered and impulsive. The part that made him attempt to smash his big brother's face in.

"Try not to take it so seriously," I said in what I hoped was a soothing tone. Which was hard for me. Generally I was about as soothing as body lotion with skin conditioners and ground glass, but this was important. "It's probably a temporary thing. He's mad at you for making the size jokes this afternoon—"

"I didn't start the size jokes!"

"You finished the size jokes. So he seduced your girlfriend. She said yes because you've been together for a whole month. Maybe things have gotten into a rut." We passed the corner of the house and reached the side yard, where no one lingering in the front yard could see us. I stopped him under the floodlight hanging from the eaves. "Let me look at your eye." I reached up to cup his face in my hands, like Cameron had.

"Is my mom going to notice?"

Yes, I thought. "I can't tell," I said. I didn't want him dashing after Sean to get revenge. "Maybe if we cleaned it up."

He pulled off his T-shirt, wet the edge of it with the faucet attached to the house, and brought it to me.

"Sit down," I said. "I can hardly see you way up there."

We sat in the grass. I leaned close, tilted his face to the light, and wiped at the half-dried blood. He watched me with serious eyes.

And I felt that tingle again. The same pesky tingle I'd felt when I hugged him in the living room, when I thought he was Sean. Only I *knew* now he wasn't Sean. And I'd seen Adam without his shirt a million times, including hours of no-shirt goodness that very afternoon. The tingle stayed.

This was only natural, I guessed. We both were still pumped full of adrenaline. We were excited about the fight and mad about Sean and Rachel, and jealous. I was leaning close to him, our lips almost touching. He still smelled like cologne, plus something sexier.

"Well?" His voice broke again. He cleared his throat and said in his deep boy-voice, "Well?"

"Well, it's not coming off." I gave the oozing blood one last gentle wipe and sat back on my heels. "I'm sorry about what happened."

He shrugged and kept giving me that intense, serious look. And I kept tingling. It was almost like he was sending me his adrenaline telepathically, and I could feel what he was feeling.

Which didn't make sense. Because he ought to be heartbroken about Rachel. But this felt *good*.

"The fireworks are starting without you." I stood up quickly and held out my hand to help him up (for show only—he weighed twice as much as me). He put his shirt back on. Pity. Keeping my hand on his back, I steered him toward the muffled noise of explosions, down through the shadowy backyard to the dock.

Boys—mostly football players my age or a year older—lit bottle rockets and held them until the fuse sparked almost down to their fingers. At the last possible second, they tossed them into the black lake. A pause. Then deep under the surface, the water glowed bright green for an instant. The lake said *foop*.

Adam would probably ask me to help him collect the bottle rocket sticks off the lake bottom tomorrow, another one of his dad's rules. I didn't want to do this, because I'd had an unpleasant bryozoa scare climbing up the ladder of their dock last year. But I preferred the boys shooting bottle rockets into the lake to shooting them toward my yard, which tended to give my dad a nervous breakdown. And I couldn't ask them to stop altogether. Adam got testy if he went more than a few weeks without setting something on fire.

The boys shouted greetings to Adam and shared their bottle rockets with him. He watched the sparks with delight and hardly a hint of evil. Then he handed me a bottle rocket and lit it for me with a lighter from his pocket. I finally relaxed. We forgot all about Rachel and Sean.

For a little while.

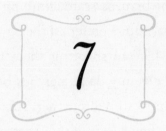

7

During the school year, Holly and Beige had said micro-miniskirts should be the official tennis team uniform because we could move better during games, and material wouldn't get bunched between our legs like it did with shorts. I'd never had the material-bunching problem myself. I figured Holly and Beige made this up so they'd have an excuse to wear micro-miniskirts to class when we had a tennis meet right after school. Thank God they'd graduated and I was (mostly) rid of them. For me, tennis and fashion didn't mix. Serena Williams I was not.

Normally I would have worn gym shorts and one of Adam's huge T-shirts to play tennis with Tammy. However, the tennis courts sat between the high school and the main road through town, which also ran past the movie theater, the arcade, and the bowling alley. If Sean was out with Rachel, he would drive right by. So it was the official tennis team micro-miniskirt for me.

"Is that part of your makeover to catch Sean? Wearing that skirt when you're not forced to?" Tammy asked as we passed each other, changing ends of the court. We were the only idiots playing tennis on a ninety-degree Saturday night, so we had the court to ourselves. Besides the ball bouncing and the rackets whacking, the only sounds were the cars swishing by on the road and the buzz of floodlights overhead. Still, the echo off the asphalt court made it hard for us to hear each other while we played. So we'd been carrying on a conversation like this for an hour, one sentence every two games when we traded sides.

She beat me twice, and we passed at the net again. "I'll admit it's not much," I said. "I need a new plan, also referred to as The Back-Up Plan When Stage Three: Cleavage Has No Effect on Cradle Robbers. Any advice?"

I won one game, and then she beat me again. As we approached the net, she suggested, "Make him jealous? I don't know. I'm no good at being sneaky and going behind people's backs."

I dropped my racket with a clatter on the court. "Don't

look now"—which of course was her cue to look—"but maybe my old plan worked after all! Sean dumped Rachel already, and the pink truck is coming for me!"

The pink truck was an enormous pickup that used to belong to the marina, so old that the red paint had faded to pink and the VADER'S MARINA signs had peeled off the sides. Cameron had taken possession of the pink truck when he turned sixteen. We gave him no end of hell about it. Then, when he graduated from high school, his parents gave him a new truck to take to college, and Sean had inherited the pink truck.

Sean, being Sean, had managed to make the pink truck seem cool. There were many rumors around school about the adventures of Sean in the pink truck with Holly or Beige. I had dreamed of my own adventures in the pink truck. Now my dreams had come true!

Except that in my dreams, I was not a dork. "Sean came to pick me up!" I groaned. "This is terrible! What do I do?"

"Act casual," Tammy said in a level tone, watching the truck park just outside the high chain-link fence. "Interested, but not manic."

"How do I do that? I don't know how to do that!"

"Go hug him hello."

Just then a breeze kissed the back of my neck under my ponytail, reminding me how hot the night was, and how heavily I'd exerted myself chasing Tammy's serves. "I'm sweaty."

"If he likes you, he won't mind." She led the way through the gate and headed for McGillicuddy's side of the truck to distract him for me.

As I walked toward Sean's side, Sean opened the door and started to get out. I had to walk all the way around the big, heavy door to hug— *"Adam!"*

He looked down at me, arms open wide for me because I'd been holding mine out. He dropped his arms when he saw the look on my face. "Nice to see you, too," he said grumpily.

I patted him lightly on one cheek—the cheek opposite the one with the blue bruise under his eye. The pats got harder until I was pretty much slapping him. "Why can't you be Sean? Oh, God." I knew almost before I'd gotten the words out that Adam didn't deserve that. I stood on my tiptoes and slid my arms around him. "I'm so sorry. I didn't mean it."

He didn't say anything. But he did put his arms around my waist.

I looked up at him. "It's just. . . . Why are you driving Sean's truck?"

"It's *my* truck."

Sean must have gotten a new truck for graduation, just

like Cameron. And now Adam was driving the pink truck, because—crap. "Oh, Adam, I forgot your sixteenth birthday!"

"I know."

Those two words told me he'd already thought everything I was thinking. Our birthdays were three weeks apart. We'd had a few birthday parties *together* when we were little. How could I have forgotten his freaking birthday? "I was preoccupied with finals," I gasped, "and summer coming up, and—"

"Sean. I know."

"Oh, I'm so sorry," I said sincerely. I hugged him as hard as I could, then started to pull back.

His hands didn't leave my waist. "I'm still kind of mad," he said.

Laughing, I tightened my hold on him. I felt him bend down and put his chin on my shoulder.

On the other side of the truck, talking with McGillicuddy, Tammy raised one eyebrow at me.

That's when I had an Idea.

I ran my hand down Adam's side until I found his hand. "Let's talk privately."

He looked down at his hand in mine like he couldn't quite believe this was happening. I couldn't either. "Okay," he told our hands.

I called across the hood of the truck, "Adam and I will be right back. We're going to talk privately."

Tammy and McGillicuddy stared at us, then each other, then us again. Finally I pulled Adam away, swinging his hand like holding hands with him wasn't the weirdest thing ever. We walked down the sidewalk, around the corner of the fence to the side of the tennis courts that faced the road. The very edge of the pool of light from the tennis courts touched us, so we could be seen from the road: very important to the plan.

I backed him against the fence. I didn't shove him or anything, but I'm sure he felt trapped against the chain links because I stood so close to him, and the determined expression on my face was so frightening.

I squeezed his hand. "I still think Sean and Rachel's little fling is fake. Sean's trying to get revenge on you, and Rachel's trying to make you jealous. She wants to heat up your romance for the summer. In two weeks, by the Crappy Festival, it'll be over with Sean, and things will be back to normal." And Sean would be free again. "But you need to up the stakes to keep her interested. To make sure she comes back and never leaves you. To teach her a lesson."

Adam breathed faster. His blue eyes widened as it dawned on him what I was going to suggest. In fact, he looked close to panic. I almost backed down. I'd be pretty embarrassed if he ran screaming away and hitchhiked with someone on the road just to escape from me. But I had to salvage my chance with Sean. I'd never gotten as close to him as I had yesterday afternoon in the lake! So I pressed ahead.

"You and I should pretend to hook up. That'll show Rachel you're not putting up with her bullshit. And it'll show Sean I'm girlfriend material. We'll drive them mad, I tell you, mad!" I made a joke out of it in case Adam burst into uncontrollable laughter at the idea of even pretending to hook up with me. Then I could say I'd been kidding all along. I knew Adam valued me as a friend. But I offered him a way out in case he thought I was a dog.

He swallowed, still watching me, alarmed. "You want to hook up with me. To make Rachel jealous, so I can get her back."

"Right," I said, wondering why this was so hard for him to understand. Maybe he didn't watch as many MTV reality shows as I did.

"You think that would work? It would make her jealous to see me with another girl?"

"Sure." It was looking more and more like my dog theory was correct. "Unless you think I'm the wrong girl for the job. I'm just suggesting you do this with me because I'm trying to hook Sean, too." Did he think being with me would ruin his chances with Rachel or any other girl at our school forever, as surely as if he'd gone out with Godzilla?

"Okay," he said quickly.

"Okay?" I had thought it would be harder to convince him. I'd missed something. Which, I'll admit, was not all that unusual.

"Okay, we'll pretend to hook up." He still watched me. His eyes traveled from my eyes to one of my ears, down my neck and further down to my cleavage (thank you sports bra!). He actually leaned back against the fence for better viewing of my legs beneath the micro-miniskirt. Then he met my gaze again. Like he was surveying what he had to pretend to hook up with, and it checked out, with no damage to his rep.

I should have appreciated this. I passed inspection! But his gaze made me uncomfortable enough that the pesky tingle returned. Worse, he seemed to sense he was causing me to tingle. He made that face with his jaw dropped, trying not to smile. Then he gave up and broke into the broadest grin I'd seen on his face since—well, since yesterday afternoon, when he beat Sean at push-ups.

A memory flashed into my mind of Adam, age eight, jumping off the roof because Sean dared him to. (Broken ankle.)

I wondered what I'd gotten myself into.

Suddenly very nervous, I rubbed my tingling hands together and looked toward the road. "Should we drive to the movie theater parking lot where more people will see us together? We could pretend to k—" I looked back at Adam at that moment, and something stopped me in the way he watched me.

"Iss," he said, nodding.

"And they'll tell everyone. It'll get back to Sean and Rachel."

Now he was shaking his head no. "That's not going to work. We can't stage it so carefully. I'm an awful actor. Something tells me you'll never win an Oscar, either."

"Hey—"

"So we need to make it look natural. We need to act like we're into each other all the time, without checking first to see if someone is watching." His hand was trembling in mine. "Maybe this is the first time we've realized we're into each other. And maybe this is our first kiss."

He leaned down. When his face got within a few inches of mine, I giggled. Not the fake giggle of a tomboy raised by wolves, either. A real, girly, high-pitched giggle that originated somewhere in my sinuses and made me want to slap myself. There was hope for me yet.

"See?" he whispered against my lips. "This is what

96

we're trying to avoid. We need to act like we *want* to do this." And he kissed me.

There were still a few inches between our bodies. So there was no embrace. Only his lips, soft, warm, on my lips.

Our fingers, interlaced.

A tingle so strong, it turned into a vibration.

A hick driving by on the road, hollering, "Get a room, Vader! Wooooo!"

Adam laughed a little against my lips. I thought I detected the slightest shudder, like he felt the vibration too. Then he backed up and looked at me. "Is that what you wanted?"

"Yes," I breathed. "Is that what *you* wanted?"

His smile faded. "Yeah. Come on." He led me back up the sidewalk, toward Tammy and McGillicuddy still talking together but never taking their eyes off us. When we got close to the truck, Adam asked me, "Will you go out with me tomorrow night?"

"I'd love to," I said, focusing only on him like I had no idea my brother was staring a hole through my head.

"I'll pick you up at seven," Adam said. "No, wait."

"That's fine," I laughed. "You can drive a hundred feet and pick me up at seven."

"I'll walk over at seven." He smiled and twisted a lock of my hair around his finger. "Seven is lucky."

McGillicuddy cleared his throat.

"That's not what I meant!" Adam roared at McGillicuddy in outrage. Adam's cheeks were bright red.

"Are we finished?" Tammy asked quickly. "Lori, didn't you lose four or five balls over the fence in the kudzu?"

McGillicuddy, Adam, and I all started for the kudzu patch. But Tammy caught me by the sports bra, and I snapped backward. She waited until the boys were out of earshot before she hissed, "Is there something you want to tell me?"

"Yes!" I said happily. "But you can't tell anybody. And I don't mean you need to keep this secret the way the tennis team kept a secret last year, by leaking it to the basketball team." I'd seen Holly and Beige work.

"I promise," Tammy said, pulling a tennis ball from her pocket and bouncing it against the truck fender. She'd seen Holly and Beige work, too. On *her* secrets. Personally, I'd never had a secret for them to work on before. I was that popular.

"Don't mention it to McGillicuddy. He might blab it to Cameron, depending on how funny he thought it was. You're the only person I'm telling. So if it gets out, I'll know you spilled it." I explained in brief the ingenious and diabolical plan. "Doesn't that sound ingenious? And diabolical?"

"It sounds hopelessly complicated. Wouldn't it be easier to hook up with Adam for real? He's adorable."

"No, he's not!" I eyed her, unsure I should have shared the diabolical plan with her after all. Granted, Adam *was* adorable. But I was after Sean. I didn't intend to *act* on Adam's adorableness. And at that moment, I realized I didn't want anyone else to act on it, either. He was part of my Adorable Special Reserve. Now that Tammy was telling me there was indeed a problem with my plan, I found that I didn't want to hear it.

She bounced the ball methodically against the truck. "You think *Sean* is adorable."

"Duh."

"And Adam looks a lot like Sean."

"True dat."

"So why don't you think Adam's adorable?"

I snatched the ball in midair and shook it at her. "Because he's Adam!"

Adam and McGillicuddy had found all the escaped balls. They stood in the kudzu, oblivious to snakes, and threw tennis balls as hard as they could at each other. The balls bounced off their arms and chests, and they dove after the balls into the vines again. Typical. I turned back to Tammy. "You said yourself that Sean was fondue."

"No, *you* said that."

99

"You said girls fall all over themselves to get to Sean. They don't do that for Adam."

"But wouldn't that be better? You'd have to share Sean. Adam would be yours."

I'd thought girls giggled secrets to each other because they understood each other. Tammy didn't understand me at *all*.

Adam had made a hangman's noose out of a length of vine and was chasing McGillicuddy down the sidewalk with it. Both of them laughed like ten-year-olds. Adam really did look adorable when he smiled.

So, maybe Tammy was half-right. I knew Adam had been kidding about seven being lucky. I knew he was just playing the part with me, like we'd planned, so he could get Rachel back. But part of me, a tiny part about the size of a candy heart, wished he dreamed about getting lucky with me.

8

Sean had the nerve to smile down at me. His blue eyes were lighter than the sky behind him, a spooky blue. He shouted above the drone of the boat motor, "Lori, when we're old enough, I want you to be my girl-friend."

I tried to speak, spluttered, and spit out a lock of my hair the wind had blown into my mouth. I was nothing if not glam. "You're old enough," I told him. "And if Rachel is old enough, *I'm* old enough."

He bent closer and said, "I'll pick you up at seven."

What a thrill! He'd asked me out! I was going out with Sean! Only, those were the words I'd *heard*. What he'd *mouthed* was something different. Like on one of those kung fu movies the boys loved to watch, with English words dubbed over the Chinese sound, and the characters' mouths never quite matching up.

"Bastard!" I sat straight up in my cold, wet bed. I wiped and wiped with my palms, but I could *not* get all my hair out of my mouth. Then I realized what I'd said out loud. "Sorry, Mom," I told her sweet sixteen photo on my bedside table. My alarm clock blared Avril Lavigne, "Keep Holding On."

Right! I vowed to move things along with Sean that day at work. I would make sure he knew I was part of the hot scene. Unfortunately, the instant I stepped into the marina office, I was presented with an obstacle to this goal in the form of a seething matriarch with pinstriped hair.

"Lori!" she roared, spinning around in her office chair.

"Good morning, boss!" I said brightly, giving her a wave.

She narrowed her eyes at me. "It was bad enough when Adam told me yesterday that Sean stole Rachel from him. He wanted me to ground Sean, or take away his Wii."

"Ground him for how long?" If Sean was grounded, he wouldn't even be able to pick Rachel up and drive her back to his own house. He could only see her if her mom dropped her off. Talk about embarrassing. Sean didn't like to be embarrassed. Instant breakup! On the other hand, if he were grounded for the whole summer, even after he broke up with Rachel, he could never go out with *me*.

"I can't *ground* him," Mrs. Vader squealed. "I can't *ground* a legal adult. And I can't *ground* one son for stealing the other's girlfriend. But I've got to do something. Adam's cheekbone is blue. Sean is holding his jaw at a funny angle and won't let me look at it. The physical fights are bad enough. They can't torture each other psychologically, too!"

Of course they could. They'd been doing it for years. Obviously Sean was careful not to call Adam ADD when their mother was around. Somehow I didn't think pointing this out would help my current situation, so I nodded like I understood her plight. "Do I have gas?"

She folded her arms. "And this morning Adam told me he's going out tonight. With *you*."

"Don't say I didn't warn you," I sang, sweeping my hand down my body in the *all this can be yours* gesture.

"You were after *Sean*," she spat.

"Who, me?" Yes, I actually said, *Who me?* I was beginning to see Adam's point about me never winning an Oscar. "I was after Adam."

"You were after Sean. You watched him moonily all day

Friday. You took an hour and a half for lunch, waiting for him to show up."

I raised my chin haughtily. "You people are slave drivers. Can't I have a break to watch *What Not to Wear*?"

"Besides," she said more calmly, examining me too closely for comfort, "if you and Adam really were about to start going out, Adam wouldn't have complained to me just yesterday about Sean stealing his girlfriend. He'd be happy to have you, and he'd forget all about her."

Good point. Where was Adam to take some of this heat? I looked around futilely for him. Then I told part of the truth. "It's the principle of the thing. Adam's also mad Sean broke his remote-control pickup that he got for Christmas six years ago."

She went limp with exasperation. "*Adam* broke that! Adam said Sean broke it on purpose, Sean said Adam broke it, and I believed Sean."

"Exactly."

She stared me down, waiting for me to crack, while I tilted my head this way and that way and fluttered my eyelashes at her. Finally she nodded at the door and said, "You're in the warehouse. With Sean."

A torture worse than death, ho ho. A second chance to move things along. Sean and I helped the full-time workers take boats out of storage. Mostly we found the boats that needed to be brought down, cleaned the seats, and topped off the fluids in the engines. As we finished each boat, Cameron and my brother delivered it across the lake. Adam had gas. More than throwing me with Sean for spite, I think Mrs. Vader was trying to keep Sean and Adam away from each other.

I did my best with Sean, but it wasn't good enough. He treated me *exactly* like he always had, except for two days before in the boat. He would do things that were so, so sweet, like get me a soda from the office when he got one for himself. But then he spoke to an old lady customer in the same loving tone he'd used on me. Also his mother.

Maybe he didn't know yet that Adam and I were going out. I couldn't imagine Mrs. Vader had shared this tidbit with him if she thought it would add fuel to the fire. So Sean didn't understand he was supposed to realize I was girlfriend material and feel jealous. Skilled though I was in the womanly arts of manipulation and talking smack, I couldn't quite figure out a way to pass this info along to him without coming out and telling him, which would blow my cover. So I was super-sweet right back to him and traipsed around the warehouse in my tank top and generally acted like he and I were just friends. Ha!

Late in the afternoon we went wakeboarding. Yesterday we'd skipped calisthenics for the first time ever, and we had no taste for them today either. My brother didn't announce it was time for calisthenics, and neither did Cameron. Sean and Adam just glared at each other as they threw life vests at each other to pitch into the boat.

I think we all were a bit on edge by the time we launched. But Sean spotted first and Adam sat way up in the bow, so we began to relax. After all, Sean and Adam weren't likely to get into it on the boat. Cameron and my brother were there to pull them off each other. My brother was bigger than any of them.

As for me, I wanted so badly to sit across the aisle from Sean. He might scoot over and share my seat with me, like two days before. But no, he would never do this and mess up his "relationship" with Rachel—not while it was having the desired effect on Adam.

Subtlety and patience were not a couple of my strong points. Perhaps you have figured this out. However, I managed to keep my eyes on the prize, which meant bypassing the seat next to Sean and hunkering down against the wind in the bow with Adam. Problem was, Sean's seat faced backward so he could spot for my brother wakeboarding. He didn't even *see* the knee-weakening look Adam gave me as I sat down.

But Cameron in the driver's seat could see us, and Sean might be so gracious as to turn around once in a while. I wondered what Adam would want to do with me. Whether he would try to touch me, and where. Maybe he was thinking the same thing I was thinking: it was a bit early for PDA in our faux couplehood. If we suddenly fell in love after almost sixteen years of being friends, it would be *obvious* we were faking to show Sean we didn't care about him and the treacherous Rachel.

For whatever reason, Adam didn't touch me. He was content to watch me, darkly. I had no idea why he was looking at me this way. Clearly we were *not* thinking the same thing after all.

Then I had another problem. Adam had told me two days before that I'd screwed my chances with Sean by taking his place in the wakeboarding show. Maybe I should face-plant an air raley so Sean wouldn't think I was rubbing it in. But you know what? I was still so thrilled with my great runs two days in a row, I wasn't willing to throw it for a boy. Even a boy this important. Maybe this was something I could work on as I matured.

Sean had another bad run. Adam did too—ouch!—but at least he enjoyed it. I had another run so fantastic, I decided I'd work on an S-bend the next day. Ideally this would involve *landing* the S-bend, unlike some adrenaline junkies I knew.

And Sean didn't seem to mind I did well and he didn't.

He was his usual pleasant self, a bit too distant for my taste, same-old, same-old. He must have *really* been basking in the fact that he'd gotten Adam's goat. I mean, girlfriend. That was okay. I would get Sean in the end.

I was feeling very hopeful about the whole situation when we docked at the marina. Maybe it was the sun again, or the lingering glow from my good run. But when Adam helped me out of the boat and we did the secret handshake, I didn't even care it was a complete waste of handshake because Sean had already gone into the warehouse and didn't see it happen. Doing the handshake made me feel like *somebody* valued me enough to do a secret handshake with me.

"By the way," I said during the high-five, "what was up with the look you kept giving me in the boat?"

"What look?" Adam asked, blushing. He knew what I meant.

"This look." I showed it to him.

He squinted at me. "I'm not a doctor, but I'd say either indigestion or a stroke."

We laughed, touched elbows, and parted ways on the wharf. I sauntered to my house, taking big sniffs of the hot evening air scented with cut grass and flowers, not minding too much that I had to spend a few minutes blowing a gnat out of my nose. I wished Sean had asked me out like he was supposed to. But if I had to go on a fake date to get him, there was no one I'd rather go on a fake date with than Adam. I might even enjoy it, as friends.

After supper with Dad and McGillicuddy, and a luxe beauty routine that included teasing my mascara-coated eyelashes apart with the comb attachment to McGillicuddy's electric razor, I was ready. An hour early. I peered out my bedroom window at Adam's house and wondered what he was doing right now. Getting ready himself? Taking a shower?

Even though the picture of him in the shower was all in my head, I took a step back from the window at the force of the picture, and the realism. I must be picturing *Sean* in the shower, because the boy in the shower wasn't wearing a skull and crossbones.

Adam wore the skull and crossbones while wakeboarding and swimming. He must wear it in the shower too. Or did he? In all the times over the years we'd worked together at the marina, when he'd bent down and the pendant had swung from the leather string, I'd never noticed a dirty patch in the shape of a skull and crossbones on his neck. Okay, I couldn't stand another hour of torturing myself this way.

I said *ta* to my dad and waded in my high heels down my yard to the dock. Then I untied the canoe and set off across the lake. Crossing the lake in a canoe, a sailboat, or anything without a motor could be harrowing. The lake was about a half mile wide at this point, and a canoe crossing the traffic pattern was likely to get T-boned by a speedboat driven by someone from Montgomery who didn't understand boating laws and was drunk to boot. But the busiest part of the day was over, and I paddled fast.

On the other side, I tied up to the Harbargers' dock. Funny that the kids weren't swimming. They'd probably been swimming all day and had brained each other several times with plastic shovels and nearly drowned once, and their nanny was about damned tired of it and had made them get out of the water. I was all too familiar with this scenario.

Sure enough, as I waded up their yard, I heard the kids laughing behind the fence. Even I, the Great Lori, Number One Seed Wakeboarder on the Vader's Marina Team, didn't think I could scale a wooden fence wearing high heels. Pitching one shoe over and then the other, I jumped up, grabbed the top of the fence, and hoisted myself up.

The kids were making castles in the sandbox. Really just mounds of sand, but I'm optimistic. Frances sat cross-legged in the grass nearby, wearing her summer hippie uniform: tie-dyed T-shirt, hemp shorts, bare feet. (Stuck in the grungewear of her college days, she also had a winter hippie uniform that involved wool and Birkenstocks.) She and the kids stared up at me.

I dropped down on their side of the fence, walked over, and sat on the edge of the sandbox. "Whatsamatter?" I asked the kidlets. "You've never seen such a vision of loveliness?"

"There's a gate, you know," Frances said.

"I didn't notice."

"It's on the other side of the house, off the driveway, where people usually put gates."

"I got in, didn't I? God, you always want me to do things *your* way." This was sort of unfair. Frances had been pretty hands-off as governesses went. Like I had anyone to compare her to. "Well, this time I've definitely done something that isn't covered in the child care manual. Go ahead, ask me what happened at the party. Ask me what happened the night *after* the party. Ask me where I'm going now, dressed to kill."

The kids gaped at me when they heard the K word. Which probably didn't reassure them about their futures as well-adjusted teens under the instruction of Fanny the Nanny. It didn't help matters that while I told Frances about Sean and Adam, she placed her hands on her knees and began one of her deep-breathing relaxation techniques.

"Well?" I shouted. Her eyes flew open. I prompted her, "Doesn't this sound like a supreme girl-adventure?

Do you watch MTV reality shows? That's a silly question, isn't it? Never mind. Maybe they have drama like this on *The NewsHour with Jim Lehrer*."

"Something else is going on with those boys," she said.

"Like what?"

"I'm not sure. It's been years since I gave Adam *or* Sean *or* Cameron *or* Bill the evil eye. You're the only one who comes to visit. Except . . . Mirabella, we do not eat the sand." She scooped up the girl and took her inside. The girl didn't protest. These children had been drugged or lobotomized.

I turned to the boy. "Don't you ever protest?"

He shook his head.

"Hold strikes? Write letters of complaint? She always told us we had permission to do anything if we could write a convincing argument for it. We tried."

He intoned in a cute little zombie voice, "We do not eat the sand."

Frances came back out and deposited the girl in the sandbox again. The girl examined some nearby dried leaves hungrily. "I guarantee you something else is going on there," Frances repeated. "Yours isn't the only plot."

"Right. Sean stole Rachel from Adam to get revenge. Sean is always the instigator of the plot. For the record, Sean is the one who started calling you Butt I Don't Need a Governess. I probably wouldn't have been half the hellion I was, if it hadn't been for Sean egging everybody on."

"I don't know," Frances said thoughtfully. "It was Adam who set off the firecrackers in my homemade cheese."

"OH MY GOD I HAD COMPLETELY FORGOTTEN ABOUT THE HOMEMADE CHEESE." I laughed until I choked. The children studied me with serious eyes. They were adapting to the Montessori method a lot better than McGillicuddy and I had.

"I always loved Adam," Frances said.

I sniffled. "You *did?*" Frances wasn't too free with the professions of love.

"But Adam had room to grow. Sounds like he still does."

Feeling strangely defensive of Adam all of a sudden, I said, "*Everybody* has room to grow."

"And I don't want you to be his field." She gave me a stern look.

"What am I, a crop of rutabagas?"

She glanced at the kids and said through her teeth to me, "Do you understand?"

"Not really. Are you forbidding me to see Adam?" This was actually kind of romantic, though ridiculous. *I forbid you to see the boy next door!*

"Mirabella and Alvin," Frances said, "please turn on the

garden hose and water your mother's beautiful flowers." Miraculously, the brainwashed kiddies stood and obeyed, taking half the sand with them. Frances watched them go, then turned to me.

"Ever since your mom died," she whispered, "your dad has been terrified for you kids. But he's gone out of his way not to be overprotective so that *you* don't live life afraid. And those were the instructions he gave me as your caregiver." She reached over and patted my knee. "No one's going to forbid you to do anything, Lori. Just . . . watch out around those boys."

9

Adam sat on the end of my dock with his shoes beside him and his bare feet swinging in the bryozoa-infested waters. Just kidding—my dock had been Sanitized for My Protection by a minnow net with a very long handle.

I skimmed the canoe against the dock and stopped myself with an oar. He stood up dripping, caught the rope I threw him, and wound it around the dock cleat. "Date or what?" he asked.

Grabbing my shoes from the bottom of the canoe, I confirmed, "Date. Ew. It's so weird to think about. Help me out, lovah."

He put out a hand to help me onto the dock. He did it in such a gentlemanly fashion, with no tickling or pinching or even a secret handshake, that I couldn't help but yank his arm to startle him. Then *he* put his weight on *me* to keep from falling, and we both came within a few millimeters of flipping the canoe over and landing in the lake.

We both managed to save at the last second. He helped me out of the canoe as if nothing had happened, except his face was bright red, and he wore that *don't make me laugh* look. "Your dad said you went to see Frances."

"Yeah. I told her about the plan, and she thinks you're only going along with it because you want to get lucky with me." We shared an uncomfy titter at this ridiculous idea as he slid his feet into his shoes, but something made me press him about this. "Did you get lucky with Rachel?"

He stared down at me, disapproving. He turned the disapproving stare in the general direction of the Harbargers' dock across the lake.

"You did," I said with a sigh. I hadn't realized I'd been holding my breath.

"N—," he started. "W— Mmph." He put both his hands into his hair. This showed me how strong and well-formed the biceps were on this tanned, beautiful boy. "I didn't, but you don't know that, okay? I have two older brothers. As far as they're concerned, I've been doing the entire cheerleading squad since I was fourteen."

He hadn't. So why was I picturing the tanned biceps straining as he braced himself above . . . who?

"Your dad's thinking the same thing," Adam said.

"About your biceps?" I chuckled.

Slowly and oh so painfully I realized no one had made a joke out loud about Adam's biceps.

Slowly and less painfully he put his arms down. "I would like some gum," he said. "Would you like some gum?"

"I would love some gum," I croaked.

He reached deep into the pocket of his shorts and drew out each of the following items in turn, placing them in his other pocket: his wallet, a lighter, a Sacagawea dollar, a plastic box of fishhooks, a four-inch-long pocketknife. Finally he produced a pack of gum so old, the company had switched to a new logo since it was made. Fine. Anything I could stuff into my mouth.

"I meant," he said, jaw working hard on a petrified square, "your dad thinks I want to get lucky with you too. At least, that was his second reaction when I rang the doorbell and told him I was there to pick you up for our date. His first reaction was to threaten to have me arrested."

"Oh, pshaw." I swallowed a mouthful of artificial flavoring. Mmmmm, igneous. "He threatens to have *me* arrested.

It's a term of endearment." I walked down the dock so Adam would follow me. When I glanced back, he was still standing at the end of the dock. I threw over my shoulder, "I'll visit you in prison."

He jogged to catch up with me, and held my arm to balance me as I slipped my heels on. I knew better than to wear heels on the dock. I'd seen too many girls wear them at the boys' parties. Heels got caught between the planks and arrested forward motion, yo.

"Why didn't you tell your dad we're hooking up?" Adam asked. "I told my mom we're hooking up." He sounded almost hurt, like he thought I was embarrassed of him.

"Would you come off it? You shouldn't have told your mom. She gave me the third degree this morning, like she knows something's up between you and Sean. You tried to get her to *ground* him? How am I supposed to go out with him if she *grounds* him?"

Adam shrugged and said with a straight face, "If you really loved him, it wouldn't matter what you did when you went out, as long as you were together." He pressed his lips together.

"You are so full of it. Anyway, I told Dad you were giving me a lift to town to buy an eyelash comb tonight, and we might hang out for a while. I figured he'd stage an intervention if I told him the whole truth. And if I told him you and I were hooking up for real, he'd give me the *fourth* degree about it, and you, and *sex*, and . . . oh."

Adam nodded. "Whereas if you didn't tell him, he'd give *me* the *fifth* degree."

"I guess I didn't think it through. It didn't seem worth the trouble, since we'll only be together a couple of weeks." Truth was, I'd focused on how our diabolical plan would help me get Sean. With an emphasis on *Sean*. Not that Adam's relationship with my dad didn't matter, because they *did* have to live next door to each other for several more years, but come on. What were a few fake dates between friends?

We walked up the hill to Adam's driveway. I opened the passenger door of the pink truck and climbed inside— and I do mean *climbed*, because when I stood on the ground, the seat was even with my head. Adam sat in the driver's seat, weirdly. He'd driven McGillicuddy and me home from tennis the night before, but I was used to sitting in the backseat with Adam while someone older drove. I wasn't used to seeing him as a driver himself.

Sean's new truck had already left the driveway. He had to drive all the way across town to pick up Rachel. No worries. We'd see them at the movies. Our biggest problem would be deciding whether to sit on the back row with the other couples who planned to make out, or further down where Sean and Rachel could see us. Then maybe there would be the additional problem of the making out. But I was getting ahead of myself. We could solve that problem when we came to it, and we hadn't even reached the movie theater yet. We were taking a detour at the dirt track, probably to show some of Adam's friends the new (to him) pink truck. And the hot prize of a girl inside! Yeah, probably not.

Instead of parking in the dirt track lot, he drove around to the mud field. It was just a huge pit of mud that the owners of the dirt track lovingly sculpted into valleys and bumps, and watered daily. Build it and they would come. Boys loved to splash across the mud pit in their pickup trucks. They didn't do this with their girlfriends, though. Girls wouldn't put up with this.

And yet here we were, perched on the lip of the pit. Scooter Ledbetter pulled up behind us in his jacked-up F-150. We couldn't even back out.

I ventured to ask, "Is this our date?"

"In all its glory." With one arm, Adam made a sweeping motion across the mud field before us.

"Great. We're trying to make Sean and Rachel jealous, besides which it's my first date in real life, and you're taking me mud riding." I'd been with the boys and Mr. Vader to the dirt track countless times to watch races. I'd always thought my first date would be with Sean. Adam wasn't too far off. But I'd never imagined my first date would be with Sean's stand-in *at* the dirt track. "You're bringing sexy back."

He stuck out his bottom lip. "Where did you want to go?"

"Didn't Sean and Rachel go to the movies?"

"Yeah, but I'll bet she made him take her to the new Disney cartoon. That's his punishment for stealing her from me. That and MTV. Endless reality shows on MTV." He cracked his knuckles.

"Adam, I don't care if it's *Mickey and Minnie Bust a Move*. We need to be there."

"We want to make them jealous," he agreed, "but we can't follow them around. We don't want to *admit* we're trying to make them jealous. And that's exactly what we'll be doing if we set foot in *Mickey and Minnie Bust a Move*."

I started to protest. But as I thought about it, I remembered every time I'd watched a DVD with the boys, Adam had left the room after thirty minutes, asking Cameron to call him back in for the juicy parts. And we were always telling Adam to be quiet. We couldn't hear the movie over his CD player, or his drum set, or the roar of the blender as he made milkshakes in the kitchen. I asked, "You can't sit through a whole movie, can you?"

He frowned, which made cute little lines appear between his brows. He fished the lighter out of his pocket and flicked it, studying the flame.

Either he couldn't sit through a whole movie, or it hurt him too much to be around Rachel while she was with Sean. This wouldn't help us make them jealous. But it *was* only the second night after the freaking shock of seeing Sean and Rachel together for the first time. Adam's heart must be breaking every time we talked about Sean and Rachel, yet he'd come with me this far. I could be more understanding and give him a few days for the wound to scab over.

"We don't have to go to the movie," I sighed, "but we need to go somewhere girls will see us. There's no one here but boys. It'll never get back to Sean and Rachel that we were together. Boys don't gossip."

"Pah! You don't know us as well as you think."

This was a disturbing prospect.

He stuffed his lighter back in his pocket. "Here's an idea. Call me crazy, but what if we actually *enjoyed* hooking up?"

"Whoa, Nelly," I said. "You scare me, thinking out of the box."

"What if we made hooking up *productive*?"

"That's what I'm talking about. Producing envy, with or without big fat teardrops."

"Forget about that, Lori. It'll come without us trying so hard." He took the box of fishhooks out of his pocket and rattled it. "You're turning sixteen in less than two weeks."

That was a low blow. "You don't have to rub it in that I forgot your birthday," I protested. "You remember mine because yours is first."

"And didn't your dad stop taking you for driving lessons after you ran his Beamer into the woodpile?"

"Only because he told me to back to the left, and I thought I did. I would have done fine if he'd pointed instead of telling me the direction. Again, you don't have to rub it—"

"I'll teach you to drive."

I blinked. He *was* a daredevil. "Around town?"

"No, right here. It's safer."

I pondered the mud field. "I might wreck the pink truck."

"Who could tell?"

"I might hit somebody else."

"If they're here, mud riding, they'd probably get off on it."

As if in agreement, Scooter Ledbetter chose this moment to start honking his horn in time to his stereo blasting Nine Inch Nails.

"Oh, what the hell," I said, spitting my petrified gum

out the window. It had turned more of a metamorphic flavor anyway. I scooted into the driver's seat as Adam crawled over me. Nose close to his shirt, I caught a whiff of his cologne.

And then, too soon, he was on his side of the truck and I was on mine. "Is it in first gear?" he asked. "Are your feet on the brake and the clutch? Look both ways and make sure no traffic is coming before proceeding carefully into the mud hole."

I screamed like a girl as the edge of the pit fell away under us. Then I bit my scream off short as we bounced over a little hill and then a big hill that sent us flying. Now I was giggling.

Adam grinned and fastened his seat belt. "Put the truck in first gear again," he said in an amazing imitation of the calming announcer voice from the films we watched in driver's ed. "Press harder on the gas to scale the side of the mud hole. As you reach the top and circle back around for another turn, don't forget to signal."

Later, waiting in line for our seventh time through, he told me, "You drive fine."

"*Really?*" I squealed.

"Yeah. Of course, I haven't told you to turn left or right."

"Right," I said, disappointed. I thought I'd been driving

fine, too. But I'd done well only because he hadn't asked me to do anything hard, like tell left from right. And let's not even *think* about starboard and port.

"When you're driving by yourself, it won't matter," he reasoned. "You've lived in this town forever. You know how to get around. Your dad won't be sitting in the passenger seat, telling you to turn left or right. The only time anyone will do that is when you take your driving test."

"That's also the only time a person taking her first road test will be banned from driving in Alabama for life." I edged the pink truck forward as a Dodge Ram dropped into the mud field in front of us.

"I have ADHD," he said. "I'm the master of cheating on tests. Just put your hands on the wheel like this." He placed his hands on the dashboard with his first fingers up and his thumbs in, pointing toward each other. "*L* is for left."

"Won't the chick giving me the test notice I've got my fingers in an *L* on the steering wheel?"

"Hold your hands like that while she's examining your car," he said. "By the time you start driving, she won't think anything about it. She'll think you have arthritis and it's none of her business."

I looked over at him. "You're a lot sneakier than I thought."

He smiled.

I said, "Frances hasn't forgiven you for exploding her homemade cheese."

His laughter rang out at just the moment I plunged the truck into the pit. He'd given me the confidence of Dale Earnhardt Jr. on holiday. I veered off the very beaten path and into uncharted mud puddles. I kicked up splashes so high, Adam rolled up his window and asked me to roll up mine to save what was left of the ancient interior. We bounced from corner to corner and were bouncing our way back again when the truck dipped lower than I expected, sending a wave of muddy water across the hood and up the windshield. I pressed the gas and heard a ripping sound.

I turned to him in horror. "I broke your truck."

"We're just stuck. It happens." He unfastened his seat belt. "Switch back."

I started to crawl over him. He'd crawled over me last time, and I figured this time he'd slide under. But he started to crawl over, too. We met in the middle, laughed, and both moved to slide under at the same time.

"Do you want to be on top or on bottom?" he asked.

"Either way," I heard myself saying. I had to remind myself that this was Adam, not Sean. This was the baby of the Vader family, who had always been the littlest, up until two days ago. At least in my mind.

He picked me up and, before I could wiggle, removed me to the passenger side. "There." He slid into the driver's seat and pressed the gas, harder than I'd pressed it, with a longer and louder ripping noise. He opened the door and stepped out, sinking much farther than he would have on solid ground. "They'll call a tractor from the racetrack to pull us out, but it might take a while. Let's wait by the concession stand. You'll ruin your shoes, though. Here, get on my back."

He stood outside the open driver's side door. His back was waiting. I hadn't been on a boy's back since . . . hmm . . . a free-for-all fight with girls on boys' backs at Cathy Kirk's pool party in middle school. If I'd been included, obviously there hadn't been enough girls to go around. And in middle school, the girls and boys were about equal in height and weight, so I'd worried I would crush the boy I rode on.

Not so with Adam. My shoes were dainty things you shoved your toes into with nothing to hold them on. I kicked them off and held them in one hand. I slid across the seat and onto his strong, solid back, feeling like a feather. A snowflake! A dainty snowflake surrounded by an acre of mud.

He nudged the door closed with his hip. I looked down. His feet had disappeared. "What about *your* shoes?" I asked. "Your mom will kill you."

"They're Sean's. I'll put them in his closet just like this."

I felt a momentary pang for Sean. Then almost laughed out loud, picturing the look on his face. They were his shoes, and he would have a right to be mad. But if anything could ever make me dislike Sean, it was how much he cared about his clothes. I cared about my own clothes only through great effort.

Sean's shoes made a *schlep* sound every time Adam took a step. He struggled getting up the hill to the lip of the mud hole, and I thought I would have to dismount after all.

He felt me start to slide down. "No!" he said, catching my legs more tightly. "We're fine." With one last *schlep* we made it to the top. The prize was a tiny Airstream trailer blowing smoke out an exhaust fan. The air smelled like fried food. "Are you hungry?" he asked.

"No, but that never stopped me before."

"Me too." He stepped up to the window and looked in. "What'cha got?"

The clerk/cook/janitor looked up from a NASCAR talk show on TV. "Cheese fries, homemade doughnuts."

With me on his back, Adam couldn't turn his head around enough to look at me, but he turned it enough to let me know I should choose from this array of delicacies.

"Strangely," I said, "I have a taste for cheese fries."

Adam reached into his pocket to pay. Putting me down on the bench beside the concession stand would have been miles easier. I was beginning to understand that he liked having me on his back. Holding my shoes in one hand, I grabbed the cheese fries with the other, and he carried a soda.

He walked to the bench, put the soda down, then put me down. I was still holding the cheese fries and my shoes. I tossed my shoes on the ground (oh well, so much for dazzling rhinestones) and picked up the soda so he could sit down, then handed it to him. It was like one of those problems on a standardized test at school. If Sean hooks up with everyone in school on Wednesday and Rachel on Friday, and Adam hooks up with Rachel on Thursday and Lori on Sunday, on what day does the nuclear war commence? One of those problems Adam would just draw an *X* through because he *thought* he would never encounter anything like it in the real world.

He crossed one leg over the other casually, as if he weren't coated with mud up to his knees. Then he took a sip of the soda, handed it to me, and pulled out a cheese fry. I took a tentative sip of soda. Not that I thought he had germs—or really bad germs, anyway—but we'd never shared a soda before. We'd shared popcorn, of course, while we watched DVDs with the other boys. Once the scoop from my ice cream cone had plopped into the lake, and he'd shared his ice cream with me. This was probably kind of gross. Mrs. Vader and Frances had rushed at us when they saw me about to take a lick. I shouldn't read too much into sharing a soda now, though. It was something people did when they went out.

"Mmph!" he hummed with his mouth full of cheese fry. Swallowing, he grabbed my bare foot and pulled it into his lap. "You painted your little toenails."

I opened my mouth to explain proudly that the toenails in question represented hours of meticulous work. Well, maybe forty-five minutes while watching reruns of *Deadliest Catch*. I'd put the polish on and taken it off three times because it tended toward gloopy. Who knew beauty regimens would be so complex?

But when I looked up, my mouth just stayed open. He was staring at me with those light blue eyes. A chill hit me from nowhere. It made the hair on my arms stand up. It raced down my body to my toes, which he was stroking with one rough thumb. And so the chill moseyed back up my body again.

I took a slow, shaky breath through my wide open, ridiculously gaping mouth. Then I realized what the problem was. His resemblance to Sean was eerie sometimes, especially the light blue eyes. I managed to say, "You're giving me the look again. Don't look at me like that."

Stubbornly he gave me the look for ten more seconds, so there. I would be lying if I said I didn't enjoy the look. I *really* enjoyed what it did to my skin. He was a super-hero with Massage-O-Vision. I enjoyed it too much for comfort. He was just going to turn his Massage-O-Vision on Rachel when he got her back, so the pleasant pricklies *I* felt were pricklies on loan. He'd be horrified to know he was giving them to me. Besides, I wasn't going to sit there and let him give me the look when I'd asked him not to give me the look.

Just as I was about to either pinch him or find the strength to look away, he let my toes go and turned away himself, gazing out over the splashing trucks. The mud sparkled in the artificial light. At first glance it might have seemed about as romantic as watching cement being poured, or a building being demolished by a wrecking ball. Nothing said *romance* like the scent of burning rub-ber. But to me, it started to seem very romantic. I almost wished Holly and Beige could see me now. Well, not really, because mud had splashed up on my calves. I scratched at a spot with my fingernail, and it smeared.

He asked, "Why does it have to be Sean?"

10

I snapped my head up and tried to gauge what he'd meant by this. I couldn't tell, because he wouldn't meet my gaze. Which was probably a good thing. I could feel myself flushing as my heart pounded.

I was attracted to Adam. Not as much as I was attracted to Sean, of course. That would never happen. But Adam had been so sweet and so fun, teaching me to drive. Tangling with me as we switched places in the truck didn't hurt either. Or carrying me on his back. I really enjoyed him carrying me on his back.

Did he mean, *Why does it have to be Sean instead of me?* And if he did . . .

Good God, what was the matter with me? Adam didn't like me that way. He just hated Sean. He wanted to know why I was so stuck on *Sean*, of all people.

And I didn't like Adam that way, either. Not really. Flirting with him was fun, but that's all it was, and I was getting carried away. I needed to remember I was on a mission. I would tell him the whole truth about the mission. I owed him that much, since he'd agreed to help me by faking a relationship with me.

I munched a cheese fry and thought about Sean sashaying his way through the school lunchroom last spring, Beige on one arm, Holly on the other. Everyone turned to watch as he passed. People called out to him from the tables. All he needed was the paparazzi behind him. Also Beige or Holly needed a very small dog that got sick when it ate too much protein. I said simply, "Sean lights up the room."

Adam still wouldn't look at me. He tried to shake one fry loose from a cheesy clump. "I can see why you'd want to watch him, listen to him. Not why you'd want to *get together* with him. He lights up the room so bright that you would just be sitting there blinking, blinded." He gave up on freeing the fry and stuffed the whole cheesy clump in his mouth. Immediately he started picking through the pile for another, like he needed something to do with his hands.

"I've always wanted to be with him," I said. "Yeah, logically I can see the drawbacks, but I don't think you or anyone could argue me out of it. I need to find out for myself, because I've wanted this so long."

"Always," Adam muttered, tossing up a bit of fry and catching it in his mouth.

"Almost always. Actually, I can remember the very day it started." The mud field in front of us dissolved into a sun-splashed view of the lake through shady branches. The roar of monster trucks faded, replaced by birds chirping, and my mother's voice. "It was before Mom died. We were all really little. But I remember it so clearly. Your whole family was at my house for a cookout in the summer. I was with Mom and your mom up on the deck. I'd wanted to play with you boys, but Mom wouldn't let me.

"Your mom said I was such a lovely little girl, so lady-like and polite. That's what pricked my ears up, of course: the praise. But I kept playing like I wasn't listening in. Then your mom said I didn't always have to stay home. I was welcome to come over to your house to play whenever McGillicuddy came over. She called him Bill. Whatever. Now I was really paying attention, and holding my breath to see what Mom would say. All I'd dreamed about my whole little life was playing with y'all."

"Why?"

I snapped out of my daydream. I'd almost forgotten Adam was sitting there.

He put one hand on my knee, watching me, and didn't even turn to look when Scooter purposefully spun his tires, coating one side of the pink truck in mud. "Why did you want to play with us?" Adam asked. "At that age, we were basically squirting each other in the face with water guns."

"Compare this to sitting in my room by myself, dressing and undressing the Barbie."

"Oh." He nodded.

"Anyway, of course I was disappointed, as always. My mom said your mom was so nice to offer, but she didn't want me playing with four boys very often. I'd grow up to be a tomboy."

"What's wrong with growing up to be a tomboy?"

"I think it's fine until a certain age. When you're young, being a tomboy may even give you a certain advantage. You can always beat girls like Holly Chambliss and Beige Dupree and, ohmyGod, Rachel in Little League softball. You can catch four fish in the Girl Scout fishing rodeo while they're still refusing to bait their hooks because worms are icky."

"Rachel will actually bait her own hook," Adam defended her.

I didn't want to hear it. I talked right over him. "After a

135

certain age, people don't know what to make of a tomboy, and you don't fit in. You end up feeling empty and lost."

Those frown lines appeared between his brows. He moved the plate of cheese fries behind him on the bench, slid over until his leg touched my leg, and put his hand on my knee again.

Strange how his touch made it easier for me to talk. I went on, "Just as Mom was telling your mom no, Sean came up the stairs crying. You and the other boys had dared him to stick bread between his toes and put his foot in the water. A fish mouthed him and he freaked out."

"Er—," Adam started.

I waved him off, because this was the most important detail. "My mom took his chin in her hand, turned his face toward me, and said, 'Just look at those eyes. He's going to be a heartbreaker.'" I found myself smiling at the memory. But when I turned to Adam and saw the look on his face, I stopped smiling.

"That sounds like a *bad* thing," he grumbled.

"People mean it as a good thing," I said, suddenly not as sure of this as I'd been for the last twelve years. But I couldn't really expect him to understand. Talking about Sean around Adam was like throwing Evian on a fire. "And then Mom said, 'Lori, just *wait* until you're sixteen.' She was stuck on the sixteenth birthday. We made a scrapbook with pictures of all my baby events, and spaces for when I would turn six and eight and ten and twelve, and a super-mondo sequined space for when I turned sixteen. She wanted me to have what she'd had, a great sixteenth birthday, exactly what any teenage girl would want. Her parents gave her a special grown-up ring, and she wore a groovy dress that's hanging in my closet."

We'd moved away from talking about Sean. Predictably, Adam took a deeper breath and relaxed against the bench. "Are you going to wear the dress on your birthday?"

"Are you kidding? It was 1979. White polyester, baby. Highly flammable. Burn baby burn, disco inferno. Unsafe. Uncool."

"I'll bet it's pretty. You could wear it wakeboarding on your birthday, during the Crappy Festival show." He was back to his old self.

I chuckled. "Unfortunately, you and I are the only two people in the world who would think that was funny."

"What does that have to do with Sean?"

I squirmed a little under the gaze of the intense blue eyes. I felt his disapproval even though I hadn't told him what he should disapprove of yet. But he was helping me with Sean, and I'd committed to telling him the whole story. "Mom died not long after that. I took it as a free ticket to Disneyworld. Yay, Mom wasn't around to stop me! I got to play with the boys! Only I always felt guilty about being the least bit happy she was gone, even when this was the one good thing about it. And I felt guilty I didn't tell Dad or Frances that Mom wouldn't have wanted me over at your house. It went against her wishes for me. I promised myself I'd clean up by the time I was sixteen. And if I could finally convince Sean to ask me out by my sixteenth birthday, I would know I'd turned out okay after all."

Adam nodded. "Because you think your mother picked Sean out for you."

"No, not exactly—"

"Like an arranged marriage," Adam interrupted. "That's very forward thinking."

"No, not like that. Mom knew what was best for me, and if she were still around, she would have taught me how to get it. She's not around, so I have to figure this out for myself. I'm transforming myself from an ugly duckling into a beautiful swan. There's much preening to be done. It's actually pretty time-consuming. I have to run my beak down every single feather to distribute the oil evenly and make myself waterproof."

"Lori—"

"And I've almost perfected my Holly/Beige imitation. At least, I *thought* I had, until the mud riding started."

"You think going out with Sean will turn you into Beige Dupree?"

"Sort of. If I hooked up with Sean, everyone would treat me differently. Everyone loves Sean. If Sean chose me, they'd think they'd always overlooked something special in me. Then maybe I really could become that girl. I know you hate Sean, but you understand why everyone else loves him, right?"

I took Adam's stony silence as a yes.

"Girlfriend/boyfriend love is totally different from brotherly love. But the effect would be the same. Like standing in his aura. Haven't you ever wondered what it would be like if Sean loved and valued you as a person?"

"I'd know Armageddon was coming. I'd brace myself for the locusts."

"I'm serious. If he just looked at you the right way, that alone could probably carry you through for a month. But if he *loved* you . . ."

Adam shifted on the bench. I thought he was standing up to stalk away, disgusted. Instead, he placed his arm around my shoulders. Lightly his finger stroked valentines on my arm, which gave me the shivers all over again.

"Every word out of Sean's mouth is meant to hurt me," he said. "And it's always been like that. Cameron says Sean changed after I was born. When I was a baby and

Mom wasn't looking, Sean threw blocks at my crib."

I almost laughed. The idea was so ridiculous. It was even more ridiculous for Adam to be angry about something like that when he was sixteen years old.

I managed not to laugh. I believed him. I knew Sean.

"But that's you," I said. "I'm sorry he treats *you* that way, but I'm the one who's going to get together with him, and he doesn't treat *me* that way."

"He will," Adam said. "If you ever let him get close to you, he will." The valentines he traced on my arm had turned to shapes with lots of sharp points, like in comic books when the superhero punches the villain. Ker-POW!

The tractor arrived then to pull the pink truck out of the mud. Adam took his hands off me—which I regretted more than I should have. He leaned forward to watch and make sure the driver didn't attach the chain to the loose side of the front bumper.

"Why does it have to be Rachel?" I asked.

"It just does," he said without taking his eyes off the truck.

"You might feel better if you talked about it."

"I doubt it."

"What do you like so much about her?"

When he turned to me, he seemed alarmed, as he had at the tennis court the night before. With wide eyes, he searched my eyes for something—which I probably would have given him, if I'd known what he was looking for. I asked, "What are you looking for?"

He shook his head and turned back to the mud pit. "I like her because she's so pretty," he said in his bullshit voice.

"That's no fair. I gave you a straight answer about Sean."

The tractor started forward. The chain to the pink truck pulled tighter and tighter and broke. One end of it flew over the tractor, barely missing the driver.

"She's cute," Adam said. "She has a nice ass. I don't know."

Now I understood. Talking about her hurt him too much. It was easier for him to pretend the ADHD had kicked in.

After two more chains and a rope, the tractor liberated the pink truck, and Adam bought the driver a doughnut. Adam and I drove through the mud field for another hour and a half, taking turns. Mostly we managed to forget Sean and Rachel.

Then we drove into town and hit all the teenage haunts: the arcade parking lot, the bowling alley parking lot, of course the movie theater parking lot. In theory this is exactly what I wanted. I was being seen out with Adam, in Adam's truck. In practice, Adam had purposefully besmirched Sean's pink truck with mud. It was like he wanted to be seen around town in it for that reason.

We rolled home at two minutes before my curfew. I'd figured he'd park the truck at his house, and I'd walk home. I was thrilled that he drove over to my driveway to drop me off. Sean wasn't home yet to see us, but maybe someone in the Vaders' house would watch across the yard and mention it to Sean later.

And then, as I was turning to Adam to thank him for teaching me to drive and allowing me to foam at the mouth about my mom, he bailed out the driver's side door. He walked around the front of the truck. I think he would have opened my door, a gentleman on a date, if I hadn't opened it first. It was too strange. I jumped to the ground, forgetting I was wearing my heels again. He caught me just before I pitched over onto the gravel.

"I'll—walk—you—to—the—door," he said slowly and clearly, like talking to someone who didn't speak English. Or didn't go out with girls much, or, like, ever. He took my hand. We walked toward the lights slanting through the shadows of pine trunks. Tree frogs screamed in the night, and the air was wet. I shivered.

We climbed the steps to the porch. Dad hadn't turned on the overhead light there, thank God. Adam stood close to me in the darkness, over me, expecting something. I expected something, too. I couldn't have stood the disappointment if we'd done all we'd done that day, hugging and giving each other smoldering looks and all, without something to show for it at the end, even if we *were* just friends. But my head felt too heavy to raise my chin.

"Hey." He put his hand under my chin and gently raised it for me. "If one of us were in love with the other, if it were uneven in some way, that would be bad." He gave me a long look I couldn't really see. The shadows on the porch were too deep. His eyes only glittered a little in the starlight.

I tried to give the look right back to him. "But we're not," I said, and what was that damned high squeakiness in my voice on *not*? I cleared my throat.

"But we're not," he agreed. "We have nothing to worry about. We can do whatever we feel like."

"Right," I said, and meant it.

The kiss was simple. He bent down and pressed his lips to mine. We stood still except for his pressure on my lips. But inside, every cell in my body turned a back flip to blind.

"Good night, Lori," he whispered. He bounced back to the pink truck, cranked the engine, drove one hundred feet to his own driveway, waved to me, and went inside his house.

I stood on my porch and stared at his house for a long

time, telling myself that I did not like Adam that way because I liked Sean and Adam liked Rachel and *I did not like Adam*. It was just that Adam was very smart, and was second only to Sean at making confusing things sound simple and death-defying stunts seem like a good idea.

Monday night, Dad insisted that Adam come over for dinner. Adam, my dad, my brother, and I ate and joked together like we normally would out in the yard, except that it wasn't normal. It was weird. Adam sat in my mom's chair at the table. We might as well have been staring at a showy centerpiece made of silk flowers and hand grenades.

Tuesday night was much more comfy. Sean was over at Rachel's and Cameron was out with his girlfriend, so Adam and I had the Vaders' living room to ourselves to watch a DVD. At least, that's what we did for about thirty minutes. Then we played CDs in his room, experimented with his drum set, and made milkshakes in the kitchen. Without anyone else around to show off for, we could just be ourselves. Friends.

Wednesday night we went mud riding. I wore my sensible shoes this time—rubber flip-flops that could be hosed off. I knew this wouldn't sound very romantic when it got back to Sean or Holly or Beige. I also knew that, just like the other nights, I would stand on my porch with Adam and get the simplest, most shiver-inducing kiss. And then it would be over. The next morning, we'd go back to being friends.

Thursday night we scored. So to speak. We'd planned to go to the arcade and see who could kick the other's ass on the snowmobile racing game, but Adam called me just before it was time to pick me up. He sounded tinny, like his hand was cupped over his mouth and the receiver. "Code green. Code green. Rachel and Sean watching DVD here tonight. Over."

The wound Rachel had inflicted on him must have healed enough that he could stand being around her and Sean. Or he must miss her so much that he was willing to take a more active role in making her jealous. Either way, this was our big chance!

Slamming down the phone, I rushed upstairs to exchange my Skechers for Steve Madden pumps and my tank top for something that said elegance, sophistication, Express. This was how I was supposed to talk about clothes, right? Naming the brands as if I cared? Another coat of mascara and a run-through with the comb attachment to McGillicuddy's razor and I was ready, baby. Snap!

Sean's truck was parked in the driveway behind the pink truck. He'd already brought Rachel over. I swallowed and tried to slow down my breathing as I pressed the doorbell with one shaking finger.

Almost immediately, I heard Adam bouncing inside. He jerked the heavy door open. "What are you doing? You don't have to ring the doorbell, dork."

Dumbass! He'd called me a dork loudly enough for the Thompsons to hear three houses over. Talk about romance.

I was about to whisper acidly that he wasn't doing a very good job of falling head over heels in love. Then I noticed he was wearing his black T-shirt printed in white with a life-size rib cage. Adam looked best in black. The color reflected darkly in the hollows under his high cheekbones, not to mention the bruise under his eye, and made his strange light eyes stand out that much more. The skull and crossbones glimmered at his neck.

He raised his eyebrows, waiting for me to say what I'd opened my mouth to say.

I was speechless. So I grabbed his arm and spun him

around at the same time. He was surprised. I managed to pin his arm behind his back for about two seconds before he shook loose and grabbed me.

"Now you've asked for it." He scooped me up, threw me over his shoulder, and held both my wrists in one hand so I couldn't tickle him. He kicked the door closed and hiked into the living room.

Pausing, he took a few steps toward Sean and Rachel watching TV on the sofa. They sat close together in the dark room. I wouldn't have been able to tell whose limbs were whose, except Sean didn't shave his legs. There was a love seat where Adam and I could have settled. Then Adam thought better of it—too close for comfort—and hiked across the room.

"Hello, Sean. Good evening, Rachel," I called cordially, upside down.

Rachel gave us a half-hearted pipsqueak greeting. Sean shouted at us, "Can you keep it down?"

Hmph! Clearly he was in a jealous rage. Adam and I exchanged a knowing look as he slid me onto the desk in the corner. Still holding my wrists immobile, he fished in a drawer and brought out a long object.

I squinted at it in the dark. "Not the stapler!" I cried.

He grinned, tossed the stapler beside me, and rummaged in the drawer again.

"Please," I gasped, "not the Liquid Paper!"

"Shut up!" Sean shouted.

Adam and I widened our eyes at each other like we were offended and hurt. I shook my wrists out of his grasp and reached behind me for a red Sharpie out of the pencil cup. Smoothing my hand across his chest (shiver), I made a red mark across the bottom right rib printed on his T-shirt, the rib I knew he'd broken. Or was it my other right? "What ribs have you broken?"

He looked down at his shirt. "This one," he said, pointing.

I made a red mark across that rib. "What else?"

"Mm." He stretched his shirt out at the bottom so he could see it better, and pointed to the opposite side. "These two." He watched as I made neat red marks across those ribs. His chin was close to my cheek.

"Both of you act crazy," Sean said smoothly, "like you're off your medication. Or like you're going to a shrink."

I didn't look at Adam. I didn't think I looked at Sean, either. But I had an impression later of Sean's face glowing white and then blue in the light of TV, and Rachel in the shadows beside him. I thought the medication comment was meant for Adam. I knew the shrink comment was meant for me.

I capped the marker and stuck it back in the pencil cup. "I'll see you later," I whispered, sliding around Adam and hopping down from the desk. I had to get across the room and outside without being further humiliated, which meant I *must not* fall down in my high heels. Or cry. I even closed the front door behind me without making any noise.

And then Adam burst through it and slammed it behind him, shaking the house. "Lori!"

"Shhh," I said with my finger to my lips, backing off the porch and into the wet grass. I didn't want to shout about what Sean had said. It was bad enough when we were quiet about it.

Adam collected himself as I watched, taking a deep breath through his nose, with his eyes closed. Then he opened his eyes and said, "The five-minute date does nothing to make them jealous." He formed his first finger and thumb into a circle. "Zero."

I swallowed. "I can't."

He stepped closer to me. "Sean has a way of finding that one thing that will make you feel so good about yourself, or so bad about yourself. That's why you love him. That's why I hate him. You knew this when you went fishing."

I was too discombobulated to make a joke about my lures. I just wanted to get away from their house. "I've had enough of boys for today, I think."

He frowned. "Are you sure?" He rubbed my arm. My hair stood on end.

Shivering in the warm night, I put my arm down by my side, where he couldn't reach it. "Too much of a good thing. It's strange, but even cheese fries can get tiresome."

"I'll walk you home, then."

"No," I said, "I'm sorry. I'm just done."

He watched me carefully for a moment, lowering his head to look into my eyes. "Okay. I'll see you tomorrow."

"Bye."

He walked back into the house and closed the door softly.

I stared at the door knocker, tree frogs screaming all around me. I had done the wrong thing. I wanted to be in the house with him. And Sean.

Sean had said something like that to me only once before, just a good-natured joke as we passed each other in the hall at school. I'd started to cry. The office had called my dad (again). Dad and McGillicuddy and I had had a Big Talk about it that night, wherein I told my dad that my business was not his to tell Sean's parents about, and wherein McGillicuddy promised to have a discussion with Sean about keeping his mouth shut. Apparently he had, because Sean never said a word to me about it again. And if he told the whole school, they were very discreet and didn't let on to me that they knew. Which would have been out of character for them, because they were bitches.

That first time happened not long after I went to the shrink, so Sean probably was just experimenting to see what I'd do. This time, he must have mentioned it because he was trying to hurt me. And if he'd tried to hurt me, he was in love with me and jealous of Adam. I knew this because when he *wasn't* in love with me and jealous of Adam, he ignored me and was quite pleasant to me.

Therefore, the plan must be working! Hooray! So I should go back in there, flirt with Adam, and press the issue.

As I stood there, considering whether to ring the doorbell or just walk on inside like I owned the place, or like they'd installed a dog door, I heard Adam holler, "Thanks, Sean."

"No problem," Sean said more quietly, because he was too courteous to yell in Rachel's ear.

I felt a flash of panic. They weren't being sarcastic. Adam was genuinely thanking Sean for getting him out of spending an evening with me. This was called a *negative self-concept*. I had learned about it in health class (tenth grade). Having a negative self-concept made me think people were making fun of me, on top of the times when they really *were* making fun of me, which I seemed to miss completely.

Then footsteps pounded up the stairs inside. Adam's bedroom light flicked on. He put his hands on the window-sill and pressed his forehead to the glass, looking for me, but he couldn't see out because of the glare.

Adam wouldn't double-cross me.

Would he?

Friday I had gas. This was fine with me. I spent most of the morning by myself on the dock, soaking up rays and feeling mentally diseased.

I didn't think I could stand a lunch hour in the office, eating Mrs. Vader's chicken salad sandwich, on edge, expecting Sean to sneak in or Adam to burst in or both. I told Mrs. Vader I was treating myself to a nice lunch out.

"Oh," she said, nodding. "Something happened between 'you and Adam'?" She moved her fingers in quotation marks.

Yeah, I didn't have the energy to argue with her this time. That was Adam's problem. I walked over to my family's dock and launched the canoe.

The open water was choppy with wind and wakes from passing speedboats. I didn't get T-boned. It was a little early for anyone to be drunk.

The wind blew me off course. I reached the far bank and needed to backtrack along the shore to the Harbargers' house. Here in the shallows, protected by overhanging trees, the water was clear and calm. Miniature whirlpools stirred around my oar. I dragged my hand in the warm water, and minnows nibbled my fingers.

I docked at the Harbargers' and ran up to the house. It was such a relief to feel the grass on my bare feet! Every toe had a blister from a different pair of high-heeled sandals. I slid open the glass door and stepped into the den.

Frances and the kids looked up. They were sitting on the floor around the coffee table. Frances didn't sit on furniture if there was a floor available. A copy of *Mother Earth News* lay open in front of her. She had stuck lengths of uncooked spaghetti into balls of Play-Doh. The kidlets were busy sliding Froot Loops onto the spaghetti, sorting by color. I couldn't believe they'd fallen for that old trick. Frances could convince children anything was a game, for about five minutes. Obviously some children were more gullible than others.

I walked into the kitchen and looked in the refrigerator. No surprises there. The meat loaf was made with tofu. Frances's strong points as a nanny included a master's degree in early childhood education and a PhD in Russian literature, but nothing approaching cooking skills, unless it was some weird hippie experiment like drying fruit on the roof. Mmmmm, rubbery apricots with a hint of tar. I filled a bowl with Froot Loops, poured soy milk over them, and joined the powwow on the floor.

Between bites I asked, "What did you mean when you said mine wasn't the only plot?"

Without looking up from the magazine on the coffee table, Frances said, "I told you. I don't know."

"What would be the metaphorical firecracker in the metaphorical homemade cheese?"

She shrugged.

"Like, Sean dared Adam to hook up with me because I'm so oafish and dog-looking?"

"You are *not* dog-looking," Frances said sternly. "Besides, a plot like that would involve a high level of organization. They would have to think it through carefully. None of you do that. Except Bill, of course, who thinks things through so carefully that he can't take action. Like his father."

My spoon stopped in my mouth at the mention of my dad, who'd been the farthest person from my mind. I swallowed and shouted, "Then what the hell kind of plot are you talking about?"

Frances didn't even react when I cussed in front of her charges. She reasoned that making a big deal out of curse words drew attention to them and caused children to use them more. So she ignored them. I'm not sure this ploy worked, but then, she'd had an uphill battle with

McGillicuddy and me. We lived next door to Mr. Vader, who could have written a dictionary of filth. She asked, calm as ever, "Have you thought Adam might really like you?"

The hair on my arms stood up, just as if Adam were sitting behind me with his hand on my shoulder.

"No, I haven't." That would be seven kinds of awful, if Adam had agreed to pretend to get together with me because he *really* wanted to get together with me. My ploy to get Sean would be ruined. I might finally land Sean, like in my dreams. But knowing I'd broken Adam's heart would be a downer and a distraction. Like making out in the movie theater, knowing the pink truck in the parking lot was on fire. My mother wanted me to be with Sean, but didn't she want me to be happy?

Frances turned the page. "Open your eyes. And watch out for those boys."

12

Wakeboarding that afternoon, I watched the boys until my eyeballs hurt from the sun glinting off the water. I could have sworn there was nothing to watch out for. Sean was a little warmer to me than usual—the way he always acted after he'd insulted me, like some friendliness here could make up for a lack of friendliness elsewhere.

Adam was *very* warm to me. While Sean drove, my brother wakeboarded, and Cameron spotted, Adam pulled me into his lap in the bow. He set his chin on my shoulder and rubbed his hands up and down my thighs. The best part of this, for the purpose of making Sean's blood boil, was that Adam did it without comment, without expecting me to comment, as if it were the most natural thing in the world for him to act like my boyfriend.

The worst part of this, for the purpose of watching out for those boys, was that if my eyelids had been duct-taped open to my eyebrows, I *still* wouldn't have been able to tell whether Adam liked me, or pretended to like me, or liked me but pretended he was only pretending.

The five of us pitched the wakeboards and life vests from the boat back into the warehouse. The Friday night party would start soon, so Sean, Cameron, and my brother headed for the houses. I ought to have been right behind them. I needed plenty of time to shower and primp and change clothes twenty times like girls were supposed to do before parties.

But I took Adam's hand and held him back from the others. I whispered what had been bugging me all day. "Frances thinks you have a plot, other than the plot with me to make Sean and Rachel jealous."

His eyes flew wide open, and the rest of him seemed to shrink back a bit. Then he stood up straighter, and his brow went down. "Frances? I haven't spoken to Frances in years. Plus she's creepy."

"Only because she's always right," I said. "And last night, something you said to Sean . . . Do you have a plot against me? Are you double-crossing me? He dared you to go out with the dog next door, and if you did, he'd give you your cute little girlfriend back?"

He snorted, then seemed to have a hard time huffing out laughter, almost as if he were *relieved*. He snatched me to his tanned chest, hugged me hard, and breathed into my wet hair, "You're not a dog. You're beautiful."

Right. I knew what he meant. Beautiful on the inside. I *had* saved a baby sparrow or two in my time. I was not someone he would want to *hook up* with, but a beautiful person. Hooray.

"Don't ever let Sean convince you you're not." He glanced in the direction Sean had gone. "Let's go for a sailboat ride."

I loved sailing. But if we went now, we'd be late for the party. "Can't we do it tomorrow?"

"This will be an investment in your future. It'll be worth it."

I waited while Adam leaned into the office to tell Mr. Vader what we were doing, and I followed him back into the warehouse. The sailboat was very old and very small. The hull was a light fiberglass platform with a hole for the metal mast. Adam and I toted the hull, mast, and sail to the edge of the wharf, threw them in, and tossed down a couple of life vests. Adam stepped carefully onto the hull, sat down, and steadied it against the concrete wall for me as I stepped on and sat down. The sitting down was very important. The boat was so small that it would tip and throw us off if we shifted our weight the slightest bit too far, like trying to stand on a basketball. Together we lifted the mast upright, slid it into the hole in the center of the hull, and unfurled the red sail.

"Do you want to drive?" he asked.

"You can drive," I said.

I scooted around the mast to the tiny bow. Adam slid to the back, taking the rope attached to the sail in one hand and the handle of the rudder in the other. He pulled the sail taut, the wind filled it—and the boat tipped over, dumping us both into the lake.

I came up quickly. The life vests were floating away on the current, but the more important thing was to make sure the mast didn't fall out of the hole and sink. We'd have a hard time retrieving it from the bottom of the lake, even here near the wharf where it was relatively shallow.

Adam had the same idea. Without a word to each other, we met under the boat. His hair floated weirdly around him and his blue eyes were bright in the dark green water as he motioned for me to turn the hull right side up while he dove after the slowly sinking mast.

I came up into the sunshine for a breath and flipped the

hull. Adam surfaced beside me, groaning with the weight of tugging the sail full of water. Together we managed to bundle it around the mast so less water was trapped in it. We pulled the sail and mast out of the water, slipped the mast into the hole in the hull, and peeled the sail into position. Water rained everywhere.

"This is romantic," I said. "You have a knack. What the hell kind of date *is* this?"

He laughed. "You'll see."

After we retrieved the life vests, I sat on the bow like in *Titanic*. But without any of that *I'm queen of the world* bullshit, holding my arms out. Come on, it was a sailboat on a lake. Adam steered us back and forth across the water. The red sail billowed above us in the strong breeze, so we wouldn't get T-boned by drunks. Unless of course they headed straight for us like in a bullfight.

Sometimes Adam jerked the boat around so fast that I slipped off the bow and into the water. Dunk! These were not accidents, I thought—the gleam in his blue eyes was too gleamy. He turned the boat only when we were very close to shore, though, where it was safe. I wasn't too concerned about getting ground to bits by a passing boat motor in the open water.

We made it to the bridge and floated under. The sound of cars zooming on the highway overhead echoed in a sucking sound underneath, with a *clack-clack, clack-clack* as they crossed from one section of bridge to another. I called over the noise, "How much farther are we going?" I looked back at the Vaders' house, tiny across the water. "The party will start soon."

"Someone there you want to see?"

I thought he sounded bitter. But when I turned around to glance at him, he was the usual Adam, quiet and intense, one finger tapping the boat with barely contained energy.

"Yes, duh. Isn't there someone at the party *you* want to see? We can't make them jealous if we're not there."

"Actually, we can." He nodded to a pile. "Catch that and stop us."

I hugged the pile and brought the sailboat alongside it. Adam opened the compartment in the hull and pulled a can of spray paint out of the pool of water inside. He popped off the cap, sprayed a little paint into the air as a test, and stuffed the can into the waistband of his board shorts. "Wait here, woman," he said, then grinned. He climbed the pile, finding tenuous footholds between the concrete blocks.

"Uh," I said. He was already at the top of the pile. "Adam?" He reached to the metal outside edge of the bridge (thank God this side faced away from the setting sun, or it would have been too hot to hold) and, using only the strength of his arms (thank God for calisthenics), hoisted himself up until he stood on the ledge. All I could see of him was his heels peeking over the edge.

I wasn't worried about him falling. Cameron had fallen off before, and it had only stung. I *was* worried about the black clouds creeping up on the sun on the far side of the bridge, and the wind picking up. A cold gust caught the sail. The boom swung around suddenly and would have decapitated me if I hadn't ducked. Not really, but I would have had a blue bruise across my neck, and how sexy is *that*? I crawled to Adam's spot in the back of the boat, untied the rope, and lowered the sail. "Hey, Adam."

The clouds blotted out the sun. Far across the lake, the shoreline looked misty with a wall of rain. Lightning forked from the black clouds to the dark green lake.

"Adam, lightning!" I called. My voice was drowned by thunder.

The paint can dropped into the lake. I fished it out and put it back in the compartment. Lightning flashed, closer.

His feet appeared, his legs, his board shorts. With the strength of a hundred push-ups a day, he lowered himself slowly until he hung by his arms from the edge of the bridge. I expected him to drop into the water, because he was like that. He would be electrocuted, just to paint our names on the bridge. Which might sound romantic, except something could sound only so romantic when it involved spray paint.

Thankfully, he swung his legs onto the pile and descended the way he'd gone. He stepped carefully onto the boat just as lightning cracked again, so loud and bright we both jumped, and thunder boomed directly overhead. I scooted toward the bow to make room for him.

He raised the sail, saying, "I'm sorry."

"It's okay!" I shouted over the noise of the rain and the deafening echo of rain under the bridge. "Not your fault."

"It wasn't supposed to rain tonight."

"Storms pop up in the summer."

Pushing the sail into the wind just long enough to give the boat momentum, and pointing the sail out of the wind again before we blew over, he steered us toward shore. Two piles spanning the width of the bridge stood between us and the bank. Twice, we both put our hands on the piles to pull the boat out into the rain and around to the other side. I bent my head under the cold deluge. Big, hard raindrops beat the back of my neck.

We made it to shore and climbed partway up the slanted concrete embankment under the bridge. Adam brought one of the ropes from the boat with him. He curled it around his ankle so the howling wind didn't blow the boat home without us. I curled it around my ankle, too, for good measure.

We both stared forward at the swaying sailboat, red sail puddled on the hull, and the pile beyond it. Rain cascaded off both sides of the massive bridge in sheets. My bikini bottoms didn't provide much padding between the rough concrete and my ass. The rain had chilled me. I moved imperceptibly (I hoped) toward Adam to bask in his heat.

The noise and echo of the rain filled my ears, but Adam's voice beside me sounded even louder. "Why'd you go to the shrink?"

I looked down. My palm was bleeding. I must have scraped it on the pile.

"Was it because of your mom?"

I wiped my palm on my other hand. Great, now I had blood on both hands. Helpful. I wiped them on the back of my bikini bottoms. Blood stains came out in cold water, and we had plenty of that.

I could feel Adam watching me.

"It wasn't right after my mom died," I said. "Actually it wasn't until sixth grade, when Frances left because McGillicuddy and I had gotten too old to need keeping during the day while Dad was at work. Frankly, I think she was glad to go. Sean calling her Butt I Don't Need a Governess probably got tiresome."

"Sean gets tiresome in general." Adam didn't meant to change the subject—he just couldn't help making this comment. He tapped my knee with his knee, prodding me to go on.

"It wasn't like I did anything so crazy," I said. "Though that's probably what crazy people always say, right? I just didn't want to sit in class anymore. The teachers were fine and the kids were fine. I just couldn't picture myself sitting in a desk in a straight line of desks for another seven hours."

"Ha!" Adam said. "You had ADHD."

"It must have been catching. So when Dad dropped me off at school in the morning, I started checking in at homeroom, then disappearing into the basement, or into the attic. I could stand over the ductwork at one corner of the attic and hear everything the principal said in her office. I could crawl above the auditorium, where the janitor went to change the spotlight bulbs, and listen to rehearsals of the school play. I was seeing this whole side of the school that other people didn't know existed."

Lightning flashed, thunder clapped. The rain pouring off the bridge into the lake sounded like static. That's what sitting in class back then had been like. Where there had been a channel before, now there was only static. I couldn't tune in, and even if I could, there was nothing to see.

"Eventually the school called my dad to say I'd missed so much school, I was going to flunk the sixth grade. My dad threatened a lawsuit because it was the school's fault they'd lost me. The upshot of it was that I went to a shrink for a while, and took some pills—"

"Pills," Adam said in utter disgust, like I would say *bryozoa* or *gelatin salad*. I hated gelatin salad. It was so ambiguous. What was it made of?

"These pills weren't bad," I said. "They helped. I only took them for a while. I went back to class and everything was fine. Really I think it never would have happened if you'd been in my class, if I'd had someone to talk to. The other kids didn't even notice I was gone."

We listened to the rain for a few moments. He said, "Lately I've been thinking about going back on my pills."

I thought he was saying this to make me feel better about spilling my secret. I *hoped* he was just saying this. Adam on his pills was no fun. He was serious and level-headed and cautious. Like everybody else. But if that's what he wanted, I should support him.

"Sean makes me . . . ," Adam said slowly, balling his hands into fists, ". . . so . . . mad." He flexed both hands with his fingers splayed. Like the anger was so great, he needed to shoot it out his fingertips before it caused him to burst into flames.

"I know," I said. "Me too." This wasn't exactly true. Sean didn't make me mad at him. He made me mad at myself.

A cool blast of wind made the chill bumps stand up higher on my arms. The sailboat rope tugged at my foot. I crossed my arms in front of me, covered as much skin as possible with my hands, and contracted into a ball.

"Hey. Come here." Adam slid his bare arm around my bare shoulders. Assuming we were both 98.6, I didn't understand how he could be so much warmer than me. His skin felt like he'd been standing in front of a fire. I slid my arm around his waist, too, and relaxed into his toasty goodness. I leaned my head against his shoulder. His fingers moved a little on my arm. I thought I heard his heartbeat speed up, but I wasn't sure.

Eventually the rain dwindled like someone turned down the volume of the static on TV. The thunder moved far away, and what was left of the sunset flung pink and orange on the scattering clouds. I hardly shivered as we edged down the embankment to the boat. Now the problem was finding any wind at all to get us home in the calm after the storm. Sitting on the hull, we both ducked as he wound the boom all the way around the mast and finally caught a little breeze.

We emerged from darkness under the bridge, into the golden light, and looked back. Partly because rain had battered the wet paint, and partly due to Adam's atrocious handwriting, the bridge didn't say ADAM LOVES LORI. I cocked my head to one side, then blurred my eyes, neither of which helped. I read out loud, "AOAN LOVES LOKI."

"They'll know what I meant." He was so proud. "Let Sean top that."

And he did.

13

The party had started. It was hard to see in the twilight, and with the mist rising off the water around us after the rain. But the gray twilight and gray mist made colors pop. Bright T-shirts and Slinky Cleavage-Revealing Tops dotted the Vaders' lawn and concentrated at the end of the dock. The faint bass beat of the music across the water was punctuated by the occasional *foop* of a bottle rocket.

Just as Adam had been waiting for me on my dock last Sunday when I canoed to see Frances, Mr. Vader was waiting for us on the marina dock. It was awkward generally for someone to wait for you on the dock like this, because you realized they were waiting for you and watching you when you were still ten minutes from reaching them. With Adam, I'd felt compelled to wave and make faces at him the whole return trip. With Mr. Vader, it was worse. He stood on the dock with his feet planted and his arms folded.

"I'm in trouble," Adam said.

"I know." I was sitting across from Adam on the hull. I didn't sit on the bow, and I didn't want to. It seemed inappropriate and frivolous now that Adam was about to get grounded.

We sailed past Mr. Vader on the dock. He followed us up the stairs and around the wharf. He helped us pull the mast and sail and then the hull out of the water and carry them, dripping, into the warehouse, all in complete silence. Mr. Vader's jaw was set. In the twilight, Adam's expression had already settled into darkness.

Finally Mr. Vader closed the door of the warehouse, locked it, and turned to face Adam with his hands on his hips.

"It wasn't supposed to rain tonight," Adam said quickly.

Mr. Vader nodded. "The storm popped up."

Adam backed off a millimeter. "Well. Since you were paying attention, thanks for coming to our rescue."

"I knew you were okay. I watched you." Mr. Vader took a pair of folding binoculars out of his pocket.

"That's creepy," Adam said.

"You know what's creepy?" Mr. Vader asked. "Two kids who are supposedly dating spray-paint their names on the bridge like they're in love. They get caught under a bridge during an electrical storm. And they don't fool around. They just sit there."

I'd planned to stay quiet and let Adam handle his dad. I didn't want to get him in *more* trouble. But this was too much. "Adam's right," I piped up. "That's creep—"

"Can you believe this?" Adam interrupted me. He didn't care I was trying to back him up. He wasn't even listening. He turned to me and said, "You're a witness to this. It's probably the only time this has happened in the history of the United States. I'm in trouble for *not* doing you."

Mr. Vader took his hands off his hips and pointed at Adam's chest. "I won't have you talking like that in front of Lori. Or in front of *me*, for that matter." Which was ludicrous, because the boys had learned all their best figures of speech from Mr. Vader. So had I.

"Why not?" Adam's voice rose. "That's what you're talking about, right? And now you don't want to talk about it? Maybe you're sorry you brought it up. Maybe you see now that it's none of your business."

"It's my business when it's part of this stupid game between you and Sean."

"Which one?" I asked.

As if I hadn't spoken, Mr. Vader said to Adam, "Your mother was right. You and Lori aren't really dating. You're trying to make Rachel jealous and get her away from Sean."

Sean made Adam angry. I could only imagine what it was doing to Adam to find out his dad *bought* Sean's act. Adam was going to explode at his dad. He would be grounded. We wouldn't get to make Sean and Rachel jealous tonight. I put my arm around him and told Mr. Vader, "Maybe he's more of a gentleman than you think."

Adam gave me a look of utter disbelief. Despite how serious the situation was, I almost laughed.

He didn't explode, but his chest did expand, until I lost my hold around him. He turned back to Mr. Vader, held out his fingers, and touched the first one. "Sean." He touched his second finger and said, "Stole." He tapped his third finger vigorously. "*My.*" He touched his pinky. "Girlfriend."

Mr. Vader hmphed and half-turned away, finished with us. "It's obvious Sean has something good going on, as usual, and you're trying to ruin it. Sean bought Rachel a wakeboard. He gave it to her at dinner, in front of your mother and Cameron and me. You don't mess with something special like that." He stalked down the pier, toward the party.

Adam and I looked at each other. Sean had been saving the money he earned at the marina to buy a Byerly for himself. He'd bragged about it every day in the boat, like all he needed was this new trick wakeboard and he'd be numero uno again. We were talking hundreds of dollars.

He'd spent that money on Rachel instead?

Adam jogged down the pier and stepped in front of Mr. Vader, blocking his way. "What about bindings?"

"Bindings too," Mr. Vader said. "They're on order."

It didn't make sense for Mr. Vader to be proud of Sean buying his new girlfriend a wakeboard instead of buying one for himself. It was a frivolous purchase made way too soon in their relationship. Right? What Adam and I knew, and what Mr. Vader knew too but clearly wasn't admitting to himself, was that this was the first time Sean had ever done something selfless.

Or so it seemed. But he'd given it to her in front of his mom and dad, like he'd wanted to impress them more than her. The *ew* factor was off the charts. Parents were bad enough. You didn't go out of your way to *involve* them.

Adam was thinking the same thing. "Her birthday isn't until March. Why'd he make this big presentation at the dinner table?"

"Because he values her," Mr. Vader said haughtily, "and he wanted to show us how much he values her."

"Couldn't he value her out in the Volvo?" Adam hollered. "Jesus!"

Mr. Vader pushed past Adam and resumed his walk up the pier. Partygoers in his yard stepped out of his way. I watched him carve a swath through the crowd until he disappeared inside the house. I couldn't hear over the music, but I could tell from the way people near the house jerked their heads in that direction that Mr. Vader slammed the door.

Adam pinched his own arm thoughtfully. He reached over and pinched *my* arm.

"Ow!" I squeaked.

He took me by the shoulders and shook me gently. "He gave her a wakeboard."

"I know."

"In front of my parents. Because he values her." He imitated his dad's tone, heavy with gravity.

"*You* could have valued her," I pointed out. "You could have given her something that meant a lot to you." I nodded toward his neck.

His eyes flew wide open. He gripped the skull-and-crossbones pendant protectively. "*You* gave this to *me*."

We pinned each other with a long look, and I wished for the millionth time in the past week that I could read his mind. He was upset all over again about losing Rachel.

He was mad at Sean about Rachel. He was outraged that his parents believed Sean over him about Rachel. But the pendant was more important to him than Rachel? Because I'd given it to him?

The boys with bottle rockets had noticed us and shouted to us. They were shooting bottle rockets near us in the water. Sooner or later they would set a boat on fire. Yet I couldn't tear my gaze away from Adam's blue eyes so bright in the gray mist. He must have seen something in my eyes, too.

"I'd better go change," I said slowly. "For the party."

"Right," Adam said, still holding my gaze.

"So." I laughed nervously. Dork. "I'll meet you back here in a while. Beauty takes patience. Ha ha ha ha."

He shook his head. "We should go to the party like this."

"Like *this*? My hair is full of lake."

"You look great in a bikini. As you know."

I was glad the dusk hid my blushing face. Or maybe it made my blushing face stand out like it made other colors pop, because I was that fortunate. "What do you mean, *as I know*? I don't *know*."

"If you didn't know, you wouldn't be wearing a bikini to get Sean's attention."

"Yeah. Fat lot of good it's done me."

"You wouldn't be flaunting it."

"*Flaunting* it! Are you sure? I have no idea what that would look like."

"Come flaunt it up at the house."

I wasn't sure why this irked me. He'd told me I looked good. He'd told me I would look good to Sean. This is what we wanted. Anyway, I couldn't stand out here and flaunt it for *anyone* in my bikini. I knew the night was hot and steamy, but the rain had done me in. I was freezing.

"Cold again?" he asked me, stepping closer.

I shivered some more. My stupid body had a mind of its own. "Toasty."

"Hold on." He took the extra key to the warehouse from the ledge above the door and stepped inside. He came back out with his zip-up sweatshirt printed with the name of our football team on the front and his number on the back. He held it up like an old man holding up an old lady's coat for her. I slipped my arms into the sleeves. Then he turned me around toward him. He pulled the hood up over my hair. Put the hood back down. Kissed me on the tip of my nose.

Foop! A bottle rocket exploded in the water just below us, illuminating a blob of bryozoa clinging to the wharf.

Adam took my hand, whispering, "We've got them right where we want them. Trust me."

He led me through the crowd in the yard, up the deck stairs, into his shadowy living room pulsing with music. Sean was surrounded by a group of people listening with open mouths to his puffed-up story of how he gave Rachel a wakeboard. Even Holly and Beige exclaimed like they were happy for Rachel instead of grumbling internally that Rachel was another in a long line and Sean was just showing off. Two feet away, Rachel was surrounded by hoydens screeching about how lucky she was to have a boyfriend like Sean.

From inside the dark room, the lights on the deck must have made Adam and me glow like a TV show. As we stepped through the door, everyone turned to stare at us.

I backed the slightest bit toward Adam. He squeezed my hand.

Then the floodgates opened. The girls who'd surrounded Rachel flocked to me to squeal about Adam spray-painting our names on the bridge. The boys with bottle rockets on the dock had seen it before the sun set and had spread the news around the party. The people who'd surrounded Sean moved to Adam and ribbed him about misspelling our names.

Adam played this perfectly. He laughed it all off like he didn't even care he was getting more attention than his stewing brother. He rubbed my shoulder and asked, "Aren't you hungry? We haven't eaten." He peered over my shoulder at the spread Mrs. Vader had laid out on the bar. "Party food isn't going to cover it."

"Starved." I followed him around the bar that divided the living room from the kitchen. There were partial walls on either side, so the kitchen was a little more quiet. At least we could raise our voices over the beat of Splender without making ourselves hoarse.

He opened the refrigerator door. "What'd they have for dinner? Chicken casserole." He wrinkled his nose. "I don't want the casserole of love, do you?"

"Definitely not."

"Hey, chica," Tammy called across the bar.

"Hey, chica," I responded, and looked over Adam's shoulder into the refrigerator again. Then I realized what I was supposed to be doing. I walked around the bar, screamed, "Tammeeeee!" and hugged her while jumping up and down. This was a lot easier in bare feet than it had been in heels, let me tell you.

"Hi there," she said, wrestling me off her. "You're insane. I'm so late. My mom made me play in a stupid tennis tournament in Birmingham today. Where is everybody?" She peered into the kitchen.

"Don't I count?" Adam asked from inside the refrigerator.

"That's Adam, right?" Tammy whispered.

"Right," I said. "Sean is holding court by the palm tree in the living room. The art geeks are outside in the grass."

"The football team is on the dock, shooting bottle rockets into the lake," Adam offered. I knew where his heart was.

"The trumpet line from the marching band is on the deck," I said. "Who were you looking for?"

"You!" Tammy said. She handed me a small present wrapped in Valentine's paper.

"Hey, thanks!" I said, ripping it open. "What's it for?" My birthday was still a week and a day away, and I didn't think anyone from school knew when it was. "How sweet!" I held up the eyelash comb, twirled it between my fingers, and slipped it into the pocket of Adam's sweatshirt. I hoped I remembered to take it out again at the end of the night. If I didn't, Adam would have some explaining to do next football season when it fell out of his pocket at practice.

"It's a hostess gift," Tammy said. "You know, when you come to a party, you bring a present for the hostess."

"But I'm not the hostess. This isn't my house." I wondered whether she'd tripped over some tennis balls, hit her head, and forgotten she'd gone with me to my house last week, scaring the bejeezus out of the father figure.

"You're the hostess because you're the girlfriend of one of the hosts," Tammy said.

Without meaning to, I glanced up at Adam. He'd

closed the refrigerator door and leaned against it, watching me.

"Or *pretending* to be," Tammy added.

Adam's blue eyes widened at me. Something told me—and I am sure this was not feminine instincts, because we have established I did not have any of those—but *something* told me my explanation of how Tammy knew about the plot might go over better if I heated Adam up. I slid my arms around his waist and pressed close to him, backing him against the refrigerator. His eyes grew even wider.

I gave him a coy half-smile that probably ended up looking like the first signs of a seizure. "You know how girls are. Girls can't make a move without telling other girls about it."

"Yeah, *girls* are like that," Adam told me, "but *you're* not."

Tammy cleared her throat.

Adam cleared his throat.

I cleared my throat, removed my hands from Adam's waist, and brushed imaginary dust off his bare shoulders, setting straight any oafish damage I might have done. From now on, whenever I got the idea that maybe he liked me a little, I would remember that he did *not* like me a little. I didn't need to read his mind.

"Heeeeeeey," Tammy squealed. She must have seen

Holly or Beige or a super-cute boy—but no, it was only McGillicuddy. They disappeared into the living room with their heads close together, shouting over the music. If she got rid of my approaching brother for me because she thought I needed some alone time with Adam to talk out our problems, she was wrong-o about me. Again. I started to follow her.

"Dinner's ready," Adam said behind me.

I looked toward the table in the kitchen. He'd set two of the places with knives, forks, spoons, and napkins. He'd placed a sandwich on each plate and sprinkled parsley flakes in a circle around it. Bam! He'd stacked the potato chips artfully in dessert bowls. He'd even lit one of his left-over birthday candles between our places. It all would have been really cute if he'd meant it. It was still pretty cute as a farce to make Rachel jealous, I supposed, but I wasn't in the mood.

"Let me help you," he said, pulling out a chair for me, as if I were a girl or something. Vivid imagination, this boy. I sat, and he scooted me up to the table.

He took a bottle of soda from the fridge and held it in front of me, like he was a wine steward. I nodded that the year was okay. He unscrewed the cap and handed it to me. I sniffed it like a wine cork, nodded my approval again, and handed it back to him. He poured soda into wine glasses for both of us, then sat down with me.

He took a gargantuan bite of his sandwich, chewed, swallowed, and looked at me. "What's wrong?"

Oh, nothing. That's what a girl would say, and she'd sulk for the rest of the night. But I wasn't capable of keeping my mouth shut. "I'm confused."

"It's not really wine," he said. "It's Diet Coke. And if anyone *ever* serves you brown wine with a foamy head, send it back."

"Thank you, Dr. Science." I took a dainty bite of my sandwich. Adam was a real gourmet. Peanut butter and strawberry jam. "I'm confused because I thought you said I was flaunting, and now I'm not even a girl? I thought you said I was a good flaunter."

"You *are* a good flaunter." He swirled the Diet Coke in his glass and sniffed the bouquet.

"Then why am I not a girl?"

"You— Shit, I *knew* that's what you were mad about. I didn't mean it that way." He leaned his head to one side and popped his neck. "You know as well as I do that you don't act like other girls."

"I'm working on it, though." I was working so hard! I felt like crying into my salt and vinegar chips, which was a step in the right direction.

"But it's *good* you don't act like other girls. Of course, I

183

don't have any say in it, because you're not after me. You're after Sean."

"You wouldn't have any *say* in it *anyway*, you patriarchal freak." I chomped a chip and said with my mouth full, "Thanks for cooking dinner. I love it when the little missus makes a house a home."

He glared at me. "Eat up. We have work to do."

"What kind of work? Devious kissing work? May I point out that we both have peanut butter breath?"

"Eat up," he said again. Sean's jovial voice escalated over the music in the living room, which made me want to speed up eating to get out of there, but also made the sandwich sit on my stomach like a rock.

We went upstairs. Adam shared his bathroom with Sean and Cameron, and the bathroom looked it. He brushed his teeth, then sipped straight from a bottle of mouthwash. As he swished it around in his mouth, he nudged my bare tummy with his toothbrush and prompted, "Hm."

"You want me to *use your toothbrush?*"

He spit in the sink. "You might as well. You're about to do a lot worse."

14

At this point, I realized what I'd thought was stress and peanut butter indigestion was actually butter-flies, which began dogfighting in my stomach at the idea that Adam and I were about to kiss some more. As I brushed my teeth with his toothbrush, I watched him watching me in the mirror. His muscled arms were folded on his strong, tanned chest. The bruise Sean had given him under his eye had almost faded, but the skull-and-crossbones pendant glinted dangerously.

If his parents hadn't been in the next room with the ten o'clock news turned way up over the music downstairs, I might have made a move on him right there in the bathroom.

Yes, I know, odds were I would have tripped and knocked him down and made him hit his head on the toilet. I was so turned on, I was almost willing to take this chance.

Instead, he took my hand again and led me down through the party, indoors and outdoors, to the end of the dock. The football team had run out of bottle rockets. The party had reached the stage where boys played quarters. The drinking game was run very professionally by experienced people. If Mr. Vader had found out, he would have shut down the party—because kids were drinking underage at his house, or because he would have known one of his sons had stolen beer from the marina. In any case, as a precaution, a wall of people stood across the dock, talking and flirting, shielding the boys playing quarters from the prying eyes of the Vaders in their bedroom.

The wall of people included Sean and Rachel, facing each other and holding both hands like they were about to dance a polka. Rachel hadn't taken the precaution of kicking her shoes off before she stepped onto the dock. She was likely to catch her heel between the boards and fall flat. (Shrug.) Rachel obviously valued beauty before balance.

As Adam and I approached the wall of people, Adam aimed straight for Sean. He brushed against Sean harder than necessary as we edged through. I felt Sean and Rachel watching us, but I didn't look back as we stepped over the boys sprawled in a circle around a cup of beer.

We sat on the edge of the dock. The wood was still damp and cold from the rain. We slipped our feet into the lake, which felt like a warm bath compared with the cool air.

"Do you want a beer?" Adam asked.

"I don't think I could handle it. I feel so high already." The warm lake, the cool air, and Adam had my body going in a thousand different directions.

Maybe he knew. He grinned at me and whispered, "I'm going to kiss you now. It'll be a big one, so don't hit me." He leaned in.

"Wait a minute," I said, putting my hand on his chest to stop him. I wasn't quite ready to kiss him with boys playing quarters right behind us, and with Sean and Rachel staring at us. We'd kissed before where people could see us if they wanted to look, but we'd never been this blatant about it. Besides, I had another concern. "I want to be prepared. Are you going to kiss me, or *really* kiss me?"

He cocked his head at me, perplexed, with those little frown lines between his eyebrows. "What would be the point of kissing you if I didn't do it right?"

"Ohhhhhh!" said the boys behind us. There was nowhere

in my life I could get away from boys saying, "Ohhhhhh!" I glanced behind us to make sure the boys were talking about beer, not us. Indeed, when the boys' quarters hit the cup and they chose someone to drink, all of them seemed to be ganging up on Scooter Ledbetter. I hadn't seen his monster truck in the Vaders' driveway, so at least he wouldn't be driving home.

Sean had moved Rachel in front of him and held her with his arms crossed over her boobs. So he could watch us over her head without her knowing. Of course, she was staring at Adam, too. I rolled my eyes at both of them, like I was *so tired* of them watching us. I almost burst into laughter at the thought, but managed to turn back to Adam in time.

I told him through my teeth, "We've been kissing all week without, you know. *Really* kissing."

"That was before Sean gave up a wakeboard for Rachel. Step up your game."

I was running out of excuses. "Look," I whispered, "when we do this stuff, we're trying to make them jealous, but it's also my first time for real. You know?"

His blue eyes focused on me. We were almost nose to nose, and our shoulders moved quickly in time with our breathing, in time with each other. "I know."

"And when I fantasize about kissing"—kissing Sean,

I meant, but I wasn't going to say this—"our mouths are closed."

"This isn't your fantasy."

I wasn't so sure about that. True, I'd never fantasized about this particular scenario, but maybe that was because I'd never imagined it. I had to remember that this was *Adam Adam Adam*, and if I could replace him with Sean from my fantasies, the warm pricklies I was feeling would make a perfect dream. Except I would probably wake up.

Adam moved in again. One more time my brain knew this would make Sean jealous, but my body sounded the alarm. I put my hand on Adam's chest and whispered, "Give me a break. I had a bad experience with this."

He looked hurt, which didn't make sense if we were only friends. He was putting on a good act. "With who?"

"The only person I've ever kissed, besides you, is Cameron."

"You kissed *Ca*—"

I hadn't expected his reaction to be that LOUD. I reached out and grabbed the back of his hair, which turned his head away from the crowd and also shut him up right quick.

I put my forehead to his forehead and whispered like a lover, "I was eleven. We were in the warehouse and he grabbed me. Very sloppy. Don't tell McGillicuddy."

Adam blinked. I felt his eyelashes on my eyelids.

"Very, very sloppy," I said. "We still can't look each other in the eye."

I let go of his hair so he could look *me* in the eye. "Let me shrug that off." He shook violently like he'd caught a sudden chill. "Okay. I'm going to *really* kiss you, but it'll be subtle." He moved toward me one more time. "And don't tell me to back off. It's starting to look like we're not really in love."

I closed my eyes automatically as he kissed me, and the word *love* blinked red and then black on the insides of my eyelids. His lips were warm. Was that all? I opened my eyes.

His eyes were still closed, and he came in again.

I closed my eyes. He kissed me like before, only I felt his tongue between my lips, opening them. His tongue was inside my mouth (ADAM VADER'S TONGUE WAS INSIDE MY MOUTH) not very far, and then out again.

I thought *that* was it, and opened my eyes. And closed them as he kissed me once more. Now I was getting it. You didn't just sit there with your lips locked with the boy's lips and the boy's tongue turning flips at the back of your throat (cough *Cameron* cough). There was constant movement and change. It was an activity, and probably one the girl could participate in, too. As Adam pulled away, I said, "Let me try."

He kissed me and whispered against my lips, "Be my guest." His low voice made me shiver.

I kissed him. Strange that the lips were so soft in such an edgy boy. I kissed him again and very gently pressed my tongue into his mouth.

He gasped. I mean, I wasn't sure, because it was in the middle of the kiss. But he seemed startled. He inhaled sharply through his nose. Then *he* was kissing *me*, deeper this time.

I pulled away, laughing. "It was supposed to be my turn."

He half-smiled. His lips stayed close to my lips.

I didn't suggest this, and he didn't agree to this, but somehow we telepathically agreed to give up on the witty conversation and make out. His tongue played with my lips. My tongue swept across his teeth. I drowned in it, and completely lost the people playing quarters behind us on the dock until someone said, "Is anybody filming Adam and Lori? You might be able to sell it." Sean laughed and said something I couldn't catch that made the people around him burst into laughter too.

Adam pulled back. He was embarrassed and saw our plan wasn't working. He would escape to his room, humiliated. He would leave me naked, or nearly so, in my bikini and his sweatshirt in the midst of these fully clothed people.

Wrong. He kissed me again and whispered, "There's something else you can do if you get bored with this."

Get *bored* with this???

"You kind of do the same thing, but move around. Here." He kissed my jaw. His tongue touched my skin just as he pulled his lips away. "Or up here." Good Lord, his teeth were on my earlobe. Very gently he slid them off. His tongue played outside my ear. His breath was loud and hot.

It felt so good, and at the same time, I could hardly stand it. I needed something to hang onto. My fingers patted the edge of the dock, finding a firm hold—but this seemed potentially splintery. My other hand felt for Adam's hand.

Strangely, he must have needed something to hang onto, too. He took my hand and squeezed.

The guys playing quarters may have made another comment about us, but it was hard to hear with a boy's tongue in my ear. Also it was hard to care.

I pulled away, shoulders shaking. Adam seemed to have a hard time focusing his eyes on me, like he was in a dream. I moved in and gave him the jaw treatment. Then the ear treatment.

"Ah," he said. He giggled and then cleared his throat before the boys heard him. "Lori."

"Mm?" I hummed in his ear.

He shuddered. And then—oh, no! He stood up. I'd done something wrong! The tongue was indeed el grosso as I'd originally thought!

"I'll be right back," he told me. He picked his way across the quarters game and pushed through the wall of people watching. He had sense enough not to push through Sean and Rachel again, or they'd know the ear was for them. At least, they'd *think* the ear was for them. I was beginning to wonder who the ear was for. It *felt* like it was for me.

He came back dragging a beanbag float and nearly knocked the legs out from under a few folks. He dragged it right over the quarters game, scattering the boys, and would have spilled the beer if someone hadn't been faster. Then he dropped the float into the lake and kicked off the part of it that sagged over the dock. He gestured toward it and grinned at me. "Your limo awaits."

I had my doubts about this. The lake was black, and the sky was black with faraway stars. But anyone who drove their boat to the party this late would know to dock at the marina where there was more room. We were safe. I shrugged off Adam's sweatshirt and—*without looking to see if Sean was watching me*, very important—slipped into the hot water. I hadn't realized my butt was frozen solid from the cold dock. The lake was such a relief. Ahhhhh.

Until Adam did a cannonball, socking me in the eyes

with water and splashing everyone on the dock, including Sean and Rachel.

"Aaaadaaaaaaaam!" they all cried. He chuckled softly to himself as we held onto the raft and kicked it out into the lake, beyond the glow of light from the house.

He stopped kicking and crawled higher on the raft, straddling it. "Come up here with me."

The beanbag raft was filled with floaty bits rather than air and always seemed in danger of sinking. This could be annoying when you wanted to stay on top of the water, getting a tan. On a night like tonight, it was perfect. It would keep us from drowning while giving us more hot water than cool air.

"Now. Where were we?" He put both his strong arms around me, pulled me close, and kissed me hard.

I hadn't thought this was possible, but it was even better than before, because no one was watching. Which was actually my new problem with it. I put my hand on his chest to stop him.

He groaned in frustration. I made a mental note to make him groan in frustration more often. It seemed like something a treacherous girl would do. Also he was really cute when he groaned.

"I just wanted to know," I breathed, "why we're doing this where no one can see us."

"We think no one can. We thought no one was watching us at the bridge. We need to act the part all the time, and never step out of character." He put his hand on my arm. "If that's okay."

I nodded. I was still nodding as he pushed me gently backward until I was lying down on the raft, and he was lying on top of me. His whole weight was on me, but he didn't squash me because I was hovering on the raft, just under the surface of the warm water. I felt him along me. Almost every inch of his skin touched almost every inch of mine.

I watched the skull and crossbones glinting in the starlight, and tried to impress it on my retinas so I'd still see it when I closed my eyes to kiss him again. This was Adam, not Sean. I was after Sean, not Adam. Adam was after Rachel, not me. And if kissing Adam was better than anything I'd ever dreamed of doing with Sean . . . well, I could see how that was going to mess up my plans.

I kissed him anyway. The skull and crossbones lay on my throat.

"And when you kiss me," I said against his lips, "you're thinking about Rachel. Right?"

Almost before I got the last word out, he was kissing me again, harder than before, so intense I got lost in it and thought I might drown in the blackness even though my head was still above water.

I pinched his ass.

He yelped, and the yelp echoed across the lake and back. Silhouettes moved far away on the dock, peering in our direction without seeing.

"Did you hear me?" I asked.

He propped himself far enough above me to be able to see me. With one finger he smoothed a strand of wet hair away from my face. He traced the line of my cheek down to my chin. "Do you want to stop? Tell me and I'll stop."

"I don't want to stop," I said. The absolute truth, for the first time in a week. "But how far are we going with this?" Adam was used to jumping off the roof. I wasn't. These were dangerous waters.

He moved to my ear again, and my body braced for the shockwaves. Just before his lips touched my skin, he whispered, "I guess we'll know when we get there."

15

"S-bend or what?" Adam asked me, grinning.

I'd just climbed out of the water after *landing the S-bend*! And even though he'd dried in the hot sun and hugging me must have been a cold, wet shock, he wrapped his strong arms around my life vest and hugged me hard. Best of all, Adam acting this way wasn't an unexpected hostess gift wrapped in Valentine's paper anymore. It was part of being his girlfriend. I was getting used to it, and I *loved* expecting it.

Saturday we'd gone mud riding. Then we'd parked in the movie theater lot, watched the trucks go by, and just talked. We'd shared a milkshake. I was totally immune to his germs by now. Monday after dinner, when I thought I'd have to spend the evening with Arthur C. Clarke, who wrote a good space story but was not the greatest kisser, Adam asked me to go for a walk around the neighborhood with him. We held hands, which no longer seemed the least bit weird. Here it was Wednesday, and I hadn't had more than a fleeting thought of Sean since Friday night with Adam in the lake.

I could have sworn Adam hadn't thought of Rachel, either. When he kissed me (often! *really* kissed me!), it felt like he was thinking of *me*, not her. Yeah, he could have been faking. But as he'd said that first night at the tennis court, he wasn't exactly drama club material.

And it would come crashing down around us any minute. Adam never looked over his shoulder to make sure Rachel was watching us when he kissed. He *did* check *Sean's* reaction. I knew Mr. Vader was wrong about which of his boys was stabbing the other in the back, but I also knew Adam wouldn't walk away after being stabbed, any more than Sean would. So I enjoyed my time alone with Adam as much as I could. Whenever Sean came around, I held my breath, waiting for the fall.

It wasn't so long a wait. The boys *looked* harmless enough this afternoon. Adam, Cameron, and my brother had had fantastic wakeboarding runs, too. They'd finally gotten their wakeboarding legs back, as good as last year.

Cameron and McGillicuddy lounged across the seats in the boat, basking in the late afternoon sunshine like big golden retrievers, watching me drip on the platform and wagging their tails vaguely. They felt what I'd been feeling since the first day we went out: sated with happy exertion. High.

Sean lay flattened across the bow seat, but not for the same reason. He hadn't taken his turn yet. He said he didn't want to miss a call from Rachel. She'd planned to come wakeboarding with us today (amid protests from the boys, because guests had never been allowed) and borrow my wakeboard since her bindings hadn't arrived yet (whatever). Her mom was going to bring her down, but they never showed. Sean had called Rachel four times from the boat (to make Adam mad, Adam and I thought) and hadn't reached her. I found this strange. Where was she? Wasn't she waiting around for Sean's call with her hand poised on the answer button of her phone?

Beyond the windshield that separated us from him, we heard his cell phone ring Nickelback's "Fight for All the Wrong Reasons." We knew it was Rachel calling him back. And when his curse word burst over the windshield, we knew what she'd said hadn't been very nice.

Adam shrugged and turned back to me. Unlike Sean, he didn't flirt with me by assisting me with things I was perfectly capable of doing myself. He didn't help me off with my equipment. He did sit on the back of the boat and watch me appreciatively. When I took off my life vest, he surveyed my bikini-clad hotness (ha) and gave me a naughty smile. I untied my bindings and lifted one foot out. He licked his lips like he had a foot fetish. I burst into laughter.

Sean charged past the windshield into the back of the boat, eyes full of tears. "She broke up with me!" he wailed. "She broke up with me because she's still in love with Adam!"

We all went quiet. Only the *clack-clack, clack-clack* of cars on the bridge and the lapping of waves against the boat disturbed the silence. The boys weren't ribbing Sean. They must have been as shocked as I was that Sean would *admit* what Rachel had said.

Sean was in love.

He sniffled. "I'm going to her house. Take me back to shore." When Cameron didn't immediately slip into the driver's seat, Sean took a step toward the steering wheel himself.

"Sean," Cameron said, standing in his way. "You haven't landed a good trick the whole week and a half we've been coming out. We only have today, tomorrow, and Friday to practice for the Crappy Festival. Take your turn first and then go to her house."

Sean cursed, and cursed, and cursed, and dove into the

lake. We all rushed to the side of the boat and watched him glide to the surface twenty feet away, already swimming. We weren't so far from the Foshees' yard that we needed to fish him out for his own safety. He swam until he could touch bottom, sloshed the rest of the way to land, and hit the grass running through the Foshees' yard, through my yard, toward his house.

Adam said quietly, "I'm the biggest."

"Adam," I scolded him.

Cameron and my brother looked from me to Adam and back to me, wondering what was going on between us. Frankly, I wondered the same thing. I wasn't sure what I'd wanted or expected Adam to say when we finally got our wish for Sean and Rachel to break up. But *I'm the biggest* wasn't it.

We drove back to the wharf still in silence—except, of course, for the deafening motor. Adam and I sat across the aisle from each other without glancing at each other. Something was about to happen.

And everyone sensed it. Cameron and McGillicuddy took more than their share of equipment into the warehouse, leaving Adam and me alone in the boat. As they came back out, Cameron looked down at us from the wharf and said, "Don't do anything I wouldn't do"—which made me wish I hadn't confessed to Adam that Cameron and I had kissed. After five years of hiding this from everyone, he had to hint about it *now*? Whatever was coming for Adam and me, it was going to be hard enough already.

McGillicuddy asked me, "Do you want me to tell Dad you'll be late for dinner?"

"No," I said. "I won't be long."

We watched McGillicuddy and Cameron walk toward the houses. They stopped to talk. Cameron took a swipe at McGillicuddy. McGillicuddy shoved Cameron. They went their separate ways. Friends to the end, the simplest relationship possible.

"What's that supposed to mean?" Adam snapped into the silence. "You won't be long?"

"It's dusk in the summer. Mosquitos," I said, slapping at a bug. While my mouth spouted this drivel, my mind worked on what I really wanted to say to Adam. But I had no more idea than I'd had out on the lake.

You know what didn't help? When he reached behind his neck and worked at the knot in the leather string. I knew what was coming. It took him a few seconds to get through that knot. Even though the whole time I was thinking about what to say when he asked me to turn around, I was speechless when the moment came. I turned around on my seat. He tied the skull and crossbones around my neck. The metal was hot against my breastbone. I pressed the skull between the eyes with my fingertips. Turning back to him, I murmured, "You're giving me a piece of you."

He looked over at me. We were together for real, and he was *so hot*. I should have been giggling with delight and dorkiness. The angry look in his blue eyes broke my heart.

"Rachel told Sean she likes you better," I said, "but you don't want her back. You've never wanted her back. All you've wanted was to get revenge on Sean. You're giving me this to show him you don't even want what he can't have."

Adam's eyes narrowed at me. I made an effort not to shrink back against the side of the boat. He said evenly, "I'm giving it to you because I want to give it to you."

"Your timing is odd. Usually a boy wouldn't laugh at his brother hitting rock bottom, then show his love for his girlfriend practically in the same breath." Now *he* was shrinking against his side of the boat, which made me brave enough to throw in still more sarcasm. "I don't have a lot of experience with this, but that's my theory."

He closed his eyes and said in a rush, "I'm in love with you."

I took a breath to tell him if he really meant it, he wouldn't have to say it with his eyes closed. But he didn't just have his eyes closed. Those worry lines had appeared between his brows. He was in pain, concentrating hard to make it go away, like the second time he broke his collarbone wakeboarding, and lay still as death in the floorboard of the boat and wouldn't let anyone touch him but me.

He opened his eyes but remained plastered against the boat. He looked small, if this was possible. "That's my plot. You were right, I had a plot, and that's my whole plot. I'm in love with you. The last nine months with McGillicuddy away at college have been freaking torture for me, because I didn't have an excuse to come to your house. If I came over without McGillicuddy there, you'd know. I hardly saw you the whole school year. I thought I might finally have a chance with you since I was about to get my license, and you were about to get your license. We could go places together, alone. I could get you away from Sean. But the more I hinted we should go out, the more you talked about hooking up with Sean. When I heard Rachel liked me, I asked her out, and I kept asking her out. To make you jealous. And at the tennis court that night when you said we should make Rachel and Sean jealous, I nearly had a heart attack. I thought you saw right through me."

He looked so hurt, and his eyelashes were so long. I had fallen in love with him. I *wished* he were in love with me too. But in telling me this elaborate lie, he'd betrayed the truth.

"You don't love me," I said. "You're competing with

Sean. Maybe you've even convinced yourself you love me, but it all comes back to Sean."

His expression changed from hurt back to anger. "Last Friday night in the lake didn't mean anything to you."

Friday night had been the best night of my life. He was picking up each thing I loved about my life, grinding it to a point, and pushing it through my heart. I'd thought only Sean knew how to do that.

"The past week and a half hasn't meant anything to you," he went on. "The past sixteen years—"

"Sixteen years!" I howled.

"You *told* me you're stuck on Sean," he shouted. His voice made the metal wall of the warehouse hum. "You think your mother chose him for you—"

"No, I don't!" Well, maybe I did. And maybe I didn't care so much anymore, but this was hard to explain while yelling. "Look, Adam. Let's say you *had* been in love with me all our lives, which, by the way, I don't believe for a second." Because why would any boy fall in love with a girl like me? "What you loved about me would have been exactly what I hate about myself. To stay the person you wanted, I'd have to stay the same. I want to change."

"You think your *mother* wants you to change," he corrected me. "Lori, when your mother said that, she was kidding."

"You weren't there. You don't know. *Your* mother didn't laugh."

"My mother *never* laughs. It's called a dry wit. You're basing your whole life on one conversation you overheard when you were four years old that you don't even remember right."

I felt like I'd been slapped. When I'd shared my deepest secret with him, it never once occurred to me that he'd throw it back in my face. Adam, of all people, had betrayed me. I stepped out of the boat, onto the wharf. "Let's end this now before we ruin our friendship."

"Too late," he called after me.

I intended to flounce across his yard and mine, but I ran straight into a cloud of gnats. I spent the rest of the walk pressing one nostril closed with my finger while I expelled gnats from the other. Eat your heart out, Adam!

Except I *didn't* want him to eat his heart out. I wanted to be friends with him. I wanted to be with him. I wanted to make out with him in the lake some more—that was for damn sure. I wanted him to stare longingly after me from the boat as I flounced to my house, which sounded a lot like I wanted him to eat his heart out. I didn't know what I wanted.

I'd made it to my garage before I realized I was still wearing the skull and crossbones. I couldn't get the knot undone. I turned the knot around to the front but still couldn't pick it apart. The pendant was searing a hole through my skin. I cut through the leather string with garden shears and tried to grind the pendant into dust in my fist like a superhero. I opened my hand and found the outline of the skull and crossbones pressed into my palm.

I didn't sleep well that night. This was probably a good thing. If I'd had to lie through one more dream about Sean being a tease, I would have had to slap him. When I woke up and found myself sleepwalking, who knew what wakeboarding posters I might have destroyed? I might even have found myself choking my childhood teddy bear, Mr. Wuggles, which would have traumatized me for life.

In the morning, I walked to the marina with the skull and crossbones in my pocket (actually, Adam's pocket, the pocket of his cutoff jeans), intending to give it back to him and say something appropriate. This would have been a stretch for me, I know. To save my friendship with Adam, I would have found a way to do it.

Mrs. Vader assigned us both to the warehouse. Great, *now* she finally believed we were together? I tried to look at the long day with him as an opportunity to have a heart-to-heart with him. Another one. Actually, the convo the evening before had been more of a spleen-to-spleen.

I could never find the right time. He was busy locating boats to take down. I was busy checking the oil. The full-time workers wandered in and out. Besides, this day of all days, he worked with his shirt off. Sweat glistened on his tanned muscles, and his brown hair fell in his eyes. He was so hot that I felt intimidated. He was telling me to eat *my* heart out, and it was working.

There were a few instances when I *could* have screwed up my courage, sidled up to him, handed him the skull and crossbones, and talked him down. But whenever I started toward him with this in mind, he flashed those blue eyes at me, and I felt that slap all over again.

It was such a relief to go wakeboarding that afternoon. Yes, I'd be trapped in the boat for over an hour with Adam and Sean, but at least I was out of the warehouse and into the strong sun and oppressive humidity. The Crappy Festival show was in two days. We all needed to nail down the course we wanted the boat to follow and the tricks we planned to do—especially Sean. Maybe thinking about the show would get our minds off each other.

Or not. Adam climbed out of the water and onto the platform after busting ass four times. He had a stare-down with Sean, who was getting in the water for his turn. If two girls had been in a fight like this, one of them would have flipped over the side of the boat rather than face probably the tenth stare-down of the day. But Sean and Adam were not two girls. And because *I* was a girl, it stressed me out more to watch them than it stressed them to growl at each other, teeth bared. I left my seat and slid into the bow, watching ahead of us as the boat drifted across the choppy water kicked up by the afternoon traffic.

The bench sank next to me, pulling me down into the hole. "So you still want Sean?" Adam hissed. "Let me give you some advice."

"No thanks." I leaned further over the bow to watch the large waves. A whitecap rolled by. A *whitecap*? You didn't see those on the lake very often. The water was choppier than I'd ever seen it.

"At first," Adam went on, "we thought we'd make him want something I had. You. Now he wants something *you* have."

"Boobs?" I asked, trying to sound bored.

"Your place at the end of the wakeboarding show. Throw a jump and fake an injury. You have to make it look like you're really hurt, so Cameron doesn't rib Sean about girls making sacrifices just to go out with him."

Cameron cranked the boat to pull Sean up, and my brother spotted. With the motor roaring and Nickelback blaring, I was free to tell Adam (loudly) exactly what I thought of that plan. I sat up and turned to face him.

Before I could get the words out, he leaned close and said, "I told you before you're not a good actress. I have a lot more confidence in you now. I thought you liked me. You had me fooled."

I stared into his blue eyes, trying to see what was behind them. "You really want me to throw a jump and go out with Sean?"

"This has nothing to do with me," he said grimly.

"It has everything to do with y—"

He put his finger to my lips. "If you want Sean, this is what you need to do, because this is how he is. Love him or leave him. I'm just trying to help." He slid off the seat with a high zipping sound of his board shorts against the vinyl and bounced toward the back of the boat. He plopped down in the seat across the aisle from my brother and crossed his feet on the edge of the boat, relaxed, satisfied by a job well done. When Sean landed a front flip, then tumbled a couple of extra times before face-planting, Adam's shoulders shook. He was laughing.

"Lori!" McGillicuddy shouted, standing directly in front of me. The boat drifted again, and Sean dripped on the platform. "I said, did you see the log? I guess you didn't see the log, since you're in a coma."

"Log schmog." I stood up and reached for my life vest.

McGillicuddy followed me as I stepped over Adam and

Sean, who didn't bother to move their feet out of the aisle as I passed. Just like old times. "There's a huge log out near the pontoon boat," McGillicuddy said. "When we get near it, I'm veering to the right of where we usually go. Okay?"

"Okay," I said, sliding over the back of the boat to the platform and stepping into the bindings on my wakeboard.

"To the *right*," Cameron laughed.

"I said *okay*." I was in no mood to be teased about my driving right now.

The drone of the motorboat was great for thinking, fortunately, or unfortunately, depending on whether you hated yourself. At the moment I wasn't enjoying it too much. I was supposed to be pinning down my routine for the show, but I just did flips and 360s automatically, my mind on Adam.

Staring at him in the boat told me nothing. He was so far away that he was just a tan face with light brown hair, and if he'd changed places with Sean, I wouldn't have known. But I stared at the boy I thought was Adam and tried to figure out exactly what he was plotting. Clearly he'd paid more attention to MTV reality shows than he'd let on.

If I pretended to get hurt so Sean could take my place in the show, he probably wouldn't ask me out. He'd watched Adam and me while we were together, that was for sure. And I'd thought at first that the light had dawned and he'd seen my ravishing beauty for the first time. Looking back, though, I thought he'd watched Adam more than me. Sean had worried Rachel would get jealous and Adam would snatch her away again.

If Sean *did* ask me out, though, I'd know for sure that my internal makeover had worked—two days before the deadline of my sixteenth birthday! And I'd also know Adam had been right. Sean was so low, he couldn't stand to ask out a girl who'd shown him up. It was almost worth throwing a jump just to see what happened and get some closure on this issue.

I could do any old jump and pretend to hurt my ankle. I'd hurt it last summer when I fell and my foot came halfway out of the binding, which was why I'd laced up the bindings so tightly since then. Faking a limp would be more difficult. But I'd need to limp for only two days, until the Crappy Festival show. The question was whether I should complain about it enough to go to the hospital and have them find nothing, which seemed like a huge waste of time and money. Adam had hurt himself before and had been in a lot of pain but refused to go to the hospital, so there *was* some precedent for this. Of course, he finally had to go, and his arm was broken in three places. There was also the small detail that Adam was like that and I was not.

Suddenly I found myself shooting farther and faster

beyond the boat than I'd expected. We were turning at the bridge, just under the words AOAN LOVES LOKI. I pulled up and took control of the run.

What had I been thinking? Had I seriously been considering throwing a jump and pretending to be hurt just to get a boy? What kind of boy did you catch with a ploy like that?

And furthermore, what kind of person was Adam to give me the idea?

I decided right then that I was *not* going to pretend to get hurt and throw this show for Sean or anybody. *Furthermore*, I would skip the party tomorrow night, because there would be no one there I wanted to see, except Tammy. Well, okay, maybe I wouldn't skip the party, because who could skip a party next door? But I wouldn't enjoy it. Or I would hang out with Tammy, ignoring the boys. And *furthermore*, sometime between now and then, maybe tonight since I obviously would not have a boy to go out with, I would ask McGillicuddy to drive me to town. I would buy the latest Kelly Clarkson album as a birthday present from me to me. I would fight and fight and fight to play it in the boat the next time we went wakeboarding. I was sick to death of Nickelback.

Something dark in the water flashed past the corner of my eye. I turned and saw an enormous log tumbling gently in the water. Just then the pull on the rope changed, and I remembered McGillicuddy was veering to the right to avoid the log. I veered to the right with him as I headed for the pontoon boat to ride the rails.

Only I was coming up too fast on the backside of the pontoon boat. I glanced over at the boys and motioned to Adam to slow down. I'd screwed this trick already.

Adam was motioning to *me*, an exaggerated wave away from the pontoon boat. And he was mouthing something. *Your other right.* I realized what I'd done then and dropped the rope. The side of the pontoon boat emblazoned VADER'S MARINA zoomed toward me, *smack*.

16

This probably would have been a lot easier if I'd gotten amnesia or at least felt a little woozy from the impact, but I didn't. I knew exactly what was happening as I slipped wakeboard-first under the pontoon boat and slowed to a stop. The buoyant wakeboard on my feet and the life vest hugging my chest stuck me like magnets to the slippery underside of the boat.

My head—I had cracked my head open when I hit the boat, and the pain was almost unbearable, but I had nowhere to put it. Blood curled around me, backlit by sunbeams streaming through the water at the edges of the boat. I needed to get out from under. I was running out of air.

I tried to kick myself over to the edge—but my feet were still stuck in the wakeboard bindings. Bending over to untie them was the only way out. I would run out of air before then. I could hardly think of anything except running out of air, the throbbing in my head, the blood forming graceful curlicues in front of my eyes.

I reached one hand as far toward the edge of the boat as I could, hoping I could pull hard with every bit of life I had left and slip out from under, dragging the wakeboard with me. My hand sank into a firm, gelatinous mass. Without looking, I knew it was bryozoa. I had died and gone to hell. This was how my mother must have felt. The water had always been my friend. The water had betrayed me.

Then they came for me. They were under the pontoon boat with me, blurry and green like ghosts in the water. One boy shoved down on the wakeboard. The other boy put a strong arm across my chest and pushed off from the bottom of the boat with his feet. He took me lower in the water—wrong direction, hello, I could hardly suppress the urge to breathe in water instead of air. I struggled. He let me go. The wakeboard and the life vest propelled me to the surface, clear of the boat.

I popped into the air, gasping. Sean put his arms around me again and held my head above the water so I could breathe. The thought crossed my mind of rejecting a boy's help and resisting the damsel-in-distress role, but really it was a little thought that had no effect on letting Sean help me breathe. The more I breathed, the harder my head throbbed, so I also had a little thought that MTV would never invite me to dance on stage during one of their Spring Break specials now that I looked like the Elephant Man.

And a little thought that I had been wrong about Sean. Mom had sent me a sign. She'd sent Sean to save my life. Maybe he *was* worth a faked injury, after all.

Of course, there was also McGillicuddy down at my feet, and the fact that the motorboat had been only twenty yards away from me when I went down, so maybe it wasn't Mom's doing. God, my head hurt like a mother.

McGillicuddy got me loose from the wakeboard. Sean held me up to Cameron in the boat, who grabbed me under the arms and lifted me in. Immediately Sean climbed the ladder and came to me. He pulled me out of the life vest, then eased me down and cradled my head in his lap.

Just like in my dream, he looked down at me with eyes lighter than the deep blue sky behind him. The sunlight turned his hair and shoulders and broad chest gold as he pressed both hands to my head.

Unlike in my dream, he dripped water and tears on my face, stinging my eyes. The blood didn't help either.

Oozing from under Sean's hand, it crawled like mosquitoes on my skin. I felt pretty.

"Calm down," McGillicuddy said. "Calm down. For God's sake, would you calm down?"

"I'm fine," I said between heaving coughs. "At least I can move my toes, so I won't have to ride the short bus."

"I meant Adam."

I stared past the pain in my head, upward at Adam's chin. Adam held me, not Sean. I hadn't recognized him upside down, without the skull and crossbones.

"Sean," Cameron called. "We've got her. Let's go."

The engine started, and the boat lurched into high speed. Down in Adam's lap, below the sides of the boat, the motor sounded muffled, more a buzz than a roar. Without Nickelback blaring, for once.

"Let me see," McGillicuddy said, bending next to Adam.

I cringed and closed my eyes and tried to go to a different place, away from the pain, as they fumbled on my forehead. Poked at my forehead. I came back from that different place and said, "DON'T TOUCH IT."

"It's going to need stitches," McGillicuddy said. "They might have to shave your hair a little. But if they do, I'll shave mine too. So will Adam. Right, Adam?"

"It's a wonder you weren't killed," Adam cried. "It's a wonder you didn't at least put your eye out."

McGillicuddy said, "Adam, would you calm down?"

I squeezed my eyes more tightly shut.

"I can't believe you actually did it," Adam said. "I can't believe you're that stupid."

"I didn't," I mouthed. That's all I could do. Sean and Adam had been my whole life for the last couple of weeks, but it was surprising how little I cared about them when I suddenly had a throbbing headache the size of the lake. Even if I'd wanted to, I didn't have the strength to fight. Adam wouldn't have believed me, anyway.

At first, all five Vaders plus McGillicuddy crowded into the emergency room with me. The nurses kicked everyone out except Mrs. Vader. They must have mistaken her for someone motherly and soothing. She barked at people and insisted on seeing their credentials before she'd let them touch me. Then Cameron came back and said Adam had taken a swing at Sean and gotten them all kicked out of the waiting room. So Mrs. Vader herded them all home where they could beat the hell out of each other in peace. She sent McGillicuddy in to sit with me.

I didn't have a concussion, and they didn't shave my head or anything traumatic like that. After the first prick of anesthetic, my head didn't even hurt much. Which was a good thing, because McGillicuddy went to buy himself some Pop-Tarts out of the snack machine. I lay there by myself on the hospital bed and stared at the water-stained ceiling while the doc stitched me up, scolded me, and left to find me some pain pills for when the anesthetic wore off. I felt very sorry for myself and very alone until Dad showed up, with Frances.

Dad grasped my hand in both of his. "Lori. Oh, my Lori." He started to cry softly.

"Dad, I'm okay." I patted his arm: there there.

"Trevor," said Frances. Her hand was on Dad's back. "Deep breaths."

Dad sniffed a deep breath through his nose while Frances held his gaze and moved her hands in circles in the air in front of her, encouraging him to breathe therapeutically. The way they were acting, people at the hospital who didn't know them might mistake them for a couple. A very odd couple, with Frances in her tie-dyed hippie costume and Dad in his lawyer costume from the office.

"Here," I said, easing off the bed. "Lie down, Dad."

He switched places with me, never loosening his grip on my hand. "I don't want you to be scared because of this."

"She won't," Frances said.

"I won't," I said.

"I want you out there wakeboarding again tomorrow," he sobbed.

"I can't, Dad. The doc said I'm not supposed to go swimming until my stitches come out in a few days."

"Then I want you wakeboarding the day they come out. And do exactly what you were doing when you got hurt."

I thought about this. "It would be difficult to replicate."

"Do you understand me?" he said, still crying.

"Shhh," Frances said, patting his shoulder.

"Yeah, Dad," I said, looking toward McGillicuddy in the doorway. He munched his Pop-Tart. I twirled my finger beside my ear: *crazy*. McGillicuddy nodded. At least I wasn't the *only* sane person around here.

A nurse brought me some pills, which I took gladly because I didn't want my brain to hurt like that again, ever. They weren't supposed to be strong enough to put me to sleep, but they did. Or it was the medicine combined with the adrenaline draining away. The fatigue from nearly drowning, touching bryozoa, being sobbed over by a couple of he-men, etc. I'd had such a busy day.

All I knew for sure was that I stretched out on the backseat of Dad's car and slept on the way home. When we got there, I wasn't moving. They prodded me, but I could *not* see myself climbing the stairs to my room. I did *not* see why they couldn't let me sleep in the car parked in the garage. The backseat felt delicious.

McGillicuddy carried me up the stairs, and Dad tucked

me into bed. Ahhhhhhh, bed had never been such a relief. Dad and McGillicuddy spoke softly in the doorway.

Dad: "She didn't even wake up. You be sure and come get her if there's a fire."

McGillicuddy: "A fire. Right, Dad."

I laughed myself back to sleep. A fire. Really! In the last twenty-four hours, I'd been through everything bad I could imagine. What else could possibly happen?

17

"Lori, when we're old enough, I want you to be my girlfriend." Sean kissed me. With his mouth still on my mouth, he pulled me off the bow seat and down into the floorboard of the boat, out of the wind.

I broke the kiss to say, "I guess this means we're old enou—"

He cut me off by kissing me. His tongue circled deep inside my mouth, and I opened for more. When I got bored with this (the idea of getting bored with making out still caused me to laugh, ho ho), I lifted my chin so he could kiss my neck. Then I turned my head so he could kiss my ear. Wow, this was the best dream ever, and so *long*! Suddenly anxious, I peered into the back of the boat to see whether the other boys were watching us. The boat was empty.

"Who's driving?" I gasped.

"You are," Sean said.

"Oh." This made me a little nervous, but not nervous enough to wake up or anything. I turned my head so he could kiss my other ear.

"Listen," he breathed. "What's that?"

"The boat motor," I murmured without thinking. "And Nickelback."

He propped himself up on his forearms and cocked his head to hear better. "Actually, I think it's JoJo." The skull and crossbones dangled above my eyes.

"Adam!" I cried, sitting bolt upright in my bed. I peered over at the clock blaring "Too Little, Too Late." No wonder the dream had lasted so long! My alarm had gone off, but I'd slept right through fifteen minutes of radio. The photo of my mother lay flat on the bedside table. McGillicuddy must have knocked it over by accident last night when he put me in bed.

"Stupid subconscious!" I slapped myself in the back of the head. "Ow!" The shock of the slap rippled through my brain and into the gash on my forehead. I cupped my hand over the stitches.

A soft knock sounded at the door. McGillicuddy leaned in without waiting for an answer. He glanced at the clock, then at me. "Breakfast is being served to the psych ward in the dining hall. You want me to send up an orderly to help you get out of bed?"

I stuck out my tongue at him. I didn't mind psych ward jokes from McGillicuddy. He was the only one who understood. Except—

"Adam came to see you."

I took in a sharp breath. "When?"

"Last night, and again this morning."

"Why didn't you wake me up?" I wailed.

"Because any other time in the history of your life, you would have snuck in my room and rearranged my sock drawer in revenge for waking you up. You know I need the argyles in the front."

"Well, what'd he say?"

McGillicuddy gathered a year's worth of wakeboarding mags and his copy of *The Right Stuff* and stacked them neatly on the floor so he could sit on the edge of my bed. "Last night he was just checking on you. This morning he came over to say he's taking the day off work. But he wanted you to know, he's through."

"He's through? With what?" With Sean? Fighting with Sean?

"With you."

Of course he was through with me. He'd told me as much while I bled in his lap yesterday. As long as I heard it with my own ears, I could hope I'd misread the whole situation. Hearing it from McGillicuddy made it real. Almost. "Are you making this up?"

"No. He's really mad at you. I've never seen him this mad. Not even at Sean." McGillicuddy thumbed through *The Right Stuff* to make sure I hadn't gotten marshmallow on it. "But I want you to know some good will come out of your crash. It's inspired me to do something I've wanted to do for a long time."

"Remove your own appendix?"

"Ask Tammy out."

My head hurt. "Tammy? Why?"

"I think she's been coming to the Vaders' parties to see me. I know, I know, this seems as impossible to me as it does to you, but I really think she likes me."

I grunted a little with the increasing pain in my head. I didn't want to tell him this, but it might save him some humiliation later. "McGillicuddy, you're wrong. She's been coming to the Vaders' parties to see *me*. We're friends."

He squinted at me. "Why do you think so?"

"She told me so."

"Couldn't it be one of those schemes, like you and Adam

are pulling on Sean? She's pretending to be your friend so she can see me without admitting that's why she's at the party."

"Tammy wouldn't do that to me," I said. My pulse began to race, and my head throbbed harder with every heartbeat. "What do you mean, one of those schemes like Adam and I are pulling on Sean?"

"I figure if you can brain yourself on a pontoon boat just to get a boy to ask you out, I can ask a girl out and brave a little rejection."

Now I winced against the throbbing in my head. "Adam told you I crashed just to get Sean to ask me out?"

"Yeah. He told me you've faked going out from the beginning. He's *really mad* about you crashing." McGillicuddy leaned across the bed and nabbed his copy of *The Hunt for Red October*, which I'd been telling him since last summer I did *not* borrow, when in actuality I had lost it under some (clean!) laundry and didn't come across it until last week. "Adam and Sean have always fought," McGillicuddy said, tucking the book under his arm for safekeeping. "But you've made it a million times worse. Can you imagine the five of us wakeboarding together for the rest of the summer?"

"No," I admitted. It sounded about as fun as getting a tooth pulled every afternoon. "But I didn't start this in the first place. Sean did. Sean stole Rachel from Adam."

"Adam never liked Rachel anyway," McGillicuddy said.

"He was madder about the insult than the girl. He was in love with you. If it hadn't been for you wanting to fool Sean, Adam would have simmered down eventually and let Sean have Rachel. We'd be back to normal by now."

"Reverse, please," I said. "Adam was in love with—"

"You. Where did I go wrong? I raised a little brother, not a femme fatale."

I didn't quite get it. Could Adam have been telling me the truth about his plot? It seemed too good to be true, and too awful if I had screwed this up. "Did Adam *say* he's in love with me?"

"*Was* in love with you. Yes, that's what he said. How the hell else would I know? I wish I didn't. This place is getting to be like that awful girls' reality show, what's it called? The chicks in my dorm call dibs on the TV in the rec center and won't let us watch basketball."

"Is it on MTV?"

"Yes!"

"Get out of my room."

As he stood, I made a weak grab for *The Hunt for Red October*, but he dodged me. He closed the door behind him.

Adam was in love with me. He wasn't just saying it to keep me with him while he made Sean jealous. He was in love with me.

Head throbbing, I looked around my room, which

still reflected the boy I'd been before I started transforming myself. I hadn't gotten around to a room makeover
with purple flowers and a fuzzy pink ottoman. As the air-
conditioning clicked on, the fighter jet models I'd built
from kits swayed at the end of their strings near the ceiling.
I was a little brother. I was a mess.

Adam had been in love with me, just like this.

And now he wasn't.

It was a good thing Advil took care of my headache. If
I'd had to stay out of work and spend the day at home, I
would have driven myself insane (if I wasn't already). As
it was, I showered faster than usual to make up for lost
time, taking care to keep my stitches out of the spray. I
ate breakfast as usual, except Dad gave me a big hug and
sobbed a little into my hair. As usual, McGillicuddy and
I opened the door to hike across our yard and the Vaders'
to the marina—

—and there stood Sean with his finger on the doorbell.
He asked me brightly, "Will you go to the party tonight
with me?"

My brain said, *Hooray! I'm going out with Sean! My time
has come!*

My body was strangely quiet. There was no happy skin.
My brain reached down through my nerve endings to poke

at my heart and make sure it was okay. My heart said, *Eh*. At this point I realized I *did* need to go back to the shrink. I sagged against the doorjamb, rolled my eyes, and uttered something very unladylike.

McGillicuddy stepped around me and wagged his cell phone between his fingers. With a pointed look at Sean, he told me, "Call me if you need me."

"I could take you," Sean shouted after McGillicuddy. "Bring it on." His voice echoed around the garage. Then he turned back to me and sighed, "I was afraid you'd say that. Look, I told my dad we'd come to work a little late this morning because we're going to fish your wakeboard out of the lake. Let's talk."

I followed him down to my pier, where he'd tied the wakeboarding boat. Clearly it *did* occur to him to dock in a certain place to save *someone* a long walk. Himself. Just not me. We stepped in, and I looked around on the floor. "Who cleaned the blood out of the boat for me? I was going to do it this morning."

"Adam," Sean said. "When we get to the pontoon boat, you've got to tell me this story. He was saying it was his fault and crying the whole time. Pussy." He slapped his hand over his mouth. "Sorry. I almost forgot you weren't a guy." Before I could offer a choice response, he cranked the motor and the Nickelback.

As we zoomed toward the pontoon boat, I noticed that a dump truck had mistakenly unloaded a pile of soot onto the side of the bridge. The closer we got, the more clearly I could see it wasn't a pile of soot after all but carefully applied spray paint marking out the letters AOAN LOVES LOKI. Adam had been busy. He must have gone out in the motorboat in the near-dark last night, or the near-dark this morning. He wanted to get the offensive words off the bridge as quickly as he could. They would have haunted him until he got rid of them. He hated me that much.

"Junior!" Sean stood in front of me, clapping his hands. "McGillicuddy Part Deux!" He'd stopped the boat next to the pontoon boat. "McGillicuddy left your wakeboard floating here, so let's check under the pontoon boat first." He handed me one of the oars that motorboats carry in case their engines stop when they run over logs. As we poked around under the pontoons, he asked, "Why's Adam so pissed at you?"

"It's complicated. We've only been going out to make you and Rachel mad." I couldn't believe I was telling him this. But my brilliant ploys had gotten me into this fix, and I'd lost hope they could get me out. Also, I must have bled out my last lick of sense. "I've sort of had a thing for you."

He pulled his oar from under the boat and put all his

weight on it, like he needed it to keep him from collapsing. "*You?* Have a thing for *me?*"

"*Had.*"

He made a face. "Ugh!"

This should have been the low point of my life, the one I'd dreaded for over a decade: rejection by Sean. Now that it had finally happened, I didn't feel humiliated. I was angry. "What do you mean, *ugh?* You flirted with me a couple of weeks ago, before your first party. Remember wiping bryozoa on me? That's the mating dance of the brain-dead Vader brothers."

"Oh, yeah! I'd forgotten all about the bryozoa." He waved his hand in the air, dismissing the bryozoa incident like a pesky yellow jacket. "Adam was acting protective of you that day for some reason. I got the idea he might like you a little. So I figured I'd push his buttons. I can't see myself really coming on to you, ever." He shoved his oar under the boat again. "No offense."

"None taken, you ass."

He glanced sideways at me. "When I said 'Ugh,' I just meant, 'Ugh, what could Buddy possibly see in little old me?'"

Sure you did. "I honestly can't remember," I said, poking my oar under the boat, too. "Anyway, Adam thinks I crashed into the pontoon boat on purpose so you could close the wakeboarding show again, and you'd like me better. I didn't, but Adam thinks I did." I ran my finger over the little dent my thick skull had made in the aluminum side of the boat. "I guess he was willing to take the fake love just so far."

"So you've faked hooking up."

I glanced toward the bridge, at the scribble that once had said AOAN LOVES LOKI. "Yeah."

"You faked flirting with each other on the desk in the living room."

"Yeah." It hadn't *felt* like faking, but what did I know?

"You faked making out on the end of the dock at the party last Friday? And disappearing into the lake? Because that was convincing."

"Yes. I mean, we really made out, but we weren't really in love." At least, I hadn't realized it at the time.

"That little shit!" he yelled so loudly that I worried about the innocent ears of Frances and the Harbarger children around the bend. I imagined Frances pretending she hadn't heard a thing as the shout echoed around their fenced yard.

"Now why are *you* so pissed?" I asked.

"Because it worked! He stole Rachel from me!"

I stomped my foot on the floor of the boat, like a girl. "You stole Rachel from him in the first place, just to make him mad. Even if you *thought* you really liked her by the time she broke up with you, she only seemed like something you'd want because Adam had her in the first place."

He brought in his oar again and leaned on it. "I may be shallow, Lori, but I'm not a monster." He gazed downstream. "I don't think your wakeboard's under here. Maybe the current caught it."

I looked downstream, too, in the general direction of the dam several miles away. My wakeboard had probably gotten stuck in one of the gates and cut off the power supply to the tri-county area. The way my morning was going, the hydroelectric police would be waiting for me on the marina dock.

"Let's try one more place." He cranked the engine, drove to the nearby bank, and cut the power again. As the boat drifted, we used the oars to shift the logs and leaves washed up against the edge of the woods. "You think I'm a monster," he said quietly.

"I think we all are."

A gust of wind blew us along faster. It swooped through the woods, swaying the trees and littering us with blossoms and leaves and delicate tree crap.

"Well," he finally said. "I didn't steal Rachel just to make Adam mad. I *pretended* that's what I was doing. That's what Adam would think anyway. But really, I've been into her for so long. I couldn't stand the thought of going to college without finding out if she liked me, too."

I was going to yell at him for being so selfish until it occurred to me that this was pretty much how I'd felt about *him*.

"I've seen the way she looks at Adam," he went on. "Girls don't look at me like that. They look at me, sure, but not like that."

Cunning as Sean was about other people, surely he couldn't be this obtuse about himself? In exasperation, I pointed out, "You don't look at *them* like that."

"I look at Rachel like that. And she says she can tell from the way I treat Adam that I have no soul. I could have sworn I did." He laughed.

Rachel might have more sense than I'd given her credit for. She'd never actually insulted me, besides calling me a 'ho to her friends when I did the secret handshake with Adam, which was understandable. I had no reason to dislike her, other than the obvious boy-ploys. And no reason at all to think she was stupid.

"But over the last couple of weeks," Sean continued, "I've seen how good you and Adam are together. And how good Rachel and I are together. Maybe Adam and Rachel are good together, too, but if they are, I'd like to rip Rachel's heart out and throw it down in the driveway and drive back and forth over it in my truck a couple of times and give it back to her. I know you feel the same way about Adam."

I stared at him and wondered what my mother had been thinking.

"I don't think we need to worry about that, though," he said. "Rachel wants to get back with Adam, but Adam doesn't want Rachel, if you can believe that! He called her last night after he dried up and had this, like, *reasonable, adult* conversation with her. He told her it was over between them, and not just because she'd made out with me when I snapped my fingers. He went out with her in the first place to make you jealous."

None of this sounded like something Adam would share with Sean on purpose. McGillicuddy, maybe, or Cameron, but not Sean. "Did you listen in on this conversation?"

Sean gave me this *how dare you insinuate such a thing* look. Which told me, yes, he had listened in on this conversation.

He went on, "So we know they won't get back together. If they do look like they're getting back together at the party tonight, Adam will be faking. All we have to do to get him back with you is convince him you're better than nothing. Which . . ." He looked me up and down, then shrugged.

The wind gusted again, lifting sections of his light brown hair, and flattening his T-shirt against his strong chest. He was a lot like Adam, and completely different. I said, "You are a sad, sad little man."

"I am what I am. So, I know this will sound kind of gross, but will you make out with me at the party?"

I poked at the shoreline with my oar. "This is a bad idea. It was a bad idea the first time I had it, and it's a bad idea now." But I might as well try something to get Adam back, right? I'd hit bottom. Nothing we did could make things worse.

"If you won't do it for yourself, do it for me. Lori, I'm in love with Rachel. That's never happened to me before. I'm not willing to let that go without a fight. And if you feel the same way about Adam, seems like you wouldn't let it go, either." He took a few steps closer to me in the boat. "He holds a grudge, you know."

I snorted. "I know." Nothing had ever been more obvious.

"You can't just hope he'll come around someday. He won't. You have to bring him back. Hey, what do we have here?" He leaned way over the side of the boat, grabbed a flower-printed edge underneath a log, and brought up my dripping wakeboard. Handing it to me, he said, "Your chariot, mademoiselle."

It was exactly like something Adam would say. I clung to the wet wakeboard and squeezed my eyes shut to keep from crying. "Okay," I said. "I'll do it. Okay."

It all would have been hilarious if it hadn't sucked.

And I couldn't go through with it. When McGillicuddy said he was heading for the party, I stayed behind. I actually started the enormous project of picking up all the books and magazines scattered three deep on the floor of my room. After about an hour and hardly any progress, I realized that by shelving them, I was messing up a filing system I didn't even know I had. Books I wanted to read again were thrown on one side of my bed. Bad books were abandoned by the window. Wakeboarding mags were strewn from my dresser to my desk in approximate order of how hot the boys were in them, and so forth. I gave up and sat downstairs in the den with my dad for a long time, watching *Dirty Jobs*.

My cell phone rang. I pried it from the pocket of my tight miniskirt. I knew girls were supposed to carry purses instead of stuffing everything in their pockets, but I needed to ease into this transition over the coming year. Sirens weren't built in a day. "Hello?"

Sean was on the other end of the line, making chicken noises.

I hung up and said bye to my dad. Again, I didn't notify him what was going on with my many suitors. I figured the situation would change anyway in the next fifteen minutes or so.

Sean stood in the doorway of the Vaders' house, letting all the air-conditioning out into the hot night. Waiting for me. "Where have you been?"

"Duh, I've been next d—"

He grabbed me, pulled me into the foyer, and slammed the door. "Rachel and Adam are inside talking. *To each other!* And I've told everybody here that you and I are together. When you didn't show up, it looked like you didn't love me as much as I love you."

"Stop the presses."

"So we need to make up for lost time." He body-slammed me against the wall and stuck his tongue in my mouth.

Well, I just let him do it. Why not? I let him slide his hands up and down my sides, too, in case that helped the cause. If he wanted to touch my boobs, I would need to take that under advisement, but otherwise I found I had a very high tolerance for a handsome ass of a boy using me as target practice.

Besides, out the corner of my eye, I could see Holly and Beige watch us from the end of the hall. They disappeared around the corner. Next a couple of guys from my algebra class walked very slowly by the opening, pretending not to watch us.

Sean came up for breath. I tried not to gasp quite as hard as I had after bashing my head and nearly drowning.

"How many gawkers is that?" he asked.

"Four," I said. "Is that enough to spread it around the party? And how can you stand to kiss a girl like that when you don't feel anything for her?"

He rubbed the back of my neck, like a lover. "I feel *something* for you. You clean up okay. Don't you feel *something* for me?"

I shook my head. "I'm not feeling you, dog."

"Don't shake your head," he said through his teeth. "We're going into the party now. Don't do anything negative. Agree with everything I say. Laugh a lot. Can you put your hands on my crotch?"

"Why, hell no, I cannot." I didn't remember anything like this happening in *Pride and Prejudice*. "Can I find

Tammy, take her to the bathroom with me, and giggle about you?"

His eyes widened in admiration. "That would be awesome!"

I was getting good at this. I gave him a peck on his stylishly stubbly cheek, patted his ass, and walked into the living room.

Every head snapped up to watch me.

Including Adam's. There were thirty-something people in the shadowy room, and I saw him right away. He sat on the couch with Rachel, exactly where Sean had sat with her the night he insulted me. Adam wasn't wrapped around Rachel like Sean had been. He wasn't touching her at all. He was talking to her. They could have been friends.

So they weren't doing anything to make me jealous. All he did was look up at me with such fury in those blue eyes that I knew I was going to throw up.

"Help," I croaked, putting a hand on Tammy's shoulder.

She looked around at me. She looked at the boys she'd been talking with: Cameron and McGillicuddy. "Can Cameron help you?" she asked me coldly. "They're his brothers, so he could help you better. *Bill* and I were talking."

Hadn't she heard Sean's blitzkrieg rumors? I wasn't pretending to hook up with Adam to get Sean. Surprise! I was pretending to hook up with Sean to get Adam, and if ever something was giggle-in-the-bathroom material, this was it. I was calculating how much of this to divulge to her while Cameron and McGillicuddy were listening, when something else clicked in my brain. "Are y'all going out?"

"Yes!" McGillicuddy beamed.

Tammy beamed too, then tried to hold the smile as she realized she'd been busted.

"So," I said to Tammy, "when you told me you came to the last party to see me, really you were using that as an excuse to see McGillicuddy."

"I didn't mean to hurt your feelings," Tammy said distantly, a tone she'd never used with me before. The tone Beige used all the time. "I guess I didn't understand you and I were that close."

"I guess it was my mistake," I said.

"I want to go back to college," Cameron said. "Linear Differential Equations class will seem so relaxing after this summer."

McGillicuddy frowned at Tammy, then moved toward me like he would pull me aside and talk to me. But McGillicuddy didn't go out much. He'd actually asked someone out! I didn't want to mess up this thing with Tammy for him. Not over some weird girl-jealousy that I didn't even understand completely.

"I gotta do something," I mumbled, pulling the skull and crossbones from my pocket. This took a couple of tries when my fist got stuck.

Across the room, Sean stood with some of his many friends. Down by his side, where the crowd couldn't see, he motioned to me. Rachel and her friends were right behind him. If I went to him, he'd make sure they saw everything that counted.

From the sofa on the other side of the room, Adam glared at me.

I took a step toward Adam. The force of his glare was like a magnet turned the wrong way against another. I took another step toward him and felt the force in my stomach. I would never be able to reach him in the face of such force. Plus Scooter Ledbetter was trying to start a mosh pit in the center of the room. So I skirted the force like I was headed out the door to the deck. Then, when Adam bit his lip and looked down, I snuck past the repellant force and plopped next to him on the couch.

"Here." I held out the skull and crossbones in my sweaty palm. Attractive! It didn't matter any more. "Look," I said in a rush, "I didn't crash into the pontoon boat to get Sean. Even I am not that unbalanced."

His mouth moved so little that I almost thought he used telepathy to tell me, "I don't believe you."

"No shit. And I'm sorry about the PDA with Sean. I don't know what I was thinking, Adam. I want another chance with you, and I *know* that wasn't the way to get it."

"That's okay," he said so brightly, so unlike him, that I knew something evil was coming. "I like Sean taking my seconds."

"See, that's the problem," I snapped, angry again despite myself. "You say you love me, but you're always looking over your shoulder for Sean."

"And you're always looking over *your* shoulder for Sean. Or Holly, or Beige." The Foo Fighters song booming through the room ended at the precise moment he said, "Or whoever's made you change from what you were into a first-class bitch."

Only a moment more of silence ticked by before Fall Out Boy started. But the damage was done. People at the edge of the crowd were slow to start dancing again. They thought we couldn't hear them over the music as they yelled in clear voices, "Did you hear what Adam called Lori?"

I told myself he wouldn't have said anything so horrible to me if he weren't jealous. Of course, I'd told myself the same thing when Sean mentioned the shrink. But Sean was Sean, and Adam was Adam. And while I was trying to use my intimidating brain power to turn myself into water vapor and vanish into thin air, Adam snatched the skull and crossbones from my open palm. "I have just the use for this," he said as he stomped out the door to the deck.

I left my sparkly shoes on the floor next to the couch. I knew that jig was up. But even in my bare feet, I didn't make it outside before Adam was on the ground far below, halfway to the dock. Possibly he'd jumped over the deck railing.

I dashed down the stairs. Sean called to me from the deck above me. I dashed faster. This was no time to save face. I had a terrible feeling about that skull and crossbones.

Sure enough, by the time I'd pushed through the crowd in the yard and the wall of people on the dock, Adam was sitting with the boys playing quarters. I stepped forward to stop him. It was too late. Instead of a quarter, he bounced the pendant on the dock. And instead of ringing the cup, the skull and crossbones slipped between two planks, into the lake.

"Ohhhhhh!" said the other boys.

"Get it," I told Adam.

He said thoughtfully, "No."

I pictured it sinking through the water, but it wasn't heavy enough to stay in one place on the bottom. The current would sweep it away if he didn't hurry. "I bought it for you!" I shrieked.

"I wore it for you," he said evenly. "And now I'm through with it."

I shoved back through the wall of people, jumped into Mr. Vader's personal fishing boat tied on one side of the dock, and grabbed a big waterproof flashlight. I didn't have to push through the wall of people on my way back because they saw me coming and got out of my way. I walked straight through the game of quarters, scattering frightened boys. I sensed rather than saw Adam's hand reach for my ankle and miss as I hopped into the lake in my adorable clothes.

The water was warm and black. Oops. I clicked the button on the flashlight and directed the beam underneath the pier. The water was only about eight feet deep here, so I was able to kick down to the rocky bottom, where I thought the pendant had fallen through.

In the eerie green light, I saw it glinting on a big branch the boys had lodged under the dock to attract fish. That was bad enough, because wood got slimy in water. But this was worse: the pendant glinted from its resting place in A GLOB OF BRYOZOA clinging to the branch. Ugh, ugh, ugh, and the pendant moved as the bryozoa bobbed in the current. Any second now, the skull and crossbones would tumble deep into the lake, lost forever.

My breath was gone. I swam toward the surface to collect one more breath. I didn't expect half the school to be peering over the side of the dock, watching for me in the darkness. That was okay. I was on a mission to PLUNGE MY HAND INTO THE BRYOZOA OH MY GOD. I took my breath and dove back down—

And someone on the dock grabbed me around the waist. Someone strong who wasn't dislodged from the dock when I struggled. Adam lifted me backward out of the water.

"Let me go!" I hollered, not looking at him, still leaning toward the water and trying to struggle free. The flashlight clattered to the dock. "I saw it. I can still get it. Let me go!"

"You're not supposed to get your stitches wet," he said.

I wanted to point out that he would not know this, since he didn't stick around the emergency room long enough to hear what the doctor had to say. Then I remembered Adam had a lot more experience with stitches than I did.

And then, out the corner of my eye, I saw a blur, and Adam was gone. An enormous splash backed everyone away from the water. Adam and Sean flailed in the lake.

"Get their parents," I said over my shoulder. If Cameron or McGillicuddy had been there, they would have stepped forward before now. And Sean's friends and Adam's friends

never intervened, like fights between brothers were somehow sacred. I watched Adam and Sean in the water to make
sure neither of them went down for too long—though there
wasn't much I could have done if they had. Nothing seemed
to be happening behind me. The crowd watched the show
as attentively as I did. I turned around and screamed,
"Go get their parents!" Three people ran up the dock and
through the yard.

I jumped out of the way as one of the boys hauled himself up the ladder. He snapped his legs up before the other
boy could drag him back into the lake. But then the second
boy grabbed the top of the ladder, swung himself onto the
dock, and tackled the first.

There didn't seem much point in explaining to Adam
that Sean had only attacked him because Sean and I were
pretending to be a couple and trying to make Adam jealous. After one of them had hit the other, it didn't really
matter why anymore, at least not to them. I bent as close
to them as I dared and hollered, "I've already told your
parents."

"Sean, stop," came Rachel's voice from the crowd, ever-
helpful.

I expected them to roll toward me. I'd have to jump
out of the way as they wrestled on the dock and caught
each other in various choke holds. Instead, the boy on top

punched the one on bottom, a pop to the nose. The fight came to an abrupt stop.

The crowd gasped. They murmured, "No, that's Adam on top. *Adam* kicked *Sean's* ass."

Adam sat on Sean's chest, his right fist clenching and unclenching. I couldn't see his face or Sean's in the dim light, but I could tell from the way they held themselves that they were giving each other the evil eye. And I knew I shouldn't be worried anymore about pulling Sean off Adam, protecting Adam from Sean.

Adam said so quietly I could hardly hear him over the waves lapping against the dock, "Don't you ever hit me again."

The murmur up the hill increased, and the crowd in the yard began to part. Mr. Vader was coming. But it was Mrs. Vader who came running in her bathrobe.

"Sean!" she called when she hadn't even hit the dock yet. "Sean, get *off* him!" As the crowd slowed her down, she said, "You two have *got* to stop doing this. You're going to kill each other." She made it through the wall of people and stopped short.

"I'm through," Adam said. He eased off Sean and stood up.

Sean sat up, looking down. His nose streamed blood.

Mr. Vader said behind us, "Hey. Is that my beer?"

I'd seen enough. I pushed my way through the crowd, up the pier, into the grass. Knots of people followed me with their eyes, turning as I passed. Cameron, McGillicuddy, and Tammy jogged down from the house. Tammy called to me. I shook my head and kept going. They didn't come toward me. They must have seen the expression on my face.

When I reached the darkest shadows of the trees between our houses, I looked back. Mrs. Vader stood in front of Adam in their yard, with her hands on her hips. He shivered in his soaked clothes. She put out her arms for him. He walked into her embrace and put his head down on her shoulder. She rubbed his back to warm him.

Furious as I was with him, I hoped he didn't get in too much trouble—about the beer, and especially about the fight with Sean. I hoped his parents understood this fight was inevitable, with or without Rachel and me and MTV reality shows. And that tonight was the first night of the rest of his life.

19

It was not, however, the first night of the rest of *my* life. It was night 5,843, and felt like it.

I stepped into the kitchen and closed the door. I dripped all over the floor. Dad freaked out about stuff like this. Someone might slip! I'd have to find a towel in the laundry room and drag it behind me all the way to the den—unless, of course, he heard me come in and called to me to ask me how my night went. Then I'd have an excuse to skip the towel. I could sit in his lap, even though I was soaked. I could break down, and he could tell me what to do about Adam.

He didn't call to me. Maybe he hadn't heard me in my

bare feet. I opened and closed some kitchen drawers gratuitously. Still he didn't call to me.

I gave up, got a towel out of the laundry room, and scooted it across the floor with my feet, catching the water that dripped from me. As I headed through the den to the stairs up to my room, I saw Dad. He'd fallen asleep on the sofa in front of the TV, cell phone gripped on his chest. I was on my own.

I walked up the stairs, which took more energy than usual. There were a lot of stairs. Thirteen, to be exact:

1. Made
2. You
3. Change
4. From
5. What
6. You
7. Were
8. In
9. To
10. A
11. First
12. Class
13. Bitch

By the time I got to the top, I was pooped, and not furious anymore. Confused and hurt about Tammy. Hurt and sad about Adam.

A long time passed before I realized I was standing in my dark room, listening to the laughter and music from the party outside.

Closing my door behind me, I slid my wet clothes off. Oh God, dead wet cell phone in my skirt pocket. There went my birthday money from my grandparents. I didn't need to turn on the light to find my mother's sweet sixteen disco dress in my closet, because it practically glowed in the dark. I slipped it on and walked to the window.

Sean and Adam lay on that strip of grass between our yards where they liked to fight each other because their mom couldn't see them from their house. Adam and Sean had finally killed each other! No—Adam's arms were behind his head. Sean's legs were bent, with one foot propped casually on the opposite knee. They watched the stars, talking.

Talking!

Adam sat up. He wore his sweatshirt with his football number on the back, the one I'd borrowed last weekend. He shook a little like he was shivering again. He stuck his hands in his pockets. He pulled out one hand and looked at it, then looked over his shoulder at my house. He'd found my eyelash comb.

Maybe he saw my dress glowing in the moonlight,

because he turned all the way around to stare. Now Sean sat up and turned around, too. Or maybe it was Sean and then Adam. I couldn't tell them apart in the dark. It didn't matter now, anyway. Bwa-ha-ha, I hope I creeped them out like Miss Havisham (*Great Expectations*, eighth grade English).

But *one* of them was Adam. Tingles crept up my arms and across my chest at the thought of him watching me. This would have to stop. Pining after Sean had been bad enough. At least I'd always thought pining after Sean would have a happy ending. I *knew* no good would come from pining after Adam. Plus it was a lot more real to me now, not a cartoon relationship lost but a real boyfriend, a real friend. I choked back a sob as my throat closed up.

I watched him for a little longer. Yes, I could tell him from Sean, even at a distance, even in the dark. The way he moved his head, the way he tapped his fingers on the ground in that fidget I'd fallen in love with. That could have been me instead of Sean, sitting with Adam in the dark. But there wasn't a way to fix this.

Ten years from now, I'd be married to someone I'd met at college. Adam would be married to someone he'd met on the bomb squad. We'd all come home to visit our parents at Thanksgiving. Adam and I would see each other out on the docks. We would feel obliged to talk for a few minutes and laugh uncomfortably about this one summer that had ruined our friendship forever. And then we'd walk away.

I looked at the clock on my bedside table behind me. 12:02. I closed the window shade, blocking out the party and Sean and Adam. I slipped off the disco dress and folded it into a big box with the scrapbook Mom and I had made to fill in with pictures of my sixteenth birthday. Standing in a chair precariously balanced on books, mags, and Mr. Wuggles—God only knew what was under there, really—I slid the box onto a shelf in the top of my closet. Where it belonged.

I woke to Kelly Clarkson's "Breakaway."

My body had gotten used to waking at this time. I didn't remember my dreams.

I would miss them.

But I tried to shake it off. I tried not to wish Adam would show up with a birthday present for me—even though I'd forgotten to get one for *him*! I would have the usual birthday breakfast with Dad and McGillicuddy, just like every year, and then I'd try to get through my first-ever day of avoiding my ex-best friend. While I worked at his parents' marina. And he worked there too. Easy.

For breakfast, Dad made me pancakes with blueberries in the shape of smiley faces, because he was a dork.

Between the butter and the syrup, McGillicuddy handed me a long tube-shaped present. Actually it was just a wrapping paper tube with the wrapping paper still on it, and something rolled up inside. Boys were like that. He saw my look and shrugged. "It would have been a waste of perfectly good wrapping paper. This worked."

Still giving him the look, I pulled out the contents of the tube and unrolled a wakeboarding poster. "Dallas Friday!" I exclaimed. "Dallas Friday shattered her femur doing a whirlybird."

"I thought it was perfect for the occasion," McGillicuddy said. "Fearless."

Dad cleared his throat and pushed a little box across the table to me. It was beautifully wrapped with an intricate bow that most girls would keep on their bulletin boards. Obviously wrapped in a store. I slipped the bow off intact and tried to unstick the paper without tearing it. It tore by accident and then, what the hell, I ripped it off.

I flipped open the velvet ring box. Inside was a silver ring with pearls and diamonds. It looked real. Was I supposed to bite it to make sure? No, that was gold coins in cowboy movies. It also looked vaguely familiar. "You didn't get this at the store."

"I had them check the settings," Dad said. "They cleaned it and wrapped it for you."

I examined the ring more closely. "It belonged to Mom."

"Her parents gave it to her for her sixteenth birthday."

I looked into his eyes, so full of concern. We had a touching moment. Then of course McGillicuddy dropped his fork and went under the table to hunt for it, and it was hard to keep the touching moment going while McGillicuddy sat on my toes. "Ow!" I kicked him.

"When you were younger," Dad said, "I thought you'd never wear it, because it wasn't your style. Lately, I'm not so sure. I thought I should give you the choice."

I freed it from the box and slipped it onto my finger. It was a crazy ring, diamonds glinting in contrast with the smooth pearls. And it was heavy. If I ever got in a fix in a dark alley, I could use it as brass knuckles. Or if I was cornered on a rooftop, I could hook it onto a clothesline and slide to freedom like James Bond. Don't try this at home.

"I'll wear it because it's a part of me," I said. "Thank you, Dad." I walked around the table and hugged him. Then I sat back down, took another bite of pancake, and stared straight ahead at the empty chair.

And I realized for the first time ever that we kept an empty chair at the table. There were three of us. You would think we would have three chairs normally, and bring in a fourth when Adam came to dinner, which clearly wouldn't be happening anymore. It wasn't like the table was square,

and a chair missing from the fourth side would be conspicu-
ous. The table was round, and could have three chairs as
easily as four or five or eight.

I was swallowing my pancakes in order to point this out
when Dad said, "I need to tell you something, Bill. I don't
want you to see me on the bank during the wakeboarding
show and wipe out because of the shock. We've had enough
wakeboard falls for one lifetime." He took a sip of coffee. "I
have a date for the Crappie Festival." He took another sip
of coffee. "It's Frances."

I sat still, thinking back to that talk I'd had with Frances.
She'd said, *You're the only one who comes to visit. Except—*

McGillicuddy didn't budge, either. Dad must have
taken our nonreaction as disapproval. "I never said anything while she worked here," he hurried on. "I never did
anything. We were coping so well, for a grieving family—"

"Except for when you sent me to the shrink," I pointed
out.

He continued more loudly, "—and I was terrified of
messing that up." He turned to McGillicuddy. "But now
you've got a foot or two out the door." He turned to me.
"And you're—" He sighed. "Grown. I thought it would be
okay now." He took still another sip of coffee, nonchalant,
but his eyes darted to McGillicuddy and me in turn. "Even
if it's not okay, I'm still going out with her."

We sat in silence a few moments more. Then McGillicuddy hollered, "Fanny the Nanny!"

"It's all very *Jane Eyre* of you, Dad," I said. McGillicuddy had read *Jane Eyre* in ninth grade English, and then *I'd* read it in ninth grade English. We'd wished we had Frances back just so we could make *Jane Eyre* jokes.

McGillicuddy snorted. "Hide the lighter fluid."

"Check the attic," I said.

Dad sat back in his chair, relaxing a little.

"No wonder she used to get so mad when Sean sang to her from *The Sound of Music*," McGillicuddy said.

"Does this mean we have to start drinking soy milk again?" I asked Dad.

"I'm glad we've gotten this settled," Dad said. "Bill, what'd you dream about?"

McGillicuddy blinked at the change of subject. "I can't tell you."

"Why not?" I grinned.

"She's a real person."

I took this as my cue to head for the marina. Dad would probably coax the dream out of McGillicuddy—Dad was a lawyer, after all—and I didn't particularly want to hear just then about Tammy beating McGillicuddy at wrestling in chocolate pudding.

But McGillicuddy stood when I did. Dad looked up at

him and said, "You take care of your sister today."

McGillicuddy shrugged. "How?"

Dad looked at me. "And you watch out for those boys."

It was way too early in the morning for a breakdown, so I squeezed my eyes shut to hold back the tears and stepped out the door, calling, "I'm afraid I have nothing to be afraid of."

20

In the garage, balanced on the handle of the seed spreader, looking out of place between the lawn mower and the tiller, was a long-stemmed pink rose.

McGillicuddy passed me. I called, "Tammy left you a gag gift."

He hardly glanced at the rose on his way out the garage door. "Pink isn't my color."

Frances must have left it as a joke for Dad, then. I should take it into the kitchen before it wilted. Almost wishing it were mine, I ran my finger across a soft petal. My hand found a pink ribbon tied around the stem, then a tag hanging from the ribbon. The tag said in Adam's scrawl, "YES it's for you." I let a little laugh escape even as my eyes filled with tears.

He'd called me a bitch. I wasn't running back to him when he left me one rose. On the other hand, there was no need to stuff it down the garbage disposal. Maybe Adam and I could be friends again after all. Someday. Besides, I adored the scent of roses: perfume and dirt. I put the blossom to my nose, inhaled deeply, grinned, and headed to work.

Another rose lay atop the woodpile.

A third was tied to an oak tree with a hangman's noose fashioned from kudzu vine.

A fourth stuck out of a broken brick in the seawall.

A fifth lay across the handles of the doors into the marina. They all smelled so lovely, my blood pressure hardly went up when Mrs. Vader shrieked at me, "Where have you been?"

She must have freaked out because the marina was already swamped with customers. The Crappy Festivities today were divided among the town swimming park and the three biggest marinas on this section of the lake, including ours. We got the crowning of the Crappy Queen. I wished we got a more interesting event, such as the Crappy Toss. I could have thrown a dead fish as far up the beach as anybody. The Crappy Queen contest was just a bunch of high school girls parading up and down the wharf as Mr. Vader called their names and announced the weights of the biggest fish they'd caught all year, and what bait they'd used. At least the event did its job of bringing customers in.

Well, if Mrs. Vader wanted me there sooner, she should have told me the day before. "Where have I been?" I repeated. "I get asked that a lot for some reason."

She took the roses from me without comment and shoved me into the showroom, where a small crowd of people in shorts and flip-flops milled between the displays. "It's been a revolving door in here since we opened this morning," she hissed. "People want to buy wakeboards, and they want to buy them from *you*."

"Wow! Really?" I'd feel a little guilty selling people wakeboards, considering my experience two days before. But after all, my wreck was caused by a brain cloud and a broken heart, not equipment failure. I patted my head to make sure my bangs hung down over my stitches.

"Yes, really!" Mrs. Vader said. "Adam's been covering for you, but he just mumbles at customers."

"Where *is* Ad—," I started to ask. Then I saw his broad back, and the door to the warehouse closed behind him. Where he'd stood, a rose protruded from behind a Liquid Force on the wall.

He'd called me a bitch. I wasn't running back to him

when he left me six roses. But I did extract the new rose carefully and put it with the others in the vase Mrs. Vader set on the counter. Then I found another rolled up in the boat twine, and still another lying across the containers of worms.

In the late morning, as I manned the cash register (after pulling out the rose inside), Dad and Frances came in. My heart pounded when I saw Frances. I wanted to vault over the counter and throw my arms around her. Instead, I asked her in a British accent, "Please, marm, are you to be my new mother?"

"Lori!" my dad burst out. Flushing red, he realized he desperately needed a new slalom ski *right then*, and bolted for the display.

Frances watched him go. "Very funny," she told me through her teeth. Then she leaned across the counter, kissed me on the forehead, and gave me a grudging smile. "Happy birthday."

"Thank you, marm."

She reached for my hand. "What a beautiful ring." She moved my finger back and forth so the ring glittered under the fluorescent lights, and smiled at me again. "Your mother would be proud of you."

"What a pretty dress," I said. "Is it hemp?"

Holding her chin high, she said self-righteously, "It's

organic cotton." She took a long whiff of the roses. "You and Adam have gotten yourselves in a mess, I hear. 'Oh, what a tangled web we weave, when first we practice to deceive!' Sir Walter Scott."

I patted her hand. "That's nice, dear."

"'An honest man's the noblest work of God.' Alexander Pope."

I squinted across the showroom. "I think I have a customer."

My dad recovered and decided he could put off that slalom ski purchase after all. He came to the counter, put his hand on Frances's back, and asked her, "Is Lori giving you lip?"

"She's making fun of me!" Frances exclaimed in mock astonishment. "I'm offering her aphorisms and she's making fun of me!"

"They do that." Dad turned to me and said, "We're going to wish Bill luck before the show. Aren't you at least riding in the boat with the boys?"

"Ha! I'd rather go shopping." Snort.

As Frances pushed open the door into the sunshine, she said something in Russian. Something long that she was determined to get out in full. Dad stood in the doorway and waited for her with a look of pure luv while she finished.

I didn't need any sage advice on honesty and I *definitely* didn't need any from Dostoyevsky. *"Do svidanya,"* I muttered. Then I realized the customer from across the showroom was approaching the counter. "Yes ma'am, may I help—" It was Tammy.

She slid a candy bar onto the counter. "Hook me up, would you? Now that I have a boyfriend, I'm trying to maintain my girlish figure."

As I scanned the candy into the register, I looked over my shoulder to see whether Mrs. Vader was listening from the office. I'd told customers off before when Mrs. Vader wasn't around, if they really deserved it. Tammy was McGillicuddy's girlfriend. I didn't want to be the annoying little sister she dreaded seeing when she came over to our house. But damn if she was going to follow me around and taunt me! She could have bought a candy bar at a gas station.

She must have seen I was gearing up to tell her off. She knew me better than I'd thought. Either that or she recognized the fixed killer stare I got before I served an ace. For whatever reason, she said in a hurry, "What draws me to McGillicuddy as a boyfriend is the same thing that draws me to you as a friend. You're both so honest, to the point of being clueless. After years of being stuck at tennis tournaments with Holly and Beige, it's refreshing."

"Eighty-three cents," I said. "You're not helping your-self here."

"And if I wanted honesty, I should have been more hon-est myself. When you left the party, I told McGillicuddy what I did to you. He didn't un-ask me out, but I could tell he was disappointed."

McGillicuddy would never un-ask a girl out. Even if he hated her guts, he'd keep his promise and act like a gentle-man about it. I didn't tell Tammy this because she was genuinely concerned about what he thought of her now. It was sort of sweet. "If it makes you feel better," I told her, "he dreamed about you last night."

"He did?" Her face glowed in the sunlight streaming through the showroom windows. Then she quirked her eyebrows at me. "He tells you about his dreams?"

I nodded. "Me and Dad, every morning at breakfast. Are you going to pay for that?"

She dug in her pocket, peered at the change in her palm, and picked out some coins. She had the same purse-carrying issues I had. "Anyway," she said, "I'm sorry for using you. I didn't mean to hurt your feelings. I didn't give it a thought. But I should have."

"Maybe I'd like to be used by a girl." As she passed me the change, I said, "I'd like to be good enough friends with a girl that we use each other without asking, and help each other without question. I'd like to know a girl always had my back." I tossed the coins in the register and slammed the drawer shut. The nickels had slid into the dime compartment, which would drive Mrs. Vader insane.

Tammy nodded. "We'll work on it. So, the wakeboarding show's starting soon. You want to go watch it with me?"

"Can't," I said, gesturing to the crowded showroom that was my responsibility. Wait a minute—it had emptied while I wasn't watching.

Mrs. Vader popped her head out the door of the office. She gazed suspiciously at the cash register drawer, like she just *knew* something was amiss in there. "Lori, why don't you take a few hours off? You should go outside and watch the boys."

"I don't *want* to go outside and watch the boys." Actually I did. More than anything. I'd never missed a show before. And I'd never missed Adam so much. But I wanted to watch them from the roof or a tree or somewhere else Adam wouldn't see me watching them. He'd called me a bitch. I wasn't running back to him when he left me nine roses.

Mrs. Vader folded her arms. "Go outside anyway."

I folded my arms too. "I don't want to go outside."

"Well, I don't want you to work."

"I want to work."

She pointed at me and screamed like I imagined real mothers did when their daughters turned out too much like them. "You're fired!"

"All *right*!" I threw my cash register key onto the counter and stomped outside.

Then turned right back around, smacked into Tammy, stepped inside, and took the roses Mrs. Vader held out to me wrapped in a paper towel. Her lips were pressed together, just like Adam's expression when he was trying not to laugh.

I stalked down the sidewalk outside. Tammy scampered to keep up with me. "Are you really fired?"

"Of course not," I sighed. "She fires me about once a week in the summers. I guess I'll take the rest of the day off, though. What's all this for?" I slowed to a stop at the edge of the enormous crowd. The air smelled like hamburgers and funnel cakes. People stood or sat together on towels, picnicking. I could hardly see a bare patch of grass or wharf, but it wasn't quite time for the wakeboarding show.

"They're crowning the Crappie Queen!" Tammy said.

"If you're going to hang around here, you need to use the correct pronunciation. It's *Crappy* Queen."

"It's Rachel."

Sure enough, down on the wharf, Mr. Vader was calling Rachel forward as the new Crappy Queen. There was some justice in the world.

And then I changed my mind. Instead of the evening gown I'd seen at Crappy Festivals past, Rachel skipped onto the wharf in cutoff jeans pulled over her bathing suit, and bare feet. She grinned while the outgoing Crappy Queen pinned a tiara in the shape of a fish into her hair. Maybe old Rachel was all right after all.

"Pardon," McGillicuddy said right behind me. He shoved me off the sidewalk. I shoved him back, then realized that when he pushed me, he'd tucked another rose into my bouquet. Walking backward down the hill, he blew a kiss at Tammy. Tammy giggled and blew him a kiss back.

Another voice behind me said, "A-choo!" SOMETHING FLEW INTO MY BOUQUET. I almost dropped my beautiful roses to avoid further contact with nastiness. But it was only Cameron, pretending to sneeze another rose at me.

"Racking up, aren't you?" Tammy asked, and I had to grin.

Right after Cameron came Sean. His nose was only a little blue. I could hardly tell it had bled the night before. Sean was like that. And he held a rose between his teeth.

I smirked at him. "Don't tell me. You want me to come and get it."

"Oh no," he said through a mouthful of stem, holding up his hands in warning. "Adam would kill me." He handed me the (spitty, ew) rose. "Did Dad crown Rachel the Crappy Queen yet?"

"Yes," Tammy and I said together.

Sean's face fell. "Oh!" He ran down the sidewalk. At the bottom of the hill, he caught Rachel by the arm and talked to her for a few seconds. His face fell further, and she shook her head. He walked away after the other boys, toward the wakeboarding boat. I almost felt sorry for him.

"I'm going to congratulate Rachel on her coronation," I said to Tammy.

"You aw?" Tammy said with her mouth full of candy bar. "Uhhh—"

"Come with me, because you're my friend and help me without question. I may need someone to call 911 if she breaks my arm."

"I'w be wight behiwd woo."

I maneuvered down the hill through the crowd, using the roses to clear the way in front of me. Now Rachel talked with an elderly couple, which might make her less likely to deck me. "Rachel!" I squealed, jumping up and down, spilling petals. "Congratulations!"

She stared at me like a fish out of water, but the elderly couple thanked me in the manner of clueless grandparents, which got us out of that embarrassing little moment.

"I need to tell you a couple of things," I said, hugging the roses to my chest and putting my other arm around her.

"Come this way," Tammy said, moving along the seawall. Rachel looked back to signal the elderly couple to save her, but I moved in, blocking her view. What a team Tammy and I made. Beyond the crowd, Tammy sat on the seawall with her legs hanging over. I did the same, and Rachel sat between us.

"It wasn't my idea to enter," Rachel spoke up defensively. "I caught a two-pounder, and my granddaddy said we could *not* let the mayor's daughter win again this year with only a one-pounder and a plastic minnow."

Rachel rose further in my opinion.

"I don't need to tell you how bizarre that is," I said. "Obviously you have a sixth sense about these things." I nodded toward Sean cranking the boat and backing it away from the wharf. My brother was in the bow, Cameron sat further back, and Adam was bent below the side of the boat, gathering something. "I needed to tell you Sean is really in love with you."

Now *she* looked toward the boat puttering across the inlet. "How do you know? You can just tell, right? You can tell by the way he acts? After the last couple of weeks, I'll never be able to trust *that* again." She tried to sound tough, but her delivery was stilted, and her eyes rolled for emphasis at the wrong place. I'd never actually talked to her before—I'd only watched her from afar—or I would have noticed this. She came off as a lot younger and more unsure of herself than I'd expected. Which made me like her even better.

"I know because he told me," I said. The boat pointed in our direction, almost like it was heading for us rather than the open water. "I also needed to tell you your wakeboard bindings came in at the showroom this morning."

"Oooh, I forgot Sean gave you a wakeboard!" Tammy said. "I wish I could learn."

"It's fun," I said. Maybe McGillicuddy could take Tammy out wakeboarding. Maybe Sean could invite Rachel again and hope she showed up this time. Of course, both Sean and McGillicuddy would have to fight the boys every step of the way. We were good together, but it would be nice to wakeboard with other people once in a while, without a freaking outcry and rumors of mutiny.

"Hey," I said suddenly. "I have a boat." There it was, tied on the side of the dock in front of my house. We hardly ever used it because we were always in the Vaders' boat. I nudged Tammy. "If you want, come over after I get off work tomorrow, and I'll teach you to wakeboard." I turned to Rachel. "You too, Miss Crappy." Of course, they probably didn't have boaters' licenses, which meant

I'd have to drive. They'd be learning to wakeboard, so I'd just take them around in slow circles. Surely I couldn't mess that up. They wouldn't suspect a thing.

"That would be great!" Tammy exclaimed. She touched Rachel's bare toes with her toes. "I'll pick you up, Your Crappiness."

In case Tammy got the wrong idea, I warned her, "McGillicuddy won't be with us. He'll be with the boys. This will be a girl trip."

"I know," she said, as if she *did* really know and wasn't trying to get out of it.

"But we could cruise by the warehouse very slowly like we need to borrow another tow rope," I said. "I have become an expert at seduction."

Rachel snorted, then gave up suppressing it and proceeded to laugh her ass off. The Crappy Crown detangled itself from her hair and would have fallen in the lake if I hadn't caught it for her. Finally she calmed enough to cough out, "I don't know. I'm not very graceful."

"Who am I," I asked, "Michelle Kwan?"

"Not hardly," Tammy said at the same time Rachel said, "I see your point." But neither of them was looking at me. They watched the wakeboarding boat float right in front of us, full of boy.

Specifically, full of Adam. He stood in the bow, one arm

cradling a bouquet of roses—a funny contrast, this muscular football player carrying pink flowers. He held his other hand out to me.

McGillicuddy leaned over the bow, too, and caught the seawall, holding the boat there so it didn't scrape against the wall and didn't drift away. The boys had planned ahead. For once.

Ninety-nine percent of me leaped up immediately and knocked Adam over, hugging him. One percent was still bitter about the bitch comment, and angry that I'd been tricked into coming out here to wait like some airhead flirt for Adam to happen by. This one percent was heavier than the rest combined and anchored me to the seawall. I elbowed Tammy. "Traitor."

"I was helping you without question," she said.

"And your mom!" I yelled to Adam. "Did you ask your mom to get me out here?"

"I told her to fire you if she had to," he called. "Did she fire you?"

"Mama Vader has some feminine wiles!" I exclaimed.

Adam laughed. "She's got maybe one more feminine wile than you, and you've got about three-fourths of a wile." He tilted his head and wiggled the fingers of his outstretched hand. "Come with us. We want you to close the show. Right, Sean?"

"Right!" Sean said with fake enthusiasm. From the back of the boat, Cameron waved my wakeboard at me to show me, again, that they'd thought ahead.

"I'm not supposed to get my stitches wet," I reasoned.

"Don't fall," Adam reasoned right back.

I wanted to go. I couldn't quite detach the heavy one percent. "You called me a bitch. I'm not running back to you when you leave me a dozen roses."

"Four more." He waved his smaller bouquet at me. "Sixteen total. Birthday or what?"

Rachel shoved me forward—which, since I was sitting down, didn't push me into the boat. It only folded me over like a movie theater seat.

"You can think about it," Adam said. "The four of us can take our turns, and we'll come back to see if you've changed your mind. But I want you to come with us now." In a singsong voice he coaxed, "I'll let you drive."

McGillicuddy and Cameron stared at Adam, eyes wide with fear. Sean coughed, "Bullshit."

"I'll let you drive when *I'm* wakeboarding, anyway," Adam said.

"It's love," McGillicuddy said, motioning with his head for me to get in the boat. "Let Tammy hold your roses so they don't go bald in the wind."

McGillicuddy's blessing was the final push I needed.

I held out my arms for the extra roses from Adam and inhaled one last long sniff before handing off the whole huge bouquet to Tammy. Then I took Adam's hand and let him help me in. McGillicuddy shoved the bow away from the seawall and walked into the back of the boat, muttering, "Freaking femme fatale."

As we puttered out of the idle zone, I gave Rachel and Tammy a pageant wave. They waved back and clapped for me. The boat reached the open water and sped up. The motor and Nickelback drowned out the clapping. Adam grabbed my waving hand, and we did the secret handshake.

As we sank to the bow seat, I touched his skull-and-crossbones pendant on a new leather string. "They still have these in the bubble gum machine?"

"Sean went under the dock and found it for me."

I nodded. "He was the best choice to rescue it for you. He has no fear of bryozoa." Squinting into the sun behind Adam, I looked up into his sky-blue eyes. "One day on the boat when we were kids, did you tell me you wanted me to be your girlfriend when we were old enough?"

He slid his hand down a lock of my hair and twisted it around his fingers. "I don't remember saying that, but I wouldn't be surprised. I wasn't lying that day in the truck. I really have loved you forever. Why else would I wear a skull-and-crossbones necklace you bought me from a bubble gum machine? It turned my skin green."

"It didn't." To make sure, I moved the pendant aside and peered at his chest, which looked the normal scrumptious tan to me. "It didn't," I repeated with more confidence.

"It did when you first gave it to me. Any metal coating that might have been clinging to it wore off on my chest years ago."

Come to think of it, the pendant *was* a funny color not found in nature. I'd probably given him lead poisoning, which was why he acted like that. I ran my fingertips down the bones, and poked the skull in the eyes. "You know, you could have told me you loved me a long time ago, before things got so crazy."

"No, I couldn't. I like to take chances. I'd blow a chance on anything but you. You didn't love *me*."

Didn't I? It was hard to believe I'd called him *little dolphin* just two weeks before. "I didn't think about you that way. Clearly I was capable of it. Because I love you now."

He grinned and took my hand. "We should add another step to the secret handshake."

"Then we couldn't do it in public." I turned his hand over and ran my fingertip lightly over his palm until he shivered. "When Sean came up to your mom because a fish had mouthed his toe, and my mom said I should just wait until I was sixteen . . . That wasn't Sean. That was you. Right?"

He put his head close to mine, watching my finger trace valentines in his open hand. "I didn't want you to like me because you thought you were supposed to. I wanted you to like me for me." His breathing sounded funny. He was about to cry—which was going to cause him a world of trouble with the boys. He could live the first time down owing to the shock of seeing me crash into a very large, very stationary object. But if he cried again, he was toast.

I knew one way to stop him. I hollered above the motor, "Oh my God, Adam, are you about to *cry*?"

"Oh my God!" Sean echoed in a high-pitched girl-voice. Cameron squealed, "Adam, don't cry!" My brother called, "No crying on the boat."

Adam laughed with tears in his eyes and kissed me softly on the forehead, the side away from the stitches. And suddenly, to my complete horror, *I* was the one crying, sobbing into his chest. I was happy, but that wasn't why I was crying. I was relieved. Relieved of a weight I couldn't even name.

He held me more tightly and kissed my forehead several more times, then made his way down my cheek, dangerously close to my ear. I giggled at the same time I cried. If he didn't stop, he was going to give me hiccups—

which would be so incredibly sexy, on top of messing up my timing for wakeboarding jumps.

He kissed my lips. "What do you want to do tonight?" he whispered.

What a question!

"Put our names back on the bridge," I said. "Only, you hold the sailboat this time, and I'll take care of the handwriting." I took a deep breath and let it out slowly, enjoying the warmth of Adam's arms around me against the wind. We sat back and watched the other boats and the crowded banks of the lake spin by. When the show started, we spotted for the other boys while they took their turns. Then it was Adam's turn, and mine.

Endless Summer

This book is for all the readers of
The Boys Next Door *who asked me*
to write a sequel. I would not and could not
have done this without you.

Acknowledgments

Thanks to Simon Pulse, for believing in this book; Emilia Rhodes, for a smart edit; my literary agent, Nicole Kenealy, for taking care of me; Erin Downing, for reading an early draft and offering terrific suggestions; and as always, my critique partners, Catherine Chant and Victoria Dahl, for sticking with me every step of the way.

1

Adam boosted me from the concrete embankment onto the narrow ledge that ran all the way down the highway bridge. From here I'd have the perfect platform to spray paint our names on the six-foot wall separating us from the cars—that is, if nothing went wrong.

I could have painted LORI LOVES ADAM right where I was, above the embankment. At least technically I was still on dry land, or over it. But his brothers would call us lightweights. They'd been more daring when they painted their own names. Using each seam in the metal wall as a handgrip, I walked carefully along the ledge. The embankment fell away. I was over the lake.

A quarter of the way across, which seemed respectable enough, I stopped. Shaking the can of spray paint with one hand and hanging onto the bridge for dear life with the other, I turned to look behind me. My house, Adam's house, and Adam's parents' marina lay across the water from us, but I couldn't see them in the starlight. Only a few lights edging the marina dock shone in the summer night, their reflections rippling in the water. Everyone must have been pooped from the festival on the lake that day. Not a single boat motor broke the silence—only the occasional *clack-clack, clack-clack* of a car passing on the other side of the concrete wall and a nervous vibration through the bridge.

"Kkkkkk," came radio static. "You on the bridge. Lori McGillicuddy. This is the police."

I glared at Adam standing on the ledge beside me with his hands cupped over his mouth to sound more like a police radio. He wasn't holding onto the bridge at *all*.

"You startled me," I said. "What if I'd fallen?" The lake wasn't far enough below to kill me, but the impact might still hurt. And we were not here for his adrenaline rush. We were doing something romantic, and we were in it together.

He touched my elbow. "I would have caught you."

He probably could have. What he lacked in good judgment, he made up for in strength and coordination. Of course, the poor judgment often trumped the strength and coordination, which accounted for at least one of the times in grade school he'd broken his leg.

But his fingers on my elbow made my skin tingle. His skull-and-crossbones pendant glinted in the starlight, and his strange light blue eyes watched me in the hot darkness. Though I was precariously balanced and about to deface public property, I used my own poor judgment to lean forward and kiss him.

He seemed surprised for a split second. Usually he was the one to start things between us. Then he slid his hands into my hair and kissed me back.

I felt the paint can slipping through my fingers. Gripping it harder, I loosened my hold on the bridge. I was falling.

He pulled me closer and held me steady. "Even *I* think this is not the best place to make out," he breathed.

"If you say so." I was kidding. Personally, my bravado had pitched off the side of the bridge along with my balance.

"*I* could have fallen instead of you," he said in mock outrage. "Oh, wait, I already fell." He touched the tip of my nose with his finger. "For you."

"Awwww!" I cried. "Adam, that's so sweet!"

He grinned. "Did you like that? I thought of it about

an hour ago, when we were in your basement looking for spray paint. I've been saving it."

"I did like it. You are a very good boyfriend. Who would have guessed?" With a final moony gaze at him— God, we were such idiots, but it was fun to be an idiot in love—I turned back to the bridge and scanned the surface for a clean space to write our names. Over the years it had gotten crowded with graffiti. Just above me was AOAN LOVES LOKI, which Adam had painted very sloppily last weekend, then crossed out when we had a fight. I could have moved farther down the bridge or reached higher up for a blank slate, but I was not as fond of playing Tarzan as Adam was. Finally I decided on a space down low that had been painted over so many times, it would make a nice dark backdrop for my red paint. I shook the can one more time, held it out to Adam to pry the top off, and crouched to write.

"You're sure you don't want me to do it?" he asked.

"No thanks. When you want your name written legibly in graffiti, you have to do it yourself."

He laughed. "I was in a hurry, and the paint ran when it rained. Besides, you knew what I meant."

Smiling, I started the first downward leg of LORI LOVES ADAM. "Yeah, I knew what you meant."

In only a few minutes I was finishing the M. "There.

Some couples swap class rings to show they're together. Some people switch their online profiles from *single* to *in a relationship*. We commit a misdemeanor."

He took the paint can from me. "The police chief's son's name is up here, so I wouldn't be too worried. Come on." He headed for the shore, placing one battered deck shoe in front of the other, but still barely holding on to the bridge, his fingers brushing the metal. Just following him seemed dangerous.

We reached land and hiked up the embankment, over to the city boat ramp, then into the parking lot. The street-lights gently lit the trucks and empty trailers of the night fishermen. No one stopped us as we walked up the steep asphalt to Adam's truck. We'd gotten away with it.

My fingers were raw from my death grip on the bridge, and my bare toes were rough. Other than that, everything had gone perfectly my whole sixteenth birthday. After our huge fight last night, Adam and I had gotten back together today. We'd had a great time at the lake festival. We and our brothers had performed a wakeboarding show for an enormous crowd. Not even Adam had broken a bone. And now we'd spray painted our love for each other on the bridge without a single mishap? This night was Too Good To Be True.

As he opened the passenger door for me—he never

locked the doors, because he liked to tempt fate—I caught a glimpse of my reflection in the window. Even after my test run in a life of crime, my hair was gorgeous, I tell you. It clumped a little in the humidity, but it looked like I'd created that piecey effect on purpose with styling gel. I was a vision of blonde loveliness.

That was the last straw. A day this happy and good hair, too? Now I *knew* something awful was about to happen.

Adrenaline had propelled me through my artistry on the bridge. That started to drain away now. Fatigue set in—from wakeboarding in the festival show that afternoon and worrying the last few days about whether Adam and I would ever get together.

"What's wrong?" he asked from behind me, tossing the paint can in the payload.

"I'm having a good hair day."

"I hate it when that happens." Gathering my hair and pushing it forward over my shoulder, he kissed the back of my neck.

I shivered in the heat. The adrenaline came rushing back, and I was not so tired.

"The night is young," he growled between kisses. "I have an idea of what we can do now. We've kissed before." Kiss. "We've made out." Kiss. "But we've never made out as an official couple, in the privacy of my Secret Make-Out Hideout."

I turned to look sideways at him. I found I couldn't do this without denying him access to the back of my neck. So I gave up on the sly look and enjoyed his soft lips on my skin. "You have a Secret Make-Out Hideout?" I whispered with my head bent.

"I do." His low voice against my neck sent chills through me. "Just for you."

"What are we waiting for?" I hopped forward through the open door, into the truck.

"You won't regret it," he said before he closed the door and rounded the truck to the driver's side.

I missed him for ten seconds, looking forward to the instant he slipped back inside the truck and we laughed together again. Decision made. It wasn't my first bad judgment leading to an Adam-Related Catastrophe, and it wouldn't be my last.

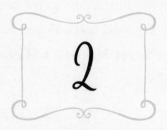

2

"Adam," Lori whispered. I'd known her all my life. I was used to her scent of warm skin and water. But in the last couple of weeks she'd started wearing perfume. I caught another whiff of it every time she shook my shoulder.

Without opening my eyes, I sniffed deeply, inhaling all the perfume I could get. Her hair tickled my face. I nuzzled her neck.

"Adam Vader." Now her voice sounded pinched, like she was clenching her teeth. "I am trying to remain calm so as not to alarm you, but wake the hell up already."

That made me open my eyes. She lay on top of me,

looking down at me. I couldn't see her features clearly in the shadowy cab of my truck. Her long blonde hair cascaded around me and glowed pink in the light of sunrise.

Sunrise!

"Oh, God." I sat up, dumping her off my chest and onto the passenger side. For the perfect end to a perfect day, I'd driven her here. My secret make-out hideout was a point of land jutting into the lake with a dirt road leading to it, a primo lot that nobody had built a house on yet. It was at the other end of our neighborhood, and we could actually see our houses and my parents' marina from here. My truck was hidden from their view by the trees around us, which was the beauty of it. I loved having the upper hand for once in my life.

But that was last night. Now the sun peeked over the highway bridge in the distance and reflected in the smooth lake.

"What time is it?" I looked toward the clock in the dashboard of my truck, which hadn't worked since probably 1995.

"I don't know," she said. "My cell phone went in the lake with me a couple of nights ago. I'd say five thirty or six."

I pulled my own cell phone from my pocket. "It's five fifty-three, and my mother's called me eleven times."

"Why didn't it ring?" Lori wailed.

"My brothers kept texting me about hooking up with you. I turned off the sound." Which was shooting myself in the foot. My brothers were good at making me do that. I turned the key in the ignition and threw the truck into reverse. We backed through the cloud of our own dust, which billowed through the open windows and glinted in the sunlight. As soon as I hit a clearing with more room, I jerked the truck around in a hasty three-point turn and hit the gas.

"Stupid," I muttered. I would get in trouble for staying out late. She would get in more trouble because she was a girl, and her dad was kind of high-strung. Plus, we'd slept all night on that abandoned point with the windows open. I should have protected her better. Maybe I'd watched snippets of too many action movies, but it seemed to me that falling asleep with a woman was just asking for snakes.

Lori crossed her arms and rubbed her hands up and down her skin, warming herself. The air was heavy with humidity, and chilly. This was the coldest part of a summer day in Alabama. "Faster," she said.

In the three weeks I'd had my license, I'd driven as fast as I could every chance I got. Most people, Lori included, thought this was not a good idea. It was a rush for her to tell me to go faster. I pressed the gas harder. "Are you sure you want me to take you home? We could run away together."

I felt her looking at me across the cab. I met her gaze and held it for one second, two seconds, three seconds longer than I should have been keeping my eyes off the road.

The truck hit gravel. I swung the steering wheel to point the truck back onto the pavement.

She laughed. "Better not."

"You thought about it, though." I grinned.

"I did." She slid her hand onto my thigh, which was bare below my shorts. "Go faster."

I put more pressure on the gas. The engine revved higher, echoing weirdly against the dense woods flashing past the open windows on both sides.

"No, wait, stop, stop, stop!"

I stomped on the brake and threw my arm in front of her to keep her from going through the windshield before I realized she had put on her seat belt. (I had not.) The truck screeched to a halt. I expected to see the huge body of a deer I'd just missed as it crashed into the woods and escaped—but outside the truck, the morning was pink and still. "What is it?"

"Sorry," she sighed. "I just realized we need to pick up where we left off last night and enjoy it for a few minutes. I have a feeling we won't get to do it again for a while."

Her eyes were sad as she said this. I should have bear-hugged her and comforted her. But when the girl of your dreams, who you've been chasing for years and have finally caught, tells you to make out with her, are you going to tell her you'd rather just hold each other for a while? Why, hell no. I put the truck in park.

Then I put my hands on her face and kissed her. She opened her mouth. Funny that she'd been so unsure about this when we'd first fake dated a couple of weeks ago, but she caught on quickly. Sometimes she even took the lead. Like now. She drew back from the kiss, touched her lips so gently to mine, licked my bottom lip with the very tip of her tongue. A chill ran through me and I shuddered.

She kissed me again. "Mmm," she said. I thought she was telling me how much she enjoyed it. I agreed completely. When her shoulders shook, I figured out she was crying.

I kissed her cheek. "Hey. Don't cry." I couldn't stand to see her cry. She'd already bawled in the boat when we got together. I'd gotten a little watery-eyed myself, which my brothers loved. It had been such a relief to call her mine after wanting her so long. For the happiest day of my life, the one I'd dreamed about forever, we sure were crying a lot.

As it turned out, we would have good reason.

But then, in the truck, I didn't know this. I wiped her

tears away with my thumb. "What are you crying about?"

"We're finally together," she sobbed, "and now we won't go out for the rest of the summer. My dad will ground me until Labor Day!"

"You don't know that." I ran my fingers through her hair. Now it was dark blonde, but as the summer went on, it would turn lighter until the front was almost white, just like every year. "We'll explain what happened. It was an honest mistake. Don't cry. Not yet." She was making me antsier than I let on, though. I pulled away from her, put the truck back in drive, and sped down the road.

"What *did* happen?" she asked. "Clearly we don't find each other as exciting as we thought."

I laughed. "I remember you were biting my earlobe—"

"I remember biting your earlobe," she said dreamily.

"—but sleep finally caught up with me."

"Me too." She scooted closer to me on the seat and put her head on my shoulder.

I drove with my left hand and slipped my right arm around her waist. For thirty more seconds, she was my girlfriend.

Finally I parked in her driveway. "I'll walk you to the d—"

She slammed the passenger door and dashed through the trees to her house. One of her pink flip-flops flew into an azalea and she never slowed down. I don't know why she was in such a hurry. Seemed to me that 6:01 a.m. was just as grounded as 6:02.

Her father was already yelling at her when he opened the door. His voice faded and the bright rectangle of light shrank as he swung the door closed behind her.

I murmured, "Happy sweet sixteen, Lori."

I backed down her driveway, drove a few feet, and pulled into my own driveway. My mom must have heard my truck. She was waiting in our own open doorway in her bathrobe with her arms crossed.

Up until the moment I saw her, I'd planned to tiptoe into the house and hope nobody had missed me. It had worked for my brothers before. If I did encounter my parents, I would tell them the truth: Lori and I had fallen asleep, we never meant to be out until morning, and I was sorry.

But there was something about seeing my mother there, arms folded, ready for a fight, that pissed me off. Instead of standing on the porch and apologizing to her, I squeezed past her into the house like nothing was wrong. And I said, "You're up early."

She grabbed the back of my neck and pointed me toward the kitchen. "Sssssssit. Down."

I huffed out a sigh and walked into the kitchen. It was a little early for everyone to be up and getting ready to go to work at the marina down the hill. My dad sat at the table, drinking coffee. He didn't share Mom's frazzled appearance, though. I doubt he'd lost much sleep over my status as a missing person. My oldest brother, Cameron, must have been asleep too—he never got up until the very last second—but my other brother, Sean, lounged at the head of the table, smirking at me. I gathered he was still mad at me for nearly breaking his nose when he jumped on me a few nights ago. The swelling had gone down and it seemed to be healing nicely, so I didn't know what his problem was.

"Sit down," Mom repeated.

I pulled out a chair and sat. I wanted some of that coffee first, but something told me I should not ask for this right now.

Mom sat directly across from me, where she could vaporize my brain with her stare. "Where were you?"

The fact that I was only two minutes away from home and could see the house the entire time I was gone might have helped me. But I had planned a whole summer of taking Lori back to that spot. I didn't want to give it away. Sean and Cameron would be lying in wait for us next time, armed with camera phones and cans of whipped cream. I said, "We fell asleep."

Sean snorted into his coffee.

Mom silenced him with her stare. Then she turned it

back on me. "Trevor McGillicuddy called me and woke me up in the middle of the night. Imagine how embarrassed I was that my son had his daughter out at all hours, after he has been so good to us. He did some fancy legal footwork to get Cameron out of that speeding ticket."

"And his second speeding ticket," I said.

"And his second speeding ticket," she acknowledged.

"And he got Sean out of *his* speeding ticket." I took the opportunity to remind her how horrible her other sons were. Since I'd been driving for only three weeks, I was still golden, at least in that area.

Sean mimicked me in a bratty tone. "And he got Sean out of *his* speeding ticket."

"That is not the point!" Mom yelled. "You expect me to call Lori's father and tell him you had Lori out until six a.m. because you fell asleep?"

"Well, we did." That's all I said, though I wanted to tell her we'd gambled away the night and my granddad's life savings at the Indian casino in Wetumpka. She was acting like we'd done something that awful.

Judging from the look on her face, you'd think I'd gone ahead and said this. Sean didn't help by prompting me, "Why'd you fall asleep? What were you doing before that?"

Mom watched me expectantly, as if she wanted to know

the answer to that question too, and as if my older brother had just as much right as my parents to interrogate me.

"Nothing," I said.

Sean laughed.

"Nothing?" Mom yelled.

No, not nothing. The highlight of the night, at least for me, had been when Lori wrestled me down on the seat of the truck, straddled me, held my wrists above my head, and kissed my neck. She'd pretended she'd overpowered me. I could have easily pushed her off me, but I didn't. It was very sexy. I could still feel her lips on my neck. God, that had felt good.

"Adam!"

I jumped when Mom hollered at me again. My hand was pressed to my neck where Lori's lips had been. I put my hand down. "Maybe not nothing, but not what you smutty-minded people are thinking."

"You just stayed out all night with the girl you've had a crush on since you were four," Mom said, "and nothing happened? What do you take me for, Adam?"

I wondered how my mom knew I'd had a crush on Lori for so long. That was creepy. But what I yelled back was, "What do you take *me* for? What do you think I did to her? You think I'm stupid?"

"No!" Sean gasped.

Normally Mom would have rushed to my defense over that sarcasm from Sean. Of all the things Sean and Cameron picked on me about, my ADHD and my tendency to flunk school because of it was the one topic that was off-limits, at least while Mom was around.

This time she said, "I'm beginning to wonder. Lori's father wants to ban you and Lori from seeing each other for the rest of your lives."

I said, "He can try."

"Adam, your father and I want to help you, but we can't if you don't help yourself. You're not doing yourself any favors with that attitude."

"What attitude? I don't think I'm being helped right now."

"This is exactly what I'm talking about," Mom snapped. "I was worried sick last night. Your father was worried sick."

Dad shrugged.

"Trevor was worried sick about his only daughter staying out all night on her sixteenth birthday," Mom shrieked, "and you don't even take it seriously."

"It's hard to take seriously when I'm in trouble for something I didn't even do," I shouted back.

"Son," my dad said.

"What!"

He stared at me for a few long seconds, letting me know I'd crossed the line, before he answered. "Shut up and listen to your mother."

"Lori's father will calm down," Mom said. "He always does. When that happens, your father and I will talk to him about letting you see Lori again. But in the meantime, you must exercise some restraint. Stay away from her, just as he wants, or we won't be able to put in a good word for you."

"Okay. I'm about to work with her for eight hours at the marina, but I'll take a blindfold."

"You will work on opposite ends of the marina until further notice," Mom said. "You may not go out with her. You may not date her. You may not be her boyfriend. Clear enough?"

Damn. Lori was right. Only it was worse than her being grounded from going out. I was grounded from *her*.

I stared at Mom, the embodiment of evil sitting across from me in a red bathrobe. Sean had told me since we were kids that I was adopted. He and I looked a lot alike, unfortunately, so I'd assumed he told me that just to be mean. Now I knew he'd told me the truth. A real mom couldn't be that cruel.

"You can't do that," I breathed. "No."

"I can," she said, "and I am. Lori's father informed me at about three thirty this morning that if we found the two of you alive, you would not date each other again. I have to agree with him until you show us more maturity."

I turned to my only chance left. "Dad," I pleaded, "this is so [cuss word you never, ever say in front of your mother] ridiculous."

Mom gaped at me. So did Sean. The difference was that Sean was half smiling, and Mom looked like she might climb over the table in her bathrobe and stab me with the butter knife.

Even Dad shook his head and said, "Consider yourself lucky. Lori's pop wants you to go to jail."

"But for now," Mom seethed, "go to your room."

Like I was five! Punished for this made-up adult behavior like I was in kindergarten. "No," I said. "I have to get ready for work, and I'm hungry."

"Go to your room!" Mom and Dad yelled at the same time.

Just as well. I was beginning to feel sick to my stomach. I scraped my chair back from the table as loudly as I could, stepped over Sean's leg, which he'd positioned to trip me, and stomped through the den to the stairs.

As I rounded the corner, I almost collided with Cameron crouching on the bottom step. His eyes widened at me. I'd caught him listening.

He recovered and said, without missing a beat, "I

thought you were going to pull it off until you said [cuss word you never, ever say in front of your mother]."

"Thanks for your support," I grumbled. "You left me there to bleed out."

He held up his hands. "I don't have a dog in this fight."

I elbowed him as I passed him on the stairs. "If you were in this shit, I would have helped you."

"How?" he called after me. "By setting the curtains on fire to create a diversion?"

At least Sean couldn't follow me. He and Cameron shared a room when Cameron was home from college. I'd had my own room since I was five and Sean wrote on my face with permanent marker while I was asleep. I reached the top of the stairs, stalked into my room, and slammed the door hard enough to bounce every football trophy on my shelves.

I leaped across the room to catch last year's tenth grade player-of-the-year trophy, presented to me at a ceremony that Sean had laughed all the way through. I carefully set it back on the shelf. But I was thinking that Sean and Cameron had a point. I was a loser. If Cameron had stayed out until morning with his brand-new girlfriend-who-was-like-a-daughter-to-Mom, Mom would have thought that was fine. Her firstborn could do no wrong. And if Sean had done it, he could have talked his way out of it. Whereas I'd dug my own grave. I couldn't do anything right.

I fished my cell phone out of my pocket and pressed the button for Lori's house. Her dad might answer, but that was okay. We couldn't get in any worse trouble.

One ring. We should have run away after all. Two rings. I'd saved a couple thousand dollars of my money from working at the marina over the years. I had known it would come in handy someday. I'd always suspected I'd end up on the run from the law sooner or later, since I was forever getting blamed for things I didn't do. Three rings. The money would tide us over until we both got jobs at a marina in a different town. Of course, we would need references from our previous employer. I doubted Mom would cooperate.

"Hello," Lori answered. She was hoarse.

"Lori."

"Adam," she whispered. "I can't talk long or my dad will catch me. He is insane. He thinks we spent the night in some kinky love grotto. It's so unfair. He has no idea what dorks we are."

"My parents are the same." In defeat, I flopped backward onto my bed. The bed Lori should have visited sooner or later. But considering the last half hour, that would never happen. "Now you can cry."

3

After a shower, I took extra time to dry my hair. Despite the fact that Adam and I had gotten each other in so much trouble—or maybe because of it—I wanted to make sure I looked as pretty for him as I had last night with my Ominously Good Hair.

Of course, this was ridiculous. All my efforts would be for naught. If Mrs. Vader stuck me in the warehouse, my blonde crowning glory would be full of boat grease and spiders by nine a.m. Also, I didn't want to be late for work. Not this morning.

I did, however, want my dad to embark on his Sunday

morning routine of going back to bed before I got down-stairs. I had never seen him as angry as he was when I came home an hour ago, and I did not want a recap.

No such luck. When I popped into the kitchen, my dad and my brother leaned against the counter with their arms folded. Dad still looked red, but at least he wasn't yelling anymore. I stepped through the doorway just in time to hear him say, "You take care of your sister today."

McGillicuddy gave my dad a two-finger salute. "Aye-aye, cap'n."

Dad turned to me. "And you." Every morning that I'd gone to play with the boys when we were little, or I'd gone to work at the marina this summer and last, he'd told me, *Watch out around those boys next door.* This time he couldn't muster the words. Focusing on me, he opened his mouth, breathed in, breathed out.

He turned to my brother and repeated, "Take care of your sister."

My brother and I closed the door behind us—softly, so as not to startle an already shell-shocked father—and walked through the garage to the yard, heading past the Vaders' house to the marina. As soon as we were out of Dad's earshot, I said, "Well! It's a good thing you're not serious about taking care of me. Dad can keep me from going out with Adam, but he'll never see me on the lake.

He won't know about anything I do at the marina, because you won't tell him. Hold up a minute."

I'd been limping behind my brother on one bare foot and one flip-flop, scanning the yard for a flash of pink as we went. I remembered having both flip-flops on at the bridge. After that, it got fuzzy. All I knew was that I'd been wearing only one when I arrived home an hour ago. My dad had characterized this as my telltale state of undress.

Now I dove into an azalea and brought out my flip-flop. I shoved my toes into it and turned around.

McGillicuddy frowned at me.

Suddenly I realized how it looked to him and to my dad. "Come on," I pleaded. "A flip-flop in the bushes does not mean anything. If you ever see my bikini top hanging from the bird feeder, I give you permission to raise an eyebrow."

He cleared his throat. "Dad *will* see you on the lake. While you were in the shower, he went out on the screened porch, dragged the lawn chair into position, and made sure he could see the lake through the trees. After work I'm supposed to get out the ladder and clip more branches out of the way."

"Oh."

"And if I see you with Adam, I have to tell Dad."

"You are not serious," I wailed.

"I promised Dad. It's a big brother's duty. Just because you've lost his trust doesn't mean that I—"

"I didn't do anything to lose his trust," I interrupted. "Adam and I fell asleep. That's the truth. You know Adam's harmless."

"I do *not*," McGillicuddy said sternly.

"Well, not harmless, but he wouldn't hurt *me*."

"He wouldn't mean to," McGillicuddy acknowledged. "But Adam's got it bad for you, Lori. And sometimes what Adam intends to do and what he actually does are two different things."

I scowled down the hill. Early morning mist rose from the smooth lake and evaporated as it touched the sun. A little over two weeks ago, I'd skipped happily toward that mist, knowing it would burn off to reveal a whole summer day working with Sean. A week ago, I'd still *thought* I was after Sean, but I'd fallen for Adam, whether I knew it or not. Yesterday Adam had won me over. It had been the best birthday ever.

We'd screwed it up already. Literally. We were the only two teenagers in the world who could get in trouble for hitting a home run when we hadn't even gotten to second base. Now the fog over the lake looked menacing. It lapped at the marina piers and curled toward the warehouse and the showroom. It threatened to grab the little love affair between Adam and me and drag it under the surface of the lake, never to be seen again.

Then McGillicuddy said, "I have to tell Dad if I see you with Adam. Just don't let me see you."

"Thank you," I gushed. I would have hugged him if that wouldn't have been weird. Instead, he turned to walk toward the marina again, and I skipped beside him.

What a relief that somebody was on our side. The situation had seemed bad this morning after Dad yelled at me. It had seemed downright hopeless after I talked to Adam on the phone and he told me he was as grounded from me as I was from him. But I figured everybody would cool down after a few days. Yesterday my dad had been happy Adam and I were a couple, and Adam's mom had helped throw us together in the first place. It wasn't logical for them to do a one-eighty just because Adam and I had stayed out all night.

Or maybe it *was* logical, but it wasn't *fair*.

Now that we had my brother as an ally, I felt better. I was sure I could fix everything. As we shuffled across the mat of pine needles, I asked him, "Can you talk to Dad for me?"

My brother eyed me. I didn't blame him. Dad had put on quite a spectacle this morning. His friendly lawyer facade had crumbled completely after a night of dead-or-missing daughter and no sleep. He yelled at me all the way through breakfast, and I had the strangest experience of being the reasonable one in the argument. Unlike him, I'd gotten plenty of rest. I'd slept through the night just dandy on Adam's chest. I had felt awful about keeping my dad awake and worried—until he started yelling.

"Can you?" I prompted my brother.

"Dad's pretty mad," he said.

"Really," I said flatly. "I did not get that at *all*."

"You should ask Frances," he said.

"I thought of that." If anybody besides my brother would believe Adam and I didn't deserve to be treated like sexual deviants, it was my ex-nanny, Frances, who was now my dad's girlfriend. I'd given her the play-by-play over the past few weeks. She knew I'd gone after Sean, caught Adam instead, and decided I'd netted the right boy after all.

But something about the idea of going to her for help made me uncomfortable. All those years she was our nanny, my brother and I thought we were pulling something over on Frances. The boys next door thought the same thing. Recently, watching her with the new family she worked for across the lake, I'd realized she let us get away with things on purpose, to learn lessons. She knew me a little too well. This was disturbing on its own, but it was doubly disturbing that this person who knew me a little too well wore hemp shorts and Birkenstocks in public.

Plus, she'd warned me a week ago that seemingly innocent Adam was trouble. And she told me that despite this, nobody would forbid me to go out with him. This was the one thing she'd been wrong about. A VERY IMPORTANT OVERSIGHT.

Plus, "Everything changed yesterday when she started dating Dad."

My brother nodded. "It's disconcerting."

"Very disconcerting." I hauled open the door to the marina office and waved him inside. "And I'm not sure she's on my team anymore." I stepped over the threshold after him, into enemy territory.

Crowded with my brother and me in Mrs. Vader's tiny office were three big, bare-chested boys wearing nothing but board shorts. They smelled better than usual, since it was so early and they hadn't spent the whole day sweating in the sun. Not that I minded their scent all that much— especially when Adam, who was standing closest to Mrs. Vader at her desk, peered at me over Sean and Cameron.

Since he'd dropped me off after our disastrous date, my mind had worked furiously to punch its way out of this box we'd built for ourselves. But now, as he looked over at me with his pale blue eyes so big and mysterious in his tanned face and his longish hair carelessly pushed back like he had no clue how hot he was—*now* I knew that if we didn't find a way to convince our parents to let us be together, this was going to seem like one endless summer.

"Adam," Mrs. Vader said. Somehow she conveyed a lot of disgust in that one name. Having raised three boys close in age, Mrs. Vader was good at this sort of thing.

"Yes, ma'am," Adam said politely, and therefore sarcastically. If he hadn't gotten a Talking-To an hour ago, he would have responded to her call with his full name, rank, and serial number like a prisoner of war.

I tried to catch his eye and give him a warning look. Our romance was at stake here. I didn't think this was a good time to be sarcastic.

"You've got gas," Mrs. Vader said.

Cameron and Sean cracked up. Some jokes never got old, at least to teenage boys whose little brother was in trouble.

"I figured," Adam muttered. Heading for the office door on his way down to the marina's floating gas station, he pushed his way past Cameron and Sean. He even shoved my brother. I would have found this angry-at-the-world act kind of sexy if things hadn't been so serious. We were in enough hot water.

He slid past me, his chest warm against my bare arm. I looked up into his eyes and watched him as he moved past me. My skin tingled wherever he touched me, like sand sparkling and swirling in the lake when the water was stirred. He filled the sunny doorway for a second. Then he was gone down the wooden stairs to the floating dock.

I turned back toward Mrs. Vader's desk. She and the three remaining boys stared at me like they'd never seen me before. Like I was Lori McGillicuddy, Teen Geek and Fashion Disaster, transformed into an underage sex goddess. Just the effect I'd been going for two weeks ago when I was trying to hook Sean. Now that I was in trouble, not so good. To assure them I was the same old Lori, I said, "Funny. I figured you'd give *me* gas."

"Ew," Sean said. Cameron fanned the air to dispel the pretend smell, and my brother took a step away from me.

"Sean and Bill," Mrs. Vader called, "you're in the warehouse."

My brother amiably headed toward the warehouse door. Sean put one hand on Mrs. Vader's shoulder. "Are you sure you don't need help here in the showroo—" He stopped midsentence when Mrs. Vader glared at him. "On second thought, I'll see if McGillicuddy needs any help in the warehouse. Good suggestion." He crossed his eyes at Cameron and me as he slipped past us out the office door.

"And you two," Mrs. Vader said to Cameron and me.

"We sold a lot of stock over the festival weekend. You're delivering boats."

Cameron took the stack of tickets she handed him. "Score!" he exclaimed, holding up his arms to signal a touchdown, because the boys considered this the choice job. Then he glanced at me. "No offense. I didn't mean you."

"Nice." I'd been so focused on the catastrophe with Adam, I hadn't even processed that there were a lot of sex jokes in my future, courtesy of rude boys. I approached Mrs. Vader's desk cautiously, because she looked like she'd had Just About Enough. "I wanted to remind you that you do not allow me to deliver boats, as I have been known to crash them."

"It's time you earned your keep around here, Lori," Mrs. Vader snapped. "You've had your boater's license for almost a year. Now you've turned sixteen. Whether or not you've learned left from right, you need to act like a grown-up. You can't rely on the boys to do everything for you. Take some responsibility."

My jaw dropped lower and lower as she said this. First of all, I worked hard around the marina, mostly, and she paid me minimum wage. What did she expect me to do, scrub the wharf with a toothbrush?

Actually, as she seemed pretty miffed, I would not have suggested this, even in jest.

Second of all, bringing up the fact that I was direction-ally challenged was a low blow, since my handicap had caused me to wreck on my wakeboard and bash my forehead just three days ago.

And finally, the suggestion that I had been careless and irresponsible in sullying her youngest child with my sexiness . . . well, that called for a Retort. I shifted my dropped jaw to one side and gritted my teeth with the effort not to say a word. I could still salvage my relation-ship with Adam and convince our parents to let us date. I knew I could if I just kept my mouth shut for now, which, let me tell you, was about as ridiculous an idea as my sud-den transformation into a teenage temptress.

Staying silent became even more difficult when, from behind me, Cameron moaned, "Woooo," like his mom had dissed me good.

I pressed my lips together and backed out of the room, without so much as a "Yes, ma'am." I was afraid of what I might say if I said anything at all.

Cameron moved past me and slid a few sheets of paper from his mom's printer. "Hey," she protested when he snagged a black marker and a roll of tape, but he just fol-lowed me out.

In the sun, with the office door safely closed behind us, he asked, "Why couldn't you and Adam hook up last summer too, and the summer before? Y'all are a riot. Sure beats three-on-two water polo for my entertainment dollar."

It was imperative that I pretend nothing about this bugged me. To Cameron, and especially to Sean, any inkling Adam and I were really worried would be like blood in the water to a shark. I waved at the paper in Cameron's hand. "What's with the school supplies?"

He handed me the tape. Spreading one sheet of paper against the side of the building, he covered it with a big black *L* in marker. He wrote an *R* on the other sheet and tried to hand them both to me. "Tape these on either side of you in the boat. They'll keep you straight."

I looked at the *L* and *R*, then at him. "I know my left from my right, thank you very much."

"Okay then." He pulled the boat tickets from his pocket and examined one. "The first place we're going is about five miles to the right."

Before I thought, I gazed in that direction. Not that I could really pick out a house so far away along the forested shoreline.

"Caught ya," Cameron said. "Your other right."

Like Adam had taught me, I made an *L* with the fingers of my supposedly right hand. If it had really been my right hand, the *L* would have been backward. Oops. "That's not fair. Now you've got me thinking about it, which is what confuses me." I took the sheets from Cameron anyway. I definitely didn't want either of us to return them to Mrs. Vader in her office just then. Judging from her current mood, I should steer clear of her for a couple of decades. We trotted down the steps to the wharf.

"So . . . ," he said. "Did you and Adam do it or not?"

Risking death by taking my eyes away from the stairs beneath my flip-flops, I looked up at Cameron.

Suddenly I remembered the one time he and I had kissed, when I was eleven years old and he was fourteen and clearly very pedophilic and misguided, or perhaps just desperate. It was an awful lip-lock, especially compared with every bone-melting kiss I'd shared with Adam in the past few weeks.

Nevertheless, that's what I thought about as I looked up at this nineteen-year-old college boy. He was asking me if I'd had sex with his brother. If I *had*, I would have been beyond mortified at this question. In fact, I probably would have refused to leave my house this morning, or ever. Frances could quit her gig with the fam across the lake and homeschool me.

However, as I had *not*, I found the question interesting. Empowering, even. People didn't consider me a child anymore, or a tomboy. They considered me Trouble in High Heels (or, at the moment, flip-flops—but I did *own* heels

323

now). Maybe being an underage sex goddess wasn't so bad. I fought the urge to pat my boobs underneath my bikini and test whether they'd grown.

"Adam told Mom you didn't do it," Cameron prompted me.

I blinked, realizing Cameron and I had paused on the stairs, facing each other. I galloped down them again, asking him over my shoulder, "Why's your mom so mad, then?"

"Mom never believes Adam," Cameron said. "And Adam didn't make it easier on himself." We'd reached the bottom of the steps. He nodded to the speedboat the boys used as a chaser when they made deliveries. "You drive the fifteen-thousand-dollar boat and I'll drive the fifty-thousand-dollar, brand-new one. Sound okay?"

"Fine," I muttered, stepping into the chaser boat. I did need to practice driving, even if it was a boat rather than a car. Every bit helped. I wanted to take my driving test this week—as soon as I could get off work for a few hours, drag a licensed driver with me, and convince someone to trust me with their insured vehicle. Adam and I had intended that licensed driver to be him and that insured vehicle to be his truck, but it looked like we'd blown any chance of that.

Or *he* had. As I puttered through the wharf behind Cameron's boat, I felt bitter that I couldn't grin and wave to a hot Adam at the gas pump. Hot as in obscenely good-looking with his shirt off, *and* hot as in an air temperature of eighty degrees at seven thirty in the morning. I couldn't risk his mom seeing me flirting with him—not that he himself seemed to comprehend such concepts as *subtlety* and *tactics*.

At least I didn't have to stare at the highway bridge all day like he did, with LORI LOVES ADAM freshly painted among the other graffiti of love. Last night it had seemed daring and romantic. Now I wished the words weren't there to taunt Adam—in red, no less—or to irk our parents further.

I throttled up to keep pace with Cameron as he arced to the right, or left, or whatever. Upstream. Away from the highway bridge. And I pondered what Cameron had said: Adam didn't make it easier on himself. *What had Adam done?*

I couldn't ask Cameron about this at the house where we delivered the boat. We had to make nice with the customer. We made nice so well that Cameron came away with money, which he pocketed. Then he saw me watching him and guiltily handed me a five without showing me what the other bills were. To determine whether I was being cheated (highly likely), I would consult with Adam later on the etiquette of sharing these tips. If I was ever allowed to speak to him again.

I couldn't ask Cameron what had transpired this morning between Mrs. Vader and Adam when we launched the
chaser boat either, because the motor was too loud. And
when we idled it back to the wharf, Mrs. Vader stood
in the office door, motioning to me with both hands
above her head and phone message slips between her fingers.

"You worried a lot of people last night," she said as
she handed me the slips and walked into the show-room,
leaving me alone in the office. I examined the messages.

For: Junior

Taken by: Sean

Time: 8-ish

From: Tammy

Message: I was at your house with Bill last night
when you didn't show up. I take it you're still alive
or Bill would have called me. Are we still on for
this afternoon?

That slip was scrawled as if Sean couldn't care less
whether I could read it (surprise). The next message,
however, he'd taken neatly, as if afraid of offending his ex-
girlfriend when I didn't get the gist.

For: Junior
Taken by: Sean
Time: 8:16 a.m.
From: Rachel
Message: Girlfriend, your dad called me last night
looking for you and woke me up! I was worried about
you! Tammy is still bringing me over to wakeboard this
afternoon and I will kill Adam for you if you want me to!
Your dad is whack!!!

I called both chicks back to confirm our wakeboarding
date and let them know I was alive. Hanging up quickly
so I didn't get run off the phone by Mrs. Vader before my
break time was up, I turned my attention to the message
that really mattered.

For: Lori
Taken by: D. Vader
Time: 8:30 a.m.
From: Frances
Message: Call me.

Frances answered the phone just as the machine picked
up. She sounded out of breath. "Harbargers' residence."

"You've got to talk Dad down for me," I whispered into the phone.

"I don't think I can do that, Lori. Excuse me." More faintly, with her mouth away from the receiver, she called, "Alvin, not on the cat. No, sir. Let kitty go." A *thump* sounded loud enough that I held the phone away from my ear, and even at that distance I could hear horrific cat noises.

Then she came back, but after I heard what she had to say, I wished she hadn't. "Your father was terribly upset last night, Lori, and rightly so. He thinks you and Adam aren't mature enough to handle the responsibility of being alone together, and I support him in that decision."

"What's the matter with you?" I demanded. "You sound like some kind of authority figure. Is someone making you say these things? Are you being held against your will? Tap once on the receiver for kidnappers and twice for spies."

"This is no laughing matter."

"It sure the hell isn't. Any other time you would have talked some sense into Dad for me, but now you refuse because you're sleeping with the enemy."

"Lori!" she exclaimed, sounding genuinely appalled at my jab at her for going on a date with my dad yesterday. Not much appalled Frances—not that she let on, anyway—so I actually squirmed in the office chair as she scolded me. "That is a completely inappropriate comment."

"No, *Sleeping with the Enemy* is a 1990s Julia Roberts movie," I backtracked. I'd never seen it the whole way through, but during puberty Sean had been very fond of the bathtub scene and had subjected the rest of us to it over and over. "Your role as my nanny was to help my dad see that it was safe and healthy for me to play with the boys. You and I have an unspoken yet binding agreement that your role should continue now that you are my ex-nanny."

"We have no such thing," she said haughtily, like an ex-nanny without a sense of humor. "Adam's mother told me Adam's side of the story and how he expressed it to her. Sounds to me like Adam needs to grow up. Mirabella, kitty does not like that. Mir—" In the background, kitty sang "The Star-Spangled Banner." "I've got to go," Frances said.

"Wait," I said. "What do you mean, Adam needs to—" Frances hung up.

I stared at the phone in my hand. A boat horn honked outside. Cameron idled a sparkling new boat around the chaser boat. I galloped down the steps to the wharf and leaped into the driver's seat of the chaser. Before switching on the engine, I shouted through cupped hands to Cameron, "What did you mean when you said Adam didn't make it easier on himself this morning?"

Cameron shrugged. "For starters, when he first came in this morning, he said to my mom, 'You're up early.' This time we're going to the left." I could have sworn he pointed to the right as he said this, and he roared off.

Over the course of the day, I was able to drag more information out of Cameron and piece together the rest of Adam's defiant act, full of sassy one-liners he would not have uttered if he were trying to get out of trouble. He'd even said [cuss word you never, ever say in front of your mother]!

Cameron shared this last tidbit late in the day as we idled into the wharf after making our final delivery. Down on the floating dock, Adam finished topping off a boater's tank and straightened with the gas nozzle in his hand in time to watch us pass.

I saw us through his eyes. Me, his girlfriend, in a bikini, wearing big movie-starlet sunglasses, behind the wheel of the boat. His oldest brother, shirtless, in Ray-Bans, whispering (well, shouting, but still) in my ear.

Though Adam was twenty yards from me, I could almost see those little creases form between his brows when he frowned. When he was worried. When he was jealous.

Sure enough, he slammed the nozzle into the gas pump, tossed one last furious look over his shoulder at me, and stomped up the wooden steps.

At this point it occurred to me that, despite my best efforts, Adam might prove difficult to date.

And I was right.

4

"Where's Lori?" I asked as I threw a life vest at Cameron in the wakeboarding boat. I was part of a line. Sean in the warehouse (where it was cool and he wouldn't melt) tossed the wakeboarding equipment we needed to McGillicuddy, and McGillicuddy tossed it to me. Then I tossed it from the wharf down to Cameron. Or threw it, because I was pissed.

Cameron caught the life vest just before it smacked him in the face. "Why the hell are you asking me?"

"I figured you'd know, since you were hanging all over her just now."

"I was *not*," Cameron insisted. He glanced around the

wharf like he was afraid his girlfriend from college, Giselle, would overhear. I wished she would. Unfortunately, she'd gone to Europe until the middle of the summer.

McGillicuddy must have shot Cameron a dark look from behind my back. They were best friends, but that went only so far when it came to Lori. McGillicuddy thought Cameron was too old for her. Damn straight.

Cameron dropped the life vest and held up both hands. "I did *not*."

Sean's voice echoed inside the warehouse: "Aw, Adam is in wuv, and he misses Lowi."

A life vest hit me in the back. I turned to pick it up and saw that McGillicuddy wasn't paying attention. His eyes lingered on Cameron a moment longer to send his warning about Lori. Then he told me, "She's teaching Tammy and Rachel to board this afternoon, remember?" He nodded toward his house.

Over at the McGillicuddys' dock, three sunkissed girls in bikinis—Rachel tiny, Tammy tall, and Lori the happy medium—loaded their boat with gear. Exactly what we were doing but prettier, and nobody was getting hit in the head.

"Ow!" I put one hand to the back of my head where the handle of the ski rope had dinged me and glared at Sean in the darkness of the warehouse door.

Lori *had* told me she was boarding with Rachel and

Tammy today instead of with us. But in the face of losing her, I'd forgotten. And all day I'd looked forward to spending an hour in our boat with her, the one place where we weren't banned from each other. Lori was the best wakeboarder we had. A good wakeboarding show in three weeks on the Fourth of July would raise interest in the sport, which would translate into sales for the marina. Maybe my mom was willing to give that up to test my maturity, or what the hell ever, but my dad was easily bought, thank God.

And now this. Lori had flirted with Cameron in the chaser boat, and now she wasn't even coming wakeboarding with us, as she had almost every summer afternoon as far back as I could remember. A hot breeze lifted her laughter across the water to me. Her boat looked small. She seemed very far away.

McGillicuddy pried my fingers from the bundle of ski rope and tossed it down to Cameron. "Relax," he told me. "There's a deep breathing exercise for that."

"There's a *pill* for that," Sean's voice echoed.

Normally I wouldn't have let the comment pass. Sean loved to jab at me because I didn't take my medicine for ADHD. If I didn't respond, he'd jab at me harder. When I was little enough to complain to my mom about Sean constantly ragging on me, she always told me to ignore him and he'd stop. That might have worked with a normal brother. Sean was not normal.

This time I hardly felt the sting. I watched Lori push her boat away from her dock with one long leg, toes pointed, and hop in at the last moment before she lost her balance.

The other guys must have been as interested as I was in what was going on in the other boat. Sean had dated Rachel until she broke up with him a few days ago. There *were* some people in the world besides me who saw through Sean's pretty-boy act. McGillicuddy and Tammy had gone out for the first time last night—and, judging from the fact that he was not grounded from her, I assumed their date had gone better than mine had with Lori. We managed to speed up the equipment line and launch our own boat a few seconds later.

And when I neglected to crank up the rock music, not one of them said a word. We preferred to hear girls.

Manning the wheel first, I steered the boat into the middle of the lake—far enough from the girls for safety, but close enough that I could hear Lori explaining to Tammy the starting stance for boarding. McGillicuddy strapped on his life vest and board and hopped over the side. I would drive him in a couple of big circles on this section of the lake, then Sean would board, then Cameron.

Lately they wanted me to board last. That way, if I had to go to the emergency room, they'd already taken their turns.

All three of them boarded better than they had all summer, which didn't take much, since Lori had been putting us all to shame lately. At least, they looked good as far as I could tell. I was driving, not spotting, so the only glimpses I caught of them were in my rearview mirror as they hung upside down in mid-trick.

And the whole time, I had one eye on the girls' boat. They were never hard to spot. They stayed in one place, with Tammy and then Rachel in the water trying to pull up, and Lori driving and instructing them at the same time. I should have been over there helping her.

Or Cameron should, I thought bitterly.

Lori did not have one eye on me. I didn't know how long I could stand this panicky feeling as I watched her across the water, waiting and wishing for her to glance in my direction. Now I knew how my friends on the football team felt when they drove around town on the slim chance they might cruise by the cute girl they liked in the parking lot of the movie theater. I'd never felt that desperate about Lori. Ever since we were kids, she'd sat right beside me in the boat. We might not have been officially together until yesterday, but at least she'd always been nearby.

Now I couldn't even tell what she was saying to the

other girls. The topic had better be boarding. It had better not be dumping me for the next Vader brother on her list.

Or for Parker Buchanan. As if it weren't enough for my brothers to talk to Lori when I couldn't, Parker roared past in a ski boat with some of his rich, spoiled friends from Birmingham. His grandparents owned the snooty private yacht club a few miles downriver. Our marina had banded with the others to host the festival on the lake yesterday, but the yacht club topped us all every year by putting on an enormous Fourth of July fireworks show over the lake.

I'd known Parker for a while. He showed up to our parties sometimes, and rumor had it he was blazing a trail through the ladies. He had dark hair and dark eyes and a habit of staring through people with his eyeballs wide open and unblinking like an owl. Girls thought this was sexy. They said it was like he could see right through them into their souls. I thought it was one of the first signs of hyperthyroidism, but I kept it to myself.

I had no reason to dislike him. I'd never considered him a threat before. Usually he water-skied on the yacht club side of the lake. Usually he didn't venture this far from home. Usually he didn't slalom through our wakeboarding course while waving to my girlfriend. Usually she did not wave back. There was a first time for everything—everything awful, that is—and every bit of it was happening to me today.

Finally it was my turn to board. Parker disappeared around the bend. I had nobody left to take out my aggression on but my brothers. Instead of buckling on my board in the boat and flipping backward over the side like a scuba diver, as I normally would have, I waited for Cameron to crawl out of the water onto the deck in back. I pretended to slip while getting in, and I shoved him with my shoulder.

"Oh, man, you have pushed the wrong brother," he told me. I thought this was more of a jab at Sean than at me. I'd whipped Sean a couple of times recently.

Then Cameron pushed me so hard, my board slid all the way across the deck, and I smacked into the water on my ear.

I shook off the pain underwater and surfaced. Now Lori watched me from her boat. She was waiting for me to come up, either because she was concerned or because she was simply paying attention to me at the precise moment I didn't want it. She gave me a thumbs-up.

"Sunglasses." McGillicuddy stretched his open hand toward me.

"I won't lose them," I said. If I'd managed to keep them on during that dramatic entrance, they weren't in danger of falling off.

"Right," Cameron said. "You never lose them."

"Adam's sunglasses are piled up like buried treasure on the bottom of the lake," Lori giggled as her boat prowled slowly by ours, headed for shore. All three girls waved to us like beauty queens on a parade float. They must have been done for the day.

Her boat sped up then. Over her motor, McGillicuddy and Sean must not have heard Cameron murmur, "Talk about buried treasure," still looking straight at Lori.

I kicked off my board, pushed it ahead of me, and caught our boat in five strokes, just as McGillicuddy started the engine. All three of the guys snapped their heads in my direction in surprise as I pitched my board into the boat and pulled myself dripping over the side. Then I punched Cameron in the jaw.

It would have connected if I hadn't been wet and Cameron hadn't slathered himself in sunscreen. As it was, my fist slipped right off his face. I lost my balance and fell on the floor of the boat. Then he was on top of me, and I knew I was in trouble. But when he tried to pin my arms behind me, his hands slid right off too.

Before he could come after me again, a second set of flip-flops approached my nose and scuffled with Cameron's pair. McGillicuddy was pulling Cameron off me. And then Sean caught me in a headlock.

"We're taking impulsive to a new level, aren't we?"

Sean shouted in my ear, over the noise of the motor.

"He called Lori buried treasure!" I meant this for McGillicuddy. Since Sean held my head down, I had to yell as loudly as I could. "Cameron was looking at Lori and he said, 'Talk about buried treasure!'"

"You did?" I heard McGillicuddy say. All I could see was the boat's carpet. I could only imagine the look on his face.

"I wasn't talking about her!" Cameron bellowed.

"Then who the hell were you talking about?" Sean shrieked.

Sean had a point, for once. Cameron had been talking about my girlfriend and McGillicuddy's sister, or McGillicuddy's girlfriend, or Sean's ex-girlfriend, who Sean was very touchy about. There was nobody else in the girls' boat. The four of us guys used to comment on girls we saw drive by on the lake (with Lori in our boat too, rolling her eyes at us). Cameron had picked the wrong girls this time.

Furious as I was, I realized something else was wrong. Even though Sean still held my head down, I was the only one who thought to ask, "Who's driving the boat?"

Over the motor, I heard girls screaming at us the instant before we crashed.

The impact threw Sean off me. There was an awful

screeching. I scrambled up and saw everybody was on the floor now but me. I jumped into the driver's seat and threw the throttle into reverse.

Too late. We'd puttered into the marina and had hit one of the newer model speedboats. As I backed away from it, I saw the black mark our bumper had made up the side.

Worse, my dad stood on the wharf, watching. Funny how whenever I broke a bone, he had to be hunted up, but whenever we damaged the merchandise, he was on hand instantly. Glowering, he showed me his binoculars. Even from a distance, he'd seen everything. Then he pointed the binoculars at me. We'd been through this enough times that I knew what he meant. Whatever the speedboat and our boat needed, I would fix them. He headed back up the steps toward the showroom without a word.

Cameron and Sean moaned at me, rubbing it in.

As I idled the boat into the usual space and cut the engine, McGillicuddy picked up my broken sunglasses from underfoot and handed them to me. "Looks like that mark will come out with buffing."

"I hope." Bailing out of the boat onto the wharf, I tossed the sunglasses into the trash before Cameron and Sean could rib me any more about this awful day. I blinked in the darkness of the warehouse until I could see, and I grabbed the wax and a cloth. Then I blinked in the bright sunlight outside and thought I was hallucinating. My first break: Lori, Rachel, and Tammy had parked their boat and were talking to the guys on the wharf. I walked over, gripping the wax and cloth hard in each fist, hoping Lori wasn't flirting with Cameron again, or Sean. Maybe I should put the can of wax down before I found out. It could really hurt somebody.

"Adam," Lori called, loudly enough for me to hear her, but not so loud that her voice would carry up to my mom in the marina office—or to her dad, who might be listening from their screened porch facing the water. "I came over to get some tips from the boys about teaching Tammy and Rachel to board. Of *course* I did not come over here to see you. How could you think such a thing? That would be disobedient."

I held up the wax. "For my own disobedience, I have to buff the boat. Then I'm going for a jog."

She tilted her head. Probably her eyes widened, but I couldn't see them behind her sunglasses. I hated not being able to see her eyes. She asked, "In this heat?"

I didn't mind jogging in the heat. The heat was a big, friendly animal that liked to wrestle and only occasionally sat on me until I lost my breath. Anyway, she was missing the point. I repeated carefully, "I am *going* for a *jog*."

"I *heard* you the *first* time," she said. "It's late afternoon in the middle of June. It's ninety-five degrees out here."

"He means he's *going* for a *jog*," Rachel and Tammy said at the same time.

"He's *going* for a *jog*." Lori still didn't get it. Normally her blondeness was one of the things I loved about her. At the moment, not so much.

Exasperated, Cameron told her, "Adam wants *you* to go for a jog too."

She said, "Oh!"

"If you two airheads have to hook up secretly for very long," Sean said, "you're not going to make it."

"Like you're an expert on making relationships work," Rachel piped up.

Now Cameron and McGillicuddy moaned, rubbing in the jab at Sean. I couldn't help but chime in. And when I saw the look Sean gave me, I regretted it. I didn't expect him to be on my side against my parents, but I hoped he wouldn't go out of his way to sabotage me. And sabotage was more likely if he and Rachel stayed broken up and he stewed in his own juices.

Lori was thinking the same thing—eyeing me, or so I thought. I desperately wanted to reach down from the wharf and take those sunglasses off her. She asked me, "Not that I have any interest in this whatsoever, but how long will it take you to buff the boat?"

"An hour," I said.

"Thirty minutes," McGillicuddy said. "I'll help him. Then I'm taking Tammy bowling, so if you go for a jog, I won't be around to see it."

Lori mouthed a *thank you* to her brother. "Okay then. Thanks for the wakeboarding tips, guys." She started the engine and cranked the throttle into reverse.

"Wait a minute," Rachel protested over the idling engine and the bubbling lake. "I thought we would really get some wakeboarding tips."

"Are you kidding?" Lori shouted. "You chicks are hopeless." Rachel and Tammy laughed with her as the boat floated backward and then idled forward, toward her dock.

We watched them go. McGillicuddy stared at Tammy's ass in that bikini. Sean pined after Rachel. Cameron seemed astounded at the whole sight—Lori had never entertained girlfriends before—but it was impossible to tell which girl he was looking at.

And I decided that if I ever went out with Lori again, I would install ten or twelve alarm clocks in the truck to wake us up, just in case. Being grounded from her was torture.

Finally McGillicuddy said, "I'll go get some wax."

"Thanks, man." I appreciated him helping me meet with Lori.

"Better you than Cameron," McGillicuddy grumbled. "I know where Cameron's been."

Sean snorted.

Cameron said, "I already told you, I did *not* come on to Lori."

He'd better not.

Half an hour later, I snagged two bottles of water from the fridge. I should have taken only one in case I was intercepted. But even though Lori and I had kissed a lot in the past week, Lori was squeamish about drinking after me. We'd shared drinks while riding around in my truck. She'd even used my toothbrush once. And I'd seen her hesitate. Probably because Sean had spit in her Coke ten years ago. If I were her, I would be grossed out for a long time too.

Then I headed outside. The heat of the afternoon would take your breath away, but after the frigid air-conditioned house, my skin drank it in. I stuck the bottles of water in the mailbox, which couldn't be seen from my house or Lori's through the thick trees. She wasn't at the road. Since hanging around our mailboxes would look guilty, she'd probably set off jogging. She was fast for a girl, but I could catch her.

Which way had she gone? We should have discussed this before. But if we'd agreed to go to the left or the right, she would have messed it up anyway. I gazed down the street dappled in shade, then turned the other way and jogged into the sun.

Normally I ran to detox my brain when Sean made me so mad I couldn't think straight. This happened once a day or so. Running got my mind off my troubles.

This time, running did not get my mind off Lori. For one thing, the skull-and-crossbones pendant she'd given me banged against my breastbone with every step. I didn't want to take it off, though. For another thing, when I finished this run, she would be at the end of it.

Three miles later, I'd returned to the mailboxes. That's when I saw her jogging toward me from the other direction. Her blonde ponytail bobbed behind her. She wore nothing but a sports bra and very small running shorts, and her tanned skin shone with sweat. It was almost as good as seeing her in the bikini. Better, in a way. Lori's body was most beautiful in action.

Lori's brain, as usual, was a couple of steps behind her body. I swear she stared straight ahead without seeing me for a full ten seconds, listening hard to her music, daydreaming.

Then she broke into the biggest smile. She pulled out her earbuds and stuffed the cords into the armband that held the player. "Mr. Vader!" she called in the awful British accent she used when she thought somebody was mad at her. "We shan't meet like this anon. 'Tisn't proper."

It was hard to stay angry. I did my best. "We weren't even apart for twelve hours, and you flirted with Parker Buchanan."

"I *waved* to Parker Buchanan."

"You flirted with Cameron."

"I knew you'd say that." She reached me and put her hands on her hips, breathing hard. "He sat close to me in the boat so we could hear each other over the motor."

I believed her. The thing was—and I knew this was unreasonable—I didn't want her talking to Cameron at all.

She bent over and put her hands on her knees. This gave me a nice view down her bra. "Cameron and I were talking about *you*," she panted. "He said that you—" She straightened and looked around us at the woods. "We need to talk, and we can't do it out here."

I stared her down, trying to stay mad at her, trying not to glance at her boobs.

She tilted her head to one side and grinned. "You're sexy when you brood."

I pressed my lips together.

"You're cute when you try not to laugh." She tickled my ribs, which were more ticklish than usual because I wasn't wearing a shirt.

I grabbed her hand. With the middle finger of my other hand, I traced the neckline of her bra. I asked appreciatively, "Sports bra or what?"

Her green eyes widened, the same color as the wild trees behind her, and her lips parted.

Suddenly it was too hot, even for me. We stood on an asphalt road that had been melting in the sun all day. I could hardly breathe the thick air. Her heartbeat raced under my fingertip.

I put my hand down. Then I walked over to the mailbox and slid out the bottles of water. "Do you ever get the feeling you're being watched?" I asked, handing her a bottle.

"Our parents may have mounted closed-circuit cameras in the poison ivy." She uncapped the water and took a long drink.

"I wouldn't put it past my mom at this point." I drank too, then poured water over my head. Then poured some over hers.

She sputtered. "My hair just blew around a boat for nine hours, and I ran a few miles on the hottest day of the year. You're ruining my look."

"You'll dry in thirty seconds in this heat." I touched one finger to her wet lips. "And you're beautiful. You'd have to work pretty hard to mess that up."

She moved her head ever so slightly. Her lips slid one

millimeter against my fingertip, and electricity rushed through my whole body. I lost my breath again.

"Come on," I choked out. With one last glance around our empty yards and the deserted road, I took her hand and pulled her away from our houses, toward the woods.

5

Adam let my hand go when we reached the side of the road. Blackberry brambles crowded the bank. As we tried to find a way through, it was every delinquent teenager for herself, apparently.

Out of habit I plucked a few berries and popped them into my mouth. Too late I remembered we were headed for a tryst in the forest together, not playing army with pinecone grenades and our brothers. I should not eat before kissing.

But three steps ahead of me, he plucked some berries on the fly too. Maybe this afternoon wasn't as strange as I thought. Maybe we really were headed into the trees for a discussion, as I'd suggested. It was innocent after all. Relieved and disappointed, I bit down on the blackberries. Sweet juice filled my mouth, and then the bitter aftertaste.

I picked a few more berries as I passed. Just as my cheeks puffed out to full capacity in mid-chew, Adam found a break through the thicket and up the hill. He turned around and extended his hand to help me up.

I froze, staring at him in the thick heat, leaves tickling my legs. Boys did not help girls. Not in my experience, anyway. When I was one of the boys, they tromped ahead of me and never once looked back to see if I was still there, much less in need of assistance. Boys had helped me only recently, when they wanted something.

No, this walk through the woods would not be innocent.

Taking his hand, I said, "Fank woo."

"Hm," he laughed with his mouth closed.

We crashed through the forest. Since we were sneaking this time together, it seemed like we should have tiptoed along, but there was no way to walk quietly through dry leaves. It also seemed like his brothers and my brother would jump out from behind a bush at any second, or that a snake would fall heavily across my shoulders. Once Sean and Cameron had told me a story about snakes in the jungle dropping down on people from trees. Then they hid in Adam's tree house with a rubber snake and waited for me to pass by underneath. If I had not been six years old at the time and in perfect health, I would have had a heart attack.

The suspense was too much. We'd walked far enough. We couldn't see the road or the houses that we'd reach if we kept going. The dark trunks of maples and oaks surrounded us, and the late afternoon sun made the green leaves glow overhead. I stopped behind a huge pine—keeping it between me and the road, because it offered extra protection from the prying eyes of boys and parents—and pulled Adam in front of me. "What I wanted to talk to you about was—"

He kissed me. At first he gently touched his lips to mine. The more exciting development was that in order to do this, he'd stepped very close. His chest was an inch from mine. I could feel his heat. He tasted of blackberries. He leaned even closer and braced his muscular arms on the tree on either side of me.

When he broke the kiss to take a breath, I whispered, "Tree hugger."

He opened his eyes, blue as the afternoon sky, and gave me this *look*. A combination of amusement and exasperation and hunger. He looked like a teenager making out in the woods. Puzzling through this, I realized that I was gazing at him from the perspective of a six-year-old girl playing army and dodging rubber snakes.

But he *was* this teenager, and so was I. I felt the same need for him that he felt for me, like a force was drawing me forward into his heat. I just didn't know how to say it.

He cupped my chin with his big hand and watched me. He breathed hard through his nose. His shoulders heaved way harder than they should have after a few minutes of kissing. I was about to suggest some additional conditioning exercises before football season started. I opened my mouth to tell him.

He kissed me again. His tongue passed my lips and played across my teeth. We'd only been kissing like this for a week, but it seemed very natural when I kissed him back the same way. My body was on autopilot as I reached blindly for his waist and dragged him even closer, his torso skin-to-skin with mine against the tree. Who *were* we? I was turning into any of the assorted older girls who'd been seen leaving the cab of Sean's truck at night. I'd always viewed those girls with a mixture of awe and derision. Sexual attraction was funny. Lust was hilarious.

Now, not so much. Those girls had my sympathy, because I totally got it. I ran my fingers lightly up Adam's bare back.

He gasped.

I opened my eyes to see if I'd done something wrong. He still touched the tree, but his muscles were taut, holding on to it for dear life. His eyes were closed. He rubbed his rough cheek slowly against mine. I had done nothing wrong. He was *savoring*.

I knew how he felt. Tracing my fingernails down his back again, I whispered, "Stubble or what?"

Eyes still closed, he chuckled. "I'm not shaving until our parents let us date again." He kissed my cheek.

"What if it takes . . . a . . . while?" I asked, struggling to talk. He'd made his way down to my neck. His tongue circled there slowly. "There are only six or seven weeks until August football practice starts, right?"

"Hm." His mouth moved up my neck, toward my ear. *Oh.*

"Will you be able to stuff your beard into your helmet?" I croaked.

In answer, he put his lips on my ear. I forgot the next joke I'd planned to make and lost myself in Adam.

I know this is hard to believe. We had a lot to worry about. My dad was threatening never to let us date again. And we were making out in broad daylight, with mockingbirds calling to each other and cicadas buzzing in the trees. We'd watched a lot of DVDs with our brothers over the years—or I had, and Adam had wandered in and out because he couldn't sit still. We'd made fun of couples who suddenly decided to make out when they'd just escaped from a hoard of alien robots bent on killing them and taking their brains back to their home planet or an insidious, sentient slime that would hunt them down and eat through their flesh to their skeletons in a matter of seconds. Who could concentrate on kissing in these situations?

Now I understood. Adam kissed his way from my ear to my mouth. He hooked one thumb in the waistband of my shorts. I kissed him harder.

I enjoyed it. *Really* enjoyed it. But in the back of my mind, I worried that if we were gone too long, our parents would find us. And I still hadn't had a private talk with him.

I pushed him away. "We need to go before our parents wise up," I panted.

He came right back for more, regaining his balance and bracing his arms on both sides of me again, caging me in. "I was just getting started," he growled in my ear.

I giggled. I'd never pegged myself as a giggler, but when Adam acted like this I couldn't help it. "Why couldn't you get started last night?"

"I was *sleeping*," he said haughtily. He buried his face in my hair and sniffed deeply. I hoped this was not too unpleasant an experience after all the running.

That was fine. I would have stood there all day and let him sniff my hair. He could take care of himself. But I couldn't shake the feeling we were running out of time.

"Seriously, Adam, we need to talk while we can." I put my hand on his bare chest and pushed him six inches away, where he couldn't reach my hair anymore.

He gazed down at my hand.

"I was talking to Cameron—," I began.

Adam grasped my wrist with two fingers, like he didn't really want to touch it, and removed my hand from his chest.

"—about how rude you were to your mom when she offered to help us," I finished. "Frances had heard about it too. I know you're mad, Adam, but it doesn't make sense for you to dig a deeper hole for both of us."

He scowled down at me. "I'm right and my mother is wrong."

"I know . . ." I almost called him "baby." *I know, baby.* I caught myself in time. Then I wondered why I'd caught myself. It just seemed foreign for this endearment to come out of my mouth. To Adam. And he would not have appreciated it, anyway. After sixteen years as the baby of the family, he did not consider it a compliment.

"I know," I said again. "But Cameron said your mom would help us if we stay apart for a while first. In the meantime, if you can keep from cussing in front of her, I have a plan that might convince my dad to let us date a lot faster."

He put his hand on my shoulder. "You make terrible, terrible plans."

"Hey," I protested. "One of my plans caught you, didn't it?"

"Yeah, but you meant to catch Sean." He took his hand off my shoulder.

I waved his concerns away, along with a cloud of gnats that had found us in the forest. "You're getting lost in the details. Keep the big picture in mind. The plan is, I will find someone to date who is a hundred times worse than you. You will be the lesser of two evils. My dad will see the error of his ways in banning me from dating you, and he'll let us get back together."

Adam nodded.

I nodded with him, grinning. "Good, huh?"

He kept nodding, but his mouth drew into a tight line. "This person you want to date. It's Sean."

"Sean!" I exclaimed. Sean hadn't even crossed my mind. "No! I was thinking about Kevin Ye. Do you know him? He's two years older than us, but he was in my driver's ed class last year because he'd flunked it twice. I'm pretty sure he didn't graduate, what with prison and all. Anyway, one day last week when you and I were driving into town, I saw him mowing the grass with a work-release crew. Maybe I could even convince him to wear his orange jumpsuit on our date. That would *really* impress my dad. Do you think Kevin Ye would go out with me?"

Adam's hand was over his mouth, hiding his baby beard. But his light blue eyes widened with horror. I did not want him horrified. He would be difficult enough to drag into the plan as it was. Instead of just the skull and crossbones around his neck, he needed a more specific warning label that said DOES NOT TAKE DIRECTION WELL.

I wasn't giving up. The plan was a good one. I could be flexible and change the details until Adam agreed to play along.

"You're probably right," I said. "Forget Kevin Ye. Sean would be easier."

"I knew it!" Adam pointed at me. "You were trying to get Sean this whole time."

I narrowed my eyes at him. "What are you saying? I planned to get Sean, I got you instead, but I was always aiming for Sean, and now I'm going in for the kill?"

"You don't fool me. You *play* dumb, but you made an A in trig. You're diabolical without even trying."

I folded my arms on my sports bra. "I'm pretty sure that's a contradiction in terms, but remind me to look up 'diabolical' later."

He put his fists on his hips, which made the bare, tanned

chest in front of me look even broader. "I won't be able to give you that reminder, Lori, because we're not allowed to see each other, and you'll be out with Sean."

"What is this business with Sean?" I insisted. "I thought you and Sean worked everything out. I saw y'all talking Saturday night."

"Worked everything out? I guess. We agreed that he would not interfere when I tried to get you back, and I would not interfere when he tried to get Rachel back."

"Oh." I'd thought they'd talked about something more meaningful and brotherly, like how Sean had mistreated Adam for sixteen years and how Adam had begun to strike back in a big way. I'd *hoped* they had, because it would have meant Sean might help Adam and me out of our latest pre-dicament. But this was too much to ask. Before that night, I'd never seen Sean and Adam voluntarily have a talk with each other. Ever.

"Well, fine," I said. "I won't go out with Sean either."

We both jumped when a bird burst from a dogwood near us and soared away. Adam watched it as it went. I watched Adam. He tracked the bird with his eyes, chin lifted as if he'd regained his dignity. I expected the next thing out of his mouth to be an apology for doubting me.

What he said was, "Who's your next choice? Cameron?"

Brilliant! I hardly even registered the sarcasm in Adam's

voice. I snapped my fingers. "That's not a bad idea. Cameron's three years older than me. He's about to be a sophomore in *college*. My dad will pass out. He'll be so happy to have me dating a high school junior again! Even if it's you."

"Plus, you and Cameron are so familiar with each other anyway, since you've already made out." His blue eyes accused me. This time his sarcasm was hard for me to gloss over.

Exasperated, I put my hands in my hair, which was a mistake because it was up in a ponytail. I only managed more of a tousled, cornered-by-my-boyfriend's-superior-logic look before putting my hands down. "Adam, we did not make out. We kissed once, when I was *eleven*. I should never have told you that." I really never would have told him if I'd had any idea he would be my boyfriend a week later and he would throw it back in my face. "I am trying to solve this problem for both of us, and all you can do is be unreasonable and furious about everything."

"I don't think it's unreasonable for me to not want you to date my brothers or a freaking convicted felon," Adam said. "What did Kevin Ye get arrested for, anyway? Didn't he steal a car?"

"He stole the driver's ed car." I laughed. Then I saw how Adam was looking at me. "He gave it back."

"They *make* you give stuff back, Lori, after they arrest you for stealing it."

I opened my mouth to respond. I was going to say something about Kevin passing driver's ed the third time he took it, despite his brush with the law. But now Adam was giving me a look that said, *I know you are not about to defend Kevin Ye.* I closed my mouth.

Adam sighed through his nose, disgusted. "I can't believe you're trying to plan your way out of this. What we do together is none of our parents' goddamn business, and if you try to work around what they say, you're just giving in."

"I'm not. It's a means to an end. You have to think like them, Adam." I poked at my head to signify *thinking*. "Think like a middle-aged man with OCD, a dead wife, and a teenage daughter. Think like a woman with three teenage sons who once ran a golf cart into the side of their granddad's house."

"Cameron and Sean shouldn't have let me drive," Adam said in his own defense. "I was seven."

"You shouldn't have *asked* to drive. You were seven."

"And I don't see why we can't just run away to Montgomery."

This idea sounded as ridiculous now as it had when he'd first suggested it last night. But the sentiment behind it—that was very sweet. As we'd argued, Adam had moved several feet away from me across the forest floor, and I'd backed against the tree. When we stood this far apart, it was hard to remember we were arguing because we wanted to be together.

Boosting myself off the tree with one running shoe, I closed the space between us, put my hand on his arm, and stuck out my bottom lip in sympathy. "I'd like to graduate from high school first."

He looked down at my hand on his arm and muttered, "I'm not graduating from high school anyway."

I stepped even closer, put my other hand on his arm, and fluttered my eyelashes at him. I was getting good at this, if I did say so myself. "I told you I'd help you in chemistry next year."

Stubbornly he held onto his anger. He didn't touch me. But he didn't back away or shake my hands off his arm, either. He said, "Even if your plan worked and they let us date again, the next time we did something wrong—"

"Why would we ever do anything else wrong? We would be very careful."

"Lori. This is you we're talking about. And me."

I laughed. "I see your point."

"The next time we did something wrong, they'd just tell us again that we couldn't date."

I stroked my thumbs across the golden hair on his tanned arm. "Not if we convince them that we're meant to be together."

"I'm not sure we are anymore."

I looked down at the diamond and pearl ring that my mother had left to me, which my dad gave me for my birthday yesterday. Of course we were meant to be together. My mother had seen this and as much as told me this before she died. It had just been a matter of me seeing this for myself. But if *Adam* didn't believe it anymore . . . I looked up at him in confusion. "You're not?"

"Not if you're that desperate to go out with Sean."

I pulled my hands off his arm. "So this is what it's about. You're still mad about Sean. What happened to what you told me a few days ago, that you've been in love with me forever?"

"*You've* been in love with *Sean* forever, and you expect me to believe you've switched from him to me in the past week, just like that?"

I'd had enough of this. If he didn't trust me when I said I wanted him and not Sean, what kind of boyfriend was he? I would tell him we should break up, as if my dad hadn't broken us up already. Things would be so much easier this way. We could enjoy the rest of the summer. Our dating ban wouldn't matter anymore, and we could go back to being friends and pretend we'd never gotten together. I hoped. Someday.

And then, something happened. The sunlight filtering

through the leaves shifted on his face. He looked different. This boy I'd been staring at in disbelief and deciding to break up with . . . I knew it was Adam. I was in the middle of an argument with Adam. But in the dim forest light, he didn't look like Adam. He didn't even look like Sean, who was so much like Adam in appearance but was two years older.

This time, as Adam pierced me with those light blue eyes and privileged me with the full view of his tanned, muscular chest and the golden stubble on his face—I couldn't quite get over the stubble—he reminded me of the senior football players whom I'd brought water and bandages to with the rest of the girls' tennis team last fall. Boys I'd considered so dreamy and so much older than me that I'd never have a chance with them, so why try?

It occurred to me that August football practice *did* begin in six or seven weeks. School would start a few weeks after that. With Sean a freshman off at college, Adam would be out of his shadow for the first time—the only Vader brother left in town. Adam would likely start for the varsity football team. He would get noticed. And he would no longer be my property all day every day like he was during the summer. I would have to share him with the other girls in my high school, including every flirtatious ditz in the lower sections of math, where he always got stuck.

I couldn't break up with him. I couldn't watch him date another girl, or a series of them, for the rest of high school. I would regret it for the rest of my life.

And I couldn't afford to argue with him like this. I had to convince my dad to lift the Adam ban before the summer was over. *And* I had to convince Adam the plan was worth it.

Unfortunately, Adam couldn't read my mind. "You know what?" he asked. "Screw this." He turned on his running shoe and crashed through the fallen leaves, toward the road. He must have thought I had no defense for switching from Sean to him so fast.

I had to fix this. But jogging after him, clinging to his arm, and begging him to be reasonable would not convince him I was a terrific catch myself, one worth all this trouble. So I used a little strategy, joking my way back into his good graces. "You have no right to dis my plan," I called after him. "Your idea of a plan is to grow a beard."

"Hey. It's a lot harder than it looks. I've only been shaving for a year."

Good. He was joking back. That meant my humor was working on him.

Bad. He didn't even call this over his shoulder to me. He yelled it facing forward as he stomped through the forest. I could hardly hear him. My humor was not working well enough.

I skipped after him until I caught up. I kept pace beside him, which was difficult. He was much taller than I was, with a longer stride, and he maintained a straight course while I had to dodge around bushes and briars.

"This is good," I panted. "We're both awful actors, as we've established. If we're genuinely angry with each other, we won't have to fake being broken up."

He never slowed down. I practically ran beside him. Branches slapped my face. Acting genuinely angry was getting easier, and I may have forgotten some of my resolve to patch things up with him. "While we're at it," I said, "why don't you call me a bitch like you did a couple of nights ago?"

"Why don't I call you a slut for hooking up with me just to get Sean?" he snapped.

"Why don't I call *you* a slut for hooking up with a different girl every month for the past year?" I yelled at him. "I'll bet your so-called Secret Make-Out Hideout isn't even a secret. You've had your license for three weeks. You probably took Rachel there before you took me."

He stopped, finally, and gave me a shocked look. Ha— he could dish out the jealous accusations, but he couldn't take them.

But I didn't want to one-up Adam. I wanted to be with him and make out with him again, preferably sooner rather than later. "Hey." I reached over to grab his hand.

Before I could touch him, he dodged away and jogged ahead again. We'd reached the edge of the forest. He barreled right through the blackberry brambles and onto the road.

"Adam," I called, determined he wouldn't get away before we could talk this out. I ran after him, hardly noticing the briars scratching my legs. I emerged onto the road in bright sunlight and the full glare of my dad and Frances, who were holding hands.

My first thought when I saw them was, *Why are they walking together?* Frances was supposed to be my dad's employee. I was used to seeing them talking, but never touching. Then I remembered Frances had not been my nanny for years, and she and my dad were dating as of yesterday. My second thought was, *Why are they walking in this heat? Nobody in their right mind would be out exercising in this heat.* And—by now you are figuring out I am a little slow on the uptake—only my third thought was, *Busted.*

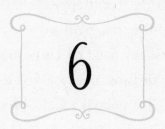

6

The instant I saw Lori's dad and Frances across the hot asphalt road, I spun around, hoping Lori was still hidden by the trees.

She stood right behind me, in full view. And if my expression matched hers, we couldn't have looked more guilty.

I turned back around. Her dad's face was even worse. Glaring at me, he worked his jaw like he was going to say something, but he wanted to make sure he'd thought of the worst possible insult first. He turned redder and seemed to swell, like all his holes were plugged up and the pressure had nowhere to escape.

He opened his mouth.

"It was my fault," I said quickly.

"I know!" he roared.

At the same time, Lori stepped in front of me and muttered, "Wrong thing to say, Adam."

"Right." I put my hand on Lori's shoulder and pushed her an arm's length away so it wouldn't look like I was hiding behind her. "It's nobody's fault, because we didn't do anything wrong."

Her dad brought his hands together and popped a knuckle.

"Trevor," Frances said soothingly, rubbing her hand on his back. But she was looking hard at *me* over her glasses, telling me upstanding citizens did not act this way. When we were kids, that look from Frances could make Lori and her brother behave, and sometimes even my brothers, but I never seemed to get the message.

"I saw you coming out of the woods," Lori's dad shouted at me. "Together!"

"We weren't rolling in the leaves or anything. Look, no evidence." I put my other hand on Lori's other shoulder and turned her around backward, hoping against hope she didn't have scratches from the tree on her bare back, or bark on her butt.

"Get your hands off my daughter."

Either I jerked away from her at the force of his words, or she started out from under my hands. I wasn't sure which. She and Frances and I stared at Lori's dad in horror. He was excitable, yes, and he had yelled at me before, yes, but always about safety issues. He thought I was going to set his house on fire with bottle rockets or run my four-wheeler into his Beamer again. When he hollered at me about that stuff, his voice pitched into a whine like a woman.

This was not that voice. This was a full-bodied boom that meant business. He looked and sounded like a big dog defending his territory.

"Here's what you did wrong, Adam," he barked. "I told your parents to make it clear to you that you were not to see Lori again. You did it anyway. That's what you did wrong."

"But—," I started.

"Shhh," Lori said beside me.

"That's—," I started again.

"Shut up," Lori muttered.

"—ridiculous," I finished.

"Adam, stop talking," Lori said.

"Adam, stop talking," Frances repeated.

I knew I was only getting myself in more trouble. Lori's dad unballed and balled his fists, daring me to talk back. I was beyond caring. I was right and he was wrong. I said,

"Of course I'm going to see her. I live next door."

"Not for long," he shouted. "Lori, go with Frances. Go home."

I balled my own fists then. Now it sounded like *Lori* was a dog.

Lori gave me a wide-eyed warning look, then obediently jogged a few steps forward and walked with Frances toward her house.

Her dad turned to me. "You. Follow me."

"Woof," I said.

Lori and Frances both stopped under the trees and looked back at me. We all half expected Lori's dad to really blow his top this time.

He didn't. His balled fists expanded into claws that wanted to strangle me. Then he turned without a word and headed for my house.

Lori widened her eyes at me and nodded after her dad, urging me to go on. Frances pointed at him and gave me the stern nanny look.

I followed. But I let him get a good thirty feet ahead of me so he'd worry. That far away, he couldn't hear my footsteps across the pine needles. He kept looking over his shoulder to make sure I hadn't escaped. We continued past my house, all the way down to the marina. He waited for me outside the office door with his arms folded. When I caught up with him, he swung open the office door, ready to feed me to my parents.

But the office was empty. He pointed me inside. I slouched past him and collapsed into my mother's desk chair. I'd been so keyed up for a shouting match, I was almost disappointed it was delayed. For a few minutes, anyway.

"Stay." He glared at me a moment more, then closed me inside the office while he went to look for my parents.

I stared at the painted metal door. Sean had drawn a smiley face on it in WD-40 when I was eight and he was ten. He blamed it on me, and Mom believed him. The huge greasy smile in the faded paint never would wash out— believe me, I'd tried. I'd been forced to try. Now it taunted me. Going in the woods with Lori had been my idea. Going parking with her last night had been my idea, too. I knew that, and yet all my troubles pointed back to Sean.

On impulse, I rolled the chair closer to the desk, snagged the phone, and punched in Rachel's number. If it hadn't been for Lori, I could have been into Rachel. As it was, I'd only gone out with her last month for the same reason I went out with any girl: to have some fun, but also hoping that Lori was watching and that she would finally get jealous. I liked Rachel, though. I felt bad about using her until she cheated on me with Sean. Afterward, I figured she deserved whatever she got, because of her infidelity and extremely poor taste.

She must have recognized the marina office number on her cell phone and thought it might be Sean, because her voice sounded tight, like she could hardly contain herself. "Hello?"

"It's only me." I hadn't meant to disappoint her.

"Hey, Adam!" she squealed. She didn't want me to feel bad for making her feel bad. Which was cute and all. Rachel was a really nice person. But if I'd gone into the woods with Rachel and then called Lori, Lori would have answered with a cackle and a "So, did you get some?" I missed her already.

"Hey," I said. I was lucky Rachel had answered her phone. Now that I had her, I needed to get what I wanted from her as quickly as I could. Lori would call her soon for a girl talk about what an idiot I was for not going along with her plan. I had to get Rachel on my side now, before my dad came in and grabbed me. "What's up with you and Sean?"

"What do you mean?" she snapped. "Did he say something about me?"

Just as I'd suspected. "He didn't say a word," I admitted.

She let out a little huff of frustration. "Then why do you think there's something up between us?"

"Not *between* you," I said. "It's all one-sided. You got mad at him and broke up with him last week. He came groveling back to you but you blew him off. You expected him to crawl back again. He hasn't. He talked to you at the festival yesterday but he didn't ask you out. Am I right?"

"Well." Her voice pitched even higher as she got upset. "I broke up with him because it seemed like he only wanted to date me to make you mad. After we broke up, I thought he would take a few days and realize how wrong he'd been, and then he'd beg to have me back and he'd appreciate me more. I never thought I would break up with him and he would shrug and say, 'Okay'!"

"I can tell," I said. "You pranced around in your bikini at the lake this afternoon and he *still* didn't ask you out. He is not acting like the boys you've dated before at *all*."

"You can lose the superior tone, Adam Vader," she said sternly. "The last boy I dated before Sean was you." She paused. "Of course, you only asked me out to make Lori jealous."

I laughed. Not a desperate-about-my-girlfriend laugh, but a cavalier laugh like Sean's. I felt ill. "That's why I'm calling."

"You want to make Lori jealous again?" Rachel guessed. "The two of you have enough problems."

"Tell me about it." The sick feeling grew. I winced at

another of those pangs in my stomach, just like this morning when I found out I was banned from Lori. Then I said,
"Lori still likes Sean."

"She does not!" Rachel squealed. I heard her swallow.
She said more calmly, "She does not, Adam. She likes you.
You should have heard her talking about you on the boat
this afternoon."

You should have heard her talking about Sean in the woods,
I thought. "Here's the thing. She's forming this plan—"

"Uh-oh," Rachel said.

"—to date other guys until I don't look so awful to her
dad."

"But she's not dating *Sean*," Rachel said.

"Not yet," I admitted. "But she will. If this goes on
long enough, I promise you she will."

"I don't believe it," Rachel said. "And even if I did—"
I had her.

"—what could I do about it?"

"Nothing yet," I said. "But when the time comes, I
want you to be prepared. I may ask you to do something
that would help me keep Lori interested or to send Sean
your way." I felt guilty as I said this. Sean and I *had* promised to stay out of each other's way when it came to Lori
and Rachel.

I talked myself out of it. I could count on one hand the

number of promises to me that Sean had kept.

In fact, upon further reflection, I couldn't think of a single one.

"I don't know," Rachel said. "Lori and I haven't been friends very long. I wouldn't feel right, going behind her back like that."

"She'll forgive you," I said. "She's very forgiving. And you'd be doing her good. You want to keep her away from Sean, don't you? He's bad news."

Rachel giggled at this. She'd always giggled at pretty much everything I said—another thing I liked about her. She was easy to please. This went a long way toward explaining her infatuation with Sean. I chuckled along with her, even though I was dead serious.

She quieted down and asked, "You think I'm an idiot for liking him, don't you?"

"No. I think you have the same taste as every other girl at our high school. I don't understand that big belt over the long shirt, either."

"It's called a tunic."

"It's called ugly. And one more thing."

She sighed. "What."

"Don't tell Lori you've been to my secret make-out hide-out. If she asks you about it, tell her that you and I never went there."

"Why would she care?" Rachel asked. "You and I went there when *we* were dating, before you and Lori got together."

"Yeah, but she thinks she was the first, and I didn't tell her otherwise."

Rachel was quiet for a few moments. In the background I could hear her little sisters yelling at each other about something. If she was trying to figure out how boys' minds worked, she was way out of her element. She was no Lori.

Finally she said, "I don't want to lie to her. Like I told you, she and I haven't been friends very lo—"

I interrupted her before she went any farther down that high-and-mighty path. Time to play the sympathy card, which never worked on Lori but was a sure thing with every other girl I knew. "Lori and I are going through a tough time right now. You would be helping, not hurting. Please help me, Rachel."

"It just doesn't make any sense," she said weakly. "I thought you *did* want to make her jealous. If you want me to conceal from her that I've been to your hideout, it sounds like you *don't* want to make her jealous."

"I don't want to make her jealous *yet*," I explained. "She hasn't gone out with Sean *yet*. Right now I want her to feel special, like she's the only girl I ever introduced to my secret make-out hideout. It's only after she goes out with Sean that I'm going to pull the rug out from under her."

"Adam Vader," Rachel said. "I had no idea you were so sneaky."

"Right. That makes me even sneakier. Deal?"

We hung up, and I felt guilty all over again. I *was* worried about Lori going out with Sean, but I was actually more worried Lori would discover she wasn't the first to experience the secret make-out hideout. I wished she *had* been the first and I'd never taken Rachel there. I didn't want to see Lori's face when she found out otherwise.

I could have admitted this to Rachel. Maybe I should have. But I didn't trust her after she'd cheated on me with Sean.

Of course, she was right that I'd only gone out with her to make Lori jealous. She had no reason to trust me, either. We made perfect partners in crime.

Suddenly I realized how tense I was, leaning forward and gripping the edge of the metal desk with both hands. I leaned back in the chair. This didn't relax me any. I found myself staring up at the bulletin board over the desk. Tacked to it were business cards for boat sales reps, a diagram of an F/A-18 Hornet that Cameron had drawn when he was about ten (and I thought he was so impossibly old), the schedule for everybody who worked at the marina (Lori was under Sean, I noticed with annoyance), and a brochure for a military boarding school. I'd almost forgotten my parents were thinking about sending me away.

I'd told Lori's dad he couldn't keep me from seeing Lori because I lived next door. When he'd said, "Not for long," that's what he must have meant. That's what he was talking to my parents about right now.

They wouldn't do that to me. Would they?

No, they wouldn't. Not yet. Not just because Lori's dad told them to.

But the threat was there. Last year when I was flunking chemistry, my mom started investigating schools. She'd asked Lori's dad about it because he had a fraternity brother who'd gone to one, and who might be able to get me into a good one for those of us with ADHD, instead of one full of actual juvenile delinquents. This was my mother's fear—that if she sent me away to clean up my act, I'd actually become more corrupted and learn to pick locks better. It was all the same to me. Prison was prison.

I'd brought up my chemistry grade by the end of the semester, though. I hadn't improved my test scores, but the longer the class went on, the more our grade was based on lab. I was *excellent* at lab. Unlike every nerdy girl in the class and half the guys, I was not afraid of the Bunsen burner.

I'd worked my ass off for that C, all for nothing.

This office had no windows.

I jumped up from the tiny chair, kicked open the door, and escaped from my cell.

Around the side of the warehouse, I fished my football out of the bushes. I jogged about ten yards up the boat ramp, aimed carefully, and fired a pass at one of the huge metal doors.

BANG.

Bull's-eye. I ran after the ball and stopped it before it rolled into the yard and down the hill into the lake. I jogged back up the ramp with it and let another pass fly.

BANG.

If Lori's dad had found my parents in the warehouse and they were looking for me now, the noise would notify them of my whereabouts. I didn't care. The more passes I threw, the better I felt.

BANG.

"Adam!" my dad roared. The sun was setting now. From where I stood on the ramp, the corner of the warehouse appeared to cut the huge orange sun exactly in half. My dad walked toward me out of that orange glow, like the devil. He hiked up the ramp and stopped near me, stroking his beard.

I can't repeat in mixed company any of what he said to me. However, I can convey the general import of the message by replacing the word I shouldn't have said in front of my mother with the word "monkey." I hate monkeys.

"Son," he said, "you monkeyed up."

"I know." I put off the rest of this conversation by running after the football again. But when I returned to my starting spot, he was still there.

"Now, I'm not going to send you to military school just because Trevor McGillicuddy has his panties in a wad."

"Thanks," I said.

BANG.

He raised his voice. "But the reason I *will* send you is the reason your mama and I were discussing it in the first place. You have absolutely no monkeying self-control. None."

"Thanks for nothing." I ran down the ramp to retrieve my football.

"That's a prime monkeying example," he shouted after me. "You're in trouble and you're still talking back. People like you end up in *jail*, son. Nobody is going to help you out then. Trevor's already so mad at you he could spit, and I'm not wasting my boat money paying for a lawyer to defend you for a crime you're likely guilty of anyway."

I walked back up the ramp, tossing the football from hand to hand. I tucked it under one arm and slapped my dad on the back. "Your confidence in me is heartwarming.

Makes me want to return all the money I stole from the little old ladies and kick the heroin."

He gave me the same look he'd sent my way that morning in the kitchen. I had gone too far.

I raised both hands and one football. I had no defense and nothing else to say.

"Why can't you stay the monkey away from her?" he burst.

"Because." This was impossible to explain. I didn't understand it myself. I put my hands down in defeat. "It's Lori."

"I know," he said. Shockingly, he sounded halfway sympathetic.

"And she's beautiful," I went on.

He nodded.

I pointed the football through the trees, toward her house. "And she's *right there!*"

"I know, son, and it's going to earn you a tour through the ass end of the South's finest secondary schools for monkey-ups."

I bounced the football on the side of my head in frustration. "What do you want me to do?"

He pursed his lips and eyed me in the dusk. "Show me you have one iota of self-restraint."

"I will," I said quickly.

"Stay away from her."

"Okay."

"Keep your hands off her."

"I'll try."

He scowled at me.

"I will," I said.

He wiggled his fingers at me. "And it might help public relations with Lori's pop if you put on a shirt and quit walking around here like sex on a stick."

I rolled my eyes. He did make me feel self-conscious about my bare chest, though. I wanted to fold my arms. Instead, I threw the football as hard as I could at the warehouse door.

BANG.

"Nice arm," Dad called after me as I chased the football. "Ever thought about throwing against the rock wall of the house? You're making a dent in my door."

That was the point. I liked making a dent. I liked watching it grow bigger with every throw. I didn't say this, though. As I walked toward him, spinning the football on one finger, I did admit, "The metal door makes a more satisfying noise. Like fireworks. I can feel it in my chest."

He reached out and stroked my cheek with his fist. "What's this scrub you're working on?"

I batted his hand away. "The apple doesn't fall far from the tree." I yanked his beard.

He feinted toward me.

I bounced the football off his chest and caught it again. "I could so take you, old man."

He chuckled and headed past me, up to the house. "You do what I said," he called over his shoulder.

"I will."

"I would hate to see you go."

I watched him walk all the way up the yard, hands on his knees when he got to the steepest part, until he disappeared into the house.

Then I looked toward Lori's house again. It was big, but all I could see between the thick tree trunks was wooden corners and white lights. It looked exactly like it always had from over here, but I felt so much different about it now.

In my earliest memory it was a scary place, because Lori and McGillicuddy's mother had died. Later it was a mysterious and wonderful place, like the Smithsonian Air and Space Museum. I didn't go to their house often, but when I did, McGillicuddy's room was full of model airplanes *still intact* because he had no older brothers to break them on purpose, and Lori was liable to pop around the corner, treating me to a little thrill.

Lately I'd hardly dared go over there because I was sure

Lori would know I liked her. When I did have an excuse to visit McGillicuddy, I walked through the halls holding my breath. The little thrill had grown into something much stronger, something that made me want to steal Lori away from McGillicuddy and get her alone. And now . . .

Now I just hoped she hadn't gotten in too much trouble.

Keep my hands off her. Right. I waved fireflies away from my face and threw the football at the warehouse as hard as I could.

BANG.

7

As the doorbell rang, I was dumping potato chips into a bowl. This was something one did when having one's friends over for lunch. This was, in fact, the only thing I could think of that one did when hostessing a lunch.

At the sound of the bell, I glanced toward the door and tried to slow my pulse. It was not Adam, miraculously freed from the wrath of his parents (and my dad). It was Tammy and Rachel, who'd agreed to come over again today to help me figure out what to do. They were conniving, like all girls but me. I figured they could troubleshoot.

"Heeeey," I wailed.

Tammy and Rachel made unfamiliar girly noises of

sympathy and wrapped me in a group hug. "Oh, no!" Rachel exclaimed. "Have you been crying?"

"I'm all cried out." My voice was muffled against Tammy's T-shirt—which was safe from stains, because I never wore makeup to work. I wished I could have enjoyed the group hug and taken them up on the implicit invitation to cry my eyes out all over again. This was why they'd driven out here on my lunch break. This was what girls did.

But I really had depleted my store of tears, and probably lost five pounds of water weight in the process, while dusting the marina showroom with Sean this morning. Plus, weird as it had been to show my emotional side to Sean, it would have been even stranger to cry in front of my brother, who would be back any second. Now that he and Tammy were together, I supposed he would listen in on all my girly confabs. Not that I'd ever had any of those before.

Plus, now that I'd rid myself of the initial hysteria at getting Adam in even more trouble, I couldn't concentrate on crying. I was thinking too hard about my plan for getting us out of this mess.

The girls and I detangled ourselves from one another and stepped into the kitchen, shutting the door on the midday heat. "It's so romantic," Rachel said. "Like *Romeo and Juliet*!"

"Romantic, no," I said. "Like *Romeo and Juliet*, yes, except that it's real. With suckage."

"Give us the scoop." Tammy slid into a chair in front of the bread and sandwich meat I'd piled on the kitchen table. "Did your dad convince Adam's parents to punish him?" She glanced around the kitchen as she said this. I knew she wasn't as interested in the scoop on Adam as the scoop on my brother's whereabouts.

"I don't know yet," I said. "McGillicuddy's supposed to be down at the gas pumps, finding out from Adam right now. I worked with Sean and Cameron this morning, but neither of them knew anything. They weren't around when Adam got in trouble. They asked him later what happened, and he told them to screw off."

"Poor thing." Rachel, who was still standing next to me, slipped her arm around my waist.

I shot a sideways look at her. "Poor thing" was right. I felt awful for Adam. But I didn't necessarily want *Rachel* feeling awful for him—not when she'd been dating him two weeks ago. I was not schooled enough in the arts of girls to know whether she was bullshitting me or not. I was about to call her on it when McGillicuddy walked in.

"Hi, Rachel," he said. "Hi, Tammy," he said in a different tone. He stepped over to the kitchen table and kissed her. At first I thought this was going to be a McGillicuddy-style peck. Historically he was not good with girls. But this turned into something more. They kissed quite deeply in the middle of the kitchen.

Rachel and I looked at each other. She removed her arm from around my waist. I walked to the table, picked up a fork, and dinged it on a glass. "Hello, no PDA in the business meeting. We are here to rescue my love life, not to advance yours."

They broke apart, glaring at me. McGillicuddy was as pink as the sliced ham on the table.

We all sat down, and I passed around ingredients for them to make their own sandwiches. All three of them shot me strange looks every time I passed something new. Perhaps other girls actually made lunch when they invited people over? Then I followed their gazes to the jars on the table. I hadn't been handing around condiments you'd usually put on a sandwich. I'd just cleared out the door of the refrigerator and plunked the contents on the table, thinking this stuff must be good for *something*, though I'd never seen anyone use it.

I picked up a Mason jar with green oozing down the sides and showed it to my brother. "Look, this is from five years ago when Frances was our nanny, not our dad's squeeze. Remember the organic muscadine chutney? Ah, memories." I hugged it to my cheek. Shocked by the cold (and the sticky), I plunked it onto the table again. "Sometimes it's good to let go."

With her finger wrapped safely in a napkin, Rachel eased the jar a few inches farther from her plate. "Could I have a knife?"

"I'm not sure even a knife will help you hack into that Mason jar," I said. "It's pretty ol—"

"For the mayo," Rachel said.

Realizing I had supplied no utensils for the grand repast, I jumped up, crossed the kitchen, and opened what I thought was the knife drawer. Clearly I had not prepared food in a while. This was a drawer full of kitchen tools we had no use for when Frances was not around, such as the avocado slicer, the garlic press, and the melon baller. I'd had a lot of fun cooking with Frances back in the day. She thought she was teaching me to cook, which made her happy. I mashed food like it was Play-Doh and learned nothing, which made me equally happy.

I grabbed a few implements in case someone needed them, sat back down, and handed Rachel a butter knife. Then I asked my brother, "What'd you find out about Adam?"

"Well," he said between bites, "there's some talk of military school."

"What!" I shouted. "Adam would be the worst person in the world to go to military school."

"I think that's the idea," my brother said. "You go into military school because you're undisciplined and unmilitary. They make you toe the line."

I felt like my insides had been scooped out with the melon baller in front of me. Adam did not toe the line. That was why he was in so much trouble. But that was also one of the things I loved about him. A disciplined and military Adam would not be a new and improved Adam. It would not be Adam at all.

"But they're not sending him yet," McGillicuddy went on. "They've talked about it before, and this latest problem"— he glanced at me, like I was the problem—"has brought up the discussion again. They won't send him if he stays away from you."

"They're saying, 'Stay away from your girlfriend or we'll send you to military school'?" I asked. "That makes no sense."

"It's more like they're saying, 'We gave you simple instructions and you couldn't follow them.'"

I threw a potato chip at my brother. Rachel and Tammy ducked, as if people did not throw food at their tables. "You don't have to act so smug about it," I said. "You helped him polish the marks out of the boat faster. You sent him in my direction."

"Isn't the issue really that your parents are watching

you all the time?" Tammy asked. "You could both quit the marina and get jobs at the same place somewhere else."

I frowned at her. I hadn't thought of this. If I got a job on land, I might dry up. I couldn't imagine a summer away from the lake. But to save Adam from military school, it would be more than worth it. I asked, "Like where?"

"You both have your lifeguard certification," Tammy said. "You could work at the city pool or the country club."

"Yeah!" I exclaimed. Work *and* water!

Rachel shook her head. "Adam wouldn't be able to stay still in that lifeguard chair for more than five minutes."

"Yeah," I said. She knew this because she'd dated Adam. However, I did not want to be reminded of this at the present time. Waving away Tammy's amateurish idea, I said, "I already wanted to talk to y'all about this, but military school makes it even more important. Adam won't follow this order from his parents. There's my irresistible beauty and allure—"

Tammy laughed.

"—shut up, and then there's the very idea of his parents telling him he can't do something. It's a perfect storm for Adam to self-destruct. I need to get us out of this mess before that happens. And I have a plan." I explained my ingenious mission with Kevin Ye, ignoring Rachel when she choked on her lemonade at several points. I finished, "Isn't that a good plan?"

"No," McGillicuddy spoke up, "but it's consistent."

I went on. "The problem with this plan—"

"*The* problem?" Tammy asked. "Like there's only one?"

"—is that I ran it by Adam, and he does not like it."

"You have got to be kidding," McGillicuddy said flatly.

"It's the Kevin Ye aspect. Adam doesn't want me dating a felon." Or his brother, or his other brother. "It could still work if I thought of someone who passed muster with Adam and horrified my dad at the same time."

"What about Parker Buchanan?" Rachel asked. "Your dad must know him by reputation. Everybody in town's heard that he made out with three different girls in the food court at the Birmingham mall and all their boyfriends tried to jump him in the parking lot."

"That's *perfect*!" I pounded my fist on the table. Rachel's lemonade sloshed over the side of her glass. "Sorry." I stood up to snag a towel.

"I was joking," Rachel said.

My brother warned her, "Do not make jokes to Lori that you don't want to be misunderstood and taken seriously."

"Why is Parker perfect?" Tammy asked. "He's a playboy who lives on the edge. Why would that be so scary to your dad? He sounds like a combination of Adam and Sean."

"Yes, but he's from Birmingham," I pointed out as I wiped up the lemonade at Rachel's place—or tried to, and ended up scooting the puddle into her lap. "Sorry. Maybe you should do this." I handed her the towel and sat back down in my place. "You know how people around here feel about Birmingham. You don't even have to explain that anything from Birmingham is more intense. If you wreck your car and people want to know how badly you were hurt, all you have to say is, 'The ambulance took me straight to Birmingham,' and everybody knows you went to the university hospital because you were at death's door. If you're going on a date and you say, 'We went to Birmingham,' people know your boyfriend took you to the fanciest restaurant in the state because he's trying to get in your pants."

McGillicuddy cleared his throat. Next to him, Tammy took a huge bite of her sandwich. He must be taking her on a date to Birmingham sometime soon.

To cover his own embarrassment—or just to make sure he understood my plan, but I doubted this—my brother reached behind him and snagged the pad and pen on the counter beside the phone. He drew a little diagram. "So an ADHD boyfriend is bad, and a playboy ADHD boyfriend would be worse, but a playboy ADHD boyfriend from Birmingham is the top of this hierarchy."

"That's what I'm counting on," I said. "I would not rely

393

on Parker's reputation alone. I would go out with him on a couple of dates, enough to let Dad know we're getting serious, and then stage a Teen Crisis."

Everybody cracked up but me. Tammy asked, "What kind of Teen Crisis?"

"I have no idea," I said defensively. "You've been watching MTV longer than I have."

"Are you just going to flirt with Parker and win him over," Rachel asked, "or are you going to explain to him what you're doing?"

"I'll explain to him what I'm doing," I said. "Otherwise I would feel awful. What if he fell for me for real?"

Rachel and Tammy looked at each other.

"It is not beyond the realm of possibility," I grouched.

"What makes you think he'll do it?" Tammy asked.

"I'll offer him something in return. I'll take him around town, introduce him to people, show him where we hang out. I will leave out the part where I am extremely unpopular and kind of socially challenged. Do you think he might believe I'm popular?"

"Depends on how long you're together," Rachel said. "He'll wise up eventually."

My brother tapped the pen on the pad. "Won't you feel guilty for lying to Dad?"

I *did* feel a twinge of guilt at that, but anger took over.

"I won't be lying to him. I *will* be going out with Parker. I might not be going out with him with romantic intensions, but I will not say I am. Dad will only infer this, and everybody knows you should not infer anything. You should get it in writing."

All this lawyer lingo reminded me that my brother was leaving behind incriminating evidence. I reached across the table, snatched the pad in front of him, and tore out the sheet where he'd made little notes about the plan. I tore out the sheet under that, too, in case the imprint of the pen was clear enough to show up if a paranoid father rubbed a pencil across it. I tore both sheets into a pile of tiny pieces while the three of them watched me as if I had completely lost my mind.

"The thing is," I said, trying to sound sane, "I need to explain all this to Adam in private. I can't get McGillicuddy to explain it to him. Something will be lost in the translation."

"Well, excuse me that I can't look at him all googly-eyed," my brother said.

"And he's liable to punch you," I said.

"Very true," Rachel agreed. I felt another twinge of annoyance that she knew Adam so well, or thought she did. That's one of the reasons I'd asked her to help me plan, but the more helpful she was, the less sure I was that I wanted her help.

My brother's eyes slid to Tammy for a fraction of a second, then back to me. He said, "Punch me? He can try."

"Right." I needed to keep my brother on my side. Best to support his machismo in front of Tammy. But he knew, and I knew, that asking Parker to help me and scaring my dad with Parker would not be nearly as difficult as persuading Adam to play along.

8

Friday night my family had Lori's family over for dinner. My mom tried to pass it off as routine. She said we'd been so busy that we hadn't invited them yet this summer, and now was as good a time as any. However, I was pretty sure she wanted to repair whatever I'd messed up with Lori's dad. Sooner or later somebody would get another speeding ticket, and then what would my parents do? *Pay* for a lawyer?

I thought I would be glad for the chance to get close to Lori. It ended up being three courses of frustration. I'd felt exactly this way wakeboarding with her an hour before. I always looked forward to being near her, but when the time came, we were both scared to exchange more than a "hi" for fear authority was watching us.

Even worse, the longer this went on, the more shy I felt around her. Not shy, exactly—I was not shy, and Lori was so friendly that nobody could feel shy around her. It was more like I wanted to impress her as her boyfriend, and for about two days I'd felt confident I could do it. Now I was regressing back to the way I'd felt ever since I could remember, knowing I liked her more than she liked me, and deathly afraid to make a move for fear of messing things up with her. Or getting sent to military school.

So when she grinned and put up her arms to slide past me in the narrow space between the refrigerator and the island in the kitchen, I didn't even put out a finger to stroke the strip of exposed skin between the hem of her tank top and the waistband of my jeans she'd cut off into shorts, with her pink bikini bottoms peeking out. I just looked longingly after her and took my second helping of catfish back to the table.

But after dinner, I got another chance.

"Run down the hill," Sean said. "Hurdle the cooler. Get sprayed by the hose. Swing on the rope. Catch the ball."

"Agreed," Cameron said. "One, two, three . . ."

"Break!" the five of us shouted, raising our hands from the pile in the center. I walked to the end of the dock, where I had a clear shot to pass the football to whoever swung over the lake on the rope hanging from a branch of the enormous oak tree. Lori followed me, dragging the garden hose. I was a little surprised her dad didn't complain about this, because she'd stripped off her tank top and my shorts to reveal her pink bikini underneath. Sean and McGillicuddy wandered over to sit with my parents and Lori's dad and Frances under the tree. Cameron hiked up the yard to get a running start.

"Oh, God," Lori said without looking at me, "what are they thinking, leaving the two of us alone out here on the dock together? We might *talk* or something."

"That would be awful," I said. "I might give you a hickey."

She laughed, still watching for Cameron's start instead of looking at me. "Just by talking to me?"

"I can talk really dirty. You'd be surprised."

She turned red. I hoped her dad couldn't see her blush from that distance. My mom had cracked open a bottle of champagne to celebrate him finally asking out Frances. Maybe that would put him in a better mood about the hood next door making his daughter blush.

"How do you like Frances dating your dad?" I asked.

"I was excited about the possibility of getting a new mother, until she started acting like one."

"Oh."

"Speaking of bizarre dates," Lori said, "I've been meaning to tell you something all week."

She was done with me. She was dating someone else. Maybe that's why I'd turned shy around her the past few days. I'd been afraid of this, and I didn't want to hear it.

Before she could spill to me, I said, "Here he comes." Cameron barreled down the grassy hill. He leaped over the big cooler. Lori gripped the trigger on the hose and released the pressure that had been building up, catching him in the side of the face with a hard stream even from thirty feet away. He put up both hands to block the water and tripped over his own feet, nearly falling as the grass gave way to the sandy beach.

"Good shot," I told her.

"Tomorrow night I'm going out with Parker Buchanan."

Cameron jumped onto the rope. His momentum carried him far out over the lake. My stomach felt like it was going with him, swinging over a bottomless pit.

I waited until the precise moment to power the football out to him. He let go of the rope at the apex of his swing just as the ball hit him in the chest. He reached his arms around it a fraction of a second too late. The ball bounced off him and plopped into the lake at the same time he did.

Everyone made disappointed noises. Only Frances

clapped for him, and when he surfaced, she called through cupped hands, "Good try, Cameron." Frances had always employed positive reinforcement with kids, which is why my family found her so weird.

I took advantage of the commotion. Still watching Cameron floundering in the water, I asked Lori, "You're breaking up with me?" If I'd been looking into her green eyes as I asked this, I probably would have broken down. As it was, only my voice broke. I hoped the splashing covered it up.

"No, of course not!" She moved her hand toward me like she would touch me, but she stopped herself in time. Her hand stayed there in the hot air between us. "I'm going ahead with my plan to date boys more insidious than you." Her hand flexed, fingers splayed, hoping I would hold off until she finished. I wondered what she thought I would do.

"I figured Parker wasn't as bad as Kevin Ye," she went on, "because he has not been to jail. Yet."

Cameron waded out of the water and tossed the ball back to me. I dried it on my shirt. Ever since my dad made the "sex on a stick" comment, I'd been careful not to expose my chest, even when boarding and swimming. Sean told me I was getting a farmer's tan.

I realized too late that I was exposing my belly as I dried

my shirt. Lori watched. I glanced toward the oak tree, but her dad was leaning forward, talking to Frances with his hand on her knee. We had fallen into a parallel universe where people who never touched each other were suddenly in love, and people who were in love weren't allowed to touch each other.

Nobody paid attention to Lori and me anyway. McGillicuddy ran down the hill. He was so big and gained so much momentum that he almost didn't leave the ground in time to jump over the cooler. His toes grazed it as he leaped. Lori squeezed the trigger on the hose. He'd turned away so the water didn't catch him in the face. She sprayed him in the back of the neck, droplets of water shooting out in all directions like an explosion. He ran that way with his face averted until he hit the beach, then caught the rope and swung out over the water, a lot farther than Cameron had gone.

I waited until the perfect moment to fire the ball at him. We made it look easy. He caught it and dropped into the water in an enormous cannonball.

Everyone cheered for him. He surfaced triumphantly and tossed the wet ball back to me.

"Great arm!" my dad yelled. He toasted me with his champagne flute.

"There's no way they'll start him on the varsity team,"

Sean called as he moved from the shade of the tree up the hill to take his turn. "Adam won't remember the plays. He won't remember what team they're playing. You can't have a quarterback with ADHD."

"We'll see," I yelled back. *You asshole,* I thought. Then I turned to Lori. "I can't believe you're going ahead with this plan after I asked you not to."

"Face forward and do not look at me."

I didn't like people telling me what to do, even Lori. But in this case, she was right. I faced forward and stared out over the lake. In the hot evening with most boats docked for the night, the surface was glassy, reflecting the sunset. No one would have suspected millions of critters lived underneath, churning the water with their complex lives. Just like no one would have looked at Lori and me then, standing side by side on the dock with a football and a garden hose, and thought we were discussing our whole future together.

"This is exactly why I'm going ahead with the plan," she said. "We've hardly exchanged two words since Sunday night. Now it's Friday and we have no indication that my dad will give in any time soon. Your parents have threatened you with military school. We have to do something. So I asked out Parker for tomorrow night. He knows it's a favor. We're only going to the movies. I'll pick him up at his grandparents' house around six thirty—"

"You're picking him up?" I asked. "In what, a boat?"

"No, silly, in my dad's Beamer. I got my license."

"You *did*?" I couldn't help exclaiming.

My dad looked up from his conversation with my mom and eyed me.

"Yes!" Lori said. "I'm sorry I forgot to tell you, with everything else going on. Actually I didn't tell you because I wasn't allowed to speak to you. Whatever."

I should have felt happy for her for getting her license. The day I got my license a month ago was one of the happiest days of my life, second only to Lori's birthday a week ago, when we'd gotten together. On my own birthday, I'd dumped my dad out of my truck at the marina and driven all over town for hours by myself.

But I didn't feel happy for her. I felt jealous. "I wanted to be the one to take you to get your license."

She nodded. "I know. I'm sorry. I would have loved to take my street test in your pink truck, but I didn't know when my dad would let me see you again, and I didn't want to wait forever. Sean drove me."

I looked at her. I knew my dad was watching us, and I didn't care. A soft breeze blew the white-blonde hair around her face into her eyes. With both hands she gathered all her hair into a ponytail in back, twisted it, and pulled it forward over one shoulder. I wished she would magically produce a clip from her bikini bottoms and pin it up. All of this would have been so much easier if I had an ugly girlfriend.

I knew she felt guilty when she went on. "My dad had a big case this week, and of course Frances was keeping the Harbarger kidlets. I begged your mom to let somebody off from the marina—anybody. Finally she said Sean could take me because he was just hanging around the showroom and hitting on the customers anyway."

I thought, *Better them than you.* I looked angrily toward Sean.

He stood on the grass with his hands on his hips, surveying the course. He didn't want McGillicuddy to show him up. "McGillicuddy and Cameron wet the grass when they came out of the lake," he complained. "It will be slippery."

"Oh, come on!" I hollered.

At the same time, Cameron yelled, "Pussy!" and quickly covered his mouth, looking around stealthily in the hope that Mom wouldn't know who'd said it.

"Teams don't get extra points for field conditions," Lori pointed out. "Take it like a man."

"Best two of three," McGillicuddy suggested.

These words weren't even out of McGillicuddy's mouth when Sean started forward, hoping he'd catch Lori off guard and avoid the hose. He hurdled the cooler neatly and ran face-first into her stream of water.

"Good one," I told her.

He continued blindly down the yard, caught the rope, and swung anemically over the lake. I threw the ball. He grabbed at it and missed, dropping into the lake empty-handed.

Everyone moaned.

He surfaced, spluttering, and pointed at me. "You were high."

I called, "You *are* high if you think that was high." Actually it *had* been a bit high, because I'd aimed for his head.

"My turn," Lori said. "Who's manning the hose?"

"I will," Sean said. He waded toward her with his hands out.

She squirted him, a hard spurt square in his belly button.

"Oh," he cried, doubling over. "You'll pay for that." He hopped up onto the dock.

"Will I?" she asked, handing over the hose.

It was a good thing I trusted her. Otherwise I might think she was flirting with him.

He slapped me on the back. "You should have seen her taking her driving test. I fastened my seat belt and took all the sofa cushions with me just in case—"

"You did not." Lori poked him in the ribs. Grrrrr.

"But you knew your left from your right?" I asked, because I wanted to know, and because I wanted to distract her and stop her from touching Sean.

"I sat in the backseat," Sean said. "When the tester told her to turn right, I tapped on the right side of her seat. When the tester told her to turn left, I tapped on the window."

This was very kind of Sean. I wanted to kill him.

Lori laughed along with him, but she kept her eyes on me. "I didn't believe you, Sean. I wouldn't put it past you to steer me wrong just for fun."

"Who, me?" He tried to squirt Mom all the way across the lawn with the garden hose.

"I used a trick Adam taught me. I put the fingers of my left hand in the shape of an *L* on the steering wheel."

"But why are you driving on the date with Parker tomorrow night?" I asked. "Why can't Parker drive you? I was hoping your first date driving would be with me." Now I sounded selfish and I knew it, but I couldn't help it.

Lori nodded. "I thought about that. My dad knows I've been bluesing for my license. If Parker drove instead, my dad might figure out this is all a set-up."

"Lori, he's going to know it's all a set-up anyway."

"He isn't. Look at me."

It was a testament to how much I'd missed her that I breathed a little faster just from looking deep into her green eyes. For a second my asshole brother wasn't standing right next to us and our nosy parents weren't watching us. Lori and I stood alone together on the dock, as we had a thousand times before, when it didn't matter.

"I'm clueless," she said. "Right?"

"Right." I wasn't going to lie to her. She wasn't a dumb blonde, but the way she acted, you'd have to know her since birth or look at her SAT scores to figure this out.

"Well, I inherited it from somewhere." She turned her back on me. I watched her go, staring at her tanned back and her perfect ass in that pink bikini. She passed Sean, walked up the dock, and continued through the grass to the starting place for the obstacle course.

I hadn't run the course yet—I would take my turn last because I was always the most likely to get hurt—but I felt like I'd run it already, the way my heart pounded.

Sean gave up trying to squirt Mom with the hose. He held it almost straight up, adjusting the stream for the slight breeze. The water cascaded on top of my head before descending to earth.

I didn't even hit him. For one thing, I was used to Sean. For another, my dad had warned me to display one iota of self-control. This was more than an iota. This was a kappa and perhaps even a lambda, the longer this went on. The cold water soaked my hair and splashed onto my T-shirt.

As if it were perfectly normal for him to annoy me for no apparent reason, which I supposed it was, I asked him, "Are you going out with Rachel tomorrow?" I didn't expect him to say yes. If they were going out, Rachel would have called me to ask my advice on how to act—as if I could advise anyone on how to deal with Sean. I just thought I would plant the seed in his head to ask her out, in case he'd forgotten about her already. He'd seemed crazy in love with her last week, which was the first time any of us had ever seen Sean act that way. But if she'd escaped his mind already, that would be a lot more like him.

He said, "You wish."

The water was so cold that my head ached. I didn't dare glance at him. That would certify how much I cared. But I was astonished he saw through me. He knew that I was worried about him dating Lori, and that I'd be relieved if he dated Rachel again. I tried so hard to be conniving and still wasn't nearly as devious as Sean when he seemed off his game.

Abruptly, he pointed the hose away from me, into the lake. Lori was about to start. I wiped the football on the only dry section of my shirt that was left.

"Girl power!" called Frances. She might have been a little drunk.

Lori dashed down the grass and hurdled the cooler, clearing it by a foot. Sean sprayed her with the hose, catching her square in the left boob. I almost cried foul. I put my hand over my mouth.

Lori just laughed. She kept running to the end of the lawn, across the sand, and leaped for the rope. She swung way out over the lake, and I threw the football.

Thinking back on it later, I didn't remember being angry with her for flirting with Sean. I would never hurt her for that, or for any reason, on purpose.

Still, there had to be some explanation. The football hit her in the chest so hard that I heard the *smack* where I was standing. She dropped into the water with the ball and disappeared under the surface. The *smack* echoed once across the lake.

"Nice arm, son," my dad called to me. He gave me a thumbs-up.

"Why are you egging him on?" my mom complained. "You never threw a football at *me* that way."

"I didn't bother. You catch like a girl. Watch, Lori will come up in a second with the ball."

A second came and went. Two seconds. I watched the spot where Lori had disappeared.

Sean said, "You've killed her."

The football popped to the surface. By itself.

I jumped into the water and swam toward the spot. At the same time, McGillicuddy and Cameron sprang from under the tree and ran into the lake. I'd only managed a few strokes by the time they dragged her up the beach, one on each side, along with half the water in the lake.

I swam after them as fast as I could and ran up the beach. She was on all fours, face white. Her ribs pulsed like she was trying to cough but she couldn't get any air in or out.

Everyone surrounded her now in a tight circle. "Lori!" her dad shouted.

"Pound her on the back," Frances suggested.

She shook her head, eyes closed, and held up one hand.

I'd seen that face plenty of times before, when we were kids. "I knocked the wind out of her," I explained.

She nodded, sucking in small breaths. She looked like she might laugh, but she didn't have the air to laugh.

My mom leaned down toward us. "Breathe," she told Lori unhelpfully.

Lori nodded again. She sat back in the sand and moved her hands in circles in front of her to show us she was trying. The skin on her chest between her breasts was bright red where the football had hit her. Her gasps got longer and longer. Finally she had enough air in her lungs to cough out, "Quarterback or what?"

The whole circle around us laughed—brothers heartily,

adults nervously. I stood up, soaked T-shirt dripping on the sand, and put out a hand to help her up.

Her dad glared at me. I put my hand down and stepped back two paces. He extended his hand to help her, then pulled her away from the group.

Now everybody stood around in knots in the fading light, talking about other times when Lori had gotten the wind knocked out of her. So I wasn't the only one who remembered this. My mom mentioned the time Lori ran into the dock on water skis and broke her arm. Frances brought up an episode even I had forgotten about, when Lori fell out of my tree house. Frances watched me as she said this, trying to gauge my reaction.

Maybe it was just me, but it seemed like none of us knew what to do until Lori's dad finished talking to her. I only half paid attention to the stories of Lori losing her breath. Underneath the laughter, I tried to hear what her dad was saying.

I couldn't catch most of it. Finally she started to walk away from him, and he raised his voice. "You're always getting hurt when Adam is around."

"That's because I'm always getting hurt," she said huskily, "and Adam is always around." She skipped back down the hill and stopped between Frances and me, careful not to look me in the eye.

"I'm really sorry," I said as quietly as I could without whispering and attracting even more attention. "I forgot you were a girl." I'd also forgotten Lori did not like to hear this. Anyway, it wasn't exactly true. I *never* forgot Lori was a girl. I just never treated her any differently from the guys when we played games, because that's what she wanted.

Maybe I should start.

Sean walked by, tossing the wet football from hand to hand. "Forgot she was a girl?" he mused. "Didn't seem like it last weekend."

With one hand I shoved him hard enough to send him reeling into the lake. He sprang out of the water and yanked me in before I could dodge him. He pushed me way underwater and held me there. I wanted to punch him, but I knew from experience that it was hard to do any damage in the water anyway. And I kept repeating to myself that I was already in enough trouble. For myself, it didn't matter so much, but Lori was at stake.

I stayed quiet under his hands, waiting for him to let me up. He didn't. I ran out of breath and still he didn't let me up. I scrambled past him toward the surface. He tried to hold me down in the darkness. I had an inch of height on him, but he had quite a few pounds on me. With all the strength I had left, I broke past him and gasped before he could dunk me again. I deserved this for knocking the breath out of Lori, but I'd had enough. "Uncle!" I yelled.

Above the surface, Lori and Frances and my mom were yelling too, hollering at Sean to let me go. He didn't listen to them, but he listened to me. Poised to put his hands on my shoulders and shove me under, Sean paused and cocked his head at me. "What?"

"Uncle," I repeated. "Isn't that what people say when they give up?"

"I don't know. You've never given up before."

McGillicuddy and Cameron splashed through the shallow water toward us, wearing familiar looks on their faces that told me they thought they were saving the day, separating Sean and me. McGillicuddy reached Sean first and dunked him.

"I already said uncle," I told Cameron just as he reached me, but this meant as little to him as it had to Sean. He turned me around and pinned my arm behind my back. He was still mad at me for trying to punch him in the boat last weekend.

We were even, then, because I was still mad at *him* for flirting with my girlfriend. I tried to jerk out of Cameron's grasp. He held me so hard that even the water didn't help me slip free. Then he pulled my arm higher behind my back until it hurt.

"That's my throwing arm," I yelled. "Get the monkey off me, Cameron."

"Isn't this fun?" my mom called in a voice bright enough to be a cartoon. "I'm so glad we've gotten the families together again. We should do this more often. Who's ready for homemade ice cream?"

At the same time the next night, I crouched in my tree house, scoping out Lori's house. Yes, I felt ridiculous, but the woods between her house and mine weren't thick enough for stealth. If I was going to watch her driveway unseen, there was nowhere else to hide except in the bushes, and I absolutely refused to hide in the bushes. That would make me a creep.

The taillights of her dad's car blinked on. She backed out of the garage and drove down her driveway, then turned toward town and disappeared.

I jumped from the tree house, ran across her yard, and burst through her front door. Maybe I should have rung the doorbell. Possibly I was no longer welcome in her house. However, I'd never rung the doorbell when I'd come to see McGillicuddy before, so it didn't seem right to start now, just because I was persona non grata.

Luckily I didn't have to deal with this. Mr. McGillicuddy didn't notice I was there. Through the glass door in the den

I could see him out on the screened porch, his favorite place lately. He was reading and didn't look up. I dashed up the stairs. With only a glance into Lori's disaster of a room—disappointing as usual, wakeboarding posters on the walls, books strewn everywhere, no underwear in sight—I ducked into McGillicuddy's room.

He sat at his desk, pecking on his computer keyboard. He didn't look around at me either, but he asked, "Yes?"

"Let's go," I said.

"Go where?"

"On Lori's date with Parker."

Now he looked at me over the nerdy spectacles he wore for reading. "I wasn't aware it was a double date. And you're not my type."

"Cut the bullshit and let's go. We've probably lost her already. We won't be able to chase her to Parker's. We'll have to intercept her at the movie and hope she was telling the truth about where she was going on this date."

He opened his mouth.

"Bill!" I hollered. "Come *on*."

He kept his mouth open and raised his eyebrows. When it became clear to me that he was not going anywhere until I let him talk, and clear to him that I was not going to interrupt him again, he finally said, "I have a date with Tammy."

"Go over to her house later," I said. "That's when the good stuff happens anyway. Come *on*."

He sighed at me, then turned back to his computer and moved the mouse.

"What are you doing?" I asked. "Shutting it down? You don't have to shut it down. Nobody is going to touch your computer while we're gone. Come *on*."

He kept moving the mouse and tapping on the keyboard like I was not standing there breathing down his neck. "There might be a fire. I don't want to lose my data."

"It's summer," I said. "There is no data. And there will be no fire. The only person who sets fires around here is me, and I will be gone. With you. Following Lori. Come *on*."

I swear it took me another fifteen minutes to forklift him out of his freaking data center. By then Lori had picked up Parker and made it all the way to the movie theater, I hoped. It would be just my luck that *now* she would decide running away to Montgomery was a good idea. Or Birmingham, where Parker was from. Birmingham would be worse.

And after I extracted McGillicuddy from his room, he slowed us down even more by sticking his head out into the screened porch and telling his dad where we were going. I couldn't hear his dad's end of the conversation, but I could hear McGillicuddy's. "Adam. . . . Why not?

I didn't stay out all night with him. . . . If he's with me, he's not with her."

"Come *on*," I grumbled under my breath.

The only reason I was able to get him through the trees, into my driveway, and into the pink truck was that he called Tammy on his cell. The second he'd ended the call with her, climbed into the passenger seat, and slammed the door of my truck, he was arguing with me again. "Why are we going on Lori's date?"

"To make sure Parker doesn't try anything with her." I cranked the engine and raised my voice over the motor. "To make sure she doesn't try anything with Parker. When she makes a plan, she gets carried away." I backed out of the driveway.

"Jesus, Vader, nobody's going to give you a prize for backward racing." McGillicuddy gripped the window frame with one hand and the edge of the seat with the other. He didn't relax until I'd reached the street. Apparently, speeding forward was not as frightening as speeding backward. He sighed, then said, "So basically, you're stalking her."

"I am *not* stalking her." I insisted. "That's where you come in. If I followed her by myself, someone who did not understand the situation and did not realize that I am so responsible—"

McGillicuddy snorted.

"—might mistake what I am doing for stalking. However, her big brother is with me. Therefore we are protecting her." Suddenly thinking I might have forgotten some equipment, I raised the lid of the console, felt around in the compartment, and came up empty. "Are you sitting on my dad's binoculars?"

He pulled them out from under him and handed them to me. I stuffed them against my thigh, where I could grab them at a moment's notice.

"You would not believe this dream I had last night," McGillicuddy said.

"I'll bet I would." I'd heard about a lot of McGillicuddy's dreams over the years. "Try me."

"I was being interrogated by the Gestapo."

This was already funny. When we were kids and we played World War II, my brothers and I were the Americans, and we made McGillicuddy be the German because he was big and blond and Aryan. In fact, I used to be afraid of him, which was ridiculous because, judging from his last name, their family was Scottish.

Anyway, he made a very scary Gestapo agent. Cameron was always the American general. Sean was the cocky captain who went against orders and saved the day. I was the private infiltrating the enemy in a suicidal sneak attack. I got killed a lot. And Lori . . . my brothers always wanted Lori to be some sort of damsel in distress, and she always refused, and then they wouldn't let her play, and she would stomp up to her house. I wanted to go after her. I knew what it felt like to be the odd one out. But my brothers would have died laughing at me for caring about her. Kind of like now.

Or, occasionally when Sean was feeling generous (Cameron did not have an opinion one way or another) and McGillicuddy defended her, she would get her way. She would be a member of the German Resistance, assisting me in the cause by sneaking me ammunition (in reality, sparklers). I understood that a day Sean let her play was a sparkling jewel in the sandbox of her childhood. I saw why she treasured every bit of attention that Sean gave her now. But just because I understood it didn't mean I had to like it.

"I was tied up," McGillicuddy said.

"Of course you were," I said.

"And then the interrogating officer came around the corner," he said. "Guess who it was."

"Tammy," I said.

"No!" he said, offended. "Natalie Portman."

"I'm not buying it. Not when you've been going out with Tammy and you haven't been banned from her." I didn't *want* to buy it. Surely to God *somebody* had a girl-friend and appreciated her! Otherwise all my own torture was for nothing.

He reached up and ran his thumb across the seam of the headliner, which was beginning to come loose from the roof of the truck and sag into the cab, as if it were full of water. "Tammy may have bandaged my wounds to ready me for more torture."

I shook my head. "I hate to be the one to tell you, but real girls do not want threesomes." Like I knew. He was the one in college.

He looked at me in horror.

I shrugged. "Sorry." Then I asked, "Was Miss Portman wearing leather?" I was just making conversation. I could predict the answer.

"How did you know?"

"I am very sneaky." I pulled into the movie theater parking lot, stopped my truck in a space nose-to-nose with the Beamer, and cut the engine.

The summer twilight was fading fast. The sky was pale pink behind the theater. Streetlights flickered overhead but couldn't quite commit to glowing at full power. The parking lot was packed full of cars and pickup trucks—it was Alabama, after all—but a lot of them were still occupied. High school kids pulled up next to each other and talked through their rolled-down windows. They held miniature tailgating parties in their trailer beds. A roving band of football players stopped at truck after truck, spreading rumors and stirring up trouble. At least, that's what I figured. I couldn't hear them, but I'd spent a lot of time in this parking lot.

"I can tell you're sneaky," McGillicuddy said sarcastically. "That's why you parked right in front of her. I hope you wanted her to know you're following her. And I'm warning you, I don't think she's going to like it."

"I don't care whether she likes it or not," I lied. In reality I was trying to figure out where she'd gone. It was common for guys from my high school to say they were going to the movies with a girl. This did not necessarily mean they were going *into* a movie. There was a lot to do *at* or *around* the movie without paying to sit indoors for an hour and a half in the dark while enormous heads talked at you and the explosions were few and far between. Often there was more violence outside the movie than inside. Possibly more sex. Almost certainly more shots fired.

Naturally I assumed that when Lori said she and Parker were going to the movies, she meant they were driving into the vicinity of the movie theater, parking in the lot, and showing off her new driver's license and her dad's Beamer to whoever drove by. That was bad enough. But she was *inside* the theater? In the *dark*? With *Parker*? I looked through the binoculars. The movie theater lobby was empty.

"Let me ask you something," McGillicuddy said. "Your short-term goal here is to monitor Lori's date with Parker. If you ruined her date with Parker, that would be okay with you too."

"Duh."

"And then what?"

I put the binoculars down on the window frame and turned to look at him. "What do you mean, 'And then what?'"

"Lori's going out with Parker because she's trying to convince Dad to let the two of you date again. If you mess up her plan, you won't get to date her *and* she'll be mad at you."

"What's your point?"

"I'm trying to figure out your long-term goal. What do you expect to happen after you scare the bejeezus out of Parker and piss off Lori?"

"Long-term goal?" I mused. "I don't have any of those."

"Maybe you sh—"

"Vaderrrrr!" Three guys from my football team finished hanging through somebody else's truck window and jogged over to mine. They poked their heads into my personal space and yelled, "McGillicuddeeeee!" They reeked of beer.

"Hello." McGillicuddy saluted them.

They retreated through the window, thank God. "What'cha doing with the binoculars?" the left tackle asked, grabbing them. "Wouldn't happen to have something to do with anybody's hot mess of a blonde girlfriend going out with Parker Buchanan, would it?"

"It might," I admitted, grabbing the binoculars back. "I need these. We're staking her out."

"Stalking her out." The running back nodded.

If there was a chance in hell I would start as quarterback in the fall, I needed to get along with the running back. I said carefully, "*Staking* her out."

"You're parked as close as you can get to her daddy's Beamer," the punter piped up. "You're waiting outside the movie for her. You have binoculars. Sure seems like stalking." The punter was a know-it-all.

"I'm not stalking her," I insisted. "I'm making sure she's safe. Besides, how could you stalk Lori McGillicuddy? She'd see you and come out to your truck and say, 'Hi, I'm Lori. Are you my stalker? It's so neat to meet you! While you're stuck here watching my every move, can I bring you anything? Sweet tea?'"

The running back laughed. "I had Spanish with her last year. You sound just like her."

"Yeah." I sighed.

"Too bad you weren't out here with your binoculars ten minutes ago," the running back said. "They were standing in the lobby, and Parker had his hand up her skirt."

The punter and the tackle backed away from the truck, doubled over with laughter. Between gasps, the tackle called to the running back, "You know that big mofo in the truck is her brother."

"I know," the running back said. "I'm just saying."

I turned to McGillicuddy. He had gone very still in the passenger seat. He gave me a dark look, asking me with his eyes whether to believe this.

I didn't know whether to believe it either.

My so-called friends were already walking away. "Reggie," I called to the running back. "Y'all come here."

Tears streaming down their faces, slapping each other on the shoulder, they sauntered over. I'm glad *somebody* thought it was funny, because I sure as hell didn't.

I grinned. "He did not," I said, trying to sound more skeptical than I was. When Lori was trying to get Sean, she'd made out with me. Now that she was trying to get back together with me, maybe she'd asked Parker to put his hand on her ass. Why not? "Reggie, come clean with me. Did he really?"

The running back held up his hand. "I swear on the Bible."

425

"You don't have a Bible." The movie theater parking lot was definitely not the place to be carrying one around, considering what went on out here.

"Here you go, here you go." The tackle pulled a receipt out of his pocket and handed it to the running back.

The running back crumpled the receipt in his fist and held up his other hand. "I swear on this receipt for bubble gum and razor blades that I saw Parker Buchanan put his hand up your girlfriend's skirt, and I wish I'd had your binoculars."

"See you at practice in August, Vader," the tackle called through the window. "Good luck with your stalking."

"Staking!" said the punter. They moved across the parking lot and stopped at the next truck with an open window. They were probably telling the people inside that they'd seen Parker Buchanan with his hand up Adam Vader's girlfriend's skirt. *Or*, they were telling the people inside that they'd lied to me about this, and now they had a bet on how fast I got myself arrested.

"Do you believe them?" McGillicuddy asked quietly.

"Of course not," I muttered. "They're just trying to get a rise out of me. They're worse than Sean." Untrue. Nobody was worse than Sean. They were pretty bad, though. "Why? Do you believe them?"

"She *was* wearing a miniskirt when she left the house,"

McGillicuddy said. "I noticed this uneasily."

I turned to look at him again. Despite his size, usually he appeared friendly, like Lori, his face honest and open. At the moment, with his blond brows down and his eyes fixed on the empty lobby, he looked like murder.

"We'd better go." I bailed out the driver's side door at the same time McGillicuddy stepped to the ground on the passenger side.

I made sure McGillicuddy had caught up with me and was hulking behind me before I approached the guy manning the ticket booth. "Let me in for just a second."

Ticket guy looked me up and down. "No way, Vader. Pay up like everybody else."

"All I have to do is beat the shit out of the dude my girlfriend is with," I said, "and then I'll leave. Promise."

Ticket guy narrowed his eyes at me. "Who's the dude?"

"Parker Buchanan," I said.

"My girlfriend *loves* Parker Buchanan," ticket guy said in a high voice that I hoped was supposed to be his girlfriend. "She thinks Parker is the shit. I am sick of hearing about Parker." He looked over his shoulder at the door into the theater, then turned back to me. "If I let you in, you have to wait a few minutes before you stick it to him. I need time to get up to the projection booth so I can watch."

I nodded, then pushed through the door into the lobby. McGillicuddy followed right behind me. I thought for a second that ticket guy would say something about McGillicuddy getting in free, too. Then McGillicuddy shot him the scary Gestapo look. I was a little frightened myself. I hadn't seen that look since we played World War II.

Ticket guy disappeared up the staircase to the projection booth. I counted to thirty, nodded to McGillicuddy, and jerked open the door to the theater.

For a few seconds, I was blind in the dark. I averted my eyes from the movie screen. Gradually the silhouettes of seats and shoulders materialized, black on black. I stayed at the back of the theater, surveying the crowd.

Luckily, because it was convenient, or unluckily, because it did not bode well for Lori being on a fake date rather than on a real one, she and Parker were in the back row. I could see right away that they weren't making out. She sprawled across her seat with one leg tucked under her and the other knee hooked over the armrest. She'd hung around boys too long. I knew this and she knew this, but I wasn't sure Parker knew it. If he looked where I was looking, he'd get a glimpse of the gaping hole in Lori's skirt, which her thighs should have blocked. And he must have been as turned on by this as I would have been if I'd sat next to her, because his arm was draped around her shoulders.

I took a few steps forward until I was even with the back row and called, "Parker."

He looked over at me, startled. Lori did too, and when her eyes slid to McGillicuddy, her mouth fell open.

"Come outside with me," I demanded. Everybody in the back third of the theater was shushing me now. They sounded like snakes. I'd fallen into a pit of them and was fighting my way out, getting madder every second Parker sat there with his arm around my girlfriend.

"Do *not* go outside with him, Parker." Lori eased her legs together as if I wouldn't notice how she'd been sitting as long as she moved slowly enough. "This is not the plan."

The movie was full of explosions. A helicopter chased a car between skyscrapers in Manhattan and nearly side-swiped pedestrians or took out police cars. It was so inter-esting that I might have been able to sit down and watch the whole movie, at least until the explosions ended and the plot started again, if it hadn't been for Lori. Even explosions and ADHD couldn't divert my attention from that.

"Let's go, Parker," I said. I didn't care what Lori thought anymore.

9

I had never been so mad at Adam, and he had never looked so perversely hot. He scowled down at me, week-old stubble on his chin making him look older than sixteen and almost authoritative. Yet light escaped the edges of the movie projection beam, softened his features, and caught in his long eyelashes.

Determined as I was to get rid of him and go ahead with my plan, he seemed equally determined to drag Parker out of the theater and start an old-fashioned duel with him, bottle rockets at twenty paces. I mean, he seemed *really* determined and confident, like he was finally comfortable with his newly broad, tall body and anxious for another chance to try it out.

I glanced over at Parker. When I'd called him about this date, he'd sounded excited about the prospect of seeing new popular venues in our town (movie theater! bowling alley! tennis court! that was pretty much it!) and meeting new people. In fact, he'd sounded a little too excited. And the entire half hour our fake date had lasted so far, he'd been a perfect gentleman. If you want to know the truth, I was a little disappointed.

Now, confronted with an angry boyfriend, which according to legend was a situation Parker was all too familiar with, he shrank into the red velveteen seat. He must have been caught off guard. Any second now, he would spring into action. And if we went outside the theater like Adam wanted, I was afraid someone would get hurt.

I had no choice. The longer Adam stood there (with my traitor brother behind him) grumbling at us in a threatening tone, the larger a fraction of the audience would turn around and stare unabashedly at us, just as the back ten rows were doing now. In about thirty seconds, somebody would snitch to the rent-a-cop the theater employed as a security guard and bouncer for unruly tween boys who threw bite-size candies at the screen.

"Pardon," I said to Parker as I reached back to remove his arm from around my shoulders. "Sorry," I murmured to the couple I slid past in the row. "I can't believe you," I whispered to Adam as I stepped into the aisle.

I was so furious with him. But the theater was dark, and I was close to him for the first time in almost a week, if you didn't count standing next to him on the dock yesterday and getting clobbered with his football pass. My skin tingled with awareness as I came within inches of him, and the hair on my arms stood up. I almost looked forward to the opportunity to tell him off.

I stopped when I reached my brother blocking the aisle. He actually looked angry at me. He was never angry at me. But no—his angry expression was directed past me, at Parker. None of this made any sense. Adam might have gotten dragged into my plan kicking and screaming, but the plan with Parker was McGillicuddy pre-approved! McGillicuddy and I had discussed it!

I waited for Parker to catch up with me. Adam fell in behind us as if he and McGillicuddy were our jailers. With Parker's reputation, I figured he probably got hauled into fake-boyfriend status every day of the week. Each weekend he probably *really* stole someone's girlfriend. He could handle himself with Adam, I was sure. But I hadn't prepared him for this level of rudeness from Adam. I took Parker's hand.

Strangely, he refused my hand. It was hard to tell in the dark, but it sure seemed to me like my hand chased his hand back and forth around his hip, and his hand conducted evasive maneuvers. I knew he did not find me so loathsome that he would refuse to touch me—he'd just had his arm around me, after all. Perhaps he needed the barrier of clothing. Perhaps he didn't want to hold my hand in front of Adam. Maybe he knew it would hurt Adam's feelings. Maybe he was scared of Adam. But none of these things was part of the Parker I knew by reputation.

So I walked up the aisle and through the bright lobby by myself, rejected from holding Parker's hand, wishing I were holding Adam's. It occurred to me that this sort of teen intrigue was exactly what I'd always dreamed about as a tomboy tween paging longingly through fashion magazines that might as well have been written in Russian, as much as I understood about hobo bags and ankle boots.

"Vader!" called the movie worker standing in the doorway of the stairs up to the projection booth. "You didn't beat the shit out of him. You owe me your admission fee."

"I was in there for two minutes," Adam said through his teeth.

"That wasn't the agreement," said the movie worker.

I truly hoped the movie worker would get a clue and shut up soon. Adam seemed to grow taller and broader every second, and I wouldn't have put it past him to sock

Parker right there, if that was the deal Adam had arranged with the movie worker, and then to sock the movie worker for good measure.

"How long is the movie?" McGillicuddy snapped.

"An hour and forty-five minutes."

"Then he owes you seventeen cents," McGillicuddy concluded, ever the engineering major, even when he was completely off his rocker. "Lori, give him seventeen cents."

"There were two of you in there," the movie worker protested. "That's . . ." He took way too long to add seventeen and seventeen.

"Thirty-four," I helped him out. "But Parker and I paid full price, and we were only in there for . . ." I pulled out the new cell phone my dad insisted I spend my birthday money on before I went on a date anywhere with anybody. I glanced at the time. "Fifteen minutes. So *you* actually owe *us* . . ."

"Fifteen dollars and nine cents."

I started to grin at McGillicuddy for this brilliant bit of figuring. Then I realized the voice hadn't come from McGillicuddy. It had come from Parker.

My astonishment at bad boy Parker letting loose with this nerd-bomb was exceeded only by Adam suddenly shouting, "LET'S GO!"

The four of us walked all the way across the parking lot. When we got close to my dad's car, I saw that Adam had parked right in front of it. He'd pulled up so close that the bumpers were within a millimeter of touching, because Adam was like that.

I turned to McGillicuddy and said, "I need to talk to Adam alone."

"I can't let you do that."

"The alternative is for Adam to get in a fistfight with Parker here in the parking lot. That is assault. You will have aided and abetted him by coming into the movie theater and dragging Parker out of there. How is that going to look on your job application to NASA?"

"Well . . ."

"Didn't you say Adam and I could talk as long as you didn't see it?"

He gestured to Adam's truck, looking ill. "Go ahead." He said something to Parker and folded his arms while Parker climbed into the front seat of my dad's car. Then my brother slid onto the hood of Adam's truck with his feet on the bumper and stared Parker down. My brother had never acted like this before, except when we were kids playing war and the boys next door made him be the evil German.

I turned to Adam. "Get in," I said as forcefully as I could. I climbed through the unlocked door of his truck, into the driver's seat. I'd been in the driver's seat all night, and it made me feel more in control of my little teenage life careening down the toilet. I wasn't ready to give up that control now—especially in the face of Adam's anger. I cranked the engine with the keys he'd left in the ignition and hit the buttons to close the windows. Bad enough that everyone in this town between the ages of thirteen and twenty-one could see us have this argument. I didn't want them to hear it, too.

Adam rounded the truck and slid into the passenger side. Except for our positions on the seat being reversed, we'd sat exactly like this lots of times a couple of weeks ago, when we were only pretending to like each other. I wanted to do that with Adam again. I was trying to get us back there, and he'd sabotaged me half an hour in!

The second he closed the door behind him, I hollered, "What part of 'I'm pretending to go out with someone worse so my dad will let me date you' don't you understand?"

He swung his head around at me, pinning me against the seat with his light blue eyes full of anger. "The part where Parker Buchanan puts his hand up your skirt."

I laughed because it was funny. It was something you would hear about a slutty girl in ninth grade or a popular girl in eleventh. I was neither.

Then I stopped laughing. Adam obviously believed this had happened. Where in God's name had he gotten this idea?

I leaned forward and said carefully, "Adam. You saw Parker and me when you so rudely interrupted our fake date just now. He did not have his hand up my skirt. And you did not give us a lot of warning that you were coming, so I would not have had time to remove his hand from my nether region. Honestly!" I blushed at the very idea of doing this in a movie theater.

"Not in the theater. In the lobby." Adam's words were still closed and angry, but the fire in his eyes had cooled a few degrees. Possibly he was realizing that he was—gasp—wrong.

"Parker did not have his hand up my skirt in the lobby," I said patiently. "That makes no sense. Even ho's do not let boys put hands up their skirts in the lobby when they have a whole dark theater at their disposal. Who told you that?"

He looked out over the parking lot, then gestured toward a group of three football players weaving among the cars. One of them stopped, put his hand over the top of the beer can he was holding, shook it up, and spewed it all over the hood of an outsized Lincoln Continental.

"Reginald Evans," Adam said.

We both watched Reggie hightail it across the parking lot, away from the driver of the Lincoln, dodging cars like they were defensive tackles. I saw why he was the star running back on our high school team.

He was not, however, somebody I would trust for personal information about my friends. I said, "Reginald Evans can't read. I was in Spanish with him last year."

"Well, maybe he just can't read Spanish." Adam tracked Reggie's path until he was looking at me again. "Miniskirt or what?" He did not sound appreciative as he said this. He sounded bitter.

"Or what?" I exclaimed. "In case you missed this when I explained it very carefully last night, I am pretending to be on a date with Parker, and I am dressed accordingly."

"Oh, yeah? You never wore a miniskirt when you went out on a date with *me*."

"I never went out on a date with you!"

"What do you call last Saturday night? You wore flip-flops and my jean cutoffs."

I huffed out my exasperation. "I call that hanging out all day at the festival on the lake, then spray painting our names on the bridge. Miniskirts are not appropriate attire for crawling around public structures. Somebody could look up my skirt and see my sexy panties."

"If you tell me you are wearing sexy panties right now, I'll—"

"You'll what?" I wasn't challenging him. I was reminding him that his anger did not match anything he was actually going to do, and his own mouth was his biggest enemy.

He glared at me for a few seconds as my words sank in. Then he sat back against the seat, let out a huge sigh, and fished in his pocket. He brought out his lighter and flicked it, watching the flame. "You didn't even wear a miniskirt for that couple of weeks when you were pretending to date me."

"That's because you were taking me mud riding!" I pointed out. "Besides, I *did* wear a miniskirt for the first Vader party of the year." It was even the same miniskirt I was wearing now, the only one I owned. It was my go-to outfit for intrigue.

He nodded. "You didn't wear it to the party for my sake. You were trying to hook up with Sean."

I banged my head against the driver's side window—on purpose, to emphasize my frustration, but a little harder than I'd intended. "Again with the Sean," I said.

"Again with the Sean," he agreed self-righteously.

Without raising my head from its resting place against the window, I said, "You're not supposed to be jealous of Sean right now, Adam. You're supposed to be jealous of Parker."

"Oh, go ahead and make an ADHD joke," he said. "Go ahead."

"Adam!" I shouted. "I do not make ADHD jokes about you. Sean does that. I am your friend."

He looked out the passenger side window. "Is *that* what you are now?" he said to the glass.

"I don't know what to say to you, Adam," I told his back and his golden brown curls, which were getting longer and looked like he was grooming them about as often as he was shaving, i.e., never. "You're determined to be mad at me no matter what."

His shoulders rose and fell slowly with a deep breath. Still looking out the window, he said, "Tell me about your panties."

I was going to tell him the sexy panties were a joke. Then it occurred to me that sexy panties were my friend. The whole thing might backfire on me if he believed I wore this mysterious lingerie for Parker. But I was hoping I'd made him feel sheepish enough about the ridiculous hand-up-the-skirt scenario. All that was left was to get Adam back in my corner. I did this by waving imaginary sexy panties at him.

"They are red lace," I said. "See-through. They are those boy shorts, do you know what I mean? They cut across my butt. They're kind of uncomfortable to sit on, actually." I made this up based on my last glance into the window of the lingerie shop as I walked toward the sporting goods store. In reality I was wearing Powerpuff Girls panties I'd had since I was twelve.

Adam totally bought my story, though. He turned toward me with his eyes wide, but little frown lines remained between his brows. He flicked his lighter and held his thumb on the button so the flame burned steadily. He dipped his head to examine my thighs sticking out of my miniskirt. He was imagining the phantom panties. His gaze traveled up to my Slinky Cleavage-Revealing Top. Finally his eyes met mine. They did not look friendly, exactly. I would not have asked him to borrow twenty dollars just then. They looked . . . lustful?

Yes, this was a lustful look, I was pretty sure, judging from the way my body answered. This look lit fuses in my heart and left trails of gunpowder down my limbs for the fire to burn along.

I wiggled on the seat, emphasizing that my imaginary lace boy shorts were cutting into my butt cheeks.

Adam's mouth dropped open.

KNOCK KNOCK KNOCK. I jumped, sure that my heart knocking against my chest in response to Adam's lustful thoughts was going to kill me.

But it was only McGillicuddy, still sitting on the truck, knocking on the hood. Then he twirled his finger in the air: *Wrap it up.* He was sweet to signal us without looking at us, so he could still tell Dad truthfully (sort of) that he hadn't seen us together. I would have felt overwhelmed with sisterly love for him at that moment if he hadn't been disobeying my direct order to help me change Dad's mind.

He was guarding my fake date like a prisoner of war.

"Are you still mad at me?" I asked Adam.

He worked his jaw, still staring a hole through me, but he didn't say a word. He flicked his lighter again.

"Fine." I opened the driver's door and slid out of the cab very, very slowly, letting my skirt ride up waaaaaaay too high to escape the notice of the parking lot. I calculated the precise height at which it would reveal the supersexiness of Blossom, Bubbles, and Buttercup and stopped there, so that my phantom sex panties remained forever my secret.

"Lori—," Adam growled.

I jumped down from the cab and slammed the door. Ha! Try that teen soap-opera business on me, would he? I was way ahead of him. I had stepped up my MTV intake for precisely this reason.

As I passed McGillicuddy, I called, "You and I are going to have a talk when we get home, young man."

He glared at me. "Are you sure you want to ride home with Parker after what he did?"

"He didn't do anything, as Adam will tell you. Both of you were taken in by a running back who can't tell *la casa* from *qué pasa*." I flounced around the back of the Beamer— Adam had parked so close to it that there was no room to slip a piece of paper between the bumpers, much less me—and slid into the driver's side, trailing my long sexy legs behind me for Adam's benefit (and accidentally kicking over an RC Cola bottle standing upright in the parking space, which somewhat ruined the effect, what with the fizz. Note to self: Sexy exits do not include fizz).

"Parker, I am so sorry," I gushed as soon as I'd closed us safely inside the car and locked the doors. "I know you've met them both before at some point, but in case you've forgotten, that's my boyfriend, Adam, whom we're trying to get me back together with, and that's my brother. They know about the plan, but their friend told them that you—" I took a deep breath. I'd just been boasting about my panties to Adam, but I couldn't even bring myself to tell Parker what the ruckus was about. It was so embarrassing, not to mention far-fetched.

Or was it? According to the rumors, the old hand-up-the-skirt ploy wouldn't have been new to Parker. However, it definitely didn't go with the vibe I'd gotten from him since I picked him up for this date. He'd put his arm around me when I'd asked him to in the theater, yes, but he hadn't tried to go down my shirt, which was standard eighth grade fare in the back row of the movie theater (or so I gathered—not that I knew this from personal experience), and which I wouldn't have put past him. I'd been willing to take the risk in the name of getting Adam back.

Parker said in a small voice, "Could you get me out of here?"

I looked over at him, his dark hair gelled just so, his shoulders broad in a preppy pink shirt that no male in town would have been caught dead in but that somehow worked on the Birmingham boy. A lot of girls said he had a mesmerizing stare that made them want to take their bras off, but to me it had always looked a lot like bug eyes, and right now he was staring bug-eyed at Adam and McGillicuddy way up in the cab of the truck. They glared right back down at him.

"Sure. Do you want to go back to my house?"

"Will *they* be there?" he asked, bug eyes never leaving the horrifying threat in front of him.

"Er, no. My brother has a date with his girlfriend. I don't know what he's doing here, come to think of it. And Adam wouldn't dare set foot in my house." I wasn't sure this was true. The longer I knew Adam, the more I realized there wasn't much he wouldn't dare do, even in the face of my extremely angry father.

Hey, great idea! "Yeah, let's go to my house." With Parker quickly losing his enthusiasm for this fake date, I needed to squeeze all the juice out of him while I could. That meant introducing him to my dad. Over the next few days my dad would ask around town about Parker and find out about the many horrors, ideally including the time Parker and his prep school friends filled the famous fountain in the center of Birmingham's Southside with cheese grits.

Sticking my tongue out at Adam—he just turned away—I cranked the engine of the Beamer, looked carefully behind me for football players and monster trucks and RC Colas, and backed out of the space. I half expected Adam to follow right behind me. Half *hoped* he would. Because that would have given me another chance to argue with him. Arguing with him seemed to be allowed by McGillicuddy and, bad as it was, it was miles better than no contact with Adam at all.

But an entire drive of watching the rearview mirror assured me I'd shamed Adam and my brother sufficiently to shake them off my tail, damn it. As I parked the car in my driveway, I turned my attention back to Parker, who was curled into a ball in the passenger seat, shaking. "Oh God, I'm so sorry about the air-conditioner. Why didn't you say something?" I'd cranked the cold air all the way up, and Parker was paying the price in frostbite. Not everybody got all hot and bothered when Adam stared at them, apparently.

Parker didn't uncurl from his ball.

"Hey." I reached over and rubbed his knee in a friendly warming-your-skin way, not a way that would earn me the

hickey from Parker that had been claimed by several sophomore girls whose stories I didn't entirely trust anymore.
"Let's go in and meet my dad."

I thought he might regain some of his bravado by the
time we got inside. But as I opened the door in the garage
and crossed from the kitchen into the den, he continued to
trail after me like a kitten with PTSD from being shot with
way too many Nerf darts. There was a reason the Vaders'
cat did not often venture out of the master bedroom. Parker
would never scare my dad while he acted like this.

I would have to rely on Parker's reputation getting
back to my dad. Then my dad would say, "My goodness,
that timid boy is actually a man-slut? By analogy, Adam
Vader, who seems to have a death wish, probably has his
shit together after all!" Of course, this was the best-case
scenario, or perhaps the in-my-dreams scenario. In retro-
spect, this was one of the reasons my plans had a tendency
to backfire.

I walked into the den and stopped so fast that Parker
plowed right into me. Dad was sitting on the couch all
right, and Frances was curled up next to him.

In a miniskirt!

Well, maybe not a miniskirt. It might have been mid–
calf length, and I got the first impression that it was a
miniskirt because she usually favored floor-length hippie

garb. She'd kicked off her Birkenstocks to reveal freshly painted red toenails. In short, for Frances, she looked adorable. I was sure this was an accident.

"Hi!" I exclaimed as if I'd totally expected my ex–au pair. But I truly hadn't bargained on Frances being there. This threw a monkey wrench in my plans, though I wasn't sure yet whether it was a big sucker like a pipe wrench or something that would be easier for me to manage like a little Allen wrench. We all exchanged greetings and I introduced Frances and my dad to Parker.

"Parker Buchanan." My dad stood and gave him the firm handshake and the full grin he used with clients. "Nice to see you again."

"Yes, sir." Parker sounded as if he might faint.

"All right then!" I announced. "Parker and I are going up to my *bed*room." I figured if this date with Parker had any thrust left with my dad, it was the fact that we were going to hang out in a room with a bed in it. I did not add that when we got to said *bed*room, we were not going to make out. We were going to have a long talk about how my dad already knew Parker and why it was nice to see him again.

We started up the stairs, Parker ahead of me, when my dad called, "Lori, can I have a word with you alone?"

Parker paused and turned his traumatized kitten bug

eyes on me. I nodded for him to go on into my room. As I bounced back down the stairs by myself, I resisted the urge to rub my hands together with glee. My dad wanted to give me a Talking-To about Parker! Hooray!

I reached the den again and my dad was still grinning, which did not bode well for the Talking-To from the concerned parent. Also, Frances hadn't budged her organic cotton—covered booty, which confused my interpretation of what my dad had meant by "alone." I could almost see her waving a monkey wrench at me.

"Young lady," he said, which was a pretty good start for the Talking-To, "I am so proud of you."

DAMN IT!

"Thank you!" I beamed at him like I knew what the hell he was talking about.

"I have been Parker's grandparents' counsel since they founded the yacht club," he said. "I've watched Parker grow up. He's a terrific student, as I'm sure you know, with designs on Yale. But his grandparents have always been concerned about his social life and frankly, his mental health. He hardly peeks out of his shell at his private school in Birmingham. Then he comes down here to stay with them in the summer, and apparently he tells a lot of tall tales, making himself out to be some sort of Lothario."

"You're kidding!" I did not need to fake my astonishment, though I was not astonished for the reason my dad assumed.

"It's wonderful that you've started a friendship with him," my dad went on. "I'm sure it will do him good."

I was sure a knuckle sandwich would do him more good, but I refrained from saying this. "Dad, your pride means more to me than you know." We gave each other a final manic grin and I headed for the stairs again, but not before I caught a glimpse of Frances watching me. She knew I was up to something.

Well, lucky for her and Dad, I was not up to a whole lot at the moment. I slogged up the stairs, into my room, and closed the door behind me.

Parker was sitting on my bed, thumbing through one of the issues of *Playboy* I'd stolen from McGillicuddy for fashion advice. He threw it back into the drawer of my nightstand and slammed the drawer shut, as if I would be completely fooled by this and had not been the one who put the magazine there in the first place.

I sat next to him on the bed and smiled sweetly at him. "You're so tense, Parker. You're not still worried about Adam and my brother kicking the shit out of you, are you? To be honest, I think they're still mad, but they don't have martial arts training like you do."

He stared at me. His eyes were so wide that I swore

they were going to rebel and pop right out of his head and wander around the room, looking at whatever they wanted. If they ventured up my skirt, I was going to step on them.

"What am I going to do?" he cried.

"What do you mean, what are you going to do?" I asked him innocently. "You trained in Japan for your black belt. Just get in a good lick or two, and maybe they'll leave you alone. Maybe, I'm saying. McGillicuddy probably will. Adam might not. Adam doesn't always respond to negative reinforcement like you'd think."

"Lori!" Parker cried. "I'm not who you think I am!"

I cocked my head and blinked at him. "You're not Parker Buchanan, grandson to the Buchanans of the Buchanan Yacht Club, student at a fancy schmancy private school in Birmingham?"

"I am all that," he admitted, "but I don't have a black belt."

I had surmised this already, but I played along. "You don't?"

"No. And . . . Lori, can you keep a secret? I have so much bottled up inside me, and the pressure is getting to me." He swallowed. "I didn't date Miss Alabama when I was in middle school."

"You didn't?" I tried to feign continued interest. But

if he wanted to self-debunk, he might go on all night, and frankly I was more interested in what Dad and Frances were watching on the Discovery Channel.

"No. I'm basically just a nerd. I have a 4.0 GPA, and I plan to matriculate at Yale and major in cognitive science with a double minor in statistics and ancient Greek."

"You don't." I stifled a yawn.

"I do. The reason I'm spending the whole summer with my grandparents is that nobody knows me here, and I can be whomever I say I am."

There were a lot of things about this statement that made me angry. The lie. The fact that I'd been taken in by the lie. His smug tone of voice when he talked about it, revealing himself to be the biggest nerd I had ever met, even nerdier than the kid from my algebra class who collected antique motherboards, and absolutely the worst person I could have chosen to drive Dad into letting me date Adam again.

I said, "Can you be a person who is GONE FROM MY BEDROOM?"

Instead of moving away from me, which I would have much preferred, he scooted closer to me on the bed. "Why are you angry, Lori?"

"Why do I have to explain this to everyone twice?" I ran my hands through my hair and squeezed my head to keep my brain from falling out. "I was trying to go out with

Satan so Adam wouldn't look as bad to my dad. If my dad already *knows* you have a 4.0 and you *know* that he knows, why did you agree to go on a fake date with me?"

"You made me an offer I couldn't refuse," Parker said. "You offered to show me around town and introduce me to people. I knew you were popular because you're always at that party next door." He nodded toward Adam's house. Those Friday night parties, ethereal and magical in my memory, admittedly had been excruciating in reality because I'd always been trying to get Sean's attention. Or, more recently, Adam's.

"And you're so pretty." He scooted even closer to me on the bed and put his hand on my thigh.

Just what I'd waited for all night. And now, not so much. I glared at him.

He wisely removed his hand without further prompting from me. "Lori, come on. Don't be mad. Aren't you basically doing the same thing, putting on this big show for your dad to get what you want? You can't be mad at me for fooling people. Besides, we have to survive another ten minutes in your car together. I don't have another way home."

"Why don't you call your family's helicopter to come get you," I suggested, "or did you make that up too?"

"My family does have a helicopter, but I didn't crash it

into the statue of Vulcan in Birmingham. I hope you didn't believe that part of the story. It only works on twelve-year-old girls."

"Why are you trying to impress twelve-year-old girls? Are you that desperate?"

He opened his mouth.

"Don't answer that," I interrupted. I didn't want to know.

A knock sounded at the door. I thought about tackling Parker on my bed, but now that I knew my dad saw through Parker's whole bad-boy lifestyle, there was no point. I didn't even leap over to Parker and snatch up his hand. "Come in," I called like a girl without issues.

The door creaked open very slowly.

My heart raced. Adam!

No such luck. It was only McGillicuddy, peering into the room with that now-familiar scowl on his face. "Leave this door open," he said.

"What are you doing home?" I demanded. "I thought you had a date with Tammy tonight."

"I do," he said. "I came home to get my car and take a shower before I go over to her house."

I thought for a second. "Why are you just *now* home? What did you and Adam do after we left the movies?"

My brother looked guilty. "Nothing." With a final dark look in Parker's direction, he disappeared.

"McGillicuddy," I called. Now I did drag Parker by the hand after me as I followed my brother into his room.

"That's why I have to take a shower," my brother admitted, opening a drawer and extracting a neatly folded T-shirt. He grabbed the center of the T-shirt he was wearing and stretched it out toward me. "Do I smell like kerosene?"

I sniffed tentatively. "A little." I wondered whether Adam was home taking a shower before his mother could ask him about the peculiar kerosene odor. "If you're going to Tammy's anyway, can you drop off Parker at his grandparents'?"

"No!" Parker exclaimed from behind me.

I turned around. I could tell from the way his eyes flitted back and forth that the look on my brother's face was not any more hospitable than the look on mine.

"I mean . . . ," Parker stammered. Suddenly he focused over my shoulder, and his eyes lit up. "Is that a B-17?"

I looked where he was looking—at the huge model of a World War II–era bomber hanging by fishing line from the ceiling. "Why, yes," I informed him. McGillicuddy had built it from a kit when he was fourteen, and I had applied the decals. It was our pride and joy.

"At home I have a B-17E, with the longer fuselage." Parker stepped farther into my brother's room, closing the

454

gap between them. Clearly he had lost his fear of being eaten.

"I always wanted a B-17G, which has six more guns," my brother said, and with that they lost me. Since I'd been trying to shake some of my grosser tomboy habits, I should have been glad that I was so easily out-boyed by a boy.

"Before I go," I informed both of them, because clearly it was okay for my brother to take Parker home now, "I have one more favor to ask of Parker."

10

I didn't talk to Lori again for a week and a day. I tried to stop being mad at her about Parker. I knew Reggie had made up the indecent incident at the movies. Trouble was, when Reggie had suggested it, I had imagined it, and in my mind it really happened. Maybe if I'd been allowed to talk to her, I could have gotten over it, but since my dad gave me the evil eye if I so much as looked in her direction, the whole insult of it continued to dog me.

Toward the end of the week I couldn't stand it anymore. I called Rachel and asked her what she'd done lately about getting Sean back. Unfortunately for her, or fortunately, depending on what you thought of Lori's plans (and I did not think very much of them), Rachel was not nearly as proactive as Lori. I could have told Rachel that Sean was patient and vengeful. If she didn't do something, the summer would end and he would go to college without ever asking her out again. He might even pine away for her, if he had room in his very small heart to do that, but it would be worth it to him if *she* felt bad about breaking up with him.

So I suggested that she have everyone over to her grandparents' place on the lake. She would see Sean and, God help her, win him back. I would see Lori.

Rachel's grandparents' house was far enough away that my parents and Lori's dad weren't likely to cruise by on the geriatric pontoon boat. It was close enough that we could all drive over there in the wakeboarding boat after business at the marina slowed down. It would look casual and spur-of-the-moment. It would not occur to Lori's dad that Lori and I could get in much trouble there, on the same lake as him, under the watchful eye of extremely old people.

And maybe, just maybe, Lori and I could slip away from McGillicuddy for a few minutes in private.

At least, that's what I figured. But Lori's dad was smarter than I thought. Even though he knew I would be there, he allowed Lori to go. But he made her go in her own boat with McGillicuddy, while I drove with Sean and Cameron.

That was okay. I wakeboarded the whole way over, which helped me get out some aggression. Cameron was driving. He kept trying to run me into shore or over big logs floating in the lake. If I were ten, I would have crashed. But I was sixteen, and I had his number. The lake was mine.

The girl was not. At Rachel's we swam, and we boarded, and we ate, and it would have been a lot of fun if I hadn't been watching Lori the whole time, trying to look like I wasn't watching her, wishing I could get her alone.

Rachel's grandmother already liked me. But she liked Sean more, because he complimented her on her peach cobbler (which was awesome, almost as good as my mom's, but it never would have occurred to me to compliment an old lady on her peach cobbler) and then insisted on helping her clean up the kitchen. He was really turning on the charm with her, but not with Rachel. Thus Rachel's grandmother would ask her a million times a day, *Why don't you date that nice boy Sean?* and Rachel would not want to admit that she had in fact broken up with Sean, and Sean had not asked her out again. I knew how Sean worked.

Late in the afternoon, the other guys went inside to watch the Braves game on TV with Rachel's granddad. I should have been there, and I would catch flak from them later for not being there. However, I was not going to miss a chance to get Lori alone. I lay with her, Rachel, and Tammy on the pier, catching the steeply angled rays of the sun.

Rachel let out a satisfied sigh. "I'm so glad Adam called me and told me to have y'all over."

Lori looked over at Rachel. Lori had her shades on, but I could imagine the shocked look in her eyes.

Rachel wore shades too. However, she was sitting next to me, because we weren't banned from talking to each other, and we had no fear of McGillicuddy looking out the window and seeing us together. Behind her shades, she cut her dark eyes at me.

Lori didn't say a word. She turned and gazed out over the broad lake. But I knew she was wondering how deep my relationship with Rachel went behind the scenes. This moved me a long way toward letting go of my anger at Lori about Parker. Now she had some idea how I felt.

After a pause, she gestured offshore. "I am going to swim out to that island. Adam is going to swim out to that island also."

"I am?" I didn't like being told what to do. But of course I would have swum across the Atlantic to see her. I pulled off my T-shirt, the first time my chest had been bare in a week.

She did the smallest double take but quickly looked away from me again, toward the girls, and pretended to ignore me. "This is all purely for calisthenics, you understand."

"Of course," Rachel and Tammy said.

"So I do not want you to look around, see us missing, and sound the alarm that we have been eaten by bryozoa."

"Bryozoa eats plankton and microscopic stuff in the water," Rachel pointed out.

"Clearly you did not watch the same space-alien movies I watched growing up." Lori pointed at Tammy. "And as for you, missy?"

"Yes?" Tammy asked drily. It sounded like she was almost as used to Lori's plans as I was.

"I can't trust my brother to keep his mouth shut about this," Lori said. "We have to make sure he doesn't see me."

"I have an idea," Tammy said in the halting speech and overenthusiastic delivery of someone reading from a cue card. "Why don't I entice your brother into a dark corner and make out with him to distract him?"

"That is a great idea," Lori said in the same tone.

Tammy stood and dashed up the dock toward the house. At least some people didn't have to be dragged into helping Lori with her plans.

"That leaves me with Sean," Rachel said doubtfully, but I could tell she was trying not to smile.

"And Cameron!" Lori reminded her. "Knock yourself out. Or . . . I guess you want to get rid of them. I know exactly how to make them forget you exist, if they haven't already with the Braves game on. Give them a bowl of Fritos and some dip. Always works for me."

"Wow, it's that easy? Thanks, Lori." Rachel got up and walked toward the house more slowly than Tammy had, watching the windows, undoubtedly hoping Sean would appear, looking for her. No such luck. I knew she held out hope Sean would throw her a bone, and I knew he wouldn't. I knew exactly how she felt.

"Race ya," Lori said. Before I could respond, she was gone. She splashed into the water and crawled at a good clip toward the tiny island three hundred yards from the dock.

I dove in after her, caught up with her in a few strokes, passed her, turned over, and did the backstroke right in front of her, kicking up big splashes in her face just to piss her off. I righted myself, treading water, looking for her.

She wasn't there.

"Sucker!" came from a long way off. I saw her wet blonde head halfway to the island already. She must have passed me by swimming underwater. Now she sank under the surface again.

I swam as fast as I could after her. As I moved nearer to the island, I saw what a genius Lori was and how brilliant a choice the island was for a place to slip away from McGillicuddy. It was possibly even more masterful than my secret make-out hideout. Rachel's grandparents' house was at the end of their neighborhood. Beyond it, the shore stretched around endless bends of red mud cliffs and pine trees, with not a soul in sight. The island sat in front of those cliffs, at the edge of the busy river channel, but a DANGER sign indicating shallow water was stuck between the island and the bank, so boats wouldn't dare float through here. It was private. It was perfect.

I touched bottom and walked through the sand, stirring up bits of mica that glittered like stars in the water. Looking back toward Rachel's grandparents' house and their pier, I watched both disappear behind the trees on the island. Now Lori and I couldn't be seen unless somebody came looking for us.

Lori sat on the sandy, glittery beach of the island, directly in front of the DANGER sign, waiting for me. I waded toward her.

"Why have you been ignoring me all week?" she called. Her voice sounded annoyed. However, she sat leaning on one hand with her long legs folded gracefully, the warm lake lapping at them. With a small wardrobe malfunction of her pink bikini, she could have been a model in one of the issues of *Playboy* she used to steal from McGillicuddy to study what kind of girl Sean was into, so she could be more like her. In fact, I thought at first that she was teasing me by pretending to be that girl. But as I waded closer, I realized she really *was* annoyed, and she was seducing me by accident. Hell, I would have been turned on no matter how she sat.

"I haven't been ignoring you," I said. "I've been obeying my parents."

"There's a first time for everything, I guess." She squinted at me and put up one hand to shield her eyes. A shadow covered half her face. The sun was peeking around my back and blinding her.

I held my ground, squishing my toes in the glittering sand, and made small movements back and forth, just to bug her. The sun was hidden by my body. Then it hit her full force in the eyes. Then it went into hiding again.

She closed one eye. "I don't buy it. You've been avoiding me. You're still punishing me for going out with Parker. And that doesn't make any sense to me, because I sent McGillicuddy over to tell you the Parker thing did not work with my dad at all. McGillicuddy came back and said you just shrugged!"

I shrugged again. "How could you and I have talked about it without somebody seeing us?"

"You managed our trip into the woods okay."

"And we got busted." Since her eyes were watering, I figured she'd had enough of my game with the sun. I sank down in the water in front of her and leaned back on my hands in the sand.

"I guess I've been expecting more out of Mr. Daredevil, Mr. Devil-May-Care." She sat up straight and looked me dead in the eye. "I'm so glad you finally called Rachel and arranged this excuse for us to see each other today."

She knew there was more to this, and she expected me to sing. Who did she think she was dealing with here, Cameron? I hoped I played this cool, but I *did* look away. I wanted to keep her on her toes, wondering if there was something going on between Rachel and me, so she'd be a little bit jealous. But she was my friend, and I felt guilty.

After eyeing me silently for a few more seconds, she finished, "Otherwise, I might not have been able to tell you what I did for you until it was too late for you to take advantage."

"Take advantage?" I looked pointedly at her cleavage. "What you did for me? It must involve underwear."

As fast as one of my brothers, she shoved me. I lost my balance and fell backward into deeper water. She jumped on top of me and dunked me. Yes, I got dunked by a girl, but only because we had trained her well, and she had surprise on her side.

As soon as I realized what had happened, I grabbed her arms above me in the water and lifted her whole body onto my shoulders. She bit off a squeal—remembering at the last moment someone back at the house might hear her. I heaved her as far as I could from the island. By the time she swam all the way back again, water spilling from her long hair, I was sitting exactly where she'd been sitting on the beach before. I was king of this mountain.

She walked up the beach until she stood directly over me. The water from her hair streamed into my eyes. "You are going to be so sorry when you find out what I did for you."

"I doubt it." I laughed. "It felt pretty good to throw you."

"Parker knew all along that my dad saw through him, but he failed to inform me of this. So I got some payback."

I wiped the water out of my eyes and moved a few feet to one side, out of range of her dripping body. "I definitely do *not* want to hear about your payback with Parker."

"Yes, you do." She followed me, stood over me again, and wrung out her hair on my head. "You know, his grandparents' yacht club puts on the Fourth of July fireworks display."

Now I had an inkling of what she was getting at. I

couldn't help smiling as I put both hands over my head to shield myself from the water. "And?"

"And you're going to help."

The splashing had stopped. I looked cautiously up at her. "I am?"

She was standing where I'd stood before. With the sun brushing the tops of the trees onshore directly behind her, I could see her only in silhouette, but I could tell by the movement of her hair that she nodded.

An explosion went off in my heart, followed by a few smaller percussions like a Roman candle. Lori was driving me batty with her plans, but it wasn't every girl who would go out of her way to get you what you wanted most in the world, besides her. Especially when it involved explosives. I breathed, "I love fireworks."

"I know!" She jumped up and down with excitement, and the silhouette of her hair bounced in long wet clumps. "But I understand you didn't want to hear this, and then you threw me into the deep water for no good reason, which hurt my feelings, so I'll call Parker and tell him no thanks."

I reached for the center of her silhouette to grab her wrist. Instead I grabbed cloth, which gave as I tugged on it. The waistband of her bikini.

"Hey." She sounded a lot less outraged than she should have. I was the one embarrassed.

"I can't see you." I rose on my knees until my head was out of the sunlight and I could see her grinning down at me. *Then* I grabbed her wrist and pulled her down on top of me.

"Which is really sad," she grunted as she fell, "because Parker was excited by the idea. He's afraid of fireworks. The yacht club hires a professional company to put on the show, but Parker's grandparents make him help every year. It's almost enough to make him give up his annual summer trip down from Birmingham."

With one hand I made a ponytail out of her wet hair and directed her lips toward mine. I kissed her.

"Mmph." She struggled to move her lips away from mine. "It would have been perfect if you'd done Parker the favor of taking that chore off his hands. Oh well."

While she was talking, talking, talking, I wrestled her down onto the beach and put some of my weight on top of her so she would shut up, and I kissed her again.

This time it worked. I heard her sigh through her nose. I felt her relax under me. Not many girls would engineer a chance for me to set off explosives, and not many girls would enjoy kissing me on this beach. I thought it was nice, but I'd kissed enough girls to predict what they'd be complaining about at this point. The sand was somewhat muddy. Bugs buzzed in the forest surrounding us and might come out to get us at any second. Boats groaned in the river on the other side of the island. They could come roaring around the side of the island without warning and wreck on the DANGER sign. Even Rachel, who put up with a lot, tended to be jumpy about these sorts of things.

Only Lori viewed them like I did, as part of every summer afternoon. She opened her mouth for mine and traced her short fingernails down my back. This made me shudder, like it always did. I wanted to be strong and unaffected every time we touched each other, but the truth was, Lori could do things to me. The only way to keep the upper hand was to do things back to her. I kissed her until she forgot about tracing her fingernails on my back. I worked my way up to her ear. Her arms went limp in the sand.

A motorboat came closer and closer. The sound stayed on the other side of the island. We lay still together, listening to it reach the peak of its volume, then fade as it went on its way downriver. But the spell was broken. I thought we had a few minutes until McGillicuddy would notice we were gone, but not so many that we could risk getting into it again and losing track of time, which we clearly had a problem with.

She looked up at me—not into my eyes, but at my

chin—and seemed fascinated with rubbing her thumb on my stubble. "It makes a crispy noise," she said.

"Admit you like it."

"It hurts." She rubbed her own red cheek. Luckily we'd come over here in the boats, and if her dad asked her about it, she could claim windburn. She pushed my chest, and I let her sit up. Then she looked out across the water toward where the dock and the house would be if we could see through the island, but she put one hand on my thigh. On the *inside* of my thigh, slowly moving up. This told me she was thinking the same thing I was thinking: We probably should be wrapping this up, but we weren't done with each other.

We should skinny-dip. That's what would happen if this were a movie. But I'd never actually known anyone who'd skinny-dipped, or admitted to it. I probably would have done it with my brothers at some point in our lives, except Lori was always around.

That was exactly my problem now. I would have given anything to see her naked, but that would mean she'd see me naked, too. I might have been the impulsive one in my family, but even I had my limits.

"Want to get naked?" she asked.

"No," I said instantly. After I'd thought for a second, I realized my first answer was the right answer for once. No, I did not.

"Me neither," she said.

I sighed with relief, then tried to turn it into some kind of offended gasp. "Why'd you ask, then?"

"You seem hell-bent on putting the last nail in the coffin," she said. "Nothing would get us in more trouble than being caught naked."

"We wouldn't get caught."

"How can you say that?" She threw her wet arms wide in exasperation. Drops of water followed her fingertips, glinting in the sun. "We get caught every time we're together."

I clamped my hand over her mouth and whispered, "That's because you're yelling."

She pulled my hand away and cupped it in both of hers. She studied it, squeezed it, ran her fingers up and down my fingers. Then she looked at me and said, "I've missed you."

I let my head sink until my lips touched her hands, but my eyes never left her green eyes. Love hurt. Honesty made it hurt worse, and I could hardly stand it.

I scooted away from her in the sand and gazed at a few white clouds, purple on their undersides in the late afternoon, in the brilliant blue sky. "This is only happening because of twenty-first-century society," I said. "Two hundred years ago, your dad would be glad to hand you over to me."

"Would he, now." She pushed me until I lay down on my back in the sand.

I thought she would kiss me again. If she did, I wasn't sure I'd let her. It would be ridiculous and uncharacteristic of me to turn down a make-out session from her—not to mention reckless, since the way things were going, I might never get another chance. But the more we kissed, the harder I fell, and the more it hurt.

She only laid her head on my chest, her damp hair spilling onto the sand around us.

I put one hand in her hair and slowly stroked. "Yes, he would let me have you, because I would be the best hunter in the forest. I would keep you clothed and fed and safe. I would be quite the catch. Your dad would be so happy. He'd throw in a cow and a couple of chickens to sweeten the deal."

"You may be right! The early eighteen hundreds were the heyday of the sixteen-year-old male with ADHD." She smoothed her hand down my belly. "The world was your oyster."

"Damn straight." I really was feeling like the world was my oyster that afternoon. In the back of my mind I always knew it wasn't, but a beautiful blonde lay on my chest, and it was easy to pretend she wouldn't be snatched away from me again before the afternoon was over.

"You would not have to do trig." She stroked higher, wrapped her finger around one of my chest hairs, and tugged gently.

"I would not have to do trig," I agreed. "Could you please be more careful with my chest hairs? I don't have many."

"So sorry." Her hand slid lower again, which I liked a lot better anyway. "In the eighteen hundreds, I would have run away with you."

I sat up on my elbows to look at her in surprise. "You would?"

She sat up too. "Yes." She nodded with certainty. "And you would die in a saloon fight and leave me with ten children and one on the way and a crop in the field."

"I would do no such thing."

"Yeah, you would never have made it that far. You would have died of infection one of the times you broke your arm." Her hand moved to my upper arm and massaged the scar where that bone had come out. Her hand moved down and lingered on the scar on my forearm. Her fingers even tickled across the position of the break that had been only a greenstick fracture, with no bone sticking out. She knew my body almost as well as I did.

"Maybe we should stay in this century and work it out," I murmured.

"No, I want to go back to two-hundred years ago, to the dysentery and the head lice. It's so sexy!" She got on her hands and knees and crawled forward until her bikini top was in my line of sight. I'd thought when we first got to the island that she was seducing me by accident. I didn't think so anymore.

"Stop it," I protested. As if.

"Say something else sexy," she purred.

"Louisiana Purchase."

She threw back her head and laughed. "And you got a D in history last semester? That mean teacher just didn't understand you."

But Lori did, and she knew exactly what to say to make me feel like the smartest guy in the world. Or maybe she didn't *know*. Maybe she just did it. Fascinated, I reached out and touched a wisp of her white-blonde hair that had blown across her bottom lip.

Her laughter stopped, and her smile faded. She said huskily, "You're only three weeks older than I am, but when you do something like that, you seem years older."

I do? I wanted to ask. This was news to me. Great news. I held her gaze like I had been aware of this already, and I rubbed my thumb gently across her lip like I'd done it on purpose all along.

"You seem so much more experienced than I am," she

said, "to make such a simple move so sexy." She closed her eyes and leaned forward.

I stroked her face lightly as she put herself into my hand like a cat that wanted to be petted (unlike my mother's cat, which did not want to be touched at all), but I wasn't watching her face anymore. I was watching her bikini top and trying not to explode.

She whispered, "Have you done this with Rachel before?"

I stopped my hand on her face, cupping her sharp chin. She went very still, green eyes on me, and the bugs buzzed louder in the trees behind us.

Of course I'd done this with Rachel. Quite a few other girls, too. Just because I'd been waiting years for Lori to notice me didn't mean I'd been waiting around the house.

I didn't want to lie to her about this. But that wasn't really what she was asking me. She was asking me if it meant more when I touched her, and if I felt more. I did.

She moved her head in my hand, forcing me to stroke her, but her eyes never left mine. She'd made herself vulnerable, and she expected me to do the same, the perfect end to a happy stolen afternoon.

I couldn't. Sorry, but the weekend before, when she was out with Parker, I'd felt vulnerable enough to last me the rest of the summer.

I said slowly, "We should go back. Wouldn't want to outstay your curfew."

"Who would do that?" she asked. "That would be stupid." She said this with no expression. I couldn't tell whether she was mad or not. She started to stand up.

I pulled her back down, rolled on top of her, and kissed her mouth one last time. It could have turned into another long tumble in the sand, and it almost did. But even I knew we really couldn't stay here forever.

We waded together into the water, dove under, and came up doing the American crawl at exactly the same time. The sun wouldn't set for another few hours, but it had weakened since the midday heat. Now the water was warmer than the air. Crawling through it was like swimming through myself. The whole lake was mine, and Lori was too. Bad as things still looked for convincing her dad I wasn't a criminal, at that moment I figured everything would work out okay. There was no way it couldn't on a beautiful day like this.

We reached the dock. She treaded water and nodded toward the ladder. "You go first. Check for bryozoa. My hero."

I climbed up. There wasn't a slimy colony of bryozoa lurking on the rungs, and I'm not sure I would have told her if there were, because I liked to hear her squeal. I reached down and held out my hand to her—not that she ever needed help, but I felt good doing it.

"Better not even stand on the dock together," she said. "The longer we stay, the more likely they're watching. You go ahead. They probably want to get going before dark. I'll stay down here and act like I've been sunning myself the whole time. If they ask whether we were together, I'll say, 'Oh, has Adam been missing too? He must have gone for a long walk. I have no idea why he would do that. Mysterious!'"

"Yeah, maybe nobody will ask you," I said, shaking my head. "Don't go offering that awful routine unless they ask, okay? Jesus." I walked up the dock, snagged my towel, and put on my shirt.

"I'm going to try out for the school play just to spite you," she called. "You'll see. I'll show you all!"

I looked back at her treading water, just a blonde head in a vast blue lake under a blue sky.

Then I jogged up the sidewalk through the trees. Because I was sneaky enough to give the alibi some plausibility, I walked around the neighborhood for a few minutes, then walked through the garage in front of the house and entered the hall. I met Rachel coming out of the bathroom.

"Hey!" she greeted me. "Did you have a nice time doing calisthenics?"

"It was okay. Did Sean ask you out?"

"I think he may ask out my grandmother before he asks me." She giggled, but her laughter died off with her smile. "If she didn't have fifty years on him, I would seriously say he was flirting with her. I think my granddad was jealous. When Sean acts like somebody he's just met is his BFF, is it all a put-on to make his ex mad and to get more peach cobbler? Or does he feel something? Does he like my grandmother as a friend, or is he making fun of her in his mind?"

"I honestly don't know." I had wondered this myself. I glanced down the hall toward the den. "Where is everybody, anyway? I hope Sean isn't in the house, the way you're talking about him. If he were, I would need to give you some lessons in sneaky."

She giggled again. Still watching the doorway to the den, I wished Lori would come around the corner and see me with Rachel when she was giggling like that. But I should have stopped thinking that way. As Lori had explained, there really was nothing to her date with Parker and no reason for me to be jealous.

"No," Rachel said, "Sean and Tammy and McGillicuddy are out on the deck. Lori was out there a minute ago. She had a text message on her phone from her dad that said he and Frances were cruising to Chimney Rock. She said it sounded like her dad couldn't sit still, worrying about whether she was seeing you over here."

"It *does* sound like that," I agreed. Good thing Lori and I had come back to the house when we did, before her dad and Frances took a detour from Chimney Rock, rode by here out of curiosity, and found a certain island hideaway.

Rachel nodded. "Lori thought it was the perfect chance to scare her dad. Things didn't work out with Parker, so she decided to try the plan with Cameron. They just left for Chimney Rock in one of the boats. What's the matter? Hey, wait—"

I was already running down the hall. Rachel's grandmother was in the kitchen, and I should have stopped and thanked her for the afternoon, but I was sure Sean had more than made up for me already, and there was no time. I dashed through the den and burst out the door onto the deck.

"Cameron made out with Lori when she was eleven!" I yelled.

Sean and Tammy looked around at me with wide eyes. McGillicuddy looked at me too, but he watched me with that war-criminal stare, waiting for the one last sliver of evidence he needed to beat the monkey out of his best friend.

"In the warehouse," I panted. "When he was fourteen.

So if you think he is innocently helping her out with her plan—"

Now McGillicuddy was the one making a mad dash. I ran after him, passed him on the dock, and jumped into the driver's seat of the only boat left. I cranked it without looking behind me to see if McGillicuddy had untied it or if Sean had made it in. But as I maneuvered into the open water, I heard Sean laughing as McGillicuddy yelled, presumably to Tammy up on the deck, "I'll call you!"

Out in the main river channel, I accelerated the boat as fast as it would go and stared ahead at the blue water, willing the miles away so we could be at Chimney Rock already. I pictured Lori asking Cameron to kiss her in front of her dad. Cameron would be more than happy to oblige. And somewhere in the middle of that kiss—she didn't mean to, you understand—she would remember why she'd always looked up to the older boys, and she would fall for my other brother.

Echoing my thoughts, McGillicuddy walked past me into the bow and stood there with the hard wind blowing his blond hair straight back, hands on his hips.

Sean sat down across the aisle and leaned toward me. If he made a snide comment, I would punch him.

He hollered at me over the motor, "Are you going to yak?"

I jerked my head around at him, ready for a fight. But his face didn't give away that he was setting me up to be the butt of a joke, like I'd expected. He looked concerned. Of course he was not concerned. Sean was not capable of this. He had contorted his face into a facsimile of concern.

"No, why?" I yelled back, still bracing myself for the other half of the joke.

"You look really pale all of a sudden." He reached across the boat and put his hand on my shoulder.

We stayed that way for approximately three seconds, him doing his concerned older brother imitation and me watching him like he'd grown another head, waiting for him to crack up.

Then he took his hand away, turned to the front, and stared into the wind like McGillicuddy and me.

It seemed like hours, but in only a few minutes we reached Chimney Rock. Here the cliffs were higher, made of granite instead of red clay. Stacks of boulders like chimneys jutted out from the bank. For their trouble, they'd been covered in graffiti over the years, just like the bridge across the lake. A path led from the shore up the side of one boulder, where you could jump three yards into the water. That was for kids. The path kept snaking up through the woods until it emerged on an outcropping where you could jump ten yards into the water. And if you were really daring, you followed the path to the top of the rock, a twenty-yard fall into the lake.

That's why boats floated in front of the colorful cliffs now: to see who would jump. A lot of people walked out onto the highest outcropping. Very few of them went off. The folks in the boats below taunted them and chanted their names if they knew them, but most would-be jumpers stared at the water for a few minutes, then made their way back down to the middle rock and jumped amid boos from the boaters. Which was probably just as well, because people had been killed jumping off the highest cliff.

But I wasn't interested in the jumpers today. Powering down the engine before I rammed someone, I scanned the crowd of boats.

"There they are." McGillicuddy pointed to the far edge of the group of boats. I maneuvered forward until I picked out our target by its high wakeboarding bar. Cameron sat behind the wheel, watching the highest rock, because he was chicken and fascinated. And Lori sat sprawled in the bow, also seeming to watch the rock behind her shades, legs spread like a boy.

At the sound of our motor coming closer, she looked around and sat up, grinning. "Hey!" she called as if nothing were wrong. We idled even nearer, and still she didn't clue in to the look on my face or on her brother's. "We've been here for a few minutes, but we haven't seen Dad. He sent that text message quite a while ago, so he and Frances must have come and gone. We were just about to head home ourselves. Oh well. It was a good idea, wasn't it?"

"Spectacular." I cut the engine and reached out for the side of the other boat so the two boats wouldn't grind together, and so Cameron couldn't get away.

McGillicuddy vaulted from one boat into the other and walked down the aisle until he stood in front of Cameron. "Hey, buddy."

"Hey." Cameron craned his neck to peer at the rock on the other side of McGillicuddy's body. "Can't see through ya."

McGillicuddy folded his arms. "I hear you kissed Lori in the warehouse when she was eleven."

"Adam!" Lori shrieked.

I didn't even care that she found out I'd spilled her secret. I focused on Cameron, who was floundering in his seat, looking at Lori and then at me looking for anybody to blame.

Finally he had to face McGillicuddy again. "I was fourteen," he said sheepishly.

"I was fourteen a little over a year ago," I said. "You give it a bad name."

"If you want to teach him a lesson," Sean called from the other side of the boat, out of the fray, "I have an idea." He nodded toward Chimney Rock.

McGillicuddy reached down toward Cameron in the seat, and I reached forward. Between the two of us, with the threat of Sean as backup, we nudged and bullied Cameron into our boat, leaving Lori alone.

"Guys," Lori called. "Y'all. Don't do anything to him for coming over here with me. It was at my behest."

"He needs to learn when to say no," I threw over my shoulder at her as I started the engine. With McGillicuddy and Sean guarding Cameron in the bow, I idled the boat forward, easing through the crowd, until we touched land. Sean jumped out and tied the boat at the base of the path.

Cameron just sat there, refusing to budge, until McGillicuddy and I stood behind him and nudged him again. He was beginning to get the idea that there was no way out of this.

If all of us hadn't been so accustomed to each other through years of bullying, he might have tried to escape into the water or to plead his case. But he knew it was no use, and if he begged, he'd be doing it in front of a crowd, which probably included some people he knew. He eased out of his seat and skulked to the bow like he had an appointment to walk the plank. Which, in a way, he did.

The three of us moved up the path. Sean fell in behind us, smirking. "Cameron, remember when you threw me off that first rock?" he called. "Remember I told you I'd get you back?"

"I was in third grade, you idiot. Only you would remember that."

This was untrue. By pegging the grade he'd been in himself, Cameron had given away that he remembered it, too. And I remembered every insult as freshly as Sean did, every blow, every time Cameron had shoved *me* off that rock. On impulse I reached forward and slapped Cameron on the back of the head.

"Hey!" he roared, turning on me.

McGillicuddy put one meaty hand on Cameron's chest to hold him off me. "Keep walking, my friend," he said with a threat in his voice.

We emerged from the trees onto the highest plateau, with more graffiti sprayed on the flat surface: GO BACK! DANGER! JUMP AT YOUR OWN RISK! Cameron eyed it as McGillicuddy and Sean and I continued to walk him slowly forward, nudging him, shoving him, stepping on his bare toes.

"People really have died jumping off this thing." He controlled his voice carefully, trying to keep face as the oldest brother, yet really, *really* not wanting to jump off this cliff. "If I die, Mom will kill you."

"You should have thought of that before you made out with my little sister." McGillicuddy pushed Cameron hard enough that Cameron stumbled dangerously near the edge, and there was a half second when I thought he would lose his balance and tumble over.

He righted himself, breathing hard. The rest of us stood in a semicircle around him—close enough that he had no escape route between us, but far enough away that he couldn't pull a kamikaze move by grabbing one of us to take over the cliff with him. I seriously doubted Cameron had the balls to do this, but stranger things had happened, and it was in the back of all of our minds as we faced each other uneasily.

"What do you want?" he demanded.

"Stay away from my sister," McGillicuddy said. "Or we will bring you right back here, and we will not be so polite about it."

I'd suppressed how I felt when I'd realized Cameron was with Lori. I'd acted cool on the boat, and I'd kept it inside for the walk up here. Suddenly I couldn't keep it contained anymore, and it burst out of me in anger. "I wish you *would* go out with her again," I challenged him.

"Adam," McGillicuddy growled. "Wrong direction."

"Touch her," I yelled at Cameron. "Just look at her. If you do—when does Giselle get back from Europe? Two weeks from now? I will drive straight to your college and tell her that you called my girlfriend buried treasure, and that you were willing to whore yourself just to make her daddy mad. And then I will take Giselle out for coffee to console her, and one thing will lead to another . . ."

I could feel McGillicuddy's eyes on me. Sean covered his mouth to keep from laughing. But Cameron watched me carefully, as serious as I was. "Giselle would not be caught dead going out with a sixteen-year-old."

"We'll see," I said.

McGillicuddy had changed his mind about the effectiveness of my threat. He chimed in, "With the beard, Adam looks older. Hell, he's taller than Sean."

"Hey!" Sean protested.

"Okay," Cameron said. "I mean, of *course* I'm going to stay away from Lori. I didn't seek her out in the first place. *She* came up to *me* and said . . ."

I took a step toward him.

He eyed me. ". . . And I was just trying to help her, and you . . ."

I took another step toward him. I didn't care whether he took me over the cliff with him or not. If he didn't swear to stay away from Lori, he was going over.

"Okay!" he exclaimed. "Yes, I was wrong. Okay?"

When I didn't budge, he turned to McGillicuddy to save him. "Okay?"

"Okay." McGillicuddy grabbed him by the back of the neck and pulled him away from the edge. "Let's go."

For all their big talk and big threats, the three of them sure did hurry away from the edge now that we had this settled. They reached the trail and disappeared into the trees without looking back to see if I was following them.

I stepped all the way to the edge. The boats were tiny, and the water was dark blue here, the deepest part of the lake. In one of the boats closest to the cliff, I picked out Lori by her long blonde hair and perfect body and pink bikini. She stared up at me with her hands over her mouth. Somebody in another boat must have recognized me, or more likely thought I was Sean, because a faint chant made its way up to me: "Va-*der*! Va-*der*! Va-*der*!

I backed up three paces, took a running start, and jumped.

The wind was what I noticed. Underneath it I thought I could hear Lori screaming, but the wind was too loud in my ears for me to be sure. It was cold on my skin despite the light of the setting sun. The boats and the lake rushed up at me. I felt high.

Then I hit the water hard—a lot harder than I expected, harder than it had felt smacking into me the millions of times I'd jumped off the middle cliff. The impact took my breath away, but only for a second. I sank so deep in the water that I hit a patch of bone-soaking cold. That woke me up again. If I sank any farther, I wouldn't make it to the surface before I had to take a breath. I clawed my way toward the sunbeams shining through the surface.

I burst into the air and sucked in big lungfuls of it. Now that I knew I was alive, the high was wearing off already. My skin stung where I'd hit the water. And when I saw Lori in the boat with her hands still covering her mouth, I remembered how angry I was. I swam over to her and hauled myself up on the wakeboarding platform in back.

She rushed toward me. "Are you okay?"

I frowned at her. "No, I am definitely not okay." I wrung out my T-shirt on her pink-tipped toes.

Her expression turned from concern to irritation as she realized I was upset about her escape across the lake with Cameron. "I mean, did you break your wrist or something? Again? You look really pale."

"I think that must be left over from the shock and horror!" I started this sentence calmly, but by the time I finished, I was yelling at her, unloading everything I felt. Luckily my brothers and McGillicuddy had descended the rock and were heading in our direction in the other boat, so

I wouldn't have to stay here with her much longer.

She flinched at my voice. Slowly she recovered, putting her hands on her hips and frowning down at me. "I thought we had a nice afternoon, Adam. I thought we fixed everything."

The other boat arrived and floated slowly past, allowing McGillicuddy to jump on next to me. I traded places with him. Then, just as Sean started the engine again to take us home, I looked her square in her green eyes and let her know exactly what I thought of her and her plan right now. I said, "So did I," and turned toward the sunset.

11

"Stay home tonight."

These were the first words Adam had spoken to me since he jumped off Chimney Rock last weekend. After the boys and I finished our wakeboarding practice Friday afternoon, I was tying the boat to the dock cleat when he jumped onto the wharf and bent to mutter this in my ear. He never stopped, just kept walking, carrying his life vest and wakeboard into the warehouse.

Of course, this was for the best. I glanced up at the screened porch of my house, where my dad was always watching—or if he wasn't, I *thought* he was, which amounted to the same thing. Adam had taken a big risk by bending down to talk to me at all.

On the other hand, you would think a boy with as much savvy and—let's face it—as many impulse control issues as Adam could have risked another tryst with me at some point during this whole week. He hadn't because he was still mad about Cameron.

Plus . . . what did he want me to stay home for? Was he sending me a message via carrier pigeon? Or did he want me to stay home just so he'd know where I was while he went out and had fun? It was like him lately not to tell me and to expect me to play along.

And I'd had enough. I decided I should go out that night, just to spite him.

Problem was, I had no one to go with. Tammy would be out with McGillicuddy. I sure wished Rachel was available. I'd been itching to milk her for more about what had happened when she dated Adam in May. In the past he'd talked like their relationship hadn't meant much, but last weekend at the island, he'd hinted at something more serious.

There would be no milking tonight. Rachel needed to spend Fourth of July holiday time with her family—which she said was an okay trade-off, since she got to take care of this on July the second. After a two-week hiatus for the beer infraction, the Vaders had reinstated the boys' weekly party, just in time for a blowout tomorrow night on July the third. Rachel would be able to come to that. And she could come with all of us to watch Adam's fireworks over the lake on the Fourth.

So nine o'clock Friday night found me sitting at my desk in my room, carefully piecing together the tail of a B-52 Stratofortress. I'd bought the model earlier in the week because McGillicuddy and Parker's convo piqued my interest again. I missed building models. It was strangely calming to construct something according to someone else's predetermined plan. A month ago I'd thought I needed to stop doing anything tomboyish so I could blend in with girls better and catch boys more efficiently. Now that I'd caught one and my dad had thrown him back, I didn't see the point in trying.

As I carefully lowered my X-Acto knife to place one of the machine guns, the gun fired a cloud of bullets! At least, that's what it sounded like. I bent to retrieve the knife, which had narrowly missed my foot, and wondered whether I'd inhaled too much glue. Then the noise came again—tiny rocks thrown against my window.

I turned out the lights, waited a few seconds with my eyes closed to adjust them to the dark, and looked outside. Adam stood between the trees. It could have been Sean—they looked enough alike—but Sean would never hike around in the woods in the hot, humid summer night without good reason. It would mess up his hair.

Adam switched a flashlight on and off to signal me in Morse code, which I'd picked up through many years playing army. The boys always made me hold the grenades. Dot, dash, dash, dash . . .

J-U-M-P

Was he referring to his fall from Chimney Rock last Sunday? Did he want a medal? I opened my window, leaned out as far as I could without losing my balance, and stage-whispered, "What do you mean, jump?"

He walked closer. I still couldn't see his face well enough to make out whether it was Adam, but his skull-and-crossbones pendant glinted in the moonlight. He stood directly under the window and held out his arms as if he would catch me.

I looked guiltily around my dark room. I'd never snuck out of my bedroom before. I didn't particularly want to be disobedient. I loved my dad. I wanted to get along with him. Being a wayward teen seemed like a lot more trouble than it was worth.

I looked back at Adam. He tapped his foot.

Decision made. I stuffed some pillows into my bed and pulled the covers over them. If this was supposed to be me, I had gained a lot of weight and I was not carrying it well, because I was looking awfully rectangular. However, McGillicuddy was out with Tammy and Dad

493

was downstairs with Frances. I seriously doubted anyone would come up to check on me and discover that I had turned into polyfill.

I lowered the window until the opening was barely wide enough for me to squeeze my butt through. Then I eased out, feet first, realizing as my toes scraped the shingles that I should have worn shoes, and realizing as my thighs scraped the shingles that jeans would not have been a bad idea either. I crawled backward down the short section of the roof and hung my legs over the eaves. This was my last chance to go back. I looked up at the dark glass.

"Drop," Adam whispered from below. "I've got you."

I took one last deep breath. I had to psych myself up to take risks. I was not like Adam. I counted in my head, one, two, three . . . and could not quite bring myself to let go. I started over. One, two, I wanted to see Adam, didn't I? Three.

"Oof!" Adam caught me all right, with the side of his head. I could tell by the feel of his skull on my foot as I kicked him. He grabbed me as best he could anyway, and we half landed, half fell in the pine needles.

He lay facedown on the ground. I flopped him over on his back to make sure he was alive. If he had a concussion, we'd have to call the ambulance, which meant we'd get caught and he'd get sent to military school. On the bright side, maybe the military school would not take him if he had brain damage. "I'm so sorry."

"Worth it," he grunted. He rolled onto his feet like a ninja and grabbed my hand. "Hurry, before they release the hounds."

We ran through the dark yard, chased by imaginary barking noises. We didn't have far to go. He stopped in the woods halfway between my house and his and made an "after you" gesture at the ladder of his tree house.

"Are you sure?" I asked. "A family of foxes lived in it last year."

"Don't worry. I've cleaned it out a little since then."

I climbed the ladder and peeked up into the tree house. His old sleeping bag covered the plywood floor. Pillows cushioned the plywood walls.

"Ohhh, this is so cool." He'd gone out of his way to plan this. I climbed the rest of the way up and slid across the soft padding to make room for him. He sat beside me. The tree house was smaller than I remembered. It had seemed like a kingdom floating above the forest when we were kids. Now we could stretch out, but just barely.

He leaned behind me and flicked his lighter. A candle sputtered to life. The soft light kissed his intense face, sparkled in his beard, smoothed the worried lines between his brows.

"We're going to catch the tree house on fire," I warned him. "And the forest, your house, the marina, the whole neighborhood. My dad will be so pissed."

"It's in a container." He showed me the candle in a jar. "And it's on a metal pie plate. Check me out. I think ahead."

"You do!" I really was impressed, because padded tree houses and candles in jars were not like Adam at all.

I sat back against the pillows and watched him. He put his hands behind his head and relaxed against the pillows too. We sat a little apart from each other, but our legs made an angle and our feet met in the middle. I stroked his broad, tanned foot with my pinky toe. He didn't shy away, but he didn't make a move on me either.

He took a deep breath and let out a slow sigh. "It's been a long time since I've sat outside at night," he said. "Well, it *seems* like a long time. I guess it was only three weeks ago, on your birthday, in my Secret Make-Out Hideout."

"That fateful night," I said ruefully.

"I forgot how loud it is out here," he said.

We listened for a long time, and I stroked his foot with my toe.

"And how many layers," I finally said. "A low hum on the bottom, then a medium, then a high hum. That's the background. Then there's the croaking, like a chanting, and every few seconds a chirp." I moved my toe to the underside of his foot, where he was ticklish.

Now he jerked away, but he still didn't take the hint and scoot in my direction.

I reached over and slid my hand underneath his shirt.

The hard muscles of his stomach jumped at my touch. I almost laughed—not because it was funny, but because I was so overwhelmed with surprise that I could make his body react like that.

"If you could draw this sound," I said, "it would look like the surface of the lake when you dribble water into it. A circle around a drop." I put my fingers together on his skin, then expanded them outward, trailing my fingertips. "Another circle." I moved my fingers and expanded them out. "Another circle." I moved my fingers. "And lines between them, as you move the water drops from one place to another on the surface." I dragged my finger up his stomach to his chest.

He gasped.

I did laugh out loud this time. "Sorry."

He put his hand on top of my hand, with only his T-shirt between them. "Don't be sorry." Then he slid his hand across his chest, onto *my* shirt, and ventured underneath. He did this very cautiously, probably waiting for me to hit him. I did not.

"I hear what you mean about the circles." He drew expanding circles with his fingertips in different places on my tummy, just as I'd done to him. "And the lines. But to me, it wouldn't look like the surface of the lake. It would look like fireworks." He dragged one finger from the waistband of my shorts upward, dipping into my belly button and out again. A bottle rocket shooting off.

My whole body was going up in flames as I watched him in the candlelight. Any second he would lean forward to kiss me, and it would be a doozy.

Instead he asked, "Do you remember this?" Sitting up again, he reached behind a pillow and pulled out a weathered wooden sign that had hung over the ladder years ago. The letters we'd scratched with a pocketknife were still visible.

"Oh my God." I laughed. "KEEP OUT JERKS. You remember that day?"

"Of course I remember," he said. "Sean told us that we couldn't play, and McGillicuddy and Cameron sided with him—"

"I hated when they ganged up on us," I mused.

"—and usually we did what they said and hung around them like abused dogs. This time we said to hell with them and came here. We made this sign and nailed it to the tree."

"And then we waited for them to notice we were gone

and come looking for us," I said. "They would see that *we* were the cool ones and *they* were the ones excluded, and they would rue the day, I tell you!" I thought for a moment. "And we ate Double Stuf Oreos out of the bag and talked, and finally we went home. They never did miss us and I doubt they rued the day, but it was a nice afternoon." I thought again. "Do you have any Double Stuf Oreos?"

He gave me a reproving look. I wished I hadn't said this, because now it seemed like I didn't appreciate everything else he'd brought.

I started, "I'm just jok—"

He reached beneath a pillow and dragged out a package of Double Stuf Oreos.

Frances had never bought Double Stuf Oreos for McGillicuddy and me. One stuff was enough, she said. All we got was single-stuff whole-wheat faux Oreos from the organic grocery store. I would not swear to it, but I'd bet the stuff was made of tofu. Mrs. Vader, in contrast, did not go to such pains for her family, or perhaps she was just tired. This would have made her home a very attractive place for me to hang out even if there had been no boys. With boys *and* Oreos, it was heaven.

I lifted the chocolate lid and dug into the icing. "Mmmmmm," I said. It was even better than I remembered. Mmmmmm, I put the rest of it in my mouth and shamefully,

I might have forgotten Adam was sitting there, until I looked up and noticed he was watching me. "Wha?" I asked around cookie.

"You look like you are really enjoying that Oreo."

Embarrassed, I swallowed. "I beg your pardon. I have been living on an athletic training diet of microwave pizza and Frances's muscadine chutney from five years ago."

"Is chutney supposed to age? Yikes." He munched his own cookie and scooted the bag closer to me. "Have another."

I dug into the bag and munched on a second cookie, happily looking around our dark, cozy nest in the flickering candlelight. "The tree house seems smaller," I said. "You seem bigger."

"Flattery will get you everywhere."

"But the Double Stuf Oreos taste exactly the same." My voice cracked from a crumb caught in my throat. I might need to bail out of the tree house and drink from the lake.

"I'm sure they have very good quality control." Then the boy who Never Planned Ahead dug under yet another pillow to produce two bottles of water. He always brought two, I'd noticed. Either he was afraid of my cooties, or he knew I was afraid of *his* cooties, ever since the time years ago when Sean spit in my Coke.

"Thank you so much," I croaked. As I sipped the cold water, I eyed him. Except for the beard, he looked relaxed and innocent, which was not like him at all. "So, what's the occasion?"

"What do you mean?" he asked too quickly. "I wanted to see you. I've been dying to see you."

"Right, but normally you would just spontaneously drag me into the woods. If you've engineered all this, something's up."

He blinked innocently at me for a few more seconds, then gave in. "Okay. It's about the plan."

"Your plan for us to run away to Montgomery? Let me guess. You've decided we can stay in the tree house and live on Double Stuf Oreos instead." I slid my hand onto his thigh. "That's actually not a bad idea."

He looked at my hand. "No, it's about *your* plan to change your dad's mind about me." He picked up my hand. "I have something important I want to ask you." He kissed my hand. "You know, when you were out with Parker and Cameron, I got angry."

"You brought me here and wined and dined me"—I nodded toward the Oreos—"just to tell me this? Your temper is not news."

He put our hands under his chin and locked eyes with me. "Sean's next, isn't he?"

He seemed so earnest, I didn't want to leave this question hanging in the air. I wanted to reassure him. But I didn't want to lie to him, either. He would have seen through it, anyway. He already did. Sean was my last resort, if only I could figure out a way to use him.

"Don't go out with Sean," Adam said. "Stop the plan. Just give your dad some time to cool down, like my parents wanted. Maybe we won't have the rest of the summer together. But in the fall, I'll do my best on the football team. Everybody loves football players, right? We seem so all-American and wholesome."

I took back my hand. "College football players have been involved in a rash of shootings."

"We'll worry about that later. This is high school, and I can be the hometown darling if Coach lets me start as quarterback."

"What are the chances of that?" I asked. "I mean, I have every confidence in you, but you have to get past that rising senior with a sixty percent completion rate in last year's postseason."

He just looked at me. Most boys seem taken aback when I spout sports statistics, as if girls aren't allowed to keep up with that sort of thing. Not Adam. He was used to me. He was staring at me because he was honestly trying to convince me his own plan would work.

"I have every confidence in you," I repeated.

He huffed out a breath through his nose like he didn't

believe me. "Plus, I swear I will not get put on academic probation this year. I will make the minimum GPA for eligibility. I might even stay a tenth of a point or two ahead."

"A 2.2?" I asked. "Gosh, Adam, don't put yourself out."

"I'm serious, Lori. I will be a model citizen all semester long, and by Christmas surely your dad will let us be together, if you'll just forget about your plan. And Sean."

"And we wouldn't see each other all that time?" I contemplated a whole summer and fall without him. We were supposed to spend the Fourth of July together. He would start as quarterback in the fall, like he said, and I was supposed to go with him to parties after games. And what about the homecoming dance?

He shook his head. "We would sacrifice the short-term for the long-term goal. We would be obedient."

"Like dogs." I hadn't forgotten his *woof* at my dad.

"Something like that."

"I think my plan would be better. A lot faster."

"I'm not playing." He took my hand again. "Tell me you'll wait for me. Please."

I probably would have tried to talk him out of it if I'd thought he was just jealous of Sean. I mean, honestly, higher than a rock-bottom C average? Adam? That would require him to make a B in something. But there was more to it than that. He lifted his chin when he talked about my dad being proud of him and our whole town worshipping the ground he walked on. He didn't just want to get out of this awful sitch we were in. He wanted to earn his way out.

I swallowed and said, "Okay."

"Okay?" He hunched down so his face was even with mine and looked straight into my eyes. "Really?"

"Really." My stomach hurt when I said it.

He sighed. His whole body went limp with relief on the sleeping bag. "Thank you. You won't be sorry. Now, there's one more thing."

"Oreos are poisonous? Then I'm screwed." I laughed. "Hey, then it really would be like *Romeo and Juliet*, if we both ate poisonous cookies and died here in your tree house together."

He stared blankly at me.

"Adam. *Everybody* has to read *Romeo and Juliet*. Did you flunk ninth grade English?"

"I made a D-minus. No, that's not what I was going to say. I was going to say, I was so happy that night we made out, and I've been kicking myself since then that we fell asleep. Now we won't get any more time together until Christmas, maybe not then, maybe . . ."

Not ever. I was afraid that's what he was thinking. I didn't say it.

His chest rose and fell with a deep breath. "Before we

say good-bye, I want a do-over of that night. Just this one last night with you."

He leaned over me. My body sparked again, like a match held to fuel that burst into flame all over. He pressed down on me. I leaned up to meet him. Our mouths met for that doozy of a kiss I'd been waiting for.

For a few minutes we enjoyed what we'd been missing. He drew back, trailing short kisses across my cheek, into my hairline. He whispered in my ear, "I love you, Lori."

I reached down and found his warm hand, calloused from wakeboarding and yard work and bottle-rocket burns. I rubbed my thumb in his palm and turned my head so I could look into his light blue eyes, which seemed to glow in the candlelight and the dark. "I love you, too."

He winced. He blinked. This was about to go very bad, because Adam was going to cry. "I miss you," he said, and his voice broke.

"I'm not gone yet." I could hardly bear the thought of being without him until Christmas or after, but seeing him cry would be even worse. So I pushed him down into the softness of the sleeping bag and tried to make him forget.

"Still alive?" I asked him an hour and a half later.

He chuckled. By now we'd been in the tree house so long that I'd become nocturnal, like the foxes who used to hang out here. The candle had burned low, but I could still see every curve of his face and every golden hair in his baby beard as he lay on his side, watching me. The worry lines between his brows were gone.

I touched the space where the lines had been, then took my hand away. "I'd better go. I wouldn't want to miss my curfew."

"You make no sense whatsoever," he said, but he must have agreed with me, because he sat up and ran his hands back through his hair to detangle his curls.

"It's the principle of the thing. I'm coming home before curfew, as I discussed with my dad. He simply does not know who I was with. Or that I was out at all. Details." I waved them away.

He caught my hand and shook it, the deceptively basic first move in the secret handshake we'd started when we were in first grade. "One last time?"

We shook hands upside down, with a twist, high five, low five, pinky swear, elbows touching.

"And add this." He traced the tips of his thumb and finger across my lips, zipping them. "Keep your mouth shut, and I promise to keep mine shut. With football stardom and my GPA in the bag, we'll be dating again before you know it."

"Sounds like a plan." I rolled over to the ladder and climbed down, reluctantly watching our cozy nest disappear above my head. Adam didn't bother with the ladder. He jumped down beside me and took my hand. We walked through the dark forest like nothing was wrong.

And nothing was. We would stay apart. My dad would come to his senses. We would get back together. But this future was predicated on Adam starting as quarterback, keeping up his grades, and generally making good. As McGillicuddy had said on the sad morning after my birthday, *Sometimes what Adam intends to do and what he actually does are two different things.*

"I worry," I admitted.

"Why do you worry?" Adam's voice came from above me. He'd been taller than me since fourth grade or so, and I'd never gotten used to it.

"You like a challenge," I said.

"Yes."

"You like danger."

"Sorry."

We reached the edge of my yard, as close as I dared come to my house without fear of being overheard. I turned to him and said softly, "I worry that you'll lose interest in me now that I'm not a dangerous challenge."

He stroked the back of my hand with his thumb. "You are the one way I'm normal. When I'm with you, I don't feel like there's anything wrong with me."

"There's *not* anything wrong with you. You're high-spirited."

"I sound like a horse."

"You *are* like a horse." He was exactly like a colt incessantly dashing around the paddock and leaping away from the fence for no apparent reason.

"Like a stallion?" He pressed his lips together, trying not to laugh. He was so adorable.

"That's a good note to say good-bye on," I said. "I will remember you just like this, feeling your oats—"

"Ha!"

"—and whinnying about yourself."

"Good." Gently he kissed my forehead. Then he squeezed my hand and let me go.

With a deep sigh of regret, I walked toward my house alone, looking up at my bedroom window. After about ten feet I stopped, turned around, and walked back to where Adam still stood. "How do I get back inside?"

He closed his eyes. Probably he was counting to ten, which was very mature of him—and I would have been proud of his self-control, except that it meant I had screwed up.

He opened his eyes. "You are mine," he said slowly, "and you are blonde, and I love you, but damn. You get back inside by using your key."

I licked my lips. "What key?"

"The house key you put in your pocket before you jumped out your window."

I glanced behind me at my house, which suddenly loomed like a haunted mansion, monsters lurking inside. Widower monsters with OCD. "I need to work on this disobedience thing, because I am not good at it." I could still joke with Adam, but my heart raced. "What do I do? Can you pick the lock?"

"I can't pick the dead bolt. Use the spare key hidden under a fake rock in the flower bed." Though his words were reasonable, I could hear the same rising panic in them that I felt.

"We don't have a fake rock," I said tightly. "My dad works with criminals and thinks he has a bead on them. Burglars know all about the fake rock. Besides, he's sitting with Frances in the den. No matter what, he'll hear me when I unlock the door."

"Wait out here with me until McGillicuddy comes home and sneak in with him," Adam said.

Now *that* was a good idea. McGillicuddy would protest, but he wouldn't really rat me out when it meant such dire consequences for Adam. I was so relieved! I grabbed Adam in a bear hug.

The kitchen door swung wide open at the same time all the outside lights flicked on, blinding us.

I jumped away from Adam.

"LORI ELIZABETH McGILLICUDDY!" my dad roared.

"The hounds caught us after all," Adam said calmly.

"Adam!" I whispered. "Run!"

"No," he said in a normal voice, even though we could hear my dad stomping toward us through the pine needles and the blinding light. "I'm not hiding from him. I won't let you take the fall for this."

"There won't be a fall. If he doesn't see you, he'll have no idea I was with you. I'll tell him I just wanted to go for a walk by myself on a beautiful summer night."

"Out your window? Anyway, he's seen me already."

"Well, he has *now*." I raised my voice to a normal tone, too, now that we were busted yet again.

Dad's silhouette loomed in front of us. Frances's was farther back, still in the garage, allowing her man to take care of family business. I felt a stab of anger at her for refusing to help Adam and me in the first place.

But it was pointless now. My dad hardly glanced at me. Focusing on Adam, he waved in the direction of the Vaders' house. He didn't prod Adam with a shotgun, but that was the overall effect.

I could tell from the looks on both their faces that Adam was going to military school.

I woke the next morning and stared at the ceiling, searching for a reason to get out of bed. Why should I go to work? If I was a no-show, my parents couldn't do anything worse than send me to military school. And I didn't need any money where I was going.

On the other hand, I could add to my stash, and the day before I was supposed to go to school, I could steal Lori and run away—not to Montgomery, but all the way to Mexico. If only it weren't for her lame idea that she needed to finish high school.

Lucky for my parents and their minimum-wage labor force, I'd always had a hard time staying in bed, or staying anywhere, for that matter. So I hauled my ass up and ran downstairs to breakfast.

The second I walked in, I wished I hadn't. My mom had spread military school brochures in front of her breakfast plate—the one that had been pinned to the bulletin board in the office for months, plus others for schools in Tennessee, Mississippi, and Virginia—so she must have been looking forward to getting rid of me for quite some time.

Then, when we walked down to her office in the warehouse, she called in a couple of the full-time employees and arranged for them to hold down the fort next week while she and Dad toured these schools. She never mentioned touring them with me. My opinion didn't matter.

"And just in case you decide to go hog wild with Lori while we're gone next week," she told me when we were alone in the office again and she was giving me gas, "just remember that some of these schools have a summer session. I'm sure they'd be willing to enroll you right now instead of waiting for August."

I slammed out of the office—oh, I was supposed to have learned to respect my parents through all this?—and walked down the endless wooden staircase to the floating dock with the gas pumps.

I stood looking out at the wide lake with mist slowly

rising into the white sky. The mist would burn off to reveal deep blue by seven thirty. Another perfect summer day.

I walked up the stairs again, just because I couldn't stand there on the dock any longer and there was nowhere else to go.

I walked down the stairs, because I'd catch hell from my dad if I stayed away from my post very long.

Half an hour later, just as the last of the mist lifted, Lori trolled the wakeboarding boat slowly out of the marina and nosed it against the pads on the floating dock. She jumped out and tied the rope to the cleat. As she bent over, I decided this was the worst punishment of all: watching this forbidden girl in my cutoff jeans.

She peeked at me between her legs. Her long ponytail touched the dock. "You're pacing like a caged tiger."

"So? Nobody gives a shit."

"Yes they do. The whole warehouse is talking about it. Your dad has been watching you through his binoculars."

If things had been different in my family, I might have thought this meant they were feeling sorry for me and my parents might change their minds about bundling me off to school. But I knew better. They watched and pointed at me like a curiosity, one that would be safely sent away from them soon enough.

Or even sooner. "If they're watching me, I can't talk to you," I told her.

She straightened and faced me. "Why not? You're already as good as enrolled in military school."

"If I screw up again, they'll send me now. As it is, they'll wait until August."

Her eyes widened, then narrowed. "I actually need gas," she said. "I need you to give me gas. Can't a girl get gas around here?" She was shouting at me for no reason. Or, she was shouting for a very good reason, but she wasn't really shouting about getting gas, and she wasn't really shouting at me.

What the hell. I took the nozzle from the pump and shoved it into the tank of the boat. It was a legitimate reason and a perfect excuse to exchange a few words with her. But I looked into her sad green eyes and could think of absolutely nothing to say.

Lori could. "August. Football practice starts in August. You'll miss it."

I couldn't stand to look at her anymore. The digital numbers ticked by on the gas pump as I said, "I don't think you quite understand. I'll miss football in general. Period."

"They don't have football at military school?"

"I seriously doubt it. They probably have varsity latrine digging."

"Boarding school. I can't believe your parents are sending you away to boarding school. I thought that only happened in *The Sound of Music*." She heaved a sigh big enough that I turned to look at her again. She watched a heron cruise low over the lake and dip its talons beneath the surface. It brought out a wriggling fish with nowhere to hide, doomed.

"What if they sent you to the military school up the road?" she asked. "Maybe I could visit you. They wouldn't have to know."

I shook my head. "When they decided to send me away, they meant *away*. Mississippi. Tennessee. Virginia. Away."

Leave it to Lori to find the bright side. She cracked a smile. "Maybe you'll like it. Will they let you shoot off cannons and machine guns?"

"No, I'm pretty sure you learn military traditions like wearing uniforms and standing at attention for hours, with all the good stuff like explosions taken out. My parents want it to be punishment because they think I'm worthless."

Her smile faded. "They don't think you're worthless."

"I don't see why not. Sean will go to college in the fall. Cameron will go back. If I was away at school too, my parents would get their empty nest two years early. I'm sure they'll be happy to get rid of me."

She considered me, frowning hard. She looked like she was racking her brain for a response to this that would make me feel better, but the evidence against me was obvious. Finally she reached up beside my ear and touched my hair. "Will they shave your head?"

I really didn't care what I looked like, as evidenced by my beard. I definitely didn't care about my hair—or, at least, I never would have admitted it.

But something about the way Lori touched it and looked at my hair rather than meeting my eyes made me care. A lot.

"My dad can see you," I said.

She started to look in the direction of the warehouse, but she stopped herself with her head half turned and her chin pointed in the air. She dropped her hand.

The gas pump clicked off, and I slid the nozzle from the tank. Lori roared off across the lake on some errand, blonde ponytail streaming behind her.

I paced up and down the stairs again, but this time it wasn't from a loss of anything else to occupy me. I was thinking.

I was thinking so hard, in fact, that when I wakeboarded with Lori and the guys that afternoon, I landed a perfect air raley and didn't even notice. The guys told me I should be sent to military school more often, and then maybe I could have a professional wakeboarding career. Their little jabs didn't touch me anymore. I was forming a plan.

After wakeboarding, I passed the office and heard Lori arguing with my mom about sending me to school. It wouldn't work, and I didn't let it faze me. I knew what I had to do.

13

The threat of Adam's parents sending him to military school had lurked in the back of my mind for three weeks, like one of those bad backdrops in a school picture, a photo of a fake library. Even if your school picture turned out great for once, there was no getting around the fact that you were grinning your ass off in front of stacks of pretend books. No matter how high the ups had been for Adam and me in the past few weeks, this threat dragged them down.

Now the threat was finally real. And I refused to accept it.

I couldn't tell whether Adam accepted it or not. Rather

than being angry about it and throwing stuff, which is what I'd expected from him, he seemed confused, like he didn't know what to make of it. Late in the afternoon he even executed a series of perfect tricks during his turn wakeboarding. The boys and I looked at one another, astounded. This was not like Adam at all. He wasn't concentrating on new and exciting ways to fall down.

Was this a preview of what military school would do to him? Even if I never got together with Adam again, I had to save him from this. After I hung my life vest and wakeboard in the warehouse, I knocked on the office door and went in to face his mother.

I slipped onto the stool behind her. She typed busily on her computer and didn't turn around. She must know what I was there for.

I said, "I broke the rules too, you know. It takes two to tango, or to spend two hours in a tree house together. Wooooo." I wiggled my fingers as if to scare her with my horrible infraction. Since she still hadn't looked around at me, the drama was reduced somewhat.

Frustrated, I said, "Why is he in all the trouble and I'm not in trouble at all? Instead of him going to military school, we could each take half the punishment. We could set up a bivouac for you on the front lawn. We both have lots of experience playing army."

"You're not in trouble, Lori, because nobody believes you would have snuck out last night if Adam hadn't convinced you." She never stopped typing as she said this to her computer screen. "Adam, on the other hand, has a long history of going out of his way to do the opposite of what we say. The fact that we're sending him to school doesn't have anything to do with you."

"It has everything to do with me!" I exclaimed.

"It did at first," she acknowledged, "but now it doesn't. Adam's father and I have given him an order that he refuses to obey. And if he *can't* obey it because of ADHD, yet he refuses to take his medicine, then he needs to learn another way to get along in the world. His father and I have tried. We can't help him anymore."

The office door screeched open. Adam filled the doorway. "ADHD is overdiagnosed and overmedicated," he said in a professorial tone. "Studies show that one in three teenagers diagnosed with ADHD and prescribed stimulants doesn't actually need treatment." He slammed the door and was gone as quickly as he'd appeared.

"You are not that one of the three," his mom hollered after him.

After her voice had stopped ringing in my ears, I said, "I don't know. You think you can outsmart him, and then he comes up with something like that out of the blue. You realize he reads the newspaper and he's not as out of it as he acts."

"Oh yeah?" Mrs. Vader asked. "Name one thing Adam has done this summer that displayed any forethought."

"He left roses all over the marina for me. You helped him do that."

"Granted, but he did that to apologize to you because he'd flown off the handle the night before. Name one more."

I opened my mouth to tell her about the sleeping bag, the pillows, the candle, and the Oreos in the tree house. I decided that evidence of advance planning for disobedience would not help his case.

Instead I said, "I think some of his problem is ADHD. I've known him forever, and he's always been that way, so it's hard to imagine what he'd be like otherwise. But some of his problem is Sean and Cameron egging him on. I know this sounds crazy, but I have seen Adam exercise extraordinary restraint in the face of incredible taunting. The first year I knew y'all, I thought his name was ADD."

Mrs. Vader hit the space bar over and over, so hard that I thought it would fly off. "Sean is not supposed to call Adam that."

"I am aware of that. Sean does it anyway."

"Why didn't you tell me this some time in the past

umpteen years?" She kept her voice low, but I could tell she was fed up with me.

"If you tattled about anything, you got kicked out of the club," I explained. "I don't want to be a member of the club anymore."

"Well." She clicked the mouse to close the document she was working on, then opened another and resumed typing. "We think this is what's best for Adam in the long run. You might as well get on board."

I sat there for a few more minutes, listening to her fingers tap on the keyboard. Since I'd come in, she hadn't once stopped typing or turned around to look at me. This told me she was upset. Normally she would have given me her outraged face a time or two during this conversation.

She was upset about sending him away. She was sending him away anyway.

And it was all my fault.

I wanted to stay and argue with her. I would have if I'd thought it would have done any good. But I was all out of vague arguments, and I was afraid if I got further into the specifics of Adam and me, he'd get sent to school faster, like he'd said.

I spun around on my stool and stalked out of the office, hell-bent on showing my dad that Adam wasn't so awful, once and for all. Mrs. Vader didn't think I was capable of disobedience on my own, did she? I was a good little girl without a mind of my own who only got in trouble if a boy led her astray? I would show them all and save Adam from military school at the same time.

Outside in the fading sunlight, Adam leaned against the wall. When he heard the door squeak open, he stood up straight and took a step toward me, worry lines deep between his brows.

I carefully closed the door all the way, then skittered toward him.

"I'll take care of it," we whispered at the same time.

"No—how will *you* take care of it?" I said quickly. We didn't have much time to talk before someone discovered us together again. "I'll go with Sean to the party tonight and horrify my dad."

"You won't!" Adam exclaimed, voice edging above a whisper, eyes intense with anger. "You promised you wouldn't."

"I did, but that was before you got sent away!" Surely he saw the difference and understood what was at stake here.

We stared each other down, stubborn, the heat from a whole day of sun breaking loose from the sidewalk under our flip-flops and rising between us.

"I will take care of it," he growled, a threat. He stepped past me and hiked along the showroom wall, up his yard, toward his house. I wished he *would* take care of it, but he did not have a stellar track record for getting himself out of trouble.

Out the corner of my eye I saw Sean sliding the big metal door of the warehouse closed for the night.

I knew what I had to do.

14

First I shaved. This was harder than I thought. I'd only shaved stubble before, not the full mountaineer beard I'd been working on. I had to hack at it for a few minutes to get it off.

Then I ironed. I dragged the iron and the board from my parents' room into mine and pressed a pair of shorts, then a long-sleeved button-down shirt. I would roll up the sleeves like an asshole. I would have worn a suit, but that seemed like overkill. I was going to see Lori's dad and I wanted to look like a presentable guy who should be allowed to date his daughter, not a criminal who'd dressed up to face the electric chair.

But first I had to get through the ironing. It took a lot of patience. I had none. It took forever, and then I had to press the whole shirt again to get out the creases I'd pressed into it.

Finally I got dressed and examined myself in the mirror. I looked like Sean.

Ready as I'd ever be.

I ran downstairs and walked through my yard, past the tree house, into Lori's yard, and across the driveway—the scenes of various crimes. I rang the doorbell.

Her dad opened the door and looked down at me. I wished the garage wasn't a couple of stairs below the kitchen, because I seemed a lot shorter than him.

I pretended it didn't bother me. I said, "I would like an audience. Sir."

He frowned at me, but he didn't send me away. He jerked his head in the direction of the den.

I followed him through the room and onto the screened porch. He sat down in the chair where he'd obviously been when I rang the bell. It looked like he'd been spending a lot of time there lately. Spy novels were piled on the table beside the chair, along with a pair of binoculars. McGillicuddy wasn't kidding about his dad watching Lori and me.

"Sit," he said.

I would not say *woof*. I would not. I sat down in the chair facing his.

"Shoot." He tried to sound casual, but he kept frowning at me.

I took a deep breath. It came out shaky. I cleared my throat. "When Lori and I stayed out so late, that was an honest mistake. And when we were in the woods together the next day, we just wanted to talk about what had happened and what we could do about it."

"That's not all you wanted," he broke in.

I paused over that. He had me there, but to admit this seemed counterproductive. To lie would be more counterproductive, because I was an awful liar.

I went on. "Last night, we were saying good-bye. We agreed not to see each other anymore, just like you said."

"I said that three weeks ago," he insisted, leaning forward in his chair.

"Yes, sir," I acknowledged, "but you seem to think we're not people. We are, and we had stuff to work through and things to wrap up."

There was a long silence. He stared at me. I tried to meet his gaze, but loud tapping on my chair distracted me. I looked down and realized it was my finger.

I would not do well under his scrutiny. I knew better than to try my hand at poker. So I threw all my cards on the table face-up. "I love Lori. I have always loved Lori. And you may be right, I may have some ulterior motives at times, which you do not want to hear about. But I would not do anything to hurt her."

He lost his cool. "You convinced her to jump out a window last night!"

I winced. "I caught her."

"And you expect me to just say, 'Okay,' and let you near her, and then tell your parents not to send you to military school?"

He might have looked taller than me when he was in the kitchen and I was down in the garage, but now I had the upper hand. Compared to him, I sounded calm and reasonable as I said, "I don't expect that. Frankly, I don't expect much out of anybody anymore. I just wanted somebody to listen to me for once." I stood up.

"Sit down," he ordered me.

I sat down.

"I hope you can see my perspective on this," he said. "When you have a teenage daughter, you won't want someone like you coming anywhere near her."

I almost said, *I can see your lips moving, but I can't understand you.* The things he was blathering about made that much sense. But I remembered what Lori told me a couple of weeks ago about shooting myself in the foot.

I was trying to solve this problem, not make it worse. I didn't say a thing.

He must have seen me squinting at him, though, because he said, "Never mind. My point is, Lori is my only daughter. Ever since her mother died, blah blah blah, very important stuff, blah blah blah, a very, very important explanation for why I have treated you like shit." I figured that was what he was saying, but I'd stopped paying attention because of what I saw over his shoulder.

A screen wall kept the porch mosquito-free. If you got near the screen, it was harder to see through, but from this distance it was all but invisible. Beyond it, bright green maple leaves rubbed against it, trying to get in. The maple leaves formed a bower, a perfect frame for Lori's dock. And on that dock stood Lori, kissing Sean. The red words spray painted on the bridge way in the distance seemed to hover above their heads: LORI LOVES ADAM.

"In addition," Lori's dad said, "blah blah blah, why I have never trusted you as far as I could throw you and how I always knew you were trouble."

Sean's hand slid down to Lori's ass.

"Some more crap," Mr. McGillicuddy said. "And an invitation to you to incriminate yourself."

Lori put her hand on the inside of Sean's thigh.

"Adam," Mr. McGillicuddy said. "Over here." He

waved his hand, blocking my view of my two-timing ex-girlfriend and my asshole brother.

"Sorry." I shook my head. "ADHD. What were you saying?"

"I was saying you and Lori can date again. And I feel responsible for the military school thing. Your parents might have been headed in that direction already, but I certainly pushed them to the doorway. I'll get you out of it."

He was telling me that he would give me everything I'd hoped for when I came over here. I won. I could at least be happy that I wasn't going to military school. My brain kept sending signals like this to my muscles, prompting a reaction, but I couldn't move. My fists gripped the armrests as I watched Lori slip her arms around Sean's waist and hug him hard.

"Why the long face?" her dad asked. "I thought this was what you wanted. Don't worry about anything. I'll call your mom right now. Trust me. I'm a lawyer."

"Yes, sir." I jumped up from my chair before I broke it into pieces by squeezing it with my fists. I extended one of my hands to Lori's dad and he shook it. What we were shaking on, I had no idea. I just wanted out.

He walked me to the door and called after me across the yard, "I am very impressed with you, young man." That was a new one on me, and I would have laughed at how ridiculous it sounded if I weren't so intent on reaching a certain point in his yard with a certain vantage point from which to see a certain dock.

I peered through the trees. I hoped what I'd seen from the porch was a trick of light on water or an all-out hallucination. But there were Lori and Sean, still standing on her dock. The kiss had ended, but they were wrapped in each other's arms.

That was supposed to be me.

Maybe it *was* me. I put my hand on my skull-and-crossbones pendant to check.

Nope, I was me and that was Sean.

I turned away. I couldn't quite get my head around what my eyes were telling me. But it was catching up quickly, and my anger simmered. I had talked to Lori's dad for her. I had shaved my beard for her—a huge disappointment, because I'd enjoyed my three weeks looking like a bank robber. I had ironed for her. I dwelled on these petty things to keep from descending into the bottomless pit that gaped in front of me. I had gotten us out of our mess. I had told her I would take care of it, but she had stopped believing in me.

Maybe she never had.

Or maybe she really was using our troubles to catch Sean, who she'd loved all along.

I wasn't sure which was worst.

I was so angry that lights flashed behind my eyes, which told me I needed to think this through before I acted. Intellectually I knew I was jumping to conclusions about her and Sean. But even if she wasn't after him, she had betrayed me again. I had fixed everything, for once. And she broke her promise to me. She had done the one thing I'd asked her never to do. I didn't need a girlfriend like that.

I walked into the kitchen of my house to yet another horror. The air was filled with the scents of pizza and bite-size egg rolls and pretty much any crappy snack my mom could find in the deep discount section of the frozen foods aisle. She was preparing an extra-special spread for the party tonight. I'd almost forgotten about the party.

When she heard the door close, she looked around the corner at me, then came out from behind the kitchen island to hug me hard. She held me at arm's length, searching my face and smiling. "Lori's dad called."

"Woo-hoo."

Her brow wrinkled in confusion, then rose. "He says you can date Lori again. And now he's trying to convince me *not* to send you to military school."

I nodded.

She put her hands on her hips. She was frustrated with

me for not showing more joy at this fantastic news, but she wasn't quite ready to let go of her own happiness yet. "What in the world did you say to him to make him change his mind?"

I shrugged. "I manned up."

"Well. I have to say, I'm bowled over."

"I'm so glad."

"You should be. Much as I hate to look like Trevor McGillicuddy is jerking my chain, he makes a very good case for you. I'll speak to your father and convince him that we don't need to take that tour of schools."

She waited for me to foam at the mouth with gratitude. I did not.

"Adam."

"What."

"I am telling you we're not sending you to school and you can date Lori again. Isn't that what you wanted? Are you hearing me?"

"What do you want me to do, thank you for treating me like a dog for three weeks?"

She stared at me really hard, and I thought she was going to lay into me. Then she asked, "Did you have an argument with Lori?"

"No!" I stomped past her, ran up the stairs, and slammed the door to my room. This time when my tenth grade player-of-the-year trophy teetered on its shelf, I let it fall. It crashed to the rug, and the football broke off the quarterback's hand.

I flopped onto my bed, fished my phone out of my pocket, and called Rachel.

"Hey, Adam!" she squealed. "I'm so glad you got your party back! I can't wait! Sean doesn't have a date, does he?"

"You could say that," I said. "I just saw him sucking face with Lori out on the dock."

Rachel giggled like she always did at everything I said. Only this time, it was a maniacal giggle, like a psychotic bluebird. I was afraid she might start hyperventilating. "Oh, God! Oh no! This is exactly what you've been warning me about all along!"

The giggle stopped abruptly, as if she'd never been on the brink of hysterics. "I'm sick of being nice," she said with determination. "I can play Sean's game. What time are you picking me up?"

I ran toward Sean at the warehouse. He looked in my direction and kept turning keys in the dead bolts on the door like he knew I was up to no good.

I snagged his hand and dragged him after me.

"Whoa there, woman," he said as he stumbled, keys jingling.

"Come with me." I led him down the grass and around the seawall until we reached my dock.

I stopped him with my hands on his chest. After an examination of my screened porch through the trees, I pushed him six inches to the left. "My dad is probably out on the porch," I told Sean. "While he's watching, I need you to act like we're together."

His eyes widened, and he put his hands up in the air. "No way. *I* don't want to get sent to military school."

"Yes way," I said. "You're going to college in the fall. You're free and clear."

He glanced toward the porch too, I thought. But I realized he was looking at the window of my brother's room when he said, "I could get thrown off Chimney Rock."

I gave him the meanest look I could muster. "Sean Vader," I seethed, "you put your hands on me in an ungentlemanly fashion this instant."

I must have looked like I was going to kill him or give myself an aneurism, because he quickly put his hands on either side of my bare waist, just above my bikini bottoms and Adam's cutoff jeans.

With my fingertip I pressed his chin until he tilted his head down. I stood on my tiptoes and balanced my forehead against his, gazing into his pale blue eyes. Close-up, he appeared to have four eyes. This was neither sexy nor conducive to a productive discussion, but I figured it looked frightening to my dad.

"You know about my plan," I said. "I've been dating boys who are worse than Adam so my dad will give in and let me date him again. You are the worst boy I can think of." I closed my eyes and kissed the side of his mouth.

Sean breathed a little harder through his nose, which made me feel powerful. But then, infuriatingly, he said, "Adam and I made a pact. I'm not getting in his way by messing with you, and he's not getting in my way by messing with Rachel."

My stomach twisted. Adam and I made a pact too. But I was trying to save him from military school, which was more important than my promise to him.

"You've already screwed up everything with Rachel," I reasoned. This might have hurt Sean's feelings, but if he still carried a torch for her, he sure hadn't done anything about it in the past three weeks. "And pact or no pact, Adam will thank you for this later. My dad will agree to let Adam and me date. Then he can talk your parents out of sending Adam away, because I was the cause of all that trouble in the first place." I kissed Sean's cheek. This was the path Adam had taught me: corner of the mouth, then cheek. Next stop, ear.

"In case you haven't noticed," Sean said, "Adam and I don't do each other any favors."

"Maybe you need to start," I said. "After all, he wouldn't be headed to military school if it weren't for you." I put my mouth on his ear.

"Me-he-he-he!" he exclaimed. Obviously he was caught off guard by the ear treatment. He gripped my waist harder, but he managed to croak, "You just admitted this was *your* fault."

"It's my fault Adam keeps getting in trouble for being with me," I whispered in Sean's ear. "It's your fault that your parents thought he was so awful in the first place. If he'd suddenly started acting out, nobody would be talking about sending him away to school. But he's been getting in trouble since I met him. You and I know about twenty-five percent of that is ADHD and the other seventy-five percent is you doing something and then blaming it on him—either just to get yourself out of trouble or specifically to screw up his life. I've known this all along, and I can't believe I wanted to be with you until recently." I kissed my way back to his cheek.

"I have issues," he whispered back. "That makes me vulnerable. Chicks dig it."

"If you say so. Shut up and kiss me." Without waiting for his decision, I kissed Sean Vader full on the mouth.

Sean was a great kisser. It would be hard to compare him with Adam because they were totally different. Sean kissed as suavely as he talked, with an understated smoothness that left me wanting more. Adam's kisses were much more intense. And that's why, even though I cracked one eye open occasionally to get a delicious peek at Sean with his eyes closed, kissing me slowly, looking so much like Adam, I never forgot who I was kissing.

He slid his hands onto my butt. I froze at first. Adam's brother's hands were on my butt. But this was great for the plan that I had dragged Sean into. I had to remember I was doing this to save Adam from military school.

Still, I began to feel guilty, and I thought I'd better lighten the mood. "Am I good at this?" I joked against Sean's lips. "Are you actually maybe a little turned on?"

"Until you started talking."

"Good." He wasn't falling for me any more than I was falling for him. I licked my lips and prepared to move in again.

But I couldn't lean forward. I stayed stuck where I was, staring into his light blue eyes that really weren't all that much like Adam's after all, now that I examined them up close.

"What's the matter?" Sean asked.

I squeezed my eyes shut against the tears. "This isn't going to work, is it?"

"No." I couldn't see him, but his low voice sounded almost sympathetic. "What are the chances that your dad is watching us right now? Or that he would care in exactly the way you need him to care? Or that he has good enough vision to tell it's me and not Adam?"

"You're right. It hasn't worked yet. I don't know why

I keep trying. I guess I just don't want to face the fact—"

I looked up into his eyes. He watched me with concern.

"—that I can't fix it!" I burst into tears. My whole world seemed so hopeless and empty and meaningless. Adam was getting a punishment he didn't deserve because of me. If I couldn't fix it, what good was I?

"Aww," Sean said. "Come here." He pulled me forward into his arms and rubbed my back, soothing. With his chin on my head he said, "I'll talk to my mom, okay?"

I was too busy sobbing and soaking his T-shirt with my tears to respond.

"I mean, Adam needs knocking around to toughen him up. I've done him a favor. But you're right—sending him to military school makes no sense. I'll try to talk my mom out of it. If anybody can do that, it's me." He patted my back absently. "Maybe it will get back to Rachel that I've done a good deed."

I sniffed gigantically. "Maybe you should *talk* to Rachel and tell her you want to make up with her, you moron."

He held me at arm's length and looked at me like he'd never seen me before. "That's an idea."

A few minutes later, I hiked back up my yard and went into my house. I had tried my best to freak out my dad, but I was used to my plans to get Adam out of the doghouse falling through, and I was resigned to the fact that my last try with Sean had not worked at all. Therefore I was astonished when my dad knocked on the screened porch door and motioned for me to come outside with him.

Cautiously hopeful, I edged onto the porch and eyed him. He relaxed in his customary chair with a full view of our dock, beaming. He would not be beaming if he'd noticed Sean and me making out right in front of his nose. Damn it, we must have won the lottery!

"I know what you did," Dad said.

"You do?" I asked carefully, just in case I had a much poorer understanding of parental psychology than I'd thought.

"Yes. And I think it's commendable."

"You *do*?" Was he talking about Sean and me? I hadn't volunteered at the Humane Society since the beginning of the summer.

"Yes. I'm not wrong about your curfew, Lori. I'm not wrong about keeping you safe." He reached forward to pat my arm. "But I may have flown off the handle about restricting your movements. Frances keeps telling me that it only backfires. I think that's what we've seen in the past few weeks. You may date Adam again, and I've put in a good word with his parents. I doubt they'll send him away to school."

'Thank you!" I screamed, throwing myself on top of my dad. "Thank you so much," I gushed. "I'm so glad. Adam is great. You just have to see past . . . a lot. Thank you, Dad." I eased off him because he seemed to be having trouble breathing, like I was crushing him or perhaps kneeing him in the ribs. "Thank you."

He took my hand and squeezed it. "Have fun at the party tonight."

"I will. Thank you so much!"

I banged into the house and ran upstairs to get ready for the party, which would start in less than an hour. In my bathroom I laid out some things I needed for the party and was liable to forget if I got too excited: mascara, eyelash comb, earrings, and my mother's diamond-and-pearl ring, which I'd only been wearing since my birthday. It still felt funny on my finger.

It wasn't until I stepped into the shower that I thought through what my dad had said, and started to have doubts. My dad thought it was commendable that I'd made out with Sean in order to save Adam from military school? That would only happen if the world were run by reality-show producers. I wanted to have another conversation with my dad about this. However, I wasn't sure how I could phrase the question. *Hey, Dad, what exactly were you commending me for just now when I acted like I knew what the hell you were talking about?* And I was afraid whatever I'd done for Adam would be reversed just because I asked.

Oh well. I was sure the mystery would be solved soon enough. Right now I would slip on the miniskirt Adam seemed so fond of and run to his house to celebrate with him.

At school my friends were always telling me how lucky I was to live next door to the Vader boys and go to their famous parties in the summer. I'd told my friends the parties were no big deal to me. I didn't elaborate on why: I felt awkward going to them. I knew I was wearing the wrong thing but I had no idea how to fix it. I wanted Sean to like me and he was in a dark corner, manhandling some other girl.

Since I'd been with Adam, of course my opinion of the parties had changed. A party had gotten Sean and Rachel together, which had opened the door for Adam and me. A party had hosted my first make-out session with Adam. The last party had been awful—Adam and I got in a huge fight, he punched Sean, and their dad discovered the tiny beer stash and took away party privileges for two weeks.

This party would be perfect. As I walked through the trees toward Adam's house, big and rambling in the orange light of sunset, I could feel the electricity in the air, even though no other guests had arrived yet. Except for the Vaders' cars and trucks, there were no vehicles in the driveway. Even Adam's pink truck was gone.

Maybe Mrs. Vader had sent Adam to town to get more food for the party. But on the off chance that someone had borrowed his truck, I entered their house without knocking. I was Adam's Girlfriend and that was my right.

In the kitchen, Mrs. Vader placed appetizers carefully on plates on the bar, and Sean quickly ate them. Without letting Mrs. Vader put down what she had in her hand, and therefore risking a grease spot on my Slinky Cleavage-Revealing Top, I grabbed her and hugged her. "Thank you so much! Is Adam upstairs? Can I see him? Is he gone? Should I wait here for him? Everything is on the up-and-up. I can sit here and wait for him and not even hide it from you! Such luxury!"

Mrs. Vader chuckled as she extracted herself from me. "Adam just left."

"Where'd he go?"

"He didn't say, but . . ." She pointed a chicken wing at me. "Adam thinks that you two are in an argument."

My body zinged into alert mode. My mind didn't know what Mrs. Vader meant, but my body already did. Even Sean glanced over at her with a cautious look.

"He does?" I asked faintly.

"A bad one," she confirmed.

"How could we be in a bad argument without me even knowing about it?"

Sean laughed nervously.

"All I know is, your dad called me to say I should reconsider sending Adam away to school," Mrs. Vader said. "Then Adam came back from talking to your dad. I told him that we weren't sending him away, and I thought he should have been happy, but he was very angry with you."

"Why didn't you tell *me* you weren't sending him away to school?" Sean asked.

"Well, Sean, I wasn't sure you'd care." Mrs. Vader's gaze switched from Sean to me and back to Sean again. She must have heard what I'd tried to tell her about Adam and Sean over all that tapping on her keyboard.

Sean gaped at her. I didn't care. They could work out their important family issues later. I had teen intrigue to manage. What I wanted to know was, "Why did Adam talk to my dad?"

She shrugged. "I don't know exactly what was said, but they had a man-to-man talk about Adam's behavior, which is what changed your dad's mind about him."

Now what my dad had said to me made sense. He hadn't commended me for making out with Sean in order to get Adam out of trouble. He assumed I'd sent Adam over for this man-to-man talk. He thought I'd dealt with my problems and Adam's in a responsible, adult manner, when nothing could have been further from the truth.

Something else made sense too. I knew why Adam was mad at me. I put my hand over my mouth. "Sean," I said through my fingers. "Sean, Adam saw us."

Mrs. Vader threw the chicken wing down on a pan and put her hands on her hips, glaring at me. "He saw you doing *what*?"

"Does it really matter, as long as it's before her curfew?" Sean said this in a snide tone, but I could hear the vibration underneath.

Mrs. Vader shook her head as she picked up a sponge and wiped the counter. "Lori, you need to watch out around these boys."

I was still miffed at her for implying I didn't have a mind of my own. "Maybe *they* need to watch out around *me*." I had thought this for a while, but I never said it out loud.

When I saw the look on Mrs. Vader's face, I wished I could take it back. "Maybe they do!" Her voice was shrill.

The doorbell rang, saving me from the possibility of the Vader matriarch throwing fried food at me. Sean clapped his hands together and said in the tone of a 1950s housewife, "There are our guests! Am-scray, om-May." He left to get the door.

With a last withering look at me, Mrs. Vader disappeared up the stairs. She passed Cameron bounding down. "Party time!" he called to no one in particular. Then he saw me. "What in the world is up with you now?"

I swallowed. "I do hope you are referring to my glamorous updo and not some bombshell you are about to drop on me about Adam."

Cameron shrugged. "Just that he went to pick up Rachel."

I nodded manically. "But not for a date, right? Just as friends, right?" I chose a pizza roll from the spread and popped it into my mouth with a shaking hand. Mmmmmm, cheese.

"I thought it was a date," Cameron informed me. "He was dressed like Sean. He shaved off his beard."

I put one hand over my heart, which was pounding in protest. "Don't you think he was just trying to make me jealous?"

"I asked him about that. He said no, he really asked out Rachel. He said you're obviously done with him." Cameron angled his head in the direction Sean had gone. "Now he's done with you. He said it was a relief because you're more trouble than you're worth. Which . . ."

"Made sense?" I shrieked.

Cameron spread his hands: *If you say so*. He walked into the living room and high-fived some of his friends.

Sean came back into the kitchen, leading five or six people who snagged hors d'oeuvres, jumped over the couch into the living room, and turned the stereo to full volume. I stepped up to Sean and grabbed him by the neatly ironed front of his shirt. "Adam saw us!" I shouted over the music. "He went to get Rachel! Cameron says he *shaved* for her and it's a real date. Please tell me you think Adam's only trying to make me jealous!"

Sean lost his natural smirk and looked concerned for once. "Sounds like they're really together."

"I don't think so." I couldn't think so. The possibility was too awful. I released Sean's shirt and smoothed it. "Adam just saw us kissing and got angry. He was always opposed to the plan. He specifically told me not to go forward with the plan. But he'll be over it tomorrow." I thought about how long Adam held grudges against me lately. "Or next week."

Sean shook his head. "They're really together. And I was going to *talk* to her!" His usual debonair grin was gone. He looked so morose that I lost all confidence I could explain my way out of my predicament with Adam.

I patted Sean on the back and said with more assurance

than I felt, "We'll sit in the front window and watch for them. The instant they arrive at the party, we'll see them and we'll talk to them just like you planned. They'll listen to reason."

Three hours later, Sean and I still shared the window seat that looked out over the Vaders' front yard. This gave us a view of anyone coming or going from the driveway and the front door. But we were afraid of giving Adam and Rachel the impression we were together, so we sat side by side on the cushions, awkwardly, and without touching, looking through the glass like eager puppies waiting for their masters to come home.

Surely they were only riding around town before the party because they knew we were waiting for them. I'd tried to call Adam and Sean had tried to call Rachel, but they weren't answering. Surely they were only punishing us. They would show up here sooner or later and we could fix everything.

"Why were you always so mean to Adam when we were kids?" I demanded. I wanted to comfort Sean in theory, but I was getting frustrated with the wait for Adam. It felt good to take out some aggression. "If you hadn't been mean to Adam, he wouldn't be so quick to lose it. For that matter, why were you always so mean to *me*? You never let us play with you. Or if you did, you made it seem like you were doing us this huge favor."

"Junior," he said gently, "you were really little. And really cute." He tweaked my nose. "And I didn't want to babysit. I wanted to play with Cameron and McGillicuddy. This is hard for me to remember, but at one time I felt, like, *honored* to be allowed to play with them because they were older than me." He leaned closer so I could hear him better over the booming bass line. "If hanging with the big dogs made you so miserable, why didn't you and Adam go hang by yourselves?"

"We did, once." I searched my memories of that summer day, the sunlight glinting off the points of waves on the lake, filtering through moving spaces between the leaves of a tall tree, threading itself into Adam's curls as we nailed a sign to his tree house that said KEEP OUT JERKS. "Normally it didn't occur to us that we could do that."

"Until now," Sean said, "when it's too late."

"Ha ha. Not funny."

"I don't think it's funny either," Sean said. "I think Rachel and Adam are really together." He glanced behind me. "Speak of the devil."

In my excitement to see Adam, I whirled around and fell off the window seat. A shadow loomed overhead, blocking out the tiny bit of strobe light that made its way through the bodies dancing in the center of the room. My brother stood over us with his hands on his hips.

I reached up and slapped Sean's leg. "I thought you meant Adam!"

Sean focused on McGillicuddy instead of me. "It's okay." Sean put up his hands. "I didn't kiss her in the warehouse when she was eleven."

McGillicuddy shook his head. "Adam and Rachel just left."

I leaped up from the floor before Sean had even made it off the seat. "We never saw them drive up! Did you tell them Sean and I aren't together?" All our assorted brothers and close friends had been instructed to tell Adam and Rachel they were wanted for a conference at the window seat.

"Apparently they never came inside," McGillicuddy shouted over the music. "I heard this from some people coming in from the dock. They said Adam and Rachel shot bottle rockets into the lake and left again."

"That's *my* date!" I turned to Sean and pounded on his chest with my fists. "Your girlfriend stole my date night!"

"Oh, God," Sean breathed.

I relaxed my fists and pressed my hands on his chest, holding him steady. Then I asked McGillicuddy, "Did they 'leave'?" I made finger quotes, which would indicate that they had put on a big show of acting like they were driving elsewhere to make out. At least, this is what the finger-quotes indicated to *me*. "Or did they *leave*?"

He frowned at me. "They left."

Tammy danced over with a big grin on her face, the kind of grin one wears when one is at a party with one's boyfriend and one's life is not going to hell in a handbasket. She grabbed McGillicuddy and pulled him onto the dance floor before I could ask him whether he'd understood the whole finger-quote concept.

"Rachel and Adam are together," Sean wailed. "I mean, really together. They've left without standing outside this window and mooning us"—he gestured to our view of the driveway—"or even waiting until we looked up at them. I'm telling you, Lori, Adam was dating Rachel in the first place. I stole Rachel from Adam. After less than two weeks, she broke up with me because of the way I treated Adam. They're not kidding. They're back together now."

"That's impossible." In my heart I knew this could not be true. Illogical as it sounded, Adam only blew up at people he loved: his parents, many times over the years; Sean, constantly. He had blown up at me quite a few times over the past few weeks. He had *never* blown up at Rachel. If he always got along great with somebody, it was a sure sign that he didn't really care what that person thought.

But I could not shake the feeling that everything we'd done together for the past month was a lie. Just as Sean had said, the first night I got an inkling that I had feelings for Adam, he was dating Rachel and he caught her making out with Sean. Why couldn't he be in love with her still, fighting to win her back? That made a lot more sense than what I'd believed for a month, that he'd dated her but he'd loved me all along. There was too much evidence that he wanted her instead of me. I suspected he'd taken her to his Secret Make-Out Hideout first, since he'd acted so suspiciously when I'd asked him about it last weekend. He'd talked her into inviting everyone over to her grandparents' house, which meant he'd been calling her. And tonight he had *said* he was with her, flaunting her at his own party. I had no good reason not to believe him.

The month we'd been together—sort of, off and on—had been an act. When I thought about the parts that *had* been an act, it made perfect sense. But when I thought about him teetering on the edge of crying in the tree house, my stomach twisted into knots. To put on an act like that, he *would* be awfully sneaky, even sneakier than Sean's wildest dreams of sneaky. He would have to be heartless. He would need to not care at all. And I knew, from growing up with him, that he cared.

Maybe he really did care about some things. Rachel, for instance. Maybe he just didn't care about *me*.

I put my palm tenderly to Sean's cheek and said, "I know where they went."

16

"Can you take off your shirt?"

I couldn't see Rachel clearly on the other side of my truck's cab. My eyes hadn't yet adjusted to the darkness of my secret make-out hideout. But I could hear her laughing her ass off. "Not even for Sean."

"Well, we have to make it look good somehow. Do you mind if I take off mine? My dad says I look like sex on a stick with my shirt off."

"Knock yourself out."

I started to pull my shirt over my head. I was used to wearing T-shirts. When it wouldn't give, I remembered I was wearing something Sean-like. As I unbuttoned it, I asked, "Want to make a bet how long it takes him to get out here?"

"Don't you mean *them*?"

I hoped. "I don't know. Sean will be here for sure. He'll come after you. He's liked you all along. But if Lori has been after Sean, she'll try to stop him from coming. I don't know whether she would come herself." I pulled off my shirt and threw it out the window for effect. "Lie down."

"I beg your pardon?"

"Thinking ahead is very hard for me," I explained, as if she hadn't found this out during a month of dating me. "I should have rigged a trip wire across the road so we'd know when they were coming. Sean won't drive up here with his headlights on. They'll walk up and surprise us. We have to be ready. It probably won't take long."

"All *right*." She scooted down and stretched out across the seat.

I lay on top of her, putting my weight more on the seat beside her so I wouldn't crush her.

"This is embarrassing," she said against my cheek.

I was halfway offended. "Why? We actually did this last month."

"We never lay down," she said softly. "My grandmother would be so disappointed in me."

"Tell your grandma you're involved in a web of deceit, that's all. They probably did stuff like this in their horse-drawn carriages all the ti—"

The door nearest our heads jerked open and strong hands dragged me out by the shoulders. I braced myself against the doorframe, first to keep from being dragged, and then, when that didn't seem possible, to keep from dragging across Rachel and hurting her.

But she was gone from under me—already out the other door. As Sean threw me to the ground on my elbow, Rachel ran around the front of the truck, yelling. "Sean, stop. It's all a joke."

"I'm not laughing!" Sean shouted at her. He stomped off through the weeds. Immediately he changed his mind, stalked back, and stood over me. I readied myself to roll away from him if he tried to kick me.

Instead, he pointed at me. He breathed in and out through his nose, collecting himself, before he said, "You are not my brother." He charged through the weeds again, down the road.

"Sean," Rachel scolded him.

"Now you know how I feel," I called after him.

Rachel turned to me. "Happy now? Is this what you wanted?" She hurried in the direction Sean had gone, calling to him. As she passed Lori at the tailgate of the truck,

she said, "I'm sorry. We'll talk, okay? But I've got to—
Sean!" She disappeared into the trees.

Lori didn't move, didn't look behind her to watch
Rachel and Sean go. She gazed down at me with her
arms folded and her jaw set. "*Were* you joking?" she asked
sharply. "Because for a minute, I sure thought you weren't."
Her eyes flicked to my bare chest and back to my face. Now
that my eyes had adjusted to the moonlight, I could see
everything I didn't want to see.

Slowly I stood, brushing the dirt off my shorts and
rubbing the elbow I'd fallen on. "What was *I* supposed
to think when you made out with Sean on your dock?"
Now that I had a few hours' distance, I realized there
were several different things I could have thought and I
should have asked her about them. But that made me feel
like the rug was being jerked out from under me, which
left me grasping for anything to keep myself upright. "I
can't trust you."

She opened her hands. "I don't understand you, Adam.
I'm with you, but you act like I'm the enemy. I see our
future like this, with you always leaping before you look
and me watching through my fingers, scared to breathe. I
can't do it anymore. When we were just friends, I feared
for you all the time, but I dealt with it. If we're something
more than friends—"

"Maybe we shouldn't be," I interrupted her. "What makes you so sure we're meant to be together, anyway?"

"My mother said so." She said this instantly, without thinking. I could tell this because she put her hand up to touch two fingers to her lips—not like slapping her hand over her mouth, but tentatively wondering where those words had come from. She brought both hands together and twisted the ring her mother had left her around and around her finger.

I said, "Your mother is dead."

She put her hands down and stared coldly at me.

Even I knew that was too much. "I shouldn't have said that."

She looked at me from head to toe, and her cold stare settled on my face again.

I took a step toward her. "Lori, I shouldn't have said that. I'm sorry."

"I can't forgive you for that." She stared at me a few moments more, to drive her point home.

She turned and walked away through the forest.

I watched her go until even her blonde hair, which seemed to glow in the dark woods, disappeared into the gloom.

Then I banged my head against the truck.

17

It was a long walk home through the neighborhood. Even if Sean and Rachel had been waiting for me in Sean's truck at the end of the dirt road, I wouldn't have taken that ride. They weren't waiting for me.

Then I spent fifteen long minutes standing in my garage, picking botanical debris off my cute outfit. Showing up with beggar lice on your miniskirt was almost as bad as coming home with a hickey. Finally I opened the door.

"Lori?" my dad called from the den.

I stopped in the kitchen and took a long, deep, calming breath, then let it all out in a Zen-like sigh. I could talk to him pleasantly now. Funny: Lovesick depression felt a lot like responsible obedience. "Yes, Father?"

"You're home early."

Oooooh, that was low.

I took another long, deep, calming breath. This one didn't work as well as the last one had. Stepping forward, I peeked at my reflection in the dark oven window. I looked like a serial killer. I manually raised my eyebrows and the corners of my mouth with my fingertips. Now I looked like bad plastic surgery.

"Lori?" he called again.

Smiling in a deathlike manner, I ventured into the den. The lights were out. The TV was on but quiet, as if nobody were paying it any attention. And Dad lounged across the couch with Frances curled up against him.

Two months ago this would have astonished me. Three weeks ago, right after they finally got together, I was happy for them, if somewhat uncomfortable. Now it made me very, very angry.

"Tell us about the party," Dad suggested. "Was your first night back with Adam everything you dreamed about?" He kissed the top of Frances's head.

I did not even try the long, deep, calming breath this time. I already was developing a headache from grinding my teeth together. Now that my eyes had adjusted to the dim light, I spied Frances's nanny basket next to an armchair in the corner. I plopped down in the chair to explore it.

The nanny basket was a bottomless tote bag overflowing with Frances's never-ending art supplies and random objects to teach and pacify small children. I tossed out a tennis ball, a long string tied in a circle for playing cat's cradle, and a copy of *Anna Karenina*.

"Didn't you always tell me to give away toys I hadn't played with in a year?" I asked Frances. "*Anna Karenina* has been living in your nanny basket for at least ten years, and it's never come in handy."

"I beg your pardon," Frances said. "Alvin Harbarger plays with that. He looks up the difficult words in the dictionary and writes out the definitions."

"Frances. Way to ensure a carefree childhood. Alvin is, like, four."

"He is five." She sounded more irate with me than she normally would have been just for messing with her nanny basket—almost as if I were barging in on her perfect date night.

OH REALLY?

Finally finding what I'd been searching for, I pulled out a sheet of red construction paper and a pair of child-safe scissors and started cutting. "Actually, Adam and I wanted some time alone, since we have been deprived of this so long. We skipped the party and saw a movie."

"Adam sat through a whole movie?" Dad asked. "What movie did you see?"

"The Scarlet Letter." The handles of the tiny scissors dug into my fingers, but I kept cutting. Big pieces of the red paper fell away. "I read the book in ninth grade. Did you?"

"I read it sometime," Dad acknowledged. "I didn't know there was a remake of the movie out."

Frances elbowed him gently. "She's not serious, Trevor. She's trying to tell you something."

Dad stared at me, slowly puzzling it out. *The Scarlet Letter.* What happens in *The Scarlet Letter*? What is she trying to tell— Oh my God!" He jumped up from the couch, dumping Frances onto the floor.

"NO, NOT THAT!" Frances and I shouted at the same time.

I tossed the scissors back into the nanny basket, fished out a roll of tape, and waggled my red paper letter at him with a wobbly sound. "It's an *I*, not an *A*. And it's not for me. It's for you." Stepping over the nanny basket and Frances, I taped the letter to his shirt. "I will make you lots of different color *I*'s to coordinate with all your suits and ties. Wear them in shame."

He looked down at his chest in confusion. "What does *I* stand for?"

I opened my mouth to form the *I* word.

And something happened to me. I had never been so angry in my life. At Adam for what he'd done, at Sean and Rachel for being in the way, at Dad for putting us in this position in the first place. At myself for telling Adam I couldn't forgive him.

I was so angry that for a second, I actually became Adam. I felt the unfairness of it all, the burden of it, living with it for weeks—or in his case, years. I understood how he could become so angry at his parents that he *had* to talk back to them and sabotage his relationship with me, even though he *did* care.

Because for that second, I was about to get grounded for the rest of the summer, maybe for the rest of the year. I was going to call my father an idiot.

From the corner of my eye, I could see Frances still on the floor, shaking her head.

Dad looked back up at me, blond brows down, growing suspicious. "What does *I* stand for?" he asked again.

I put my hand in the center of the *I* on his chest. Did he know he had ruined my summer by banning Adam and that changing his mind now didn't help? Did he know he'd ruined my relationship with Adam forever?

Did he know he'd ruined my life? My mouth still formed the shape of an *I*.

I opened my mouth a little wider. "Irony," I forced out.

I took one more long, deep, calming breath, and I sighed.

And then I headed upstairs to my room.

When I reached the steps, I heard Dad say from behind me, "What's eating her? I told her she could date Adam again."

"And now they've had a fight," Frances said. "It's ironic."

"I'll go talk to her," Dad said.

"No," I whispered to the steps.

"No!" said Frances. "I'll go."

I was near the top of the staircase by then. I could have run into my room and slammed the door. I had that impulse.

But I didn't do it. I walked into my room, sat on my bed, and waited for Frances to come up the stairs. She hadn't even poked her head through the doorway before I started to cry.

"Oh, Lori," she cooed sympathetically, which just made me cry harder. She sat beside me on the bed and held out her arms to me, and I totally lost it.

I never dared shed a tear around the boys growing

up, even when I got hurt playing with them. I wanted to be like them, and *they* didn't cry. Even if I had cried, I wouldn't have sought solace from Frances. She was not my mother.

Or was she? I cried into her lap as if she were, and I learned what people meant by a "good cry." As I cried, I thought about everything Adam had done to me and everything I had done to him. Offenses leveled at both of us by Sean, the Vaders, my dad, and even Frances herself in refusing to take my side. One cry led to another until I truly was all cried out. When I'd said that to Tammy a few weeks ago, I had no idea what I was talking about. I sat up, feeling empty, with a headache but no desire to cry.

"Tell me what happened," Frances said.

I sniffed. "Adam hurt me as badly as he possibly could, and then . . ."

Behind her big ugly glasses, Frances's brows went down. "And then *what?*"

"And then I told him I would never forgive him!" Whoops. I was *still* wrong about being all cried out. I found some more tears and cried them into my hands.

Frances waited until I was done. Again. "So you're not crying over what Adam did. You're crying because you told him you couldn't forgive him?"

"I guess!" I wailed.

"Does that mean you *can* forgive him?"

"I might, if he would never do that to me again."

Frances put her hand on my knee. "I think he's going to do it again."

"Why?" I demanded.

"All the years I've known you, you and Adam have been consistent. You seem alike in many ways. No wonder you've always gotten along so well. But you arrive at that similar place from opposite directions, which is why you argue. You want the best for everyone, Lori. You want everything to work out. You fix things. You have no malice."

"Adam doesn't fix things," I said ruefully. "He has a lot of malice."

"Adam feels much more deeply than you or I can understand," Frances said. "He will find your buttons and push them. He will hurt you. I think it's a defense mechanism he developed growing up behind Cameron and Sean."

I felt guilty talking about him this way, though I knew it was true. "He's not always mean like that," I said.

Frances nodded. "He can also be the sweetest, most thoughtful young man I've ever met. His highs are very high, and his lows are very low. For an even-keeled person like you, it's fine to be friends with someone like that. It's harder to be in love. Then you're on the receiving end of the lows as well as the highs."

I laughed. "Nobody's ever accused me of being even-keeled."

"In comparison with Adam," Frances clarified.

"The *Titanic* while sinking was even-keeled in comparison with Adam."

She smiled. "The next time you hurt him, he will turn around and hurt you again. Maybe when he's done that to you enough times, you will get tired of it, and you really won't be able to forgive him. You'll walk away for good. I don't think you're there yet."

I ran my hands through my wreck of an updo. My fingers found more beggar lice. I flicked them behind my head and put my hands down before Frances saw. "How do I fix it?"

"You don't fix it, Lori," Frances said. "Stop trying to fix it. You're liable to do more damage, because you're both still angry. Let him cool down, and when the time is right, you'll know."

My brother knocked on the doorframe. "Just came from the party. Eventful night. So! Sean and Rachel are back together." He nodded at Frances's happy exclamations and follow-up questions, but he watched my reaction.

"Good," I sighed, meaning it. I bore Rachel no ill will. Or maybe some, but not enough to begrudge her her relationship with Sean. Sean was an excellent kisser, which

I had always suspected. He was also a halfway decent guy, which had never crossed my mind.

My brother cleared his throat. "Lori, did you and Adam have a fight? I mean, another fight? A humdinger?"

I snorted. "No, I'm sobbing in Frances's lap because she will marry our father someday and bring back the vegi/soy mayonnaise."

"What's the matter with vegi/soy mayonnaise?" Frances asked.

McGillicuddy wrinkled his nose at the memory. Then he said, "Adam asked me to call him if you weren't home safe. And he's trying to put a hole through the warehouse door with his football."

I hopped out of Frances's lap and rushed to open the window. I couldn't see the big door from this angle, but I heard the BANG of the football on metal, and then Mr. Vader hollering, "Adam! It's eleven thirty at night! Put that football away! [Cuss word you never, ever say in front of your mother]!"

I shut the window. "I have to go!"

Frances shook her head at me.

"Right," I agreed. "I have to stop trying to fix it."

But after she and my brother had left my room, I opened my window again. I thought about Adam and let the periodic BANG of his football lull me to sleep.

18

My mom tapped at my door. I knew it was
her because she had this special way of drumming her long
fingernails on the wood.

She wanted to talk to me about Lori. I did not want to
talk to her. But after being banished to military school and
then reinstated as a member of the family all in the space
of twenty-four hours, I decided now was not the time to
insist on privacy.

"Just a minute." I rolled off my bed, where I'd been
lying facedown for an hour with a book about living with
ADHD balanced on the back of my head. I checked myself
in the mirror. I hadn't cried, but I looked like it anyway,

all haggard and kind of green. Or maybe that was from lying down with a book on my head. I crossed the room and opened the door.

Sean stood there with a mischievous grin, hand still forming a claw. He'd tapped on the door with his fingernails to fool me.

I slammed the door in his face.

Before the latch caught, the door bounced open again. Cameron stood just behind Sean with the rubber toe of his shoe blocking the door from shutting. "You look like hell," Cameron said.

"I look like Sean." This was a joke from my darkest memory. If Sean told me I was ugly, I could deflect the insult easily, because he was calling himself the same name. If Cameron told me I was ugly, he was also insulting Sean, and Sean would get revenge on him without me having to do a thing.

Sean smiled briefly at me to show I wasn't funny. Then he said, "I came to apologize."

"What's the punch line?" I asked. "Did Rachel put you up to it?"

"Rachel didn't tell me to say this. But she does make me see myself differently." He leaned against the doorframe and managed to look cool and collected, even when debasing himself. "I'm sorry I said you weren't my brother, because you are. I was just so shocked when I saw you with Rachel. I've never gotten naked with her like that."

I glanced nervously down the hall. My parents' bedroom wasn't far. I didn't want them to overhear the word "naked." I stepped out of the way and let my brothers into my room. They belly flopped onto my beanbag chairs. As I closed the door behind us and crossed the room to sit on my bed again, I told Sean, "You broke the pact first."

"I did break the pact," Sean admitted, "but only because your wheeling, dealing girlfriend convinced me you'd want it that way."

"That's exactly what she did to me at Chimney Rock!" Cameron exclaimed. "We pushed her around for years, and now she's finally morphed into a more powerful creature bent on revenge! Reooouur!" He held up his paws, bugged out his eyes, and imitated a giant she-creature stomping across the marina. Sean made noises like fighter planes strafing the creature with machine-gun fire.

I rolled my eyes. "Guys. Hello. I'm sorry too."

That got their attention. They put down their hands and looked at me.

"I know I fly off the handle," I said. "I'm going to try really hard not to do that before I lose everything." Probably it would help if I read the book on ADHD rather than just balancing it on my head, but at least I'd found it on the shelf, which was a start.

"You're two years younger than I am, and you've always been able to do stuff I can't do. I mean, this is fine." Sean slid the book from my bed and hefted it in his hand. "Know thyself, or whatever." He tossed it across the room. "But a lot of guys would kill to be more like you. I think you should embrace it. I mean, you will jump off Chimney Rock. That's got to look good on a job application, if it's the right job, and if you can figure out how to explain it."

I nodded. "Are you sorry for calling me ADD my whole life?"

"No, it's funny."

Oh well. I couldn't expect Sean to make a complete one-eighty. I turned to Cameron. "What are *you* here to apologize for?"

"Nothing," he said. "I'm here to make sure you're not really going to ask out Giselle."

I'd never had any intention of doing this. However, I decided to let Cameron sweat it for a few more minutes. I leaned back against my headboard, put my hands behind my head, and crossed my ankles. "You could have prevented this, you know. If I were still dating Lori, I'd have no interest in Giselle. But when I first got in trouble, I wanted your help, and you said you didn't have a dog in this fight."

"You can't date Giselle!" he exclaimed. "You can't be with her. You would ruin her life. Screw what Sean said. Nobody is going to employ you for jumping off Chimney Rock. What kind of job are you going to get when your professional football career flames out? How are you ever going to get life insurance? Nobody is going to give you life insurance when they look at your health record and see you broke your arm four times before you were sixteen."

"I'm not messing with Giselle," I assured him. Then I moved my arms and bounced my head against my headboard. "I just want Lori back. I don't know what to do."

"Nothing," Sean said. "I would *not* suggest doing nothing for three weeks and waiting for the girl to make a move. This didn't work out well for me, at least not at first. But I *would* suggest doing nothing for a few days and thinking about it."

"The entertainment value for us will be much reduced." Cameron looked at Sean and they both cracked up. Then Cameron turned to me again. "But it will be better for you."

"And Lori," Sean added.

"What the monkey!" My dad slammed through my door and burst into my room wearing nothing but his bathrobe.

We all looked up at him in surprise. "You tell us," I said.

"Oh." My dad actually looked sheepish. "It's one o'clock in the morning and I was going to tell you to shut the monkey up and go to bed. I didn't realize what was going on in here."

"What's going on in here?" Cameron asked suspiciously.

"Maturity." My dad backed out of the room and closed the door.

19

"Lori is quiet."

I looked up at Tammy sharing a seat with McGillicuddy
in the back of the boat. Even in the starlight before the
fireworks, the whole distance of the boat away from her, I
could see she was poking her bottom lip out, feeling sorry
for me. McGillicuddy leaned around her to watch my reaction too.

I appreciated their concern. Theirs and everybody else's
I knew. That morning I'd discovered that even the regular
workers in the warehouse had heard about the big blowup
between Adam and me and were rooting for us to get back
together. McGillicuddy had come into the showroom a

million times and given me a play-by-play of the lovelorn noises Adam was making in the warehouse—the one time I didn't want to know. Rachel had driven over in her grandparents' boat to eat lunch with Sean, and they had grilled me about my plan to get Adam back, as if they couldn't stand for us to be apart now that they were together.

In fact, every molecule of my body wanted to do something to fix this. I could feel my molecules like a full stadium at a football game, standing up and cheering me on and dancing to a fight song.

But Frances was somewhere out there in the enormous crowd of boats gently bobbing in the darkness. She was with my dad on the Vaders' pontoon boat, and they were in love. She must have fallen in love with him while she was my nanny, but she never did anything about it. She was patient, and now she had her reward.

Actually, as I thought about this, I realized it wasn't much of a reward, waiting around for YEARS to hook up. I was not down with that. But I had been content to spend my Fourth of July passing Adam quietly at work, watching him bust ass in a spectacular failure of a discombobulator during the wakeboarding show, and generally letting some more water flow under that bridge.

I took a deep breath through my nose and pictured the water flowing, calming myself as I tried to be one with the water. It was a good thing I didn't have to pee. "Lori is meditating," I said.

"Lori has picked a strange place to meditate," Cameron called from behind the wheel of the boat.

I sighed again, and this time it wasn't because I was one with the lake. "Lori would like to be left alone."

"Lori has picked a strange place to be left alone," Sean commented. He sat in the bow with me, on the other side of Rachel, holding her hand in a death grip like their lives depended on it.

He did have a point. I was glad they'd finally gotten together. Again. And I wouldn't have missed Adam's fireworks for the world. Just thinking about him doing something he loved—setting off explosions—made me smile. But I did wish there were some way for me to see this show that did not involve proximity to other people, especially people determined to pick on me and draw attention to the fact that I was not myself.

I sighed yet again, a looooong sigh that encompassed my extreme fatigue exacerbated by being stuck in a boat with boys. "Lori has had a bad day."

"Lori's day is over." Rachel reached over and patted my knee.

And just what the hell did THAT mean? On the one hand, it sounded soothing. There was a comfort in knowing your bad day was coming to an end, and all you had left to do was watch fireworks, ride back home in someone else's boat, brush your teeth, and go to bed.

On the other hand, it sounded ominous, like Adam and I had already enjoyed our day in the sun, and now Rachel was signaling me to move over, Rover. When she'd come to the marina for lunch with Sean, she and I had talked a little. We'd told each other we were sorry for last night's Xtreme Dating. But I could tell it would take a while for us to truly forgive each other.

And now she had that look in her dark eyes that she'd gotten a couple of times in the last few weeks when I'd asked her about Adam. The one that said she knew more than she was telling.

I didn't want to go ballistic on her while all of us waited patiently and contently for the explosions, but God! "What do you mean," I started, my voice rising over the eerily quiet lake, "my day is o—"

BANG!

We all jumped in our seats at the first explosion. Because the sound was delayed, we looked up to see the bouquet of golden light already spreading across the black sky.

In the pause before the next explosion, the crowd in the boats actually said, "Oooooh."

More rockets snaked trails of smoke through the gold, then exploded green and blue. The percussion of their explosions reached us at the same time the strings of "My Country, 'Tis of Thee" waltzed through the loudspeakers.

"Wow," Rachel said. I looked over at her and Sean, gazing up at the sky with their heads close together, fireworks reflecting in their eyes. Everyone in the boat was gazing up. Everyone on the whole lake was gazing up. It would have been a great time to be a pickpocket. But only Adam would think of something like that, or the girlfriend of Adam who had gotten used to him over the years and missed him awfully.

Rocket after rocket zipped into the night sky, paused, then turned itself inside out in a rain of light. "My Country, 'Tis of Thee" ended and "America the Beautiful" began. "America the Beautiful" gave way to "You're a Grand Old Flag." I would have time enough to pine away for Adam when I lay awake in bed tonight, but right then I enjoyed the beauty of the fireworks and the fact that Adam was helping set them off from the grassy hill next to the yacht club and having the time of his life.

I jumped again—not at an explosion this time, but at my cell phone buzzing in the back pocket of Adam's cutoff jeans. Maybe my dad was texting me that he and Frances were staying out later than me—but couldn't he wait until the fireworks were over? I glanced at the screen to see who'd sent the text.

Adam.

I suppressed the urge to look around and make sure nobody was watching. Adam and I might not be together anymore, but the ban had been lifted. He was free to text me if he wanted. Again, his timing was not good, but then again, he might be asking me to call him an ambulance. I opened the message.

This one's for you.

"You're a Grand Old Flag" ended. The next song over the loudspeakers wasn't a patriotic tune at all but a new rock song Adam and I both liked. A love song.

A smaller rocket cut across the sky, trailing smoke. It exploded in a red heart.

"Awwwww!" said the crowd.

"Upside down," said Sean.

The heart was, indeed, upside down. It grew and grew, upside down, until its lights trailed and faded.

A bigger rocket exploded in bright golden sparks, and then came another red heart.

"Upside down," said all the boys.

Three explosions layered on top of one another, gold,

blue, pink. Then still another red heart exploded, growing and growing before it faded.

"Upside down," said everyone in the boat but me.

My own heart expanded for Adam. I whispered, "I know what he meant."

I stood up and started to put one foot over the side of the boat.

"Where are you going?" Sean grabbed me by the wrist. "Are you bailing on us? You're not upset, are you? Adam's planning to ask you to go to Birmingham with him in a couple of weeks. He thought you needed a while to cool off but the fireworks would soften you up."

"Birmingham!" I exclaimed. "That's serious!"

"That's what I said to Adam." Sean raised one eyebrow at me.

I watched a Roman candle pulse into the air: *foop, foop, foop,* with very bad aim, too low. In silhouette, the people in the boats closest to the shore ducked and covered their heads with their arms. "Adam makes terrible plans," I said.

"Oh, come on," Sean said in his most persuasive voice. "Wait a few weeks like he said, and maybe you'll feel differently. He'll explode something else to impress you. It wouldn't be my choice of method to get Rachel back if I were in the doghouse with her, but there's no accounting for taste."

Rachel batted her eyelashes at him.

And I gaped at him. It was hard to concentrate on what he was saying with fireworks flashing and booming above us, but I did believe that, while trying to put in a good word with me on his brother's behalf, Sean had managed to insult both of us. Then I shook my wrist out of his grasp. "It's a terrible plan because I'm not waiting a few weeks."

Before Sean could stop me again, I leaped out of the boat and into the one next to it. The men relaxing in lawn chairs in the bow hardly had time to turn around to see what blonde goddess had descended on them before I traversed that boat and leaped over the side, onto a pontoon boat loaded with drunks. They braced themselves as the boat shifted under their feet, but they were inebriated enough and fascinated enough with Adam's light show that they assumed it was the alcohol making them sway rather than a teenage pirate on a mission. They never turned around.

Quite a few boats were like that. A few had more alert passengers who stared at me. One old lady tried to lecture me about boat-hopping among strangers at night, a nice girl like me. And a couple of times I had to convince people to start their engines and putter a few feet forward so I could make it to the next boat without going into the lake. At the beginning of this summer I would have sworn I was not capable of drowning, but my last wakeboarding accident had convinced me I was wrong about that. And it would be my luck to go out that way: floundering in the lake and succumbing under the boats to the jaunty tune of "Stars and Stripes Forever."

The boats always obliged. Whether I knew the people in the boat or not, the driver idled closer to the next boat, just to stop me from interrupting the fantastic show overhead. I chose a safe path through the boats that would put me onshore at the yacht club wharf, rather than heading straight for the hill where the fireworks were coming from. It would be just our luck for me to get stabbed through the heart by a wayward rocket just as I was making my way back to Adam.

Come to think of it . . . wasn't Adam the one more likely to get killed by a rocket, since he was the one setting off rockets? The detail was different, but our luck was the same. I pictured reaching the hill a few minutes too late and the other pyromaniacs pointing to the chalk outline sprinkled with ashes that was the only evidence left of his body.

I leaped from the last boat, hit the yacht club wharf, and ran.

Thick ropes anchoring huge white sailboats crisscrossed the wharf, but I was a master at dodging maritime obstacles. I skittered toward shore as fast as my flip-flops would carry me, all the time watching the hill. Between explosions, the hill was dark and silent. Adam had been killed, and the show was over. Then pink light flickered through the grass, and silhouettes ran away from the light with their ears covered. Funny that I recognized Adam from the way he ran in silhouette. I would have known him anywhere.

I slowed to a walk now that I knew he wasn't in (immediate) danger of dying. I hadn't realized how hard I'd been running, but my lungs felt like they were about to fall out as I turned backward to watch the latest rocket arc impossibly high into the air. It paused, quiet. Then it burst into a million golden sparks, and the thunder came afterward to thump me in the chest and take my breath away all over again. The sparks faded into the black sky, then came back in a lovely surprise, bursting suddenly brighter and chasing one another around in circles as they fell. The entire bouquet of golden light reflected in the water. The lake looked like it was rising to meet the light instead of the other way around.

Foop, foop, foop. Three more rockets left the hill. I looked in that direction for Adam's silhouette.

That's when I saw him running down the hill—*oh no, massive explosion, every man for himself, run for your lives!* I did have that thought for a split second, but as I watched him,

I saw he wasn't running away from anything. He was running toward me.

The fireworks exploded in midair and lit him up. Two new burn holes had appeared in his T-shirt, giving me a peek at his chest. Soot streaked his tanned face, and his curls were dotted with small lengths of white straw—courtesy of ducking and covering on the ground, I guessed. He grinned at me.

We were on a collision course. Unless a rocket crashed down to explode just above our heads in the next ten seconds, we would meet in the middle, and I had no idea what to say. I'd told Sean that a few weeks was too long to wait to see Adam again. Now I wasn't so sure. Maybe I should suggest we forgive each other but let things cool down between us before we started up again. We could have some long talks and discuss where we'd been and where we were going. That would be the adult thing to do—

He threw down his lighter, grabbed me with both hands, and kissed me.

I let him kiss me for a few seconds, shocked and relieved.

Explosions startled me. I'd gotten so lost in Adam, I'd forgotten we were standing in a fireworks display.

Then I moved forward, into him. I kissed him harder and put my hands in his hair, my fingers slipping past the pieces of straw. I wanted him closer.

More and bigger explosions went off behind him. I couldn't tell whether the percussions in my chest were from the fireworks or from being chest to chest with Adam himself.

He kissed the corner of my mouth, kissed my cheek, and growled in my ear, "Fireworks or what?"

"Stars and Stripes Forever" ended with a flourish of horns. The silence grew, waiting for another rousing patriotic tune to fill it. The silence stretched. Then there was another noise—*foop, foop, foop, foofoofoofoofoo*—endless launches of rockets. The music had stopped because no one would hear it over the grand finale of explosions.

I put both hands on his chest and backed him up a pace. The black sky behind him was filled with color. I said, "Go. Hurry. You can still help. You're missing it."

He pulled me close again and gazed down at me, tracing one finger so tenderly along my cheekbone. His finger was black, and he might be leaving an attractive black streak across my skin. I didn't mind. The way he was looking at me with those light blue eyes, I had never felt more beautiful.

He bent his head close to my ear again so I could hear him whisper, "I'm not missing anything."

Check out another
romantic and fun book from
Jennifer Echols:

The Ex Games

seat belt

(sēt′ belt) *n.* **1.** a trick in which a snowboarder reaches across the body and grabs the board while getting air **2.** what Hayden needs to fasten, because Nick is about to take her for a ride

At the groan of a door opening, I looked up from my chemistry notebook. I'd been diagramming molecules so I wouldn't have any homework to actually take home. But as I'd stared at the white paper, it had dissolved into a snowy slalom course. The hydrogen and oxygen atoms had transformed into gates for me to snowboard between. My red pen had traced my path, curving back and forth, *swish, swish, swish,* down the page. I could almost feel the icy wind on my cheeks and smell the pine trees. I couldn't *wait* to get out of school and head for the mountain.

Until I saw it was Nick coming out the door of Ms. Abernathy's room and into the hall. At six feet tall, he filled the doorway with his model-perfect looks and cocky attitude. He flicked his dark hair out of his eyes with his pinkie, looked down at me, and grinned brilliantly.

My first thought was, *Oh no: fuel for the fire*. About a month ago, one of my best friends had hooked up with one of Nick's best friends. Then, a few weeks ago, my other best friend and Nick's other best friend had gotten together. It was fate. Nick and I were next, right?

Wrong. Everybody in our class remembered that Nick and I had been a couple four years ago, in seventh grade. They gleefully recalled our breakup and the resulting brouhaha. They watched us now for our entertainment value, dying to know whether we'd go out again. Unfortunately for them, they needed to stick to DVDs and Wii to fill up their spare time. Nick and I weren't going to happen.

My second thought was, *Ah, those deep brown eyes*.

Maybe snowboarding could wait a little longer, after all.

"Fancy meeting you here, Hoyden." He closed the door behind him, too hard. He must have gotten in trouble for talking again, and Ms. Abernathy had sent him out in the hall.

Join the club. From my seat against the cement block wall of our high school's science wing, I gazed up at him—way, *way* up, because I was on the floor—and tried my best to glare. The first time he'd called me *Hoyden*, years ago, I'd sneaked a peek in the dictionary to look up what it meant: a noisy girl. Not exactly flattering. Not exactly a lie, either. But I couldn't let him know I felt flattered that he'd taken the time to look up a word in the dictionary to insult me with. Because that would make me insane, desperate, and in unrequited love.

He slapped his forehead. *"Oh,* I'm sorry, I meant *Hayden.* I get confused." He had a way of saying *oh* so innocently, like he had no idea he'd insulted me. Sometimes new girls bought his act, at least for their first few weeks at our school. They were taken by the idea of hooking up with Nick Krieger, who occasionally was featured in teen heartthrob magazines as the heir to the Krieger Meats and Meat Products fortune. And Nick obliged these girls—for a few dates, until he dumped them.

I knew his pattern all too well. When I'd first moved to Snowfall, Colorado, I had *been* one of those girls. He'd made me feel like a princess for a whole month. No, better—like a cool, hip teenage girl who dated! The fantasy culminated with one deep kiss shared in the back row of the movie theater with half our English class watching us. It didn't end well, thus the aforementioned brouhaha.

I blinked the stars out of my eyes. "Fancy seeing *you* here, Ex."

He gave me his smile of sexy confidence, dropped his backpack, and sank to the floor beside me. "What do you think of Davis and Liz?"

My heart had absolutely no reason to skip a beat. He was *not* asking me out. He was asking me my opinion of my friend Liz and his friend Davis as a couple. That did not necessarily mean he was heeding public opinion that he and I were next to get together. Liz and Davis were a legitimate topic of gossip.

I managed to say breezily, "Oh, they'll get along great until they discuss where to go on a date. Then he'll insist they go where she wants to go. She'll insist they go where *he* wants to go. They'll end up sitting in her driveway all night, fighting to the death over who can be more thoughtful and polite."

Nick chuckled, a low rumble in his chest. Because he'd sat down so close to me and our arms were touching, sort of, under layers and layers of clothing, I felt the vibration of his voice. But again, my heart had no reason—repeat, *no* reason—to skip two beats, or possibly three, just because I'd made Nick laugh. He made everybody feel this good about their stupid jokes.

"And what's up with Gavin and Chloe?" he asked next.

"Chloe and Gavin are an accident waiting to happen." I couldn't understand this mismatch between the class president and the class bad boy, and it was a relief finally to voice my concerns, even if it *was* to Nick. "They're both too strong-willed to make it together long. You watch. They're adorable together now, but before long they'll have an argument that makes our tween-love Armageddon look like a happy childhood memory."

Suddenly it occurred to me that I'd said way too much, and Nick would likely repeat this unflattering characterization to Gavin, who would take it right back to Chloe. I really did hold this opinion of Chloe and Gavin's chances at true love, but I'd never intended to share it! I lost my inhibitions when I looked into Nick's dark eyes, damn him.

I slid my arm around him conspiratorially—not as titillating as it sounds, because his parka was very puffy—and cooed, "But that's just between you and me. I know how good you are at keeping secrets."

He pursed his lips and gazed at me reproachfully for throwing our seventh-grade history in his face, times two. Back then he'd brought our tween-love Armageddon on himself by letting our whole class in on his secret while he kept me in the dark.

Not that I was bitter.

But instead of jabbing back at me, he slipped his arm around me, too. And I was *not* wearing a puffy parka, only a couple of T-shirts, both of which had ridden up a little in the back. I knew this without looking because I felt the heat of his fingers on my bare skin, above the waistband of my jeans. My face probably turned a few shades redder than my hair.

"Now, Hoyden," he reprimanded me, "Valentine's Day is a week from tomorrow. We don't want to ruin that special day for Gavin and Chloe or Davis and Liz. We should put aside our differences for the sake of the kids."

I couldn't help bursting into unladylike laughter.

I expected him to remove his hand from my hip in revulsion at my outburst, but he kept it there. I knew he was only toying with me, I *knew* this, but I sure did enjoy it. If the principal had walked by just then and sensed what I was thinking, I would have gotten detention.

"Four years is a long time for us to be separated," he crooned. "We've both had a chance to think about what we really want from our relationship."

This was true. Over the four years since we'd been together, I'd come to the heartbreaking realization that no boy in my school was as hot as Nick, nobody was as much fun, and nobody was nearly as much of an ass. For instance, he'd generated fire-crotch comments about me as I passed his table in the lunchroom yesterday.

Remember when another heir called a certain red-haired actress a fire-crotch on camera? No? Well, *I* remember. Redheads across America sucked in a collective gasp, because we *knew*. The jokes boys made to us about Raggedy Ann, the Wendy's girl, and Pippi Longstocking would finally stop, as we'd always hoped, only to be replaced by something infinitely worse.

So when I heard *fire-crotch* whispered in the lunchroom, I assumed it was meant for me. Nick was the first suspect I glanced at. His mouth was closed as he listened to the conversation at the lunch table. However, when there was commentary around school about me, Nick was always in the vicinity. He might not have made the comment, but I knew in my heart he was responsible.

Now I chose not to relay my thoughts on our four-year-long trial separation, lest he take his warm hand off my hip. Instead, I played along. "Are you saying you didn't sign the papers, so our divorce was never finalized?"

"I'm saying maybe we should call off the court proceedings and try a reconciliation." A strand of his dark hair came untucked from behind his ear, and he jerked his head back to swing the hair out of his eyes. Oooh, I *loved* it when he did that! I had something of a Nick problem.

His hair fell right back into his eyes. Sometimes when this happened, he followed up the head jerk with the pinkie flick, but not this time. He watched me, waiting for me to say something. Oops. I'd forgotten I was staring at him in awe.

A reconciliation? He was probably just teasing me, as usual. But what if this was his veiled way of asking me on a date? What if he was feeling me out to see whether I wanted to go with him before he asked me directly? This was how Nick worked. He had to win. He never took a bet that wasn't a sure thing.

And if he'd been listening to everyone in class prodding him to ask me out, the timing was perfect, if I did say so myself. He was between girlfriends (not that I kept up with his dating status) and therefore free to get together with me. Everett Walsh, my boyfriend of two months, had broken up with me last week because his mama thought I was brazen (no!). Therefore I was free to get together with Nick.

Playing it cool, I relaxed against the wall and gave his puffy parka a squeeze, which he probably couldn't feel through the padding. With my other hand, I found his fingers in his lap and touched the engraving on his signet ring, which he'd told me back in seventh grade was the Krieger family crest. It depicted bloodthirsty lions and the antlers of the hapless deer they'd attacked and devoured—which seemed apt for our relationship in seventh grade, but *not* for our relationship now, in eleventh. I was no deer in the headlights. Not anymore. Coyly I said, "I'll mention it to my lawyer." Ha!

He eyed me uneasily, like I was a chemistry lab experiment gone awry and foaming over. But Nick was never truly uneasy. He was just taken aback that I hadn't fallen at his feet. Then he asked, "What are you doing for winter break?"

Winter break was next week. We lived in a ski resort town. It seemed cruel to lock us up in school the *entire* winter. They let us out for a week every February, since the base might or might not start to melt by spring break in April.

Was he just making convo, whiling away our last few minutes of incarceration at school, or did he really want to know what I was doing during our days off? Again I got the distinct and astonishing impression that he wanted to ask me out. Perhaps I should notify Ms. Abernathy of a safety hazard in her chemistry classroom. Obviously I had inhaled hallucinatory gas just before she kicked me out.

"I'm boarding with my brother today," I said, counting on my fingers. "Tomorrow I'm boarding with Liz. Actually, Liz skis rather than boards, but she keeps up with me pretty well. I'm boarding with some friends coming from Aspen on Sunday, the cheerleading squad on Monday—"

Nick laughed. "Basically, anyone who will board with you."

"I guess I get around," I agreed. "I'm on the mountain a lot. Most people get tired of boarding after a while, which I do not understand at *all*. And then on Tuesday, I've entered that big snowboarding competition."

"Really!" He sounded interested and surprised, but his hand underneath my hand let me know he was more interested in throwing me into a hot tizzy than in anything I had to say. He slid his hand, and my hand with it, from his lap and over to my thigh. "You're going off the jump? Did you get over your fear of heights?"

So he'd been listening to me after all.

My friends knew I'd broken my leg rappelling when I was twelve. That actually led, in a roundabout way, to my family's move from Tennessee to Colorado. My dad was a nurse, and he got so interested in my physical rehab that he and my mom decided to open a health club. Only they didn't think they could make it fly in Tennessee. The best place for a privately owned health club specializing in physical rehab was a town with a lot of rich people and broken legs.

Though my own leg had healed by the time we moved, I was still so shell-shocked from my fall that I never would have tried snowboarding if my parents hadn't made me go with my little brother, Josh, to keep him from killing himself on the mountain. Josh was a big part of the reason

I'd gotten pretty good. *Any* girl would get pretty good trying to keep up with a boy snowboarder three years younger who was half insane.

And that's how I became the world's only snowboarder with the ability to land a frontside 900 in the half-pipe *and* with a crippling fear of heights. Not a good combination if I wanted to compete nationally.

"This competition's different," I said. Growing warmer, I watched Nick's fingers massaging the soft denim of my jeans. "For once, the only events are the slalom and the half-pipe. No big air or slopestyle or anything that would involve a jump. Chloe and Liz swore they'd never forgive me if I didn't enter this one."

"You've got a chance," Nick assured me. "I've seen you around on the slopes. You're good compared with most of the regulars on the mountain."

I shrugged—a small, dainty shrug, not a big shrug that would dislodge his hand from my hip and his other hand from my thigh. "Thanks, but I expect some random chick from Aspen to sweep in and kick my ass." And when that happened, I sure could use someone to comfort me in the agony of defeat, *hint hint*. But Nick was only toying with me. Nick was only toying with me. I could repeat this mantra a million times in my head, yet no matter how strong my willpower, his fingers rubbing across my jeans threatened to turn me into a nervous gigglefest. Sometimes I wished I were one of those cheerleaders/prom queens/rich socialite snowbunnies who seemed to interest Nick for a day or two at a time. I wondered if any of them had given in to Nick's fingers rubbing across their jeans, and whether I would too, if he asked.

"Anyway, those are all my plans so far," I threw in there despite myself. What I meant was: I am free for the rest of the week, *hint hint*. I wanted to kick myself.

"Are you going to the Poser concert on Valentine's Day?" He eased his hand out from under mine and put his on top. His fingers massaged my fingers ever so gently.

Nick was only toying with me. Nick was only toying with me. "That's everybody's million-dollar question, isn't it?" I said. "Or rather, their seventy-two-dollar question. I don't want to pass up a once-in-a-lifetime opportunity to see Poser, but tickets are so expensive." I may have spoken a bit too loudly so he could hear me over my heart, which was no longer skipping beats. It was hammering out a beat faster than Poser's drummer.

Nick nodded. "Especially if you're buying two because you want to ask someone to go with you."

I gaped at him. I know I did. He watched me with dark, supposedly serious eyes while I gaped at him in shock. Was he laughing at me inside?

We both started as the door burst open. Ms. Abernathy glowered down at us with her fists on her hips. "Miss O'Malley. Mr. Krieger. When I send you into the hall for talking, you do not *talk* in the *hall*!"

"*Oh,*" Nick said in his innocent voice.

I was deathly afraid I would laugh at this if I opened my mouth. I absolutely could not allow myself to fall in love with Nick all over again. But it was downright impossible to avoid. He bent his head until Ms. Abernathy couldn't see his face, and he winked at me.

Saved by the bell! We all three jumped as the signal rang close above our heads. On a normal day the class would have flowed politely around Ms. Abernathy standing in the doorway. They might even have waited until she moved. But this bell let us out of school for winter break. Ms. Abernathy got caught in the current of students pouring out of her classroom and down the hall. If she floated as far as the next wing, maybe a history teacher would throw her a rope and tow her to safety.

Chloe and Liz shoved their way out of the room and glanced around the crowded hall until they saw me against the wall on the floor. Clearly they were dying to know whether I'd survived being sent out in the hall with my ex. Both of them focused on the space between me and Nick. I looked down in confusion, wondering what they were staring at.

Nick was still holding my hand.

I tried to pull my hand away. He squeezed even tighter. I turned to him with my eyes wide. What in the world was he thinking? After the insults Nick and I had thrown at each other in public over the years, we would have been the laughingstock of the school if we *really* fell for each other.

And now he was holding my hand in public!

He wouldn't look at me, though I pulled hard to free myself from his grasp. He just squeezed my hand and grinned up at the gathering crowd like he didn't care who saw us.

Which was *everyone*. Davis sauntered out of the classroom and slid his arm around Liz. Unlike the train wreck that was Chloe and Gavin as a couple, Liz and Davis were the two kindest people I knew. They deserved each other, in a good way. But even Davis had a comment as he casually glanced down at Nick and me and did a double take at our hands. "That's something you don't see every day," he understated to Liz. "Usually at about this time, Nick is going around the lab, collecting whatever particulate has dropped out of the solution so he can throw it at Hayden."

"We didn't do an experiment today, just diagrammed molecules. Nothing to throw," Nick said in a reasonable tone, as if he and I were not sitting on the floor, surrounded by a two-deep crowd of our classmates. They had all filed out of chemistry class and joined the circle. They peeked over one another's shoulders to see what Nick and I were up to this time.

Then Gavin exploded out of the classroom, and I knew Nick and I were in trouble. He whacked into Chloe so hard, he would have knocked her off her feet if he hadn't grabbed her at the same time. Over her squeals, he yelled at Nick, "I knew it!" while pointing at our hands.

"Oooooh," said the crowd, shifting closer around us, totally forgetting they were supposed to be *going home* for *winter break*. If Davis, Liz, Gavin, and Chloe hadn't made up the front row, the rest of the class would have overrun us like zombies.

"I was just shaking Hayden's hand, wishing her luck in the snowboarding competition Tuesday." Nick stood, still gripping my hand, pulling me up with him.

"See you tonight," Davis mouthed in Liz's ear. Then he turned to Nick and said, "Come on. I'll fill you in on what Ms. Abernathy said after you got ejected from the game." Of course Nick didn't give a damn what Ms. Abernathy said in the last ten minutes of class before winter break. But that was Davis, always smoothing things over.

Nick *finally* let go of my hand. "See you around, Hoyden."

He pinned me with one last dark look and a curious smile. Then he and Davis made their way through the crowd, shoving some of the more obnoxious gawking boys, who elbowed them back.

But a few folks still stared at me: Liz, Chloe, and worst of all, Gavin. One corner of his mouth turned up in a mischievous grin. Gavin was tall, muscular, and Japanese, with even longer hair than Nick. I would have thought he was adorable if I didn't want to kill him most of the time for constantly goading Nick and me about each other. I certainly understood what Chloe saw in him, even though he drove her crazy too.

Gavin turned to her. "Give me some gum."

"No."

Liz and I dodged out of the way as Gavin backed Chloe against the lockers and shoved both his hands into the front pockets of her jeans. You might think the class president would find a way to stop this sort of manhandling, but actually she didn't seem to mind too much.

By now the crowd had dispersed. Nick and Davis were walking down the hall together, getting smaller and smaller until I couldn't see them anymore past a knot of freshman girls squealing about the Poser concert and how they were working extra shifts at the souvenir shop to pay for the expensive tickets. Go home, people. I resisted the urge to stand on my tiptoes for one more peek at Nick. If I didn't run into him on the slopes, this might be the last I saw of him for ten whole days.

"I don't have any gum!" Chloe squealed through fits of giggling, trying to push Gavin off. "Gavin!" She finally shoved him away.

He jogged down the hall to catch up with Nick and Davis, holding the paper-wrapped gum aloft triumphantly.

"That was my last piece!" Chloe called.

I never would have admitted that Gavin's gum theft made me jealous. Nick was bad for me, I knew. He was the last person on earth I wanted to steal my gum. Still, I stepped to one side so I could see him behind the Poser fangirls. I watched him turn with Gavin and Davis and disappear down the stairs, and I couldn't help but feel like a little kid on Halloween night, standing in the doorway in my witch costume with my plastic cauldron for trick-or-treat candy, watching the rain come down. Such sweet promise, and now I was out of luck. Damn.

Chloe stared after the boys too. I assumed she really wanted that gum. Then she looked at me. "Oh my God, did Nick ask you out? It sounded like he was asking you out, but we couldn't quite tell. Ms. Abernathy finally came to check on you because the whole first row got up from their desks and pressed their ears to the door."

I answered honestly. "For a second there, I thought he was going to ask me out."

"But he didn't?" Liz wailed.

To hide my disappointment, I bent down to stuff my chemistry notebook into my backpack as I shook my head.

"At least you got a *see you around*," Chloe pointed out. "Normally if he bothered to say good-bye to you at all, he would do it by popping your bra."

"True," I acknowledged. And then I realized what was going on here. Chloe and Liz had been hinting that I should go out with Nick now that they were dating Nick's friends, but at the moment they seemed even more eager and giddy about it than usual. I straightened, folded my arms across my chest, and glared at Chloe and then Liz. "Please do not tell me you put Nick up to asking me to the Poser concert."

Chloe stared right back at me. But Liz, the weakest link, glanced nervously at Chloe like they were busted.

"Come on now." I stamped one foot. "Even y'all aren't going to the Poser concert with Gavin and Davis. It's too expensive."

"Nick has more money than God," Chloe pointed out.

I turned on Liz. "You really want me to go out with him after I told you he made that fire-crotch comment about me?" Liz was all about people being respectful of one another. We were in school with teenage boys and this was asking a lot, I know.

"That *did* sound disrespectful," she admitted. "Are you sure he didn't mean it in a friendly way?"

Incredible. Even Liz's sense of chivalry and honor was crushed under the juggernaut called Wouldn't It Be Cute/Ironic If Nick and Hayden Dated Again.

"What if he *did* ask you out?" Liz bounced excitedly, and her dark curls bounced with her. "Oh my God, what if you saw him on the slopes over the break and he asked you to the Poser concert? What would you say?"

I considered this. Part of me wanted to think Nick had changed in the past four years. I would jump at the chance to go out with the boy I'd made up in my head. In real life Nick was adorable, funny, and smart, but in my fantasies he had the additional fictional component of honestly wanting to go out with me.

Another part of me remembered his dis four years ago as freshly as if it were yesterday. When I recalled that awful night, the image of Honest Nick dissolved, even from my imagination. That Nick was too good to be true. I couldn't say yes to Nick, because I was scared to death he would hurt me again.

"It doesn't matter," I declared, "because he's not going to ask me out. If he really liked me, he wouldn't have treated me the way he did back in the day. So stop trying to throw us together."

"Okay," Liz and Chloe said in unison. Again, too eager, too giddy. The three of us turned and made our own way down the hall. We discussed how low Poser tickets would have to go before we sprung for them, but the subject had changed too easily. I was left with the nagging feeling that, despite their promise, they were not through playing Cupid with me and Nick.

About the Author

Jennifer Echols grew up on beautiful Lake Martin in Alabama and learned to water-ski when she was five years old—wakeboarding wasn't invented yet! Currently she lives with her husband and son in Birmingham. Please visit her online at www.jennifer-echols.com and sign the guestbook!

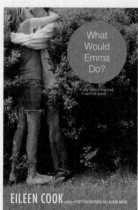

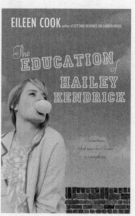

Sweet and Sassy Reads

One book. More than one story.

Which will be *your* first?

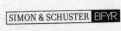